With a rush and a rattle, the spate of water spilled from the hand pump into the tin pail that hung on its peg below the spout. Andrew cupped his hands and sloshed the soothing water over his face, directing most of the spray onto the new and sizeable lump on his brow. His formerly buoyant mood had vanished.

The pain when he accidentally brushed his nose with his fingers brought him close to shouting a long line of curses to the heavens. Instead, he grabbed the top of the pump with both hands and hung his head, waiting for the pain to diminish.

When the nettling stings blunted to a dull ache, he shook his head to clear the cobwebs.

He hadn't anticipated that it would be such a difficult thing to find his way home in the dark. "You'd think she'd have picked a better location for her establishment," he growled to himself, having observed that it wasn't exactly a well-worn path to her door. "Bull probably kept his end of the path worn smooth," he muttered, displeased for being bothered by what the town boss did with his ladylove.

Maybe he deserved the knot on his head for ignoring their differences. As much as he hated to admit it, they were worlds apart.

She had been right to remind him that she was a whore and he was a do-gooder. The only consolation; she was an unhappy whore and he was a happy do-gooder.

NOVELLAS BY NORA FLETCHER

A Song for Him

Maria,

Blessings, Best Wishes,

Nora Fletcher

Let me know how you like it.

WWW. norafletcher - com

CACTUS ROSE

by

NORA FLETCHER

Echelon Embark

Echelon Press

Crowley, Texas

Echelon Press
P.O. Box 1084
Crowley, TX 76036

Echelon Embark
First paperback printing: November 2002

Trade paperback ISBN 1-59080-102-4

Printed and bound in the United States of America.

www.echelonpress.com

DEDICATION

Authors through the ages have likened writing a book to becoming pregnant with the germ of an idea until the last bit of punctuation of the final edit terminates in delivery of their creative baby. In this case, the pregnancy of *Cactus Rose* lasted sixteen years. It was Christmas of 1986, when my children were small that we bought my first word processing typewriter and I began the saga of Andrew and Avis. My children are now grown, with children of their own. I suppose one could say that I wrote from one generation into the next.

The first person I wish to thank is Theron White, omnivorous reader and computer genius for discovering my first twelve pages on the kitchen counter and being impressed. There after, he insisted I learn to use a computer maintaining that WordPerfect and keyboarding would make my writing easier. It did, and I am ever in his debt.

Next, a big thanks goes to Jack Howell, and Gary Edwards for their outstanding support when times got hard and the system crashed or the computer quirked in a new and unique way.

Another note of appreciation to my muses, Pat Pellemeier, Pat Menar, and Nancy Switzer, who share my DNA and have a passion for words. They have been invaluable to me for critique and encouragement.

My sincerest thanks and deepest gratitude goes to my mentor Karen Syed of Echelon Press. A woman for all seasons, Karen saw promise in my work, and held our hands as we took baby steps into the business of *word smithing*.

My most profound, and inexpressible gratitude goes to the man I married. Howard is a man who knows how to keep a promise even through great sacrifice, and, who with quiet determination, does the really hard stuff to inspire me and to keep going.

Finally, to the 3 A's who grew up generously allowing their mother the time to create.

PROLOGUE

New Mexico 1900

Avis Hollis recoiled at the chilling details of her husband's murder. She could hardly reckon the news of her widowhood, for the mounting horror at the circumstances Bull had devised to have Albert killed.

She had thought there could not be anyone as evil as her black-hearted husband, but wasn't Bull reciting the details of the contrivance in the same unemotional way he bought a fresh load of timber?

Keeping the coil of fear at bay, she listened intently. She had to understand everything that Bull was saying to comprehend the more important, but unspoken things.

Back rigid, not yielding even a glance, her body betrayed her when familiar tingles forked through her breasts. She did not have to look down to know that twin spots of sticky moisture sprouted on the front of her cotton blouse.

Shifting the sleeping infant in her arms away from the milky dampness, she prayed little Amanda would not awaken at the scent of nourishment.

"I think you will find, my dear, that your life will be much improved by avenging the attack upon your person. A pity that I was forced to deal with Albert in such a final way, but he had become a damned nuisance and provoked too much talk around town," recited Bull, his voice absent of feeling or care for his kin. "I did this for you."

Her mind reeled at such wickedness. Raising her head, she matched his glacial gaze. "Stop!" she hissed, her chin notching upward. "If the reason you brought me here is to tell me that my husband is dead, you have delivered your message. I do not want to know what happened or even how. It is enough that Albert is gone."

Bull did not immediately reply, but stared at her with unblinking eyes. His tongue snaked over his lower lip. Nauseated, she looked away.

The office was hot, stifling and Avis swept the strands of hair from her forehead with her free hand. Shutting her eyes, she counted slowly to herself, willing her heart to calm its awful thumping.

She opened her eyes. Her vision faded so that she peered down a long tunnel. Digging down deep to find courage, she surged from the chair. Head high, and shoulders squared, she locked her knees so that he would not see how truly afraid she was.

Otherworldly music surrounded her. She halted, amazed to be enveloped in a golden glow. Everywhere she looked was bathed in the shimmering haze. The radiance became liquid, flooding her with peace.

Her senses lifted away from her body, and she floated above, adrift in the purest of light. Surely, this could not be real. She blinked again, but the vision remained.

Avis watched herself, as she stood with sleeping babe in arms, daring to face the man behind a desk. Eyes locked, in confrontation, she stood courageous, unbowed. She stared, astonished to watch the man behind the desk swirl into a coiled snake.

His head broadened and flattened to that of a serpent poised to strike across the table. Entranced by the lidless eyes, she held her breath, waiting to feel sharp fangs sink into her flesh.

The light pulsed brighter. A lance-like bolt splintered, striking the snake, shriveling the serpent to a worm.

The radiant haze vanished leaving only the shriveled worm. She blinked, again and the illusion departed.

Avis did not know that she had been gaping until she thirsted, her mouth parched. "We will go. The child's mother will be worried," she croaked out before turning toward the door.

"Sit down, damn you! You're not going anywhere," hissed Bull from behind her, his voice deceptively soft.

Avis hesitated, the threat implicit. More afraid to back down than to go through the door she fortified her courage by summoning her abiding hatred of this man and this place. Death would be better than living in hell.

How very well she knew that Bull preyed on weakness. Her weakness had been her own child: a babe not much older than the one in her arms. The greatest fear a woman could have could only be for her child. In the end, she had sent her precious Tessa far away from the malignant wickedness of her own father.

Indeed, she knew well that Albert and Bull were the vilest of monsters! Old men or young children, no one was free in Bull's town, from his control.

Tugging on the doorknob, she cracked open the office door. The heat of the desert afternoon flashed upon her face. The street was deserted. A scream from her would bring no help.

Bull's eyes narrowed. "I am warning you, niece, this is my territory. If you leave this office too speedily, you will not live to see another day."

Carefully, she closed the door and turned about to face him. His overfull lips twisted into a smirk. Refusing to cower, she held herself proudly and raised her chin to look down at him.

Bull smiled at the defiant toss of her flaming mane of hair. The daunting glint in her blue eyes challenged his superior thinking. He had thought her the handsomest of women from the moment she stepped from the train with his nephew by her side. Upon occasion, he had even envied Albert his stunning wife. Never did he covet her more than when she was provoked, for then she was like a finely blooded animal with an arrogance that begged for taming.

Though Avis could be contrary, he had grown to respect her. She was, above all, a survivor. Such a desperately poor, but thoroughbred pragmatist could be useful to him. That is, provided she heeled to his wishes.

His eyes assayed her face, pleased with the straight, classic line of her nose. The porcelain complexion was near flawless and her eyes were the refined and rarest blue of Wedgwood china.

There existed one small, but curious imperfection staining the crease of her lower lip. The wine-colored birthmark only served to draw attention to the sensual fullness of her lips, and entice those so inclined into seeking her other womanly charms. Most men craved to possess such a sweet blossom of the South.

Her profile, the classic image of a cameo, belied the heart cut from quarry stone. By the time their game played out, either they would be a matched pair, or he would rid himself of her sooner, rather than later. Could he, he wondered, bring her to absolute obedience? How tragic it would be for the frosty arms of the grave to embrace such beauty so prematurely.

Although Bull admired beauty, he felt no passion for Avis or for females in general. His aversion for women had become a problem that, if discovered, would make him a pariah in his own town. The world was full of provincial people who disdained a man of his hidden persuasions.

The damp spots on the front of the cheap blouse repulsed him. Pursing his lips, he averted his eyes, once again reminded that women were foul creatures.

Bull was a man's man with preferences for bodies, perfected in pain. He pursued fine cigars, cards, and other unspoken, but highly pleasurable manly lusts that had nothing to do with females.

There were others like him: Men who paid for dark diversions to be satisfied and even more handsomely for keeping their secrets. He would not relinquish his pursuits, or the money they paid for his silence.

He had contrived this elaborate ruse to keep his true passions securely hidden. His worst nightmare could never be death, but exposure. Too much depended on his success.

For the first time in his life, he had need of a woman. He had chosen his nephew's wife for a number of reasons. The disowned daughter of a rich widow with a passion for opiates, Avis Hollis had nothing to lose and everything to gain by this arrangement.

He sensed no pity for Albert in her icy gaze. He, on the other hand, recalled his ardent and devoted nephew with great fondness.

Bull remembered with much pleasure, Albert's elation upon finishing the test of the labyrinth. He proudly wore the symbol of gold upon his finger, the sign of his acceptance into the Fraternity of the Minotaur.

Albert's loyalty had been unswerving, even to the smallest assignment. His adoration for the Beast remained to the end and he would prove more valuable, dead than alive.

Avis presented a more complex problem. Like all females, she could be difficult in the extreme. Unlike Albert, if she did not surrender, she could not translate into another life.

The foul-mouthed, godless, and tough-minded woman was more interested in gold than the pettiness of provincial ideas of right and wrong. She was the goddess Pasiphae, and he was the Bull. Together, they would rule the world.

His mind searched for a weakness to prod the female to

his will. The woman might be stubborn now, but fear and blackmail usually worked. His eyes narrowed at the child in her lap.

The infant squirmed, as if knowing he was watching. Avis, he observed as she bent her head to soothe the child, seemed peculiarly fond of a baby not her own. Wearied of the woman's attachments, Bull sighed at the thought that just as he had once pressed Albert to separate the woman from her own child, he would eventually have to separate her from this little leech.

Through the months since she had come to his territory, he had kept her from what few relations she had in the east. A prime source of opiates from China for her mother, and crafty diversions to keep her snotty-nosed brother in Europe had proved successful.

Avis had broken the bond with her daughter, sending her east without a piteous whimper or contest. There was something peculiar about a woman who would not fight for her own child.

They had fixed her so she could never produce any more brats. Albert fixed her too well. Bull frowned. His nephew had not been light handed at all and nearly killed her. The fuss over the attack had traveled through the town like prairie fire.

They had miscalculated. The plan had been for her to come to him. Instead of going a few steps down the hall to beg for his help, she had crawled all the way to the preacher's doorstep. Stuck, Bull allowed the preacher and his family to care for her, proving even they could serve his purpose until his plans for Albert were complete.

His eyes traveled downward to where the splotches dried into the front of her shirt. The blouse clung disgracefully to her undergarments in a most disgusting way. All women were cows.

He arched his brow at her. "Tell me, Avis, I am curious.

Are you required to have special feelings for someone else's *get* to provide your milk, or are you like an animal in that it only requires that the teat be manipulated in the correct manner?"

Avis could not stop the hot blood that rushed through her veins no more than she could stop her heart from slamming against her chest. This time she would escape. She fit the baby closer to her and hurried to the door.

"Sit down, woman! I'm not finished with you yet!" thundered Bull, his booming voice making the baby flinch. Glancing down, she held her breath as Amanda, thankfully and miraculously, remained asleep.

"You open that door and I swear to you that little parasite in your arms will be dead by sunrise."

Stricken with the terrifying certainty that he meant every word, she gazed down at the cherubic face framed with damp wisps of curls. The picture of innocence made Avis' heart overflows with love, then twist with fear.

She knew the baby should not be in the presence of this ogre. When he had trapped them at the post office, she had begged Bull for the chance to take her home. He had denied her even that, merely ushering them to his waiting carriage and taking them the few blocks to his office.

In the past, she had seen Bull's revenge work swiftly, and to defy him would put Amanda's life in danger, but if she remained, then what? Avis shivered at the thought of the things Bull Trumbull could do to herself, or to others.

Slowly, she faced Bull where he sat basking in the afternoon sun that shafted through the window. She did not look at him, but studied the reverse side of the black and gold lettering where his name was proclaimed along the windowpane. A fly buzzed his head. Limply, he shooed it away with a careless wave of his hand.

How fitting, she thought, to see Beelzebub, Lord of the Flies, Prince of Demons, being plagued by a nasty black fly.

Only Lucifer, fallen to earth, could be so twisted and perverse.

How could she have known before she married that Albert's life had been cursed from the beginning? One wrong decision had brought her from purgatory, in North Carolina, straight to hell in New Mexico.

"I do have ways to bend you to my wishes, don't I?" His pale eyes, too big, and bulging in a face too narrow, focused upon her.

The shiny ring on his left hand winked at her while bloodless fingers twisted the band. She recognized the ring, which bore the emblem of man and bull, as one identical to the one Albert had worn. The very ring she had asked about, but never received an answer.

"You will attend to me," he hissed, the icy shards of his eyes looking through her. "Or the consequences will be grave, even lethal."

"You bastard!" she swore, subduing her voice into a whisper. Perching on the edge of the chair, she tucked the baby protectively into her side.

Again, Bull observed the motherly way she cosseted the child. She had given him the lever he needed to precipitate her surrender.

Plucking the ivory handled riding whip from the tulip-shaped brass urn at the end of the desk, Bull hunkered down in his gold studded leather chair. Reclining, he propped his booted feet on the desk and stroked his ankle with the limp leather thongs at the whip's tip.

"Niece," he began, following the sinuous caress of rawhide against the ankle of his boot with his eyes, "simply because my nephew is gone, does not mean that our kinship has ceased. You see, I have it in my mind that our relationship has merely changed directions." He lifted his hands into the air, spreading them wide, and grinned. "Grown, you might say. Another way to put it is that we, as dear Albert's survivors, have progressed upward, a step or two, in our family intimacy."

Bull swiveled his seat to face her, but before the curtain dropped inside those palest of eyes, she glimpsed the fires of hell at the center of his rotten soul. When the point of his tongue followed the crease of his lips, she shuddered inside, reminded of a toad on a lily pad whose slithery tongue darted at the passing fly.

Balancing the whip, he adroitly rotated the ends, watching the slim, gold-stemmed rod turn between his fingers. He manipulated her, she realized, in the same way his fingers danced along the whip. "Oh, Lord," she murmured under her breath, "Help me get out of here."

No walls fell, nor did lightning strike. Only silence reigned. Again, she felt the sting of the hopelessness that had so far ruled her life. Why should this time be any different? Had the fickle god of fools ever answered even one of her prayers? Gritting her teeth, she determined to find a way to do battle for herself.

Bull rose from his chair. The deliberate and ponderous thud of his boots echoed on the pine plank floor. Standing before her, he pressed the tip of the whip beneath the soft underside of her chin to provoke her face upward until she met his stare. Her eyes dropped and he pressed harder.

Avis gasped at the sharp pain in her neck. Her gaze flew to his face, trying vainly to read the intentions in the soulless eyes.

Delighted at the fear he saw there, he brought the tip up to caress the wine stain on her bottom lip. She shivered and he grinned. Not long ago, they would have called the seductive little wine stain a devil's mark. Most fitting now that he was the presiding devil in these parts.

"You must understand, my dear, that you are privileged. Here I am king and I have planned for you to be my queen." He paused a moment to enjoy the horror in her blue eyes.

The tip of the whip traced an intimidating trail from her chin, down the side of her neck, finally circling her breast. "Since I would prefer not to marry, you may be my consort." Bull leaned forward, his leering face insinuatingly close to hers. "However, you may be my wife, if you like."

Bull perched on the edge of the desk. "Either the position of wife or whore would be a step up for you, don't you think?" He flipped the whip back and forth into the palm of his hand, waiting.

After taking the measure of the fury he saw etched in every line of her body, he turned his back on her. He had to remember that obstinate though she might be, she remained a petty problem.

The match for her flaming temper was to dash the fire with cool control. "I need to reinforce my reputation with the ladies and you will help me build my name as a lover. Your lover." He turned to watch the play of emotions on her face. "But, since I am uninterested in your charms, you will show your devotion to me in other ways."

"Devotion?" she repeated softly, her brows drawn together. She dropped her gaze, trying to understand.

"I see you are confused. Let me explain." Bull steepled his fingers before his lips, while he paced a line from the window to his desk. Abruptly, he stopped pacing to raise his head and bestow her with his seeking gaze.

"You see, as Shakespeare once said, 'The play is the thing'. All you need to do is gossip about my charms and praise my prowess in the grandest sense, making me the envy of every man in the Southwest. You will play my gracious mistress at the important meetings I shall occasionally have for business purposes. Naturally, I will confide a few lurid tales about you to my fellows."

Bull watched her face pale, and she did not speak. Her shrewish tongue must have been captured. He rubbed his hands together.

"Sometimes you will entertain my acquaintances, but not at all as a common whore might. I am a clever man and know that if I were interested in your sex, sharing your charms would be beneath me, unless, of course, there was a purpose behind my generosity." His shoulders moved down in a negligent shrug. "Sometimes there will be a purpose and I will share you, but that will only be when it is in my best interest." He tilted his head to gaze into the distance. "At those comparatively few times, you will be obliged to fornicate on my behalf."

He paused, allowing her to plumb the depth of his intent. "Albert was too heavy handed, but no more will you have to worry about the complicating attachments of motherhood. Considering the haste with which you unloaded your child, you may consider your fixing Albert's departing gift to you."

Unloaded her child? Only fear for her child's life had caused her to part with Tessa!

Avis stared wide-eyed at Bull, afraid to blink at the shock of his words. The hardest deed she had ever done had been to part with her baby, and she had done so expecting to make good her own escape when Tessa was safely thousands of miles from this place. Albert had known she was about to escape, and attacked her. At least that is what she had thought until now.

She had been fixed? She had known the beating had put an end to hopes for more children, and she had grieved, but, heaven-help her, until now, she had not fully realized the attack could have been planned.

The hidden part of her died. It drew its last breath, shriveled, and escaped in her sigh. Perhaps it had been a tender, sprout of hopefulness that the preacher was right and life just could not be so damned bad.

Maybe it was her soul that had departed. She certainly could not find anything inside herself, but the desire for revenge, and the numbing cold of the purest of hatred.

What a twist that she now knew what prompted gentle souls to murder. No longer confused, she leveled her gaze upon him.

Bull shrugged, judging from the malignant loathing in her eyes, that it was well that Albert had met his end, for certainly she would have killed him herself. "You may find life much more enjoyable with me. Certainly, richer and you would even have privacy more often than not."

Rising from his chair, Bull went to stand by the window. "I am waiting for your answer." He turned to gaze out at the window at Main Street. Hands behind him, rocking back and forth on his heels, he flipped the quirt up and down impatiently.

Avis licked her lips, afraid that the lump in her throat was going to strangle her before she could reply. How could she go from being Albert's widow, and freedom, to Bull's woman in the space of a few minutes? Impossible! "No, I refuse to marry you," she squeaked, her voice sounding humiliatingly timid.

He turned, arching an eyebrow and smiled at her in a tolerant manner. "I see. I thought for all your fine ways, that you might prefer being my whore."

This was outrageous! "No! And I'll not be your whore, either!" she shouted without thinking.

Startled, the infant jumped, whimpered and looked at Avis in a sleepy daze. Instinctively, before Amanda could cry out, she moved the baby to her shoulder. Gently, she patted Amanda's back and forced her own voice into quiet tones.

"You can't make me do that either, Trumbull. I refuse to be your kept woman," she informed him through clenched teeth.

Warm dampness seeped through to her skin. Dimly, she comprehended that Amanda needed changing, but not yet, and not in this place.

"What are you going to do? Kill me like you killed Albert

if I don't make myself available to your base perversions?" She drew back. "I would rather die, than submit to your charade. It is time people found out just what you are!"

Spit welled, but she realized spitting at him would be bearding the lion in his den. She could not afford to take chances with Amanda in her arms. "I will kill myself before I let you make me into your wife or your whore," she vowed keeping her voice low, but firm in her resolve to die rather than surrender.

Bull observed the uncompromising determination that had marked her as his adversary. She would do just as she had vowed, but everyone, he had discovered, had a price, even stubborn Avis Ashton Hollis. The woman's determination had driven Albert to divide his loyalties between them once too often. Turning away from her, he smacked the tip of the whip flat in his palm while his mind focused upon the voices speaking in his head.

His eyes drifted away from her. "No? I hear you--" he answered softly. The voices in his head reminded him that fools would often sacrifice self to protect those they loved. "I see. Of course...sacrifice?" he answered his attention on the counsel of his muses, the voices that directed his life.

Avis watched the one sided conversation and trembled. Trumbull could only be mad to be talking into the thin air!

He faced her, eyes narrowed. "It won't be you who dies if you will not abide by my wishes. You might escape in death, but I promise that before your corpse lies cold in the grave, there will be others to suffer in your stead."

Bull stood before her, pointing the whip at the baby. "I would start subtracting with that bundle in your arms and then progress to her father. Popular and a good minister from what I hear, but a puny and weak man. That finished, I would see that the death angel is dispatched eastward, to your mother, brother and lastly, to your daughter. I would have Albert's daughter linger a bit."

He turned away from her, mumbling, conversing with the unseen.

The next moment, he spun around, startling her. She gasped.

"If you chose to maintain your willful attitude, your suffering will worsen until you learn that no man or woman stands in Bull Trumbull's way."

He pointed the whip at her, his eyes like shards of blue ice, impaling and, then probing, intent upon stealing her life. She wanted to die, ached to die, but the master of Hades would not even allow her that escape.

"I promise you that if you persist in your stubborn ways, alive or dead, I will have my revenge. If not on you, then those you love."

Avis knew from the calm, assured way he threatened that he would fulfill his vows.

Head reeling, her body ached as though she had been pummeled with fists. A pulsing thrum in her ears increased the pressure in her head. She feared she might explode and burst into a thousand small pieces never to be whole again.

Amanda, sensing the tension filling Avis, began to fuss and root on Avis' cheek for her nourishment. Defeated, Avis slumped. Bull had won. Just as surely as the sun would come up over the Sacramento Mountains in the morning, the bastard had won.

Frantically, her mind searched for a way out of his wicked scheme. "Lois--" she began, her mouth dry and her tongue thick. She licked her lips.

Anticipating what she would say, Bull cut her off with a flourish of his hand. "A petty problem. The Preacher's wife will soon be gone."

She flinched when the whip clattered onto the desk. Long, slender fingers spread out, spider-like, on the desktop. He leaned forward, crouching like a buzzard before carrion. "In my generosity, I have decided to give you sufficient time for her to die."

How could Bull know about her sickness? Did he know something about the preacher's wife that she did not? "How do you know she's d--?" she stammered, not wanting even to say the words. Amanda's moist mouth rooted against her neck, and the infant's ringlets bobbed against her cheek.

Bull stared at Avis for a moment as he considered his next words. He could not tell her too much. She must, however, believe him.

He did not look at her, but sank back into his chair. Eyes riveted on the brass bull on his desk, he licked his lips. "I saw many cases such as hers when I was studying medicine in France. When tuberculosis progresses to that degree, there can only be one result, and that is death."

Medical school! The pervert had been to medical school! Outrage knotted her stomach. Bull, not Albert, had been the calculating mind behind the attack that had nearly killed her. Anger and hatred fused in a moment, forging the grit necessary to destroy the loathsome demon before her. There could be no price too dear for her to give him what he deserved.

She met the opaque eyes without wavering. Everything she had suffered was because this unholy and wicked man had coveted his nephew's wife. She would have her revenge.

Steely calm settled over her. Bull was too clever to try to outwit without playing the game long enough to gain his confidence. "Before I agree, I want Albert's death certificate," she demanded coolly.

She watched Bull calmly roll the whip in his fingers. There remained this uncertainty about him. Bull was far too smart to rid himself of an obedient, adoring pettifogger like Albert. More likely he had him hidden away, ready to blackmail her.

Bull nodded, smug in having all the answers to her questions. He had known the proof of Albert's demise would be the key to gaining her cooperation. "Certainly, that is a reasonable request. I have ordered the document be sent in your name and the proof should arrive to you within a few days." His eyes leveled with hers. "Understand that a certificate attesting to your freedom is to my benefit, as well."

"You are saying that the death certificate is on its way to me?" she repeated, relieved that this was one battle she would not have to wage.

The hard proof of Albert's death would be in the death certificate, not in Bull's words, or someone else's stories. Whether Albert Hollis was yet breathing did not matter, because he would legally have ceased to exist by proof of a death certificate.

"The demise of my favorite nephew has its price, Avis." He pursed his lips thoughtfully. His fingers tapped on the desk. "I will give you until the day that one's mother is buried, and if you do not come to me by the end of that afternoon…"

He fell silent again, nodding his head as though some unseen voice whispered in his ear. His eyes rolled to her, and he raised his finger. "On second thought, I will give you one hour, precisely, to come to me. If you are so much as five minutes late, I shall start subtracting, just as I have detailed. Their blood will be on your head."

Avis stiffened and Amanda squalled, her piercing shrieks rising to the pine beam rafters above them.

"Do something about that brat, or I will," he threatened.

Loath to feed or change the baby in the presence of a troll, Avis slowly rose to her feet and carried the baby to the door of Trumbull Mercantile. After juggling Amanda to a more comfortable position, she grabbed the knob.

"Very well, leave then, but listen to what I have to say. I will give you anything and everything you want, Avis Hollis, except your freedom from me. You will become a wealthy woman in your own right, and I would not expect you to live with me. To prove that, I will deed you a house, plus a generous income."

The chair creaked, followed by the ominous thud of his boots closing in on her. Avis held her breath until, mercifully, the stalking steps halted behind her. If he touched her, she would scream.

"Be assured, that I would never be interested in darkening the door of your private quarters. On the other side, as my property, I would protect you from other manly distractions." He chuckled, a low rumble that chilled her. "Outwardly, you would be a kept woman, but you and I would know better. You would be kept, but not in a conventional sense."

Head raised, she turned the knob, preparing to cross the threshold. His imperious voice sounded a final warning to her already frazzled nerves and she stopped.

"Remember what I told you, Avis, about subtraction. I will see you no later than one hour from the time Mrs. Bristow is in the earth, or the subtraction process begins. I warn you not to seek to fool me Avis, for you have to remember my duty will be to attend the burying of the preacher's wife."

Avis shoved through the door, leaving it gaping behind her. Holding the squealing babe to her bosom, she fled into the bright sunshine, panting for the purity in the high desert air. She slipped into an alley, and hid in its shadowed coolness to press her back against the wall. Gradually, her heart slowed.

Surprised by her new surroundings, Amanda glanced about, rammed her thumb into her mouth, and ceased fussing. Avis planted a soft kiss on the moist round cheek made salty with baby tears. "Thank you, Amanda Rebecca for being so good. I am sorry you had to meet that awful man."

She resettled Amanda on one hip and hurried for the preacher's house. "That mean old man is not going to get anyone, because I will ruin him first, Amanda," she vowed, moving the baby to rest on the other hip.

Before she set foot on the veranda of the Bristow's home, she had figured out how she would destroy Trumbull. The process could take months or years, but she would get to him before he got to them.

She had to! Bull could not afford to lose. When he finished with her, he would arrange not to leave her around as a witness. Everyone's life depended upon her ability to act the part.

The first step to entrap him, as painful as it was, would be to appear to play his game. She would allow nothing to stop her. If that meant she sold what remained of her soul, so be it.

When she opened the heavy door of the Preacher's home, she was met by the fragile wraith, Amanda's mother. Rescuing her baby from Avis' arms, Lois ventured into the cool dark living room, pulled a dry napkin from the fresh stack of linens and began to change the baby on the thick pad stationed on the immense horsehair sofa. "I was worried when you didn't come right home from the post office," whispered Lois.

The meager effort to speak was too much. The spasm of coughing brought on the shaking so that she could not finish folding the diaper. Frantically, Lois delved for the handkerchief she kept in the sleeve of her blouse.

Avis watched her friend's body shake and jerk with the wracking coughs. She noticed the bloodstains on the crumpled handkerchief. Her spirits plunged even further. Gently, she nudged her friend aside, and reached for the swatch of muslin. "Here let me, Lois"

Quickly and efficiently, Avis folded the muslin into a triangle and fit the absorbent cloth around the baby's hips, fastening the muslin neatly in front with one knot. She glanced down the hall, and saw, by the closed door and light shining beneath, that the preacher was in his study.

Leaning back on the sofa, Avis untied the strings and dropped the shoulder of the simple blouse. Baring one breast made knotty and feverish from the overdue feeding, the baby began to nurse while her mother averted her eyes.

Avis' shut her eyes and sighed at the welcome and immediate relief for her breast. Resting her head on the back of the deep mauve sofa, she forced herself to relax as the child suckled.

"Albert is dead, Lois," she informed her friend without opening her eyes. "Bull cornered us at Dixon's when I picked up the mail. He refused to allow me to bring Amanda home and took us to his office to tell me that Albert was killed in a brawl somewhere in Texas."

"No," whispered Lois, her eyes wide, and cheeks flushed. Gentle, like the kiss of a butterfly, her hand rested on her lips. "My poor Amanda. Imagine, having to be alone with that awful man." She sighed, allowing her hand to drop onto her lap.

"After he got us to his office, can you believe that man proceeded to tell me how he had set Albert up to be killed? Right down to the last, ugly detail." Avis took a deep breath. "Thank God, Amanda fell asleep and slept through most of the ordeal. Bull would not even let us go, until she started raising a rusty."

Avis shook her head, unwilling herself to believe that her battle had only begun. If she thought about the staggering consequences of what she was going to do, she would be lost. Some things she would not even share with her dearest friend.

Avis opened her eyes to see Lois clasping and unclasping her frail hands in her lap. Her nail beds were tinted blue, and a blue tinge lingered around her lips.

"I hate to say it, but I am glad Albert is dead," admitted Lois with what Avis thought might be guilty preoccupation, as if she knew she was not long for this earth. Lois' lips tensed and a rare fire sparked in her blue eyes. "I don't know why the

Lord allows such evil to thrive on this earth."

The strangled gasp portended more coughing that rocked Lois until Avis thought her friend would collapse.

Avis steeled herself to deliver the rest of the news, but looked away. She could not bear to watch Lois' face flush pink, then purple as though giant hands were throttling the very breath out of her.

"That means," gasped Lois, between spasms, bringing the handkerchief to her mouth as she struggled for air, "that your troubles are over."

When the spasm stopped, Avis opened her eyes, noting the lingering blue around Lois' mouth. Tears nettled her eyes and she transferred the baby to the other breast. She strengthened her resolve.

Bull is right. Lois is dying and I cannot do a damn thing about it! Shaking her head to shed the morbid thoughts, she stared down at pink-cheeked Amanda, who radiated health. The child's gaze roamed Avis' face as she nursed and kicked her bare foot playfully against side of the sofa. "Babies are so precious," she whispered, thinking of her own child.

Avis turned to her friend. "No, Lois," Avis replied while reaching for her friend's hand. Clutching the cold fingers in her warm ones, she held them as if keeping her only friend from slipping away from the people who needed her. "I am afraid Albert's murder means that my problems have only begun."

Eyes widening, Lois removed the handkerchief from her mouth where she had been dabbing at the corners. "I don't understand." Lois crumpled the handkerchief in her hand.

Avis watched Lois' chest heave up and down in her fight for breath. Every day seemed more of a struggle.

"Albert was the monster who did those awful things to you and--" began Lois, battling for one more breath.

"Hush! Don't try to speak, Lois. I will tell you all, but first I want to make sure you understand that Brother Andrew cannot know. The last thing I need to do is get the preacher involved in this mess."

Avis turned to look down the hall to make sure he remained in his study. She was certain he would feel obligated to interfere and, if he did, Bull would have the kindly preacher laid out for the undertaker in the wag of a tail.

Avis watched as Lois closed her eyes, her mouth tightening into a firm line. She tilted her head back as if dreaming. Opening her eyes, she stared beyond Avis. "I saw that man, Avis, but I see him not as a snake, but a worm that lives in filth."

Avis stared at her friend, shocked. "How did you--" she wanted to ask, but knew that her questions would only lead to more questions that could not be explained. She knew what Lois would say, and she could not abide one more word about Lois' God.

Avis shook her head, ridding herself of all thoughts except those of revenge. "Lois, never mind." Lois was not looking at her, but pouring her a glass of water. She handed Avis the glass. "I don't want to hear your fairy tales about angels and such," she said softly accepting the drink.

Lois gave her that infernally understanding smile she always gave her, as if she knew a secret. Feeling unreasonably guilty for not wanting to listen to the same old story, Avis shifted away from her. Did not the existence of such evil belie the existence of a good god?

"Just let me explain, Lois. We don't have much time before the preacher is done and I have a lot to say."

"Very Well. Whatever you care to share."

In the quiet of the Saturday afternoon, while the preacher worked on his Sunday sermon and Amanda played quietly on the sofa, Avis explained how Albert came to die in that saloon brawl and Bull's diabolical plan for her life. She told her friend everything, leaving out only the matter of Lois' death, and her own determination to destroy the man.

When she had finished, and all Lois' suggestions for escape resulted in dead-ends, Lois bowed her head. She raised a trembling hand toward heaven, the lace of the handkerchief trailing downward from the palm.

"May God help us all," prayed the frail, wisp of a woman in an unusually strong voice.

Avis jumped at the answering clap of thunder. If there was a God, He might have heard this prayer after all. She trembled.

CHAPTER ONE

August 1904

A hot burst of wind sent loose desert sand spinning a fragile twisting funnel that meandered through the lonely streets of town. The spiraling dust devil skipped past the adobe homes and shuttered windows of the local businesses, spending itself in a peppering spray against the whitewashed facade of Dixon's General Store.

The long and blistering hours of the day when the sun traveled its unrelenting course above the thin air of the desert basin were spent in siesta. During siesta most folks preferred to sleep on their good ear, unwilling, come marauding Apaches or hell, itself, to be dragged away from the cool sanctuary of their homes.

Avis' dainty pump-heeled eastern boots fired rapid taps on the hardwood deck of the sheltered boardwalk that fronted the businesses of town.

Avis frowned when the curled feather of her hat dangled in her eyes instead of over her ear. She halted to pin the red silk hat more firmly atop the French twist of her hair, then picked up her red, white, and blue striped silk skirt and marched to the saloon.

The white, silk purse dangled from her wrist in the sort of carefree manner that presented good advertisement, but belied the angry bent of her thoughts. "He'll freeze in hell!" she swore, fuming at Bull's vulgar demands.

The sick old cur-dog thought he could think up any scheme to make her dance, did he? Since when had she whored in the basest of ways by flaunting her body?

Bull might as well water cactus, or paint the white sands blue. Stripping off her clothes and prancing before a rowdy bunch of men was not part of the deal between them and she had made that clear to him four years ago.

She suggested he get Delilah and her *silver dollars* for the night's entertainment. Delilah delighted in flaunting her unusual attributes. Bull, with his fancy for pretty boys, didn't understand how a whore with nipples too big, and too round to be normal, could inflame any man into selling his soul for a nibble. Finally, her words sank into Bull's convoluted cow paddy brain, or he gave up. She didn't know or care which, but she won.

She had been winning a lot lately. Bull was a sick old varmint, declining every day. Growing more forgetful, he had left the actual running of the mercantile and lumber business to her, while keeping his own darker dealings private.

Incapable as he was, she suspected that someone else was running the evil side of Bull's empire. Until she penetrated the *brotherhood* and discovered that name, she would be unable to end her quest. She had come too close to have the disease snatch her victory from her.

If there was any doubt lingering in Bull's mind as to the eventual outcome of one of their disputes, then a little blackmail laced with fear changed the course of his thinking. How ironic that he did not even realize that his own methods were being used against him.

She would take her place as mistress for tonight's shindig. Delilah would gain the biggest part of the night's benefits. Every buck from fifty miles each side of Alamogordo would be lined up out the door, over the Sacramento Mountains, across the Pecos and clear on to Texas, for a look at her *silver dollars*.

This occasion might be a chance to gain more information about the next transport into Mexico. She had long suspected the army had to be involved in getting the captives across the border.

How things had changed. She recalled the times she had been ashamed and afraid to walk down the street and face the cruelties of the townspeople. Her war had extracted a high price, but she was close to the end.

There was the matter of the symbolic rings, and the men who wore them. They were important men who disappeared under cover of festivities, to return days later to board the train.

Curiosity about the rings advanced when she had learned from a book that the Minotaur was part Greek mythology. The man-bull lived in a Labyrinth, and was a peculiarly hideous monster known for the human sacrifices made to appease the monster.

Avis shuddered to consider the awful implications of the bond these fellows of the ring shared. If she had learned anything, it was that the world could be impossibly wicked.

Tonight, while all eyes would be on Delilah and her entertainments, Avis would attempt to follow the men to discover their destination. If she succeeded, she would expose their secrets and Trumbull's treachery would be revealed.

Bull was right about one thing. Through the years, she had become rich and saved much more than she had sent back east. Smarter, too, stashing her money elsewhere besides Bull's bank in Bull's town.

The years had changed much about her mother, but for one constant: Mavis Ashton wrote long lists of needs, in hopes that Avis would send more money. Money for the mansion, the property, new furniture, and hundreds more excuses, but Avis was not fooled. Her mother's single comfort, that unchangeable thing, was the expensive, ever-increasing doses from a little bottle that kept her body present and her soul far distant from this world.

The moment Avis gained her freedom she would return to

North Carolina to reclaim her daughter and end her mother's habit. Right now, she had no way to help her mother, except to keep her life as peaceful as possible.

Unbidden tears misted her eyes at the guilty knowledge that she was helping her mother destroy herself. What else, she wondered, could she do from more than a thousand miles away?

Avis frowned, remembering the rambling and incoherent letter that had arrived a few weeks before. Barely readable, the writing smudged and spotty bore no resemblance to the delicate and precise script that her mother had perfected as a child and prized as an adult. The letter must have been written while in a stupor.

Avis had taken great pains to see that Tessa had little to do with her grandmother. The one exception was the monthly visit her mother made to the boarding school. Thankfully, the Catholic sisters had recognized her mother's condition and always had a chaperon present. Never would they allow Mavis Ashton to take Tessa anywhere for any reason.

Every month Avis sent a generous donation directly to the academy for Tessa's room and board. Separately, an allowance was sent to her mother. Because her mother was untrustworthy, the servants communicated with her directly, advising her. They, too, complained of being helpless in the face of her mother's decline.

Still, with all the precautions, some question lingered. Perhaps it had been her mother's deep melancholia, but there persisted a new uneasiness; a dark and fearful expectancy.

Breathing deeply, then mounting a smile on her face, Avis put her hand on the swinging door of the cantina. She paused to listen when she heard wrenching shrieks coming from around the corner. The strident wailing sounded like a wounded animal.

Searching, she saw nothing and no one else in the streets.

She had passed naught but a few languishing horses tethered to the shaded hitching posts in the few blocks she had walked from her home to the cantina.

Irritated with herself for caring about a dumb animal, she whirled about to search out the source of the agonized cries. She could at least put the wounded animal out of its misery with the pistol holstered at her thigh.

She stopped abruptly. Before her, a huge, dirty man add lash upon lash of his long, black whip onto the crumpled and bleeding form of a girl-child. The whistle of the whip dulled to a sickening thud each time it deepened its bite in the already hemorrhaging flesh.

Gripped by the scene, she stifled her gasp. Nearly gagging at the stench of blood and the filth that filled the air, she covered her nose with her hand.

As she watched, the girl quit screaming. Even the cicada's paused their noisy chorus to listen to the whistle of the strop as it sliced its way through the air.

Engrossed in the violence, he did not know she stood behind him. Avis seized the chance to make a dash for help.

Quickly, she hastened down the boardwalk, through the saloon, out its rear door and across the alley. She had been like that girl once, and the preacher saved her. Maybe he could help this girl as well.

Head down, her hands holding the hem of her gown up from the dirt, she nearly collided with the preacher emerging onto the verandah from the office door.

"Oh!" yelped Avis in surprise, stepping back, her hand over her heart.

"Sorry," mumbled Andrew stepping back from the near collision.

He blinked once, and then gazed at her with a bemused smile. What must he think, wondered Avis, to encounter the profane Miss Hollis standing before him on his very own doorstep?

She watched him tense. The chiseled lips flattened. Her hand swept the dampness from her brow. She shouldn't have come.

"Miz Hollis? Surely, my eyes must be deceiving me. Could it really be you? Such a pleasure to see you again," he announced with a bow, and the with same false cordiality he would welcome Jack the Ripper into his congregation.

Really! Bowing to a harlot, just to rub it in. Avis bit her tongue. A quick glance showed his hazel eyes dancing with, of all things, humor. The man was imperturbable.

After folding his arms across his chest, he cocked his head to the side, and watched her, like he would a dirty little bug. Clearly, he waited for her to speak, but words escaped her. She had no business being around the preacher, but who else would help the girl? She opened her mouth to retort, but snapped it shut, not knowing how to ask for help.

"To what do I owe this honor? And so dressed up, too," he observed. His eyes dropped to survey the fancy gown and linger over the fulsome creamy mounds shamefully pushed up, nearly spilling out of their lacy nest.

He really wasn't thirsty, but the longer he looked at the professional seductress, the less spit he could muster. A flush climbed up his neck when he caught her aloof gaze upon him. If the brazen woman had not wanted to be ogled, she should have covered them up!

Was he mistaken or did a light blush stain her cheeks? Surely, she was beyond being shamed by her brazen appearance.

Hands fluttered to her brow. She did not look at him, but stroked her forehead.

It was her fault that he was feeling these urges. She was a soiled dove, a temptress from a long line of Eves, come to stand on his porch and entice him into eating forbidden fruit.

Arms dropped to his sides, hands curled into fists, he studied her face for changes the years had made. Four years of debauchery should have left a few creases at least, but the years had been good to her. She had grown more beautiful and, perhaps softer.

Had she softened towards him, he wondered, thinking that something must have happened to bring her to his doorstep? The next moment, he questioned why the feelings of a hussy should be important enough to concern him?

Maybe because he could not forget her? What would happen if his congregation knew that their pastor preached against sin from the pulpit, but dreamed of the town's foremost sinner at night?

Enough! Andrew met her gaze and shifted his stance. "Well?" he said again, folding his arms across his chest determined to present as close to an implacable attitude as he could muster. "As I understood, when last we met at the store..." He stepped back. "I am sure you remember that occasion of my public humiliation?" He hoped he sounded distant and not at all weak minded or peevish.

Her hair, he noticed, had every bit the radiance of the live coals he remembered in his dreams, when she was warm and wet beneath him.

Before she had worn her hair down, allowing the brilliant curls to fall, touchable and not swept up in a fancy pile on the top of her head. Certainly not covered by a foolish hat.

His eyes traveled to the awful red silk hat with a blue feather that sat on the back of her hair. The droopy feather that curled around her left ear was nearly insulting in its lack of starch.

"Well!" Andrew cleared his throat to stifle his amusement. "I see by the blank look on your face, Miz Hollis, that you have forgotten that occasion? Let me remind you, because you were very clear to everyone within hearing distance, that you never wanted to see this-- What is that name you like to call me?" Andrew screwed his eyes shut as if he were struggling with his memory, but, instead, keenly recalling the biting insults periodically been hurled at him for more than three years.

His index finger shot into the air. "Ah yes! Now I remember. You don't seem to know me as anyone but that cowardly, yellow-bellied muck worm. Since then, you have been shouting to all within hearing distance that you never wanted to see this *muck worm*, again. Now, you must explain how you come to be on this lowly muck worm's veranda?"

She dropped her head, embarrassed. For mercy sakes! Everyone understood he was a preacher and she only humiliated herself by shouting that he was a spineless, no account worm that lived in manure. If anyone lived in cow dung, it was herself and the mayor.

Andrew expected another round of undeserved imprecations. When he saw that the usual onslaught was not forthcoming, he stepped back, spreading his hands wide. "But let us forget all that is past, and now, tell me what brings you to the abode of this self-same, but now more humbled, man?" he chided, dropping his voice into his best sermonizing manner.

Avis opened her mouth to speak, but words failed. Noting the anxious lines around her mouth, Andrew paused and studied her eyes. If eyes were the windows to the soul, then these eyes usually hard and unreachable were open like blue velvet pansies. What he saw in their depths was fear. Could it be that the hussy was afraid?

"Please, not now," whispered the woman, with a flick of the tip of her tongue over her lower lip. "Come, follow me, Preacher," she urged grasping his arm and tugging at him.

Andrew winced as claw-like nails gripped him, digging into the sensitive flesh under his right forearm. He had seen that panicked look of desperation before on others, but Avis, he already knew, was not given to fits of hysteria.

She relaxed her grip and he stared down at the hand on his arm. Her touch gentled, but remained insistent in its warmth and urgency. When he glanced back up into the depths of her eyes, years of rancor slid away. She needed him and maybe that was all that mattered.

"Please, Andrew, if you don't come someone is going to die," she begged, her blue eyes pleading.

"Very well," he replied, softly with a nod of the head. He allowed her to grab his hand and lead him from his porch, and across the ally.

When they walked through the rear door of the saloon, Avis quit towing him, but charged ahead.

He followed, realizing that he had no idea where he was going. What was new about that? He never did know where he was going with that particular female, anyway.

Andrew had lived across from the back door for years, but had never before seen the inside of the local pleasure palace. Try as he might, he couldn't curb the temptation to eyeball the bawdyhouse as they marched through.

The dim, open hall of the lower room was dark, and cavernous. A finely crafted, glossy pine, brass railed bar ran the length of one end, behind which hung the usual oversized painting of the ample-breasted naked woman.

The last painting he had seen like that was in Virginia. The buxom nude, he recalled, had been of the pink skinned blond variety, but this one was a brunette. Closer inspection showed him that she was a brunette from head to toe.

The facial features of the reclining full-bodied beauty of the portrait looked strangely familiar. This supported his long held theory that in every sporting house the same blowzy body was plastered across the wall for the bleary-eyed lustful to ponder while they swilled their drinks. The only changes were to the color of furry patches and the eyes.

He had yet to see a naked female mounted for carnal

rumination, which didn't have the color of her hair, matched to the thatch between her thighs. Why, he wondered, had he never seen a painting of a flaming red head, like Avis Hollis, with a black patch betwixt her thighs?

One thought led to another and the next moment he caught himself staring too long and wondering too much about the female marching ahead of him. He tried to visualize how she looked under all those clothes.

A man of discipline he glanced away and swiveled his head to smile at the barkeeper. The wizened older fellow had been busying himself by drying the fruit jars neatly arrayed before him.

Surprised at the procession, the barkeeper paused in mid-swipe to watch the parade pass before him. Andrew grinned sociably at him. "Just passing through," he announced as casually as he could.

It probably never occurred to the preacher that a body might well be wondering exactly what the preacher was doing following a whore around at all, let alone letting her parade him through a saloon. Sal grinned and the preacher looked away.

Andrew averted his eyes, trying not to think about much, but keeping up with the sashaying bottom ahead of him. He marveled at how delightful the sway of a curvy female could be to a starving man.

He breathed deeply, observing that the pungent odors of soured spirits, stale smoke from countless cigars and the rank cuspidors that dotted the saloon, remained the same. The pernicious odors fouled the air.

Ever looking for a good sermon, he compared the lingering stench of tobacco to a legacy of evil. Maybe not evil, but a lesson on lust! Lust was always good for a message! Maybe he would build a sermon around pernicious lust for Sunday. My, my, but wouldn't that be a popular sermon!

Andrew glanced at the bartender once more, following his gaze to see that Avis' shiny red hat pitched, and bobbed atop the pile of hair very nearly the way a cock's comb would as he strutted around the coop. Humored by the comic sight, Andrew shared the joke with the bartender.

Sliding his eyes downward, he admired the play of her bustle as it moved with the womanly sway of her hips. *My goodness Miz Hollis, but you are one fine example of female pulchritude!*

Instantly his wicked thoughts shamed him. Andrew rolled his eyes heavenward. *Lord, I am sorry, but You have left me a bachelor too long and see what happened*! He silently apologized while dropping a complaint to Providence for leaving him high and dry for more than four years.

Suddenly, the right half of the swinging gate smashed directly into his face. Squeezing his eyes shut, the stinging shards of pain lanced up through the bridge of his nose and sharp needles clustered behind his eyes. Silently, he notified the Lord that he had gotten the message.

Clutching at his nose protectively, he endured the pain until it ebbed into a dull ache. When he was certain there was no blood, he placed his hand on the offending door, only to have Avis barrel through the other side and send him sprawling at her feet.

"Hell's bells, Andrew!" she scolded, forgetting to whom she spoke, "I don't know what your game is, but you'd better get up or you're going to be too late to do any good at all!"

It was not every day a beautiful woman spouted ugly curses at him. Amazed, he rocked back on his elbows to stare up at her. There she stood, hands fisted on hips, swearing like an old salt. All he could do was marvel that such ugly words could come from such a dignified looking woman.

Putting aside his irritation with the mouthy woman, he scrambled to his feet. This time, he kept the palm of his hand cupped over his nose as he walked through the swinging doors.

Sal watched the lively and amusing little comedy, cheered to see Hollis putting the preacher through his paces. He didn't know this particular preacher, but he had decided a long time ago that all preachers were useless and he disliked them in general. In his opinion, a preacher was only good for marryin' or buryin' and he had never met a preacher who had an ounce of spine to him at all.

Convinced that this preacher wasn't any different from the rest, he was enjoying seeing him jump, like a frog's leg in a frying pan, to a fire lit by a woman who most of the gentry considered a sportin' floozy.

She was just opposite of what folks thought. Someday them cackling hens who looked the other way when they met her on the street would know it right a long with the preacher.

CHAPTER TWO

Andrew heard the unmistakable hiss and pop of the whip before he rounded the corner to see the stranger, who wielded the long black strop. Stroke upon stroke fell, as the big man flailed the life out of an Indian child crumpled into a bloody mound curled almost entirely under the stoop of the meeting house.

He did not know if the child was alive or dead. Mangled as she was, the only way he could discern that the bloody lump was female, were the tattered remnants of her deer-hide dress and an extraordinary length of black hair that lay tangled and matted beneath a veneer of fine, tawny colored dust.

Andrew observed the frenzied mania with which the madman delivered the lashes and knew this was not a situation when the stranger would listen to reason. A quick survey of the area told him the law was nowhere near, and there had not one second to spare.

Andrew knew that nothing short of violence would counter the merciless attack. He had to act quickly, and do so in such a way to prevent a worse tragedy.

While Andrew considered his options, the truth of the situation dawned upon Avis. A mindless dolt could see that the peaceable man was no match for a Goliath who towered at least a foot taller and two hundred pounds heavier. Besides, the preacher was too nice and she didn't think he had it in him to win in a face off with a piss ant.

The more she considered the situation, the more anxious

she became that her hastiness had jeopardized his life. Then, again, she reasoned, trying to excuse the rashness of her actions, if the girl were to have a chance to live, there hadn't been time to summon help from anyone else.

How long, she wondered, did it take to whip a body to death? Indeed, Avis turned her attention to the motionless form, glad to see that while she was gone, the child had crawled half under the protection of the steps. But did she live or would all this been for naught?

At the very moment Avis was about to suggest to Andrew that they try and find more help, Andrew surprised her by yanking her back into the shadows of the walkway. The next second, he crammed her into a doorway with her arms bowed up and pinned between them. The air was pushed out of her lungs with a muffled whoosh.

He flattened himself against her, squashing her into the nook, as she wrestled beneath him. Grabbing her chin in one hand, he captured her face with the other to still her wiggling body long enough to listen to him. "Stop squirming, woman," he growled between clenched teeth, "I need to talk to you and I can't do it while you are fighting me."

"If you want to talk to me, then let me breathe," she hissed in shallow pants.

A look of surprise crossed his face before he obliged her by stepping back and relaxing the hold on her face. He did not fully release her, but leaned forward, binding her between himself and the wall by posting his hands on either side of her head.

"Sorry," he whispered, nose to nose, and barely separated from her at all. "Do you still carry your buddy, Avis?" he asked, aware that she never went anywhere without the pistol.

Her jaw dropped and she quickly clamped it shut. She sucked in a deep breath making her bosom heave against his chest. "What the hell! You can't be serious. Nobody can hit a damn thing with my pea shooter from this distance and you know it," she hissed, vainly trying to reason with him while pushing his hand away from the wall. "Especially you, a preacher. Why, I don't even think you know the butt end from the barrel end."

When he refused to budge, but outstretched one palm, she crossed her arms in front of her bosom and raised her chin. She refused to look anywhere, but beyond him.

Precious moments slipped by. "We are wasting time. Forget what happened between us. You asked for my help, and now I'm asking for yours," he growled, his voice hard as the desert pavement. "Or don't you care about that poor girl out there. Pretty soon that stranger is going to go under those steps to get to her and then we won't have a chance to save her."

He was right. She was being petty, unthinking, and worse, uncaring of the poor child who had no one else to defend her. "You are going have to get right up on him, Preacher," she said, mentally cursing them both for a pair of idiots. "Step back and give me some room." After pushing him away, she hiked her skirts, and reluctantly extracted the tiny, silver, double shot pistol from her black lacy garter.

Andrew turned away to peek around the corner. He did not turn back until she dropped the pistol into his palm.

"If you miss with this thing and that stinking goat charges you, you best believe I will be out of here faster than a coyote can mess in a cocklebur patch." Avis dropped her skirts. "It's your butt, Preacher Bristow."

Andrew studied the weapon while trying to ignore the unladylike language. "I cannot believe that such a beautiful woman should have such a nasty mouth," remarked Andrew, not seeing her face redden before she laid upon him a new string of whispered swear words.

Andrew flipped the safety off. "I thank you for your vote of confidence and your overwhelming concern, Miz Hollis. I am touched, really I am, that you have expressed more concern for my hinder parts in the past five minutes than you have for my family in the past four years."

He smiled, but with no real humor, just determination and, she suspected, years of resentment. She watched as he turned from her to face the Goliath.

Avis, nose in the air, turned to abandon him to his just desserts. She hesitated. Truly, she did bear a certain loyalty to the man who saved her life. It wasn't his fault he was too damned nice. Never mind what he said, she owed it to him to stay until the job was finished.

Avis stepped off the walkway beside him. Andrew halted surprised, the last thing he needed was to have to worry about her safety as well as his own. Immediately he stepped back, to jerk her by the arm backward with him.

He shoved her into the cove of the storefront, his hands gripping her shoulders. When he jerked her around to face him, enough pain lanced through her to make her wince

Disgusted with himself for his unintentional roughness with the obstinate woman, he grit his teeth. "Will you stand still and listen. You stop this insanity long enough to let me do this!"

One look at the fiery darts in her eyes and the stubborn set of her jaw showed him that she would not willingly do anything for him. He peered down at her and shifted his stance.

"Look, allow me to explain," he said too calmly, his eyes boring into hers. "You may run for help now, or stay back here, in any case you are to do nothing, but pray. Do not step any further than the end of this boardwalk. We have taken too long as it is."

Andrew watched Avis' cheeks heat; probably humiliated that he treated her the same way he would a disobedient child. He was drawing a line in the sand that he commanded her not to cross.

The contrary set of her mouth and those sullen eyes were familiar. She was not about to co-operate with anything that he had to say. His eyes narrowed and he gripped her arm.

"Your are hurting me," she softly cried.

"Dammit, woman! We are wasting time! Either, you keep your pretty ass out of my business, or I am going to move my butt out of here faster than you can call me a son-of-a-bitch again! Do you understand me?" Andrew watched disbelief and surprise creep into her eyes. He released her with a purposeful shove backward and walked away, knowing what she was thinking.

Shocked to her toes that the preacher would sink to using profanity, Avis could only stare after him.

The minute he turned the corner to confront the filthy pig of a man, she wanted to run after him and beg him to stop before he got hurt. Her heart dropped to realize she was too late.

Ever expecting the worst and disbelieving in prayer, she could only hold her breath as Andrew drew nearer to the evil beast. She knew that he had to be close to make the shot count.

She listened to the Spanish curses flung over the crumpled body while the big man flogged the child. She understood when he called the child some kind of witch. Such a superstitious people to believe such a child could really be a witch.

A few feet behind the stranger, Andrew realized that he probably could have come on like a herd of thundering buffalo and the stranger would not hear. His confidence grew.

With the skill honed by youthful years of competition and practice, Andrew carefully figured the angles and awaited the rise of the whip hand. He marked the knothole at the middle of the porch support, just beyond his chosen target. The hand drew back to repeat its path, and Andrew fired the instant it crossed between himself and his mark.

Not seeing any contradiction between the violence of the moment and the virtue he strove for, Andrew muttered a quiet thank you when the tiny bullet blew a small perforation in the back of the hand. He watched as bits and pieces of flesh spat from the wound, and the flattened lead chunked up a puff of dirt to spend itself in the sand.

The bloody damage immediately apparent, the wounded hand flung the whip far way, landing with a thud in the dirt.

Andrew watched the big man twist about, staring, but not really seeing. Instinctively, he grabbed his wrist, holding his hand up before his eyes.

The tightened grip, Andrew knew, would do nothing to soothe the pain or stanch the flowing blood. Rivulets streaked down his forearm to mingle with the girl's blood on the thirsty ground.

Roaring, and eyes wild, the stranger lurched forward to attack. Others emerged from their homes to group about Andrew. The big man shrank back.

Manuel moved to stand beside his boss, carefully scanning the surrounding area for any surprises lurking in the shadows of the town. "I see I am tardy. What can I do for you now?" he asked, his eyes never straying from the fat pig of a man. The preacher had never before used a pistol since he had known him.

Relieved to have Manuel by his side, Andrew continued to keep the small pistol aimed slightly to the left of center of the prisoner's chest. "I may have been too late and he might have already murdered her."

Manuel looked to see the body of an Indian child sprawled nearly under the steps of the church. "It is sick to attack one so young," he commented, shaking is head.

Together, they watched Father Juan hurry to the girl's side, his long, coarse brown robes flapping around his ankles. The priest did not stop to greet Andrew.

"If she is alive, the *chica* needs our help, Manuel. After the priest is finished checking her over, it would be best for you to take her to our home. You may put her in my room and see what kind of help you and Maria can get for her."

"*Si*." Manuel motioned with his hands toward the quiet form. "Do you think she is yet alive, *Senor*? For myself, I am sorry to say that she does not look to be breathing."

The priest's lips moved in prayer, while he reached under the stoop to push the veil of tangled hair back from the face that lay turned away. Manuel waved his hand at the girl. "You see, the padre is likely bestowing last rites."

Andrew shrugged. "Don't know, but we have to try to save her. If you look at the dirt around her and see how it's kicked up, I think he went so *loco* he missed his mark about half the time. That and the way she nearly crawled under the porch might make the differences that could save her life."

The air was dry and the sun beat down on Andrew's bare head, causing sweat to roll down his face. He raised his arm and quickly swiped the dampness from his forehead with the long sleeve of his shirt. "I think Father Juan should be able to tell us something here in a minute." They remained silent watching the priest minister to the girl.

Andrew contemplated just how far he needed to carry this new burden of holding a man at gunpoint. He was a preacher, a minister of the Lord, not a lawman, but he appeared to be trapped holding a gun on the prisoner until the law showed up and that might be a while. There had not a badge visible anywhere in the rapidly emptying streets.

He needed a better gun. "I think, rather than trust this goober plunker of Miz Hollis' again, I'd better borrow one of your Colts. I'm a little rusty, you know, and the forty-five will give me more of an advantage." Andrew wiped his face again with his sleeve.

"Rusty?" remarked Manuel with a snort to think of what amazing shooting that the man could do if he were not so "rusty." He shook his head at the preacher's unintentional foolishness and handed him the heavy, long-nosed revolver, butt first, as Andrew passed the derringer back to him.

"Please see that Miz Hollis gets this, tell her *gracias* for me. Warn her that she has one shot remaining. I would hate for the thing to fire off and accidentally shoot her in some delicate place," commented Andrew as he sighted in the bigger gun, missing entirely the amused speculation in his friend's eyes.

The crowd mumbled a few irritated complaints at being awakened over something insignificant. Avis watched the few onlookers drift away, thinking how like mice they were. Fat mice fleeing to the comfort of cool dark holes without a care for the wounded one." At least Manuel is here," she said to herself, blessing him for having a gun that could do some real damage to the bully.

Lost in thought, she tried to sort through the amazing event she had just witnessed. She marveled that a man who had made it his business to preach against guns handled one so well. The man, who she had thought too cowardly to fight, had just brought down a giant with an impossible shot from an equally impossible distance, with a weapon designed for threats of an intimate nature.

The only comfortable explanation for his keen shooting, in view of her past accusations, was that the shot was a lucky one. Mentally, she retraced the way he seemed to wait for just the right moment to fire. She had to admit that there had been a method, which meant that the preacher might have known exactly what he was doing. How pathetic to have believed her lying insults about his supposed cowardice.

Years past, they had often argued about owning a gun, and she had assumed he could be too nice to do what was necessary to defend himself. The lies she had spread about had been invented to protect and not to harm him, but some time, in the last four years, she had begun to believe them.

What if she had gone to him, and explained to him that she was trapped? Could he have, or would he have stood against Bull? Could he have come out from a showdown four years ago alive and whole? She guessed that now she would never know. Too much had gone on for things to ever be right between them.

As she waited, she watched Andrew, broad shoulders squared and muscular legs planted wide apart, adjust his stance. His auburn hair, turned rich russet in the brilliant light of the afternoon, began to corkscrew. Before long, she knew, the curls he kept shellacked to his head, would be popping out all over from sweat.

The only undisciplined thing about the man was a full head of rebellious hair. If he ended up with a whole head of screwy curls, looking like a bandito, it would serve him right for being too stuffy by far.

Damn! Andrew didn't even have a hat! A sure way to go down with the stroke was to be out here bareheaded. Worried, now more than ever, she anxiously sought a way out of this predicament. Maybe Manuel could help when he finished whatever he was doing.

Manuel flipped the safety on and examined the dainty type pistol that a woman could carry concealed almost anywhere on her body. He grinned; thinking that some places a woman could hide the little thing was more interesting than others. Turning around, he quickly spied the pretty woman standing behind the *senor* looking sad and too worried.

As long as Manuel had known them, an odd strife existed between the preacher and *La Bonita.* They did foolish things to each other. Sometimes, the two would pass each other on the street and never speak, but, later, wheedle for information about each other from Maria and him. Then, after they had given over every morsel of information, he and Maria were required to swear themselves to secrecy.

Christmas was always most interesting with its loco exchange of gifts. As far as the town was concerned, there existed nothing, but hostility between them. He and Maria knew better and had always suspected fire of another sort sparked between them. They went along with the silly game, expecting that, one day, something would happen. It was not good for *Senor* to be so long alone.

Manuel glanced up to see that Father Juan was not ready for his help. "Before Padre Juan calls for help, I need but a moment, to return the pistol to *La Bonita,* who is behind you."

Andrew shrugged, feeling a momentary stab of whatever it was he always felt whenever Manuel called the lowly harlot 'pretty woman.' "Just make sure you don't tarry too long. Father Juan should be finished *pronto,*" he growled, wondering why he should begrudge Manuel his moment with Bull's woman. Andrew shook his head to clear it of all the memories of the times the tramp had made him feel like a *gauche* kid who couldn't say or do anything right enough to please her.

Manuel's grin, thought Avis, was like a scoop of vanilla, against tanned, swarthy features. She had always thought that when the tall, jovial, and aristocratically handsome Manuel smiled that way, it was almost impossible not to feel better, and smile in return. Often, after one of Bull's orgies, when the darkness in her soul was tarry thick, and her view of humanity the most jaded, she would think of Manuel and Maria. Filled with self pity, she would wonder why the simple happiness of the loving bond between two people, was lost to her.

"*La Bonita,* the preacher says '*gracias'* for the use of your pistol," said Manuel, bestowing a courtly bow upon her as though she was a lady worthy of respect. When she reached out to take the silver derringer, he straightened. "The boss also says to tell you that there is one bullet left, and to be most careful how you replace it."

She smiled with a flirtatious wink. She should have been embarrassed by his insinuating grin, but she had long ago forfeited modesty as the ante of the game.

The preacher hadn't personally delivered his thanks, but

there was no reason for him to thank her for a damn thing, but trouble and that with a capital "T." She frowned to recall how she had only ever been trouble to the man, and she could not rightly blame him for not wanting to meet up with her again.

Manuel leaned down to speak softly in her ear. "Do not be so confused, I was surprised by his fine shooting as well, but then I remembered that none of us can truly know another. He has his reasons for not taking up a gun and we know very little about the person he was and what happened to him before he came to this place."

Avis pulled back from Manuel. She held her breath, listening intently, trying to gauge how much he knew about her feelings for the preacher and his child.

"Forgive me for saying this, but I think you are disturbed to find out the man is not the coward you have despised him for being, no?" he said with a wriggle of dark eyebrows.

She did not reply, but lowered her eyes.

"Because, until now, he has refused to pick up a gun, you have given the man an undeserved reputation in this town. Now you are ashamed and wondering."

Bothered that Manuel should know so much, she remained silent. Glancing up, she met dark eyes tendered by his concern for her. If no one else understood the hell her life had been, she knew the tall Spaniard did.

"I do not know what is between you two, but I think you have you had your reasons for saying such things," he said softly. "Many people misjudge him because of his gentle nature and thoughtful ways. I believe the man is far stronger and wiser than either of us can know.

"Manuel…" she began only to be stopped by his upraised hand.

"One moment, *Bonita*. I have to say this now. That he is more the stalking cat, the kind that wisely waits for his moment and chooses his fights. Though I am not of his faith, I know that this preacher is a good man and not a coward, as you have said. Perhaps that is just as you are not what you seem, eh?"

The winning grin flashing at her again. A too friendly grin that intimated they shared a secret. Her heart beat faster at the thought that Manuel might know too much. Did he know that she was collaborating with the government in Santa Fe? Avis was about to inform Manuel that he could know nothing at all, but was spared by Father Juan's call for help.

Learning to dwell in silence and build a case against Bull had been difficult. Bull might cease to be a threat, but there remained that most devious of minds behind him. She must never divulge her secrets until the end. To slip, or raise any question, would mean certain death for the few people closest to her. She had to be certain that when the trap closed upon the cult, not one would be missing.

No other person could know how, over the years, she had watched Bull's organization grow into an octopus, its enormous tentacles spanning states, oceans, and even continents. How he trafficked across the border in human souls

Even though disease was gobbling him alive, his influence was bigger now than had been four years ago. Another had taken his place, and if he was whom she suspected, then her life could not proceed until he was carted away.

She had done right by not seeking protection from the preacher, a gentle soul, who could never have conceived of such evil. Andrew, she decided long ago, was too damn good for this world and, unless a heaven really existed, maybe for the next. Then, as now, there would be only danger for anyone she allowed into her thoughts.

Manuel bowed to her with a flourish, by sweeping an imaginary hat across his waist. "Now, I must go, *Senorita*, but someday I must tell you of my former life as a pirate."

Manuel disappeared, to return a few minutes later lugging the weather-beaten back door of the meetinghouse in his arms.

She watched him ease the pine door onto the ground beside the girl, who lay on her stomach.

Avis followed the hand motions as the priest and Manuel discussed in Spanish, how best to lift the broken body. Hope flickered inside her, for surely, if the child were dead, the men would not be quite so careful in transporting her. Just maybe they had done the right thing and the situation wasn't as hopeless as she thought. Maybe, with the proper attention, the girl would survive.

Avis watched them work and considered Manuel's odd sense of humor. She knew it to be a device he used, particularly with Amanda, to give ease to a bad situation. A dart pierced her heart at thoughts of the little curly topped child she had loved as her own. She reminded herself that it is better to put Tessa and Amanda out of her mind than to yearn for the children she could not have.

He had called himself a pirate! She giggled at the preposterous vision of Manuel as a devil-may-care rogue of the sea, leaning into the wind while shouting orders to a crew of blackguards.

She thought to help Manuel and Father Juan care for the child. The good citizens of town had faded from sight and she knew the preacher was stuck. She certainly did not at all like the cunning way in which the fat man had leered at Manuel, as they huddled over the girl.

Avis resolved to stay behind Andrew, thinking that two watchdogs had to be better than one. She raised the derringer, aimed it over Andrew's left shoulder, pointing the barrel in line with the center of the biggest part of the bastard's belly.

Avis, unlike the preacher, was not known for mercy and it did not concern her one whit that she did not know the *hombre's* name. Unlike the preacher, she had no misgivings about shooting a living thing. The world would be better off, she was sure, with one less vile abuser of women.

Manuel, on his knees, gently lifted the fragile form onto the makeshift stretcher. Laying her on her stomach, the girl's face toward her, Avis could see that the girl might have been a few years older than she had thought. Not quite a child, but not an adult, either. The priest captured and folded the girl's dangling arms to rest them above her head.

Perhaps, more dead than alive, the child did not even groan or protest during a process that must have caused considerable pain. Cautiously, the two men bore the battered girl away to the preacher's house.

She gnawed at her lower lip, confused at having no idea what to do. Where, she wanted to know, was the sheriff? She had a good idea where the deputy was resting his worthless hide. If someone didn't come to help the preacher pretty soon, either the heat would get him or the prisoner would get away. He couldn't very well take the bad man to his house. Avis heard steps behind her.

Sal, hands fisted in pockets overlaid by his snowy apron, came to stand beside Avis. She could hear him working over a plug of tobacco, and her stomach revolted against the churning of the tobacco in his jaws.

The sweet scent of blood was drawing swarming, shiny bluebottle flies. Bile rose in her throat as visions of the torn child played through her mind. Avis' free hand went to her mouth as beads of sweat burst upon her forehead. She had to get hold of herself because she would be no good to anyone retching in the street. "Sal, you have got to help him," she whispered, "I'm afraid I am going to be sick."

Sal glanced at Avis. "Gol' darn it, Hollis! I thought all that miserable howling was some damn she cat looking for a tom," explained the bartender, while he shuffled his feet in the dirt.

"'Pears like there is just the four of us crazy people left out here in this heat. Seems like an Injun ga, ain't worth losin' sleep over, according to the Bull." Sal splattered the dirt with a stream of tobacco juice. "But if you need some help, Hollis, I'll be glad to run and fetch the sheriff or somethin'."

Avis considered his offer, for a moment, mildly surprised that Sal offered to get involved. Sal, she thought, must really be feeling guilty to volunteer.

She scanned the shuttered storefronts on either side of the street. How odd it was when something like this happened it fell to a priest, a preacher, a former gunslinger, a bartender, and a whore, to care about the misbegotten.

"Come to think of it, Sal, I haven't seen the sheriff in a couple of days. Hasn't he dropped by the cantina at all?"

"Nope, Usually stops by once or twice an evenin', but I ain't seen him in about a week. Now that I think of it, I ain't seen that good for nothin' deputy around here since last night, either." Sal noticed the tremble in her gun hand.

"You want me to take that double barrel cannon you got there, Hollis?" offered Sal, figuring that she could use some relief. He tilted his shiny pate toward the preacher who was working up quite a sweat.

"That preacher sure is standin' still out there, in all this heat. I give him fifteen minutes 'fore he hits the dirt."

"Hmm. I am afraid you are right." Damp patches had sprouted under the preacher's arms, and his face, she noticed, was turning pickled beet red. "I know," she sighed, "that's why I'm staying. I can't desert him after getting him messed up like this."

"Honey lamb, it's a fine time for ya' to keep watch. I mean, it's hot enough out here to pop hominy." Sal's voice softened, "Maybe ya' should let me stand your duty for awhile."

Avis shook her head prompting the feather on her hat tremble like a leaf in a windstorm. "Thanks. Maybe later, but for right now I'm just fine. Just help me keep an eye on him," she replied her eyes focused on the preacher.

CHAPTER THREE

The blistering sun beat down on his head, his nose ached and the noisy locusts were a plague on his senses. Not usually one to complain, if someone asked him, he would have been forced to admit that never had he known such misery or felt so trapped.

Stubbornly, he waited for the sheriff or somebody to tell him what to do with his prisoner. His predicament worsened in the onslaught of voracious flies. The pests were biting flies that busied themselves with sorties about the wounded man, enticed by the blood turned to doughy splotches in the dust.

One thing the desert had a plenty, was flies, observed Andrew stoically, as he watched the stranger shoo the pests away from the fresh blood. The giant flies sure didn't seem to bother him as much as the incessant buzzing bothered Andrew.

The sun, weakened him, turning his bones to jelly and making him feel like he was melting in the heat. Andrew used all the mental tricks he had practiced to keep awake while riding his frequently long circuits through the desert. Unfortunately, it had not taken him long enough to recite the sixty-six books of both Testaments, the generations of "begets," and all one hundred and seventy-six verses of the longest chapter of the Psalm.

When he switched to singing familiar hymns, the words choked in his throat. He could smell the spilled blood sending up a cloying stench that made his stomach roil. Even one stanza of "Shall We Gather At the River?" taunted him to allow the beast to escape and dunk himself into the scummy water in the trough a few paces away.

Andrew had gotten a closer look at the girl as they carried her past him. He could plug him and be done. Angered by the attack on the child, he forced down the compulsion to rid the world of such an animal.

Who would blame him for a well-placed shot to the head that would surely put a quick end to all lingering miseries. However, shooting a wounded, unarmed man was not a memory he wanted to struggle with for the rest of his life. Lord knows that he had acquired enough bad memories to last his lifetime.

Listening to the man's moans and watching him coddle his hand, even knowing the pain to be real, produced no charity within him. Thoughts of the girl made him want to inflict even more suffering on the abuser.

Then, there was the matter of his vow. Shouldn't he have some remorse for breaking the first vow he had made before God? A vow he had kept until a few minutes before. But when he remembered the man's frenzied attack on the girl and the extent of her wounds, he felt no guilt. There had been no other way to deal with the enraged madman but to use force. Didn't laws exist for the lawless? Maybe God would forgive him by reason of aiding another more helpless.

If the sheriff had been here, none of this would have happened. Where was Sheriff Bookhout, anyway? His heart sank to suddenly remember that the sheriff had gone to El Paso and would not return for a day or two.

Everyone knew you couldn't count on the malingering deputy being any help. Herb loved his liquor and his popularity with Bull, making his estimation lower than a snake's belly in the eyes of most everybody else in Bull's town.

The streets, from what he could tell, had emptied. Good Samaritans, one and all, he thought ruefully as he committed himself to sermonize about true charity come next Sunday morning in the very same meeting house in front of him. Of course, he could be wrong and there could be hundreds of people in back of him, but that was doubtful. He listened, hoping that he was wrong.

Gradually, above the heat and the stink of blood and sweat, he could detect people talking behind him and, over his left shoulder. One of the voices was female. It should have made him more comfortable to know that he had not been deserted, but realizing who stood behind provoked only further aggravation.

Unbelievable! The woman stuck closer than a tick! Miz Hollis had ripped him up one side and down the other for years with her tongue, but now she would not use good sense to leave him and find help. The last thing he needed was for his fallen, but newfound guardian angel to become prey for a wounded man. Vexed angry men had been known to do amazing things when frightened.

That bright hair and womanly shape would surely be a beacon for trouble: like waving a red flag in front of a bull. Unhappy though she might be, he needed to think of a way to get her out of here and put an end to this situation before the pig charged, and the day ended in disaster for all.

If the deputy didn't always make it a point to carry the keys on his belt, they could lock the prisoner in the hoosegow. Herb was probably in some dark hole, with a bottle and a not too particular female. But, if anyone could find Herb's rat-hole, it was Miz Hollis, who, he had heard, had more connections in this territory, than the Southern Pacific Railroad.

With a jerk of his left hand, he pulled the shirttail out of his Levi's and used the end to make a hasty swipe at the stinging sweat running into his eyes. At least he was still sweating; it was when he quit sweating that he had to worry. "Avis," he called, realizing too late, that she would probably balk because he forgot to address her formally.

Hot and tired as he was, he did not appreciate how long it

took her to make those few steps to help him. Resentment increased, while he waited for the fickle lady to make some sign that she had heard him. The precise moment he knew he was going to rupture with anger at her contrariness, he caught a whiff of rose perfume and glimpsed the silvery glint of her precious derringer out of the corner of his eye.

His parched throat forced him to speak in low, raspy whispers that she had to bend closely to hear. The cloying scent of roses was almost dizzying to a man in his depleted condition.

"Miz Hollis," he began, rolling his tongue around, trying to muster up a dab of spit while keeping his eyes on his captive. "I just remembered that Sheriff Bookhout is in El Paso with Garrett for the next couple of days. As for Herb ...well, unless you can find Herb, and we can lock this *hombre* away, I'm going to be stuck here. It is getting hotter by the moment, and right now this six shooter is at least five pounds heavier in my hand than it was to begin with." Andrew paused, watching the stranger shift his position. "If you can't find the deputy, at least get me out of this heat where there is water."

There were a few moments when he could hear the swish of silk and again, smell beyond the stink of his own sweat, her female scent. Just as he predicted, she hesitated and he wondered fleetingly, if she really thought he needed her protection. Couldn't she see he was in more danger with her around than without her?

"Listen, Miz Hollis, I am a desperate man and you seem to be the only one available amongst the good citizens of this town to help me. I need you to go--" he whispered, his throat dry and scratchy. He passed his tongue over his lips and coughed. "As much as I appreciate your loyalty, this is the way I need you to help me now and you are the only one who can do it." Again, he coughed. "Do I need to remind you that you got me into this situation and I am depending on you to get me out of it."

After a moment, there came another rustle of silk and he

glanced down in time to become distracted by a pale, white thigh netted by a lacy black stocking angled in his direction. He gazed, entranced as she deposited the pistol in the beribboned garter. How could he have missed the shapely thigh when she removed the gun to give it to him?

His jaw dropped in awe of the enticing part of a woman's anatomy he hadn't experienced in a very long time. He stared until he heard his prisoner shift position. Looking up, he discovered the hairy ape hushed and leering at the same thigh in like manner as he had a few seconds earlier.

"For heaven's sake, put your dress down," he growled out the side of his mouth. All he needed was for his prisoner to get the same lustful ideas and charge towards her.

She dropped her skirts, instantly regretting her thoughtless lack of modesty. Tears of shame smarted at the cruel edge in his voice. She looked up to see the hulk had quit his caterwauling, and ogled her, his black eyes filled not with pain, but with blatant lust. An apology on her lips, she looked back to Andrew, who glared angrily back at her.

"I know you are used to parading yourself in front of others, but this is not the typical whore-house situation we have here, and you could get us killed for showing your...a...self." Andrew's eyes narrowed. "Unless, of course, you are deliberately trying to embarrass me with your harlot's tricks."

Hurt by the sneer in his voice and feeling foolish at her impetuous occasion of immodesty, she tried to cover her embarrassment with humor. "Come on, Preacher," she cajoled, in a husky and seductive voice tapping him in his side with her elbow "You've seen a lot more of me than my leg, or can't you remember back that far?"

Andrew did not have to look at her to know she was trying to goad him into another argument. That taunting and familiar, *I can get to you*, tone was implicit. "Unfortunately, yes, Miz Hollis," he replied coldly. "Much to my regret, I do recall those occasions. However, I do try to forget those difficult times and so should you."

His eyes were hard and unyielding; his mouth set in the most disdaining of frowns. She stifled a gasp and looked away. He could not have hurt her worse had he pointed his finger directly at her and denounced her for being a whore. She had always wondered if he ever regretted saving her life, and now she had a pretty good idea that he did.

Avis searched her heart knowing some of his feelings about her were justified, while others were not. Rather than risk a defense, she straightened, angled her head so that she looked down her nose at him, turned and left him to his vigil, convinced that the least she owed him was to get him out of this mess.

Andrew listened to the reassuring tap of her step along the boardwalk. For a moment the noise stopped and he had the dreadful feeling that she would just leave him to fry like an egg on a tin roof. He wiped the sweat from his forehead with his sleeve, hoping that she did not plan to get even with him by leaving him standing all by his lonesome in the middle of the afternoon.

Thankfully, the tap of her shoes resumed, but coupled with heavier thuds. Andrew's spirits lifted when he calculated that she had passed the saloon.

He clearly heard the *hombre* beg for mercy in Spanish. Andrew remained unmoved.

He raised his eyes to the cloudless sky. A brazen haze engulfed everything. Salty patches were drying into his shirt, but the persistent, stinging sweat that dripped into his eyes nearly blinded him. The next moment, dizziness seized him causing the pistol in his right hand to droop, while his left hand went to his head to stop the reeling.

Vaguely, he heard shuffles in the dirt. The next second, a steadying hand gripped his shoulder. Lifting his eyes, he saw the saloonkeeper offering him a glass of water.

He grabbed the glass eagerly with his free hand, asking the Lord to bless the old man real good for his thoughtfulness. "Don't drink it all at once or you will get stomach sick," Sal cautioned.

"Listen, Preacher, Hollis said that ya' needed some water and some help. I'm here to spell ya', but ya' gotta make it snappy because my bald head will fry quicker than *mamacita's* tortillas," he explained in a reedy voice that Andrew took to be something between Deep South and carnival huckster.

"Then we're gonna see how to get this bastard into the saloon, 'cause I ain't never seen a female ever get in a real hurry for nothin' and we surely cain't stand out here all day a waitin' for Hollis to come back."

Shaking his head to clear it, Andrew gladly relinquished the heavy pistol to Sal and sipped the last of the liquid refreshment. Then, thinking he needed his whole body wet down, he took the empty glass with him to the shaded trough, and set it on the hitching post. He yanked at his shirt, sending the buttons flying.

After dredging the shirt in the torpid, murky water of the horse trough, he wrung the water out to swab his burning face and neck with the cool dampness. He dunked it again, this time, leaving the shirt slack with water.

Momentarily flustered to find the buttons gone when he tried to put the shirt back on, he knotted the loose ends of the shirt around his waist, leaving the sodden shirt to fall open. He looked down and thought wryly that exposing ones chest was not exactly the proper dress for the parson, but at this point, he didn't care. Especially when there was no one about to see him anyway.

Ignoring the muck that bobbed on the surface of the water, he drowned his head in the liquid. The coolness soothed his half-baked brain.

He raised his head, flinging his hair away from his eyes, spraying the area with a fusillade of droplets. His gaze lingered on the water, but, even as thirsty as he was, he was unable to find the nerve to actually drink the vile stuff.

Slogging back to the bartender he could see by the light pink tint on the bartender's brilliantly shining pate that he was already feeling the effects of the August sun. "Thanks, barkeep," he said, as he regained the gun, "but what happened to the crowd?"

"Dunno," replied Sal, "but old Bull stepped out himself sayin' somethin' about an *Injun* not being worth the trouble. Tell you what. Let me get myself a little coolness for my poor head and we'll move that *gordo* right on into the saloon."

Andrew set eyes on Sal, and chuckled at the soggy turban mashed on his head, then, winced in pain to be reminded of his wounded nose.

"You'd be surprised at what ya' gotta do when the grass don't grow there anymore," explained Sal, enjoying his own little comedy.

Andrew refrained from even smiling.

"Say, I haven't seen Hollis so het up about anything in quite a spell," said Sal between bites of his chaw. "Yep, she was like Sherman, just a marchin' to the sea, all right."

Andrew heard him give a juicy little chortle and laughed along with him, until another stinging jolt of pain shot up his nose. He would have to remind himself not to laugh.

"Ya know, Preach, them other gals don't like Hollis much. Come to think of it, her bossy ways can be a might irritatin' to me, too." Sal slipped his hands into his pockets and jiggled change around. "Them gals call her the *norther* 'cause she's kinda cold and don't really give a hang about the others. Oh, she takes care of her few see-lect high rollin' customers better than they all do. She is friendly with Miss Kate, but she don't give a damn, excuse me, Preach for sayin so, about anyone else. Leastwise, I didn't think so till today."

Andrew did not know why the man thought he should tell

him about Avis Hollis, but Sal's jaws were working hard to get that fresh wad of tobacco down to a lump to stick behind his lip. Something about the sound of all that watery chewing revolted his stomach. He turned his thoughts to his daughter Amanda.

"If Hollis is having one of her bad days, her monthly or somethin', she can swear a streak as long and wide as the Rio Grande. Then, them other hussies say we are having a *blue norther*."

Funny, but Andrew would never have compared the arrogant woman to a long spell of icy weather out of the north.

Sal snickered. "But still, there are some things about her that just flat out don't make sense. It's like she just don't enjoy herself, at all."

For his part, Andrew did not think there was anything that Miz Hollis enjoyed at all. Unless it was that she did purely enjoy making his life miserable. "Pretty and as prickly as a cactus rose, alright," agreed Andrew not trying to hide the sour note in his voice.

Then next moment the memory of a happy and laughing young woman flashed across his mind. It was the occasion of Amanda's first play in the courtyard fountain, when the infant had just done herself proud by splashing her daddy's Sunday suit with water while Avis made sure he was in the splatter zone. Andrew smiled at the remembrance and he winced. "Tell me, sir, is my nose red?"

"Name's Sal, Preacher. Call me Sal," he urged, as he examined Andrew's nose from just about every angle.

Finally, Sal stopped his perusal and spat a juicy stream of tobacco onto the ground with a force that might have shaken the Rocky Mountains. Andrew watched him maneuver the plug behind the front of his lower lip.

"Let's just say, you best stay away from strawberry patches or somebody's libel to pick it," chortled Sal.

Andrew rolled his eyes heavenward. What a time to be

beset with a funnyman. "Fine." he replied irritably. "You tell funny stories. Now, since I am fresh out of ideas, have you got any ideas on how to get this ape inside, without having to wrestle him down or plug him first?"

"Let me think on it a minute." Sal returned to the trough and saturated his apron again. "Don't take long for anything to dry in the arid desert air."

Andrew glanced at Sal thinking that he looked like a sheik. Maybe even the Pharaoh of Egypt. His mind strayed. Was Moses bald? He was certain that he remembered that somebody in the Bible was bald, but who was it? Andrew shook his head.

"It's funny about being bald," Sal began conversationally, peering anxiously down the street.

"I guess we might as well talk about being bald as anything else," he growled, wiping the sweat from his eyes with his arm.

Sal heard the peevishness in the voice. One glance told him that the preacher wasn't looking too damn happy or very healthy with that pink face. Hollis would make him pay hell, if the preacher went down.

"When I used to have plenty of hair it was all kinky and curly, just like yours, and I never did worry about my poor pate roasting like a Christmas turkey. I'm a tellin' ya, man, if we don't get out of this sun quick like, you, me, and the animal here are gonna go down with the stroke!"

"Maybe we should pray for rain, Sal," he suggested seriously, while trying to decide whether it was Elijah or Elisha who was bald.

Mortified, Sal stopped ruminating over his pithy wad of chaw long enough to gape at the preacher. "Pray? Hell no, Preacher! I quit prayin' a long time ago. You can sure as hell stand out here, roast like a spitted goat and pray all you want to, but I have a better idea.

Gently, Sal eased the weapon from Andrew's grip, trudged over to the keening prisoner, and pointed its dark, blue-tinted barrel threateningly. Promptly, the big man quit groaning, and listened to Sal. A few seconds later, Sal stepped back, keeping the weapon trained on the stranger, as he lurched upward.

Before Andrew knew what was happening, Sal had the big man ambling meekly down the street, while Sal followed, letting the pistol dangle lazily at his side. "We're gonna have us a party, Preach, and you're welcome to come along. That is, if you're done prayin' and don't mind drinking water in a devil's den."

"Huh?" he mumbled. He shook his head clear of the cobwebs and hustled to catch up to the slow moving pair.

"How did you get him so agreeable, Sal?" he queried, feeling the coolness inside. Maybe it was a den of iniquity, but right now it looked pretty heavenly to him.

Sal squirted the stream of tobacco juice through his yellowed teeth directly into one of the strategically placed cuspidors. "T'warn't nothin' to it. I just told him that I could blow his balls off now, or he could behave himself while we get inside."

Sal snorted when Andrew flinched. "Works every time on men, but it don't work so well on females. I tried usin' it once on one of them hussies upstairs and she laughed in my face. Cain't understand why it didn't work." Sal noticed the preacher's amazement. "Whatcha' thinkin', Preacher?"

Crude, though it might be, for the first time in the long afternoon, Andrew wanted to let loose with a gut busting kind of laugh, but refrained. "Well, you might not have done it the way Moses led his people to the Promised Land, but I'm not going to argue with the results."

CHAPTER FOUR

Sal returned the Colt to Andrew. He pushed tables and chairs around, enlarging a round space in the center of the worn pine floor. When he was done, he motioned for the prisoner to sit in the middle of the makeshift island.

Andrew half listened while Sal palavered with the stranger in heated Spanish. Keeping a watchful eye on the exchange, Andrew observed that although the man complained, he answered Sal in subdued, but peaceable tones.

Immediately, Andrew found himself a table at the fringe of the circle, collapsed into the chair, and sprawled his legs before him. He sighed deeply, relaxed to be out of the heat.

He listened, catching a few of the more familiar words in the same manner a man might catch a few flies by leaving his mouth open in a garbage dump. "What's his name, Sal?" he called, as the bartender made his way back to the bar.

"Said his name is Xavier, and he is a trapper from way up Capulin Mountain way," he shouted back, while banging around behind the bar.

Andrew heard the unique ratchet-like noise of a water pump, and the clink of glasses. Soon Sal returned with food and drink.

Andrew dubiously eyed his beans and tortillas before pushing them away. He looked to see the prisoner gracelessly and loudly shoveled the food into his mouth. "His hand hasn't seemed to affect his appetite," he observed.

"Said that his hand burns like fire and I told him he should be glad that you did not shoot at his *cajones* because you were a bad *hombre*, even if you were a priest."

Sal cackled, but Andrew didn't find shooting humans anything to laugh about. He didn't like being called a "bad *hombre*" either, but he had the uncomfortable feeling that the crotchety barkeep purely enjoyed needling him just to see how far he could push a preacher.

Kinky screws of hair dangled before his eyes. Too miserable to care, he jumped to his feet, tore his shirt around its hem, and tied the strip around his head to hold the hair out of his face.

He sat back down and propped his chin on his hand. What, he wondered, made Avis Hollis tick? How he would like to unravel the puzzle that was the beautiful Avis Hollis. He could not understand why the woman made a habit of pushing people away from her, and himself the farthest of all.

Sal knelt to care for the prisoner's hand. Andrew nearly shot the stranger again when Sal poured cactus whiskey over the wounded hand, and the man let out a bellow that could be heard clear to the Oklahoma Territory.

"I hope you suffer real good, fat man," taunted the bartender taking a swig out of the bottle of tequila before he put the stopper back in the neck.

When the hand was neatly bandaged and the stranger settled, Andrew's mind returned to envision Avis as she had been before Trumbull got his hooks into her. The year when her hair, a wild coppery mass of curls, dipped past her waist, and the wide, almost cornflower blue eyes could be soft and merry.

Then she had been a gentle and even tender woman. Not brittle as slate or honed to an edge sharp enough to cut Amanda from her life. The day Avis Hollis walked out of his home without so much as a thank you for saving her, he had actually regretted saving her life.

The same day he buried Lois in the consecrated ground just

outside of town, she had made it very clear that she liked Trumbull's money and power. He recalled that her eyes had roamed over his body in a leering way telling him what it was she really wanted.

Clearly she did not consider him a man. That morning having put his wife to rest, all he could do was let her go. But her words stung as no other words had before or since.

Now, from the stories he heard, she was getting every bit of what she wanted from Trumbull. She might be getting what she wanted, but he had to agree with Sal; Avis Hollis was one prickly floozy and likely because she lived a miserable existence.

Andrew's eyes roved the big room, thinking of the loose women and lusty rowdies who would play here in a few hours.

Once he had been like them. He thought of Ella. Ella, who had blithely pleasured him, teaching him what women did and didn't like. Her bosom, he recalled, had been lush, and one fine place to rest his head.

Sighing, he leaned back in his chair. Propping his feet on the table, he put his hands behind his head. The next moment he was sitting on his behind. Startled, and sitting on the floor, Andrew looked around him, confused by the sudden pain in his backside.

"By the way, I plumb forgot to tell you 'bout that chair bein' dangerous, Preach. Guess it wouldn't do any good to tell you about it now."

Andrew moaned, and draped his arms over his knees. He hung his head, ashamed to be caught in vain imaginings. He picked himself up off the floor noticing that he had succeeded in waking the prisoner.

"Lord help," he begged silently, gazing heavenward. "It's been more than three years and I don't know how much longer I can remain in this condition." He picked the chair up with one hand and beat the leg piece back into its hole with the palm of his hand.

"Okay, so I am guilty of lust," he complained under his breath. He had no one but himself to blame for his own wicked thoughts. Truthfully, he could only pray so much, and he was running short on prayers.

Ella probably hadn't been as wonderful as he remembered, but never in his adult life had he had been so long without a woman. Abstinence was the curse of a righteous man.

Maybe he should find a mother for Amanda first and worry about himself second. Any woman good to Amanda could be a decent wife.

With a determined grunt, Andrew grabbed the gun off the floor. "This chair okay to use, Sal?" He held the gun down at his side in one hand and lifted the chair up with one hand for Sal to see. "Sal," he ground out between his teeth, but Sal didn't even give it a glance.

"All them other chairs are fine, as far as I know, Preach," he replied, intently sweeping the area behind the bar. Andrew sat down gingerly, testing the chair, not at all convinced that Sal wouldn't enjoy seeing him fall on his rump again.

Andrew watched the stranger close his eyes, and settle his bandaged arm across his chest. After a few minutes, his jaw went slack, and he commenced to snore loud as a lumberjack.

"Hell's fire, Preach! You mean we are gonna have to listen to that shit until Hollis gets back?" yelled Sal, stopping and stationing the broom in front of him.

Andrew shrugged and relaxed. Snoring that loud, meant the whole basin could hear him and everyone would know when he stopped.

He closed his eyes and a flame haired vision of the seductive kind drifted before them. Unbidden, a vision, no, a memory of her sitting on the edge of the fountain, cooling her feet in the water while Amanda splashed at her feet.

He had seen the bared curve of her legs. Then she turned

70

her splendidly blue eyes upon him and grinned, inviting him to share in the sunshine and frolic.

"Sit down," she had said, moving over for him, her eyes had been bright with delight. "Look. Amanda likes the water. I think she is a water baby, after all," she said, smiling up at him. "Maybe even a beautiful baby water sprite." She turned her face to smile at him, and that was the first time he could recollect noticing the wine stain on her lower lip.

Andrew opened his eyes and hunched forward. How humbling for him to admit that he had been lusting after a harlot. But it was only lust, after all.

Doubtless he could buy her. He could beat the financial arrangement Bull had offered her, but he refused to pay a cost that was far greater than any monetary price. She might be negotiable, but his self-respect was not.

Seven years ago he had changed his mind. Turned his back on his wild ways, and now he wanted no part of that kind of misery.

Even so, he had to admit that he had this crazy attraction for that particular harlot. Was he doomed to want what he couldn't have?

Still, he deserved better from her. She certainly despised him. He had fed her, clothed her, and cared for her until she was well.

Fine thanks he got. When Lois died, Avis cursed him. She even forbade him from calling her by her given name. Just to let him know she meant business, she repeatedly humiliated him at the store, barbershop, ice cream parlor, or anywhere he happened to try to exchange pleasantries with her.

That was how she treated the person who had bathed the blood and filth from her body, bandaged her wounds. He even got on his knees and prayed all night when the doctor did not think she would survive the internal wounds.

Even knowing she was purely wicked, there were times

when he closed his eyes, and she floated before them, a shimmering vision with arms outstretched, blue eyes bidding him come to her. When he reached for her, she would vanish into a hazy mist.

Heat surged through his body and he looked around for a distraction. He found none, only disgust to be stuck in a saloon with nothing to do but feed his vain imagination.

It was all Miz Hollis's fault that he was not home preparing his sermon for the next service, or helping Maria sort through the donations of food and clothing. He should be most anywhere, but sitting in a saloon getting randy over old memories of the carnal kind.

Andrew straightened, his thoughts interrupted by a particularly obnoxious string of thunderous snorts and snuffles.

Fed up, he hit his fist on the table, jumped to his feet, and toppled his chair. "Where in thunderation is that woman!" he bellowed. A volley of doors opening and closing echoed above his head.

Presently, there appeared along the horseshoe shaped gallery above his head, all the women any man could ever want in every state of dress and undress imaginable. Blondes, brunettes, redheads, and everything in between stood, arrayed before him in full battle dress, or in this case undress. Even Xavier perked up when he saw the awesome display.

Andrew surveyed beauties ranked above and uttered a low and miserable groan.

Inevitably, one female, a husky voiced brunette spoke up. "Which one of us do you want, honey?"

Next came a higher pitched and shrill-voiced blonde, "Hey girls, ain't that the preacher yellin' for one of us?"

Still another voice answered, "Sure is, Maybelle."

Unseen, another voice exclaimed, "Well, I'll swannie! But I never thought to see that man come here."

"You'll swannie horsy pucky, Emma! He's a man ain't he

and all men get hard peckers sometimes, don't they?"

Much to Andrew's horrified amazement, a sultry voiced silvery blonde, clad in nothing but pink lace underwear with straps to hold up her stockings, and pumped up shoes, picked her way down the staircase. Wiggling, she sashayed around the tables and headed straight for him.

Andrew's eyes widened, as her bosom loomed closer. He refused to look at her and retrained his aim on the prisoner, but he could not have felt more trapped if the pistol had been trained on him.

Once he got a whiff of musk perfume and a close up gander of whipped cream-colored breasts the size of Pecos cantaloupes, his common sense departed. His gun hand trembled.

"Lord, help me! I am about to backslide," he murmured, his face reddening. He couldn't have moved if his life depended on a simple shift to the left or right.

She opened her mouth to speak. His gaze shifted from the inviting bosom to assessing her blue eyes. They were forward eyes, void of depth: the kind of eyes that promised a good time with no consequences.

"It's a little early, honey," she said in a low, cat-like purr, "but like they say… Hmm--" she taunted, strutting around and giving him a lurid appraisal.

"Hey girls!" she yelled, giving him her stamp of approval by delivering a few quick pats on his rump, "He is short, but he's got a damned nice ass, and look at all those yummy curls. Makes my fingers itch just to look at them," cooed the voluptuous woman wrapping one of his curls around a glossy red claw of a nail. "And ain't that headband so cute!"

Andrew heated underneath his already sunburned face when he heard the giggles from the gallery. The blonde released the curl, set one foot upon the chair, and pressed her knee into his groin. She leaned forward to trace a scarlet nail down the center of his chest. Her lips were close and he could smell the faint scent of cloves on her breath. "Like I was sayin' sugar, you got the money, honey, and I got the--"

His eyes glazed over at the intensely pleasurable massage of her knee against his manhood. She was really good, he thought, closing his eyes to savor the building fire. Just a few more seconds and four years of abstinence would be shot all over.

Amazingly, he watched her cupid-bow lips transform into a gaping hole outlined in red rouge. She shrieked a bursting scream as cold water cascaded over her head and down the front of her scantily clad bosom.

"I realize you have probably never seen a real preacher before and corrupting one is too much of a temptation, so I thought to save you some disappointment and cool you down, Delilah," admonished Avis as she swaggered into his view with the water pitcher in her hand.

"This Samson doesn't need his hair cut by you or anyone else." Avis put her fists on her waist and then turned her haughty stare toward the audience in the balcony. "Seems to me, sisters, it is time you ladies got back to your *dos*, 'cause the fun is over and we have got a big night ahead," she yelled, glaring up at them until they skulked off to their rooms.

Delilah scurried back up the stairs, holding her sodden hair back from her eyes. As she wiggled her way up the stairs, Andrew could not help but stare, entranced by the jiggle of the finest pear shaped bottom he had ever seen.

At the top of the stairs, the buxom temptress spun around. Throwing her head back she unhooked the front hooks of her corset to her waist.

Avis reached for the filthiest spittoon she could find, while Andrew gaped at the grandest pair of nipples he had ever seen. They were dusky nipples, big as Texas crabapples; his mouth watered.

"Like I said, Preacher," Delilah called down to him,

"anytime you want more than a mouth full, you just holler and ask for Silver Dollars. They'll know who ya mean. Then Delilah will take care of you in a mighty way."

Andrew, although momentarily distracted by Delilah's bounty, saw Avis head for a spittoon. He had a pretty good idea what she was going to do with it. In three strides he was behind her, and the moment she raised the nasty missile to lob it at the woman, Andrew neatly plucked it from her hand.

Surprised to find her hand empty, Avis turned, looked at Andrew, and blinked once. Good thing he caught her. She would never have been able to lob the filthy thing to the top of the staircase.

He expected at least a few choice words to be flung at him, but she smiled sweetly at him, and gave one of his springy curls a playful tug.

"Maybe you do need your hair cut after all, Preacher man," she said coyly, as her eyes flickered down to the evident bulge in his breeches.

Andrew felt the uncomfortable flush of embarrassment creep up his neck. The woman was bound and determined to humiliate him again! With a painful jerk, Andrew extracted her hair from his hand. "No more jokes, Miz Hollis," he said, his jaws clenched tight. He seethed, shamed that he had besmirched his calling amongst all these lost souls just because of a temptress with the biggest nipples he had ever seen.

"I do not enjoy being put on your level, and if anyone should know that, that person would be yourself!" He spat the words out at her, between clenched teeth, his square jaw hard and thrusting.

Avis stared at him. She had never seen him so angry. And he was blaming her, and not Delilah. That was not at all fair!

Eyes lowered, she shifted her stance. Somehow, now, with a pistol in one hand and her wrist imprisoned by the other, baiting him was not so funny anymore.

She must have humiliated him but good for him to be so close to blowing the lid off his celebrated self-control. But it was Delilah who had no respect for him, not herself.

Andrew thrust her hand away from him, ashamed that she had noticed his aroused state. "Where have you been anyway, or were you just waiting for the other whores to find me here?" he accused certain that she had intended to prove his weakness and publicly shame him. Why was it that she enjoyed humiliating him? What had he ever done, except save her life what seemed eons ago? The anger raged through him. "Maybe some of your keeper's meanness has rubbed off on you."

She had never seen Andrew's eyes so hard and cruel. The sharpness of his words, and the cruel way he called them all whores as if they were little better than pesky insects stung. How, she wondered, could he ever breathe her name and Bull's in the same breath?

Could he charge her with meanness? Trying to battle Bull, could she have become hard and evil just like him? The thought that she could have become wicked and perverse nearly overwhelmed her with self-loathing.

It was true; she had made everyone around her unhappy at one time or another. Forced, as she had been to protect those she cared about from Bull's vengefulness, she could not have done otherwise. Andrew's do-gooder ways would have ended him in big trouble with Bull. She had seen it before. One night, one or two of his men would have taken Andrew out in the desert and left him. Only rebuff and public disgrace on her part could have kept him from butting his nose where it didn't belong.

Poor Andrew, the way he stood there; his hair falling in his eyes and his shirt shredded, looking like a befuddled and sorrowful little boy touched her heart, making her ashamed. Resisting the urge to touch him with a soothing pet, she smiled instead.

"I am sorry I took so long," she said, her Carolina accent

dripping sweetness and sounding calmer than she felt. She hated her life and the rotten things she had to do, but she did them for the best of reasons. "But I could not find Herb at all, and I knew that you would want me to go get the doctor. Then, I had to wait for Doctor Glenn to show up, because Miz Glenn is laid up expecting a new baby."

Andrew eyes narrowed in thought and he pursed his lips. What she had to say was very reasonable, and she said it so sweetly, with her blue eyes open and trusting, that Andrew felt guilty for his own selfish anger. The bottled up rage dissolved and his shoulders relaxed.

"Were you afraid one of the girls was going to attack you and force you to defend your honor?" she inquired, softly?

Did he detect a fresh note of sarcasm in her voice? "No, not really," he replied wearily, suspecting that she was baiting him again. "Did you think I was afraid?"

"No," she responded with equal calm, her eyes alight with an impish glint, "but I just can't figure out why you have got that gun in your hand."

"What do you mean? I have the gun to keep the prisoner from taking off or attacking someone else. Andrew turned to where the prisoner should have been, only to find him gone. "Thunderation! Where did he go?" he shouted. No one watching answered him, only returned blank looks.

Defeated, he sank into his chair. Disgusted with himself and the wasted afternoon, he placed the pistol on the oval card table and pushed it away from him.

Andrew sighed and rubbed his eyes. He felt as if he'd taken a dive, and just hit the rock bottom of the cistern behind his house. He took the band from around his head and ran his hands through his hair, only to replace it when the curls before his eyes bobbed worse than a spring wagon.

"Well, I guess that's the end of it and there's no reason for me to stick around here now." The chair rasped across the floor as he stood. Glad to be quit of this place, he grabbed Manuel's pistol, and headed toward the front door. He craved a breath of air without the tang of smoke or soured spirits.

Avis watched him leave, headed for the wrong door. His shoulders slumped, and he looked every bit like a deflated pirate come in from a long voyage.

She nearly called to him, but the next moment, realizing he was going the wrong way, he changed direction making a beeline for the back door. Poor man was so upset he had forgotten the closest way home was out the back door and across the alley.

Life just wasn't fair. The preacher had saved a life, but sacrificed by spending a miserable couple of hours in a place where he had no business.

His shirt was torn, and he had looked the savage with that band around his forehead, but also a little silly with his poor nose as red as a radish. She certainly had not helped his manly pride at all.

Now that the ladies had returned to their rooms, the saloon had quieted. There were only the tinkles and thuds of Sal's setups and the retreating sounds of Andrew's boots. There was nothing more she could do for him.

Avis mounted the stairs to her office. Perhaps she could do something else for him after all. At the top step she whirled around to see Andrew open the back door.

"Preacher," she called, holding her breath, knowing that he had good reason to ignore her. If their positions were reversed, she would probably ignore him, as well. Avis watched his shoulders, as he pulled the door toward him.

Stopping, he then reversed himself, to stand woodenly, his back to her for a few moments. Turning slightly, he tilted his head back and stared at the ceiling for what seemed a very long time. Poor man. She thought he was either pondering his next course of action or counting to ten.

Finally, he shrugged and wheeled around to face her, the Peacemaker, like an unwanted appendage, dangling forlornly at his side. He looked up at her expectantly, but with a fresh wariness about him. "Yes?" he replied, stepping forward.

She smiled down at him, still thinking of the little boy all worn out from his good deeds.

"If you will wait just a few minutes for me to a-rearrange some plans, I will be glad to go with you and help you with the girl," she offered as she tilted her head to one side to watch him. Whether Andrew knew it or not, she was making a big sacrifice. Kate and Sal could keep their eyes and ears open for her, but Bull would be angrier than six scorpions in a cigar box full of mirrors to learn she would not be here for his fandango.

Andrew didn't answer her outright, but stared at her as if she were a three-headed beast from the Dismal Swamp. Of course, her offer was out of line. It just didn't do for the town preacher to keep company with the town whore. He looked so woebegone, she felt sorry for him.

He moved closer to her, not speaking, his eyes intense and probing. Her hand came up, motioning him to stop. "That's all right, Preacher. You did a wonderful thing for that Indian girl and you need to go home. I have other plans anyway." She squared her shoulders, holding her head higher and turned toward her room.

Andrew watched her leave and stepped toward the stairs. "Wait, Miz Hollis!" he called.

She stopped, still holding the hem of the gown off the floor, to peer down at him. She waited, her head tilted in a question. He smiled "We would be very glad for you to come help us. In fact," he added, as he strolled over to the bar and laid the pistol down with a soft thud. "I cannot think of anyone better able to lend us a hand in this situation than you."

She didn't answer him or smile, but gave a slight nod, and hurried to a door located in the center of the gallery where she disappeared.

"Strange female. Now she wants to help," he muttered to himself. Sal snorted behind him.

Andrew turned his attention to the crusty old man behind the bar. Remembering the expert care he used to tend the prisoner's hand, he suspected there was more to Sal. "I guess I owe you a big vote of thanks, Sal," said Andrew, thrusting his hand towards the older man in a gesture of friendship.

Sal answered the preacher's smile with one of his own before grabbing the preacher's hand to shake it enthusiastically. "I ain't shook a preacher's hand ever before, but its my pleasure to now. My helpin' t'warn't nothin' at all, just pure pleasure to help that poor thing. Just sorry the ugly bastard got away."

Andrew placed his elbow on the bar to hold his head in his hand. A few moments of silence lapsed while the barkeep puttered around behind the bar and Andrew meditated on the rosy breasts of the naked woman in the painting. He rolled his eyes, disgusted with himself, reminded of what a poor showing he'd made when he allowed a bunch of soiled doves to distract him into letting the prisoner to get away.

Sal plunked a glass of liquid on the bar. "Made it special for you just like I do Miz Hollis. No liquor in it, at all," he said.

Andrew took a drink. So the intrepid Miz Hollis did not imbibe? Well, that was one sin he could not lay at her feet. "Hmm, lemonade. Thanks, Sal." He took a swallow of the tart liquid, snapping his taste buds to attention. Did he put any sugar in the lemonade at all, he wondered? "When did the *hombre* get away, anyway?" he choked out, his mouth puckered from the sour refreshment.

The saloonkeeper barked insinuatingly. "Whatcha' bein' so quiet about it fer, Preacher? There ain't a soul in here but you and me. Feelin' a mite guilty?"

Andrew thought to distract him by complaining about his sour lemonade, but the telltale flush started at his neck and moved upward. Maybe he should keep his mouth shut.

"Now just when do ya think the pig made his escape?" scoffed Sal, chuckling when he saw embarrassment overtake the preacher's face. "Could it be that you're ashamed to be distracted by them beauties and not thinkin' too clearly?"

Andrew took another drink, then choked on a lemon seed.

"Yes, sir-ee! When Delilah sets her mind to have some man's curls, she can be a mighty distractin' little floozy!" continued Sal.

Plunking the glass down at the bar, he snapped his damp towel at a passing fly. "But, just b'tween you and me, Preach. I'd rather put a snake in my bedroll, than to hook up with that varmint." The barkeeper walked out from behind the bar and scrubbed down the last dirty table.

"If you're hankerin' for a piece of that jezzy, you'd be better off to tie a knot in it," he suggested, his voice quivering with every scrub, "Or if you've a mind, you could use your hand and get just as much pleasurin'."

That bit of coarse jesting and Sal's accompanying laughter, lead Andrew to decide that he needed to wait outside the door.

After taking the final swallow of the sweaty glass of lemonade, he dried his hands by wiping them on his pants. He shoved the Colt in his belt.

"Thanks for the drink. Tell Miz Hollis that I will be out on the front bench," he said, figuring the last thing he wanted to do was become gossip in the local din of iniquity. Andrew headed for the swinging doors, shaking his head.

The first bonafide customers of the day, a couple of saddle bums, eyed him suspiciously as they brushed by him going through the swinging gates. Andrew gave them a businesslike nod of the head.

The gates still squeaked behind him when he sat down on the bench, bone tired. The gun rested on the bench beside him, while he settled his head against the cantina wall. Too tired to be irritated with the wait, he folded his arms and watched the purpling shadows of evening lengthen across the street.

Delilah? What a name for a comely woman. But to ever take her seriously, or be desperate enough to take up on her offer was unthinkable and too sinful to consider. The more he thought about her, the less her shameful ways attracted him.

People were beginning to stir. He sure wished she would hurry up. He yawned, thinking how much he did not enjoy being found on the bench in front of a saloon, and looking like an outlaw. Andrew sat forward to gaze at the bustling street and yawned, again.

Oddly, he could not remember why he had been on the veranda when Avis had grabbed hold of him. "Must be all that sun today." He sighed as his head gradually lolled forward to rest on his chest.

From very far away, a voice called, "Would you look at that, the preacher's done passed out in front of the saloon!"

A firm hand on his shoulder prodded him awake. He opened one eye to find those same bottomless blue eyes that had so often graced his dreams, peering down at him. He smiled the addled grin of a fool and closed his eyes. "Not now. Come back to bed, honey." He shifted to a more comfortable position, resting his elbow on the bench and his cheek on his hand before he fell back to sleep.

"Well, I never!" Vaguely, he heard a horrified gasp and struggled to open both eyes. When he brought himself around, he saw Avis laughing as elderly Miz Trumbull, the mayor's tyrannical mother, hustle away in a cloud of dust.

Andrew shook his head, completely mystified by the odd behavior of the not so sweet old lady. His puzzled gaze shifted to Avis. "What's wrong with Miz Trumbull?" asked Andrew innocently, as he continued to watch the ample-bodied, gray haired harridan, huff and puff her way toward Trumbull's offices down the avenue.

Avis could see that the preacher had no memory of the incident, so she simply hid her humor and answered demurely, "I'm sorry, Reverend, but I am sure I don't know." Andrew closed one eye and stared at her with his really good eye, wondering at the sudden sweetness.

He stretched himself, trying to shake off the lethargy, and sat forward, slapping his hands on his knees. A few moments later he wiped the sand from his eyes, swept up the weapon, and stood. "Well, Miz Hollis, are you ready?"

Avis thought he looked rather endearing, with his tired, puppy dog eyes, tousled hair, and poking the long nose of the pistol into his pants. "Yes, Andrew, I'm ready," she answered, her eyes dropping to check to see if she looked proper enough to be seen in public with the preacher.

Andrew had to wonder why she suddenly turned tame and switched to calling him by his Christian name. Could she be hiding that old sucker punch behind all that sweetness?

"I appreciate you doing this for me," he informed her, being more used to being dosed with her vinegar than her virtue. "I know this is a sacrifice for you. I mean losing the money from your business and all," he finished lamely, trying to shrug out of the unintentional gaffe.

He watched her eyes harden, her back stiffen, and he had that feeling so similar to stepping into warm manure with bare feet, that he looked down to see if he still had his boots on. "I'm sorry. I didn't mean it the way it sounded," he explained lamely, trying to figure out for himself how not to insult a woman who made her living servicing the male gentry.

She shrugged and fixed her sleeves, so that the lace draped straight. "No harm done, Reverend Bristow. We both know what I am." She spoke lightly, but Andrew could tell that the *icy norther* had blown in.

"Now that the town has seen you sitting here, let's not go through the cantina again," she suggested. "There are too many people around to see you go in there."

"Very well," he replied, seeing the reason behind her caution. Sometimes she seemed to care more about his reputation than he did. He mulled over this contradiction in the silence between them as they walked through the alley and around the corner.

Earlier, when he had first awakened, she had been laughing. Her lovely face had been glowing, and her eyes alive with mirth. What had been funny enough to make her come out of that forbidding shell she built around herself, he wondered?

Tonight might be difficult for her because of Amanda. He was certain that Avis would always be sensitive about his daughter. They mounted the steps to the veranda, Andrew leading the way. As he opened the door for her, he overheard her mumble, "I don't understand why you couldn't just hog tie the animal, instead of letting him get away."

Andrew watched her shapely backside disappear into the subdued light of the foyer. He did not want this evening to be subtle torture for them. Reaching out, he planted his hand firmly on her shoulder and whispered in her ear. "Do you really want me to explain why the captive got away, Miz Hollis? But, on the other hand, why should I explain, when I am sure you already have figured it out? I should have realized that this must be part of a plan to needle me the rest of the evening and make me feel more foolish than I already do," he hissed.

She turned to face him, one elegant burnished, brow raised. A smile threatened at the corners of her mouth, making the small birthmark on her lip more alluring. "So you admit you aren't so perfect after all?"

Andrew ignored the words and tempting lips, seriously trying to avoid any of the sparring that plagued their relationship. "I never said I was perfect. You now know I am not. If you are planning to badger me with your strange sense of humor, you may carry your womanly charms back to the cantina and use them on Bull or upon whomever you bestow them these days. I am too tired for this game."

His eyes narrowed to see her reaction in the dim lamplight of the entryway. Instead, he found himself lost in unexplored depths.

Instantly, her eyes came alive with mischief. He almost smiled at her propensity for seeing his words to be opportunities for new rounds of cunning and cutting remarks.

Andrew studied his hand where it rested on her shoulder. The flesh under the palm of his hand was soft, but there existed certain, unfamiliar warmth.

His gaze strayed back to the birthmark at the corner of her lip. If he kissed her there, what would the spot taste like, he wondered? Would the wine-hued mark be the flavor of port or have the richness of sherry?

A woman like her, would she, he wondered, object if he did sample the wine stain? Just one touch would do. His mind lingered on that pleasant thought. He raised his index finger, but catching himself, he ran his hand through his hair. Ashamed, he looked away.

Maybe, it was the effects of the shadowed hallway, but Avis had never seen the preacher's hazel eyes turn smoky. If she didn't know better she would say that Andrew was on the verge of passion. This was altogether a different Andrew than she knew. Could he have been about to kiss her? Surely she had been mistaken. His experience with Delilah surely had put those forbidden thoughts in "Mister Simonpure's" head.

Andrew had been without a woman much too long and probably more years than she knew. Lois' illness had begun when she but a young girl. But perhaps he was better at sneaking around than she knew.

For some reason the thought that Andrew could be a philandering widowed preacher displeased her. Contrary to her past feelings, perhaps Delilah would be the candidate most likely to end Andrew's long celibate streak. At least Delilah was clean, unlike most of the others.

She drew closer to him, blending their shadows into one. Maybe she could do him a favor after all.

Andrew sensed the heat of her body as she closed the gap between them. Her womanly scent warmed him. Lost as he was in the nearness of her, he did not notice his arousal until it was fully erect and straining against the fabric of his trousers

"You are a damn good shot," he heard her say, as her hand pressed gently on his chest making a new battery of sparks shoot through his blood. "That is, for a man who hates guns." She stepped closer to him. His heart beat furiously under her palm, and he wondered if she could feel the pounding through the cotton of the shirt.

Andrew fought for control, his arms as eager to embrace her as his tongue to sample that odd little speck on her lower lip. Instead he heard himself mumble something about being glad to be of service.

She smelled sweet and all fresh and rosy, with eyes filled with soft acceptance of what was this moment between them. He hadn't yearned this way for a woman's touch in years. Would she or could she even understand?

"You deserve a prize for that kind of shooting, and I tell you what I am going to do for you," she declared softly as she fit herself closely against him. "Come closer, I want to whisper in your ear."

Entranced by the soft allurement of the woman, he leaned his ear toward those perfect lips, his senses alive at the way her breasts thrust against him, increasing the heaviness in his loins. Oh the pleasure of a woman…this woman.

"I'll set you up with Delilah, you just say the word. I mean that I can assure you that nobody has to know."

His mind abruptly collided with his anatomy and disappointment shrank any desire lodged in any part of his brain or body. The ugliness of the offer repulsed him and he stepped away from her. Trying to clear his mind, he pressed his hands to his face, and ran his fingers over his forehead. "Just exactly what kind of a man do you think I am, Miz Hollis?" he countered stiffly, gravely disappointed. "Can you honestly believe I would ever be in a bad enough way to stoop to the likes of her and your kind?"

Too late, Andrew realized his words, although true, were ill chosen and possibly cruel. She stiffened and, he knew she was raring to let him have a piece of her mind.

Her blue eyes flashed fire at him as she went nose to nose with him. "I was wrong, Andrew, you are not a coward, but a hypocrite and I loathe hypocrites even more than I despise cowards." Her hand pointed below his waist with a flourish. "I mean, it was obvious that you had this--"

She never finished what she intended to say because he placed his hand over her mouth. "Shush. I'm sorry. I did not mean to sound cruel, but I'm warning you woman, drop it, or go back to the saloon." He gave her no time to reply for he immediately traipsed into the glare of the sick room, and she quietly followed, wiping her mouth with the back of her hand.

When he saw the fragile nature of the girl and the gravity of her wounds cleaned up, he winced. His stomach churned at the raw gore. But before his mind completely made that adjustment to the singleness of the life and death struggle before him, he had the fleeting insight that Avis had a point and may have meant a kindness, after all. Somehow, before the night was out, he vowed he would make amends.

Even if her kindness had not been his particular variety, it was the thought that counted. She had been generous to even consider such a thing.

He had not meant to be cruel at all. This was a free country where a person earned a living. What else could one expect from a whore's point of view, but to supplying the needs of a randy man?

CHAPTER FIVE

The small knot of people clustered about the girl spared the late arrivals not even a glance. The doctor and his makeshift group of helpers, their heads bowed, continued the gruesome process of probing and cleansing the gore.

Andrew noticed the mingled, unpleasant odors that assailed his nostrils. He moved across the warm, stuffy room, opening the patio double doors and windows, lowering the netting to allow the evening air.

Although the evening was slipping into twilight, the bedroom glared garishly bright with artificial light. Andrew scanned his bedroom, guessing that someone must have pilfered the parish of every lamp and candle not tacked down, or burning, to add to the single electric light in the ceiling. He smiled when he noticed that even some of the votive candles from the mission's altar had not escaped their search.

The doctor mumbled to himself, while he patiently probed the ribbons of shredded flesh. Padre Juan, stationed across from him, used fresh rags to sop blood as it wept from places where the doctor dug for the tiny pieces of grit embedded in the pulp of her back.

Little conversation passed between them. Occasionally, the doctor would give instructions to one of his helpers. He did so without ever lifting his eyes from his patient.

Andrew watched the priest's lips move in prayer for the sleeping girl. He respected and appreciated the kindly, but overworked priest, who was always available, when they needed him.

Maria, her thick dark hair swept into a tight knot at the back of her neck, stood to Padre's right with a basin of fresh water and clean compresses. She exchanged the freshened pads for spent pads, returning them to another bowl of rust colored water to soak.

Events such as this had led him long ago, to conclude that his housekeeper to be a keenly intelligent woman and that he was blest to have her managing his home. But then, Andrew thought that the redeemed bandit, Manuel, was an even smarter man for marrying her and letting her keep him on the straight and narrow. I should be so blest; he thought with a sigh, his fingers tugging loose the protective window screens from where they were stored in rolls above the windows.

Manuel leaned against the wardrobe, his attention fixed on the girl. If she suddenly shifted while the doctor worked to clean the deep wounds, she could hurt herself even worse. During the course of the past hours, he had been kept busy enough to forget about everything else, but keeping her still.

Manuel had held her down both times while the Doctor carefully measured drops of strong smelling medicine onto a cloth that he placed over the child's nose and mouth. Immediately, she had ceased to struggle and lapsed into blessed unconsciousness, but Manuel took no chances.

Because he was standing by the door, he was the first to hear the soft slap of bare feet on the hardwood floor, and a plaintive voice call "Daddy?"

Manuel stepped out of the room, to greet the child standing in the darkened hallway. "What is wrong, *Meja,*" he asked, scooping the curly-topped five year-old into his arms.

She went to him willingly, delighted to be picked up by the tall man. "Did Daddy come home yet?" she asked before placing a dimpled hand on each of Manuel's cheeks to stare into his black eyes.

"*Si*, little girl," he answered in a most serious manner. "But your father is very busy now helping someone who is most ill."

Amanda gave him an unblinking stare. "But did he find my baby?"

"That I do not know. If you will tell me where you last saw her, I, the best finder in all of North America, will locate your baby."

Amanda smiled at the big man, her blue eyes sparkling. She kicked her feet, insisting to be put down. After he set the child on her feet, she turned to stare at him until he opened the heavy oak door for her. Following her into the lamplight as she scurried down the outside gallery, he watched her duck behind the potted cactus-rose bush to retrieve a rag doll. Hugging her doll closely, she popped her thumb into her mouth. Manuel lofted them both into his arms and carried the pair back into the house.

The hour was late, and Manuel stood in the doorway of the bedroom. "*Querida*, I am hungry," he called to Maria. "What do you say to some tortillas and frijoles, *Si*?" he asked juggling both doll and child in his arms.

Amanda and baby perched on one arm; he motioned for Maria to come join him with the other. Avis, who stood at Maria's side, wordlessly stepped into Maria's place and began relaying the compresses back and forth.

Andrew, by this time, held a lamp over the doctor's working area. Feeling eyes upon him, he glanced up to see his daughter nursing her thumb and intently staring at him. Thankfully, she could not see fully into the room, only him holding the lamp.

When she spied her father looking at her, she pulled her thumb out of her mouth with a slight pop and wagged the yellow yarn haired doll in front of him. "Looky, Daddy," she sang out to him. "Manuel helped me find Miss Lizzy."

Only then did he remember why he had gone out on the veranda in the first place. "I am so glad," he told her enthusiastically, but feeling guilty because he had forgotten such an important thing to her. "But did you get a nap?"

"*Si, Senor,*" answered Maria for the child, swiping her dripping palms and backs of her hands on her apron. "When you did not return pronto, she found me in the living room, and fell asleep on the sofa while I dusted the furniture." Maria shook her head, having grown used to her master's sudden disappearances. "I assure you, *Senor* Andrew, she did not fret for too long this time," she informed him while dumping the mound of soiled rags and water into a tin bucket and pouring more fresh water into both basins.

Andrew dropped his eyes. Maria had a way of making him feel lower than pond scum during a drought. "Daddy is so sorry, Sugar, that I did not come right back, but there was not time. Can you understand how time can be so important when it is somebody's life?"

Bright curls dancing, Amanda plugged the thumb back into her mouth, and stared accusingly at him over Manuel's shoulder while he carried her to the kitchen. His daughter had not forgiven him at all. Fickle females!

Poor Amanda. It must seem to her that he was always being called away to some emergency and forgetting his little girl. Lord! But he needed a mother for Amanda in the worst way. Unquestionably, the child's needs should come before everything else. If he had to marry to see that she had a mother, then so be it. After all, many people out here married for just such reasons.

Marriages of convenience were no less sacred, nor did the convenience part mean that love couldn't develop over time. Andrew's lips thinned to a flat line. He knew better than most that many of those marriages endured through years of mutual misery.

He could not convince himself that he needed to settle for a nice arrangement for Amanda's sake. He had hoped that he would not have to settle for anything less than the undiminished and unconquerable love his mother and father had for each other. This intertwining of two souls was what he had experienced as a child and he was reluctant to settle again, for anything else.

Perhaps that kind of love only existed for a chosen few. Was he wrong to seek that special quality in marriage?

The Doctor cleared his throat. "If you are through feeling lower than a snake's belly for forgetting that doll, Andrew, I need all of your help while I disinfect the area. I also need to explain a few things to you all about her care before I go," he informed them, rinsing his hands in yet another bowl of water and wiping them on a fresh towel.

"The chloroform should begin wearing off soon, and I want to do this antisepsis procedure while she is still under. The alcohol will sting those torn places like fire, but it will be better than cauterizing such large amounts of open flesh." He tilted his head to the side and pointed to the open wounds on her back. He looked over the rim of his glasses, his gaze encompassing everyone in the room.

"Naturally, if we see that it is getting infected we will burn the areas, but I don't want to do that unless I have to. I mean, we can only burn so much and then cauterizing can become a hazard in itself." Dr. Glenn peered around at them for understanding, and Andrew nodded his head.

He stationed Andrew, Avis, and the padre at certain points to keep her down. He opened his worn alligator-hide medical bag and fished around for the alcohol. When Avis saw the corked bottle of antiseptic, she winced in sympathy for the girl.

Obediently, but with her eyes closed, Avis gently, but firmly held the girl's head, as Andrew held the right side. Manuel returned from the kitchen to brace her legs, as Father

Juan prayed a litany in Latin to petition the mercy of God.

Their patient did not so much as whimper or stir when the alcohol flowed over the wounds. After a few moments, they looked around at each other, and sighed with relief. "It was your prayers for God's mercy, Father Juan," said Andrew with a smile.

"Or perhaps yours for peace, Padre Andrew," countered the Catholic priest.

After the doctor finished the procedure, they waited before releasing her to determine if the patient would attempt to roll on her back. Thankfully, she remained still.

Seeing them through the worst, Father Juan made his apologies and hurried back to the mission, promising to return for the night watch.

The doctor's gaze fell on Avis. "Are you going to be able to help with this patient, my dear?" he asked tersely, never having been one to have much time to mince words.

She looked confused for a moment and then brightened. "Why, yes Doctor. I suppose so. At least that is why I came here tonight."

Her answers were cool, but Andrew heard the underlying apprehension in her voice. He had noticed a wariness about her years before. A fear of commitment perhaps, or probing questions that revealed too much.

Doctor Glenn turned to his bag. "Well, I can't think of a better nurse for this one, unless it was my Em and you know she is too far down the pike with carrying this baby to be of much help." As he continued talking with Avis, the doctor selected another smaller, fragile looking blue bottle and set it in her hand. She recoiled from the pretty bottle.

"This is laudanum, and it is made from a powerful drug called opium. Always remember," instructed the doctor, "that a little is sufficient, but too much will kill. Also, if a person uses the drug too long, the body will crave it so that they would even sell their soul." He scanned their faces seeing if they understood the import of the information.

"However, it is the most powerful painkiller I have." He noticed that she had accepted the small bottle with trembling hands.

The burly doctor waited, expecting her to explain. What, wondered Doctor Glenn, did Bull Trumbull hold over the girl? Why had she snapped up the mayor's offer as quickly as she had? He would have thought her too damn smart to get involved with the pervert.

He was one of the few who suspected Bull's stories about Avis' wild ways to be nonsense. The doctor had good hard information that the Bull did not like girls and he had never seen any evidence of debauchery on Avis' person. Could it be the money Bull provided, or a deeper mystery? Was she addicted to an opiate, herself?

He held a small pretty blue hobnailed bottle. "Do you know what this it, Avis?"

Avis backed up. Her eyes skimmed from the doctor to Andrew, who, both, clearly expected some kind of explanation. She bent her head to deliver a gentle puff of her breath and extinguish the votive candle that sat on the bedside table. She walked to the next candle, trying to avoid the pain of bringing up the childhood tragedies that shaped her life. She halted, knowing this was one occasion when she had to communicate them, to help the good doctor to understand.

"Actually Doctor, that is opium. First it brought my younger brother's death by accident. Then, a few hours later delivered my father suicide. He achieved his purpose, but with a huge cost. My mother, unable to care even about her my brother and me, craves the stuff. Mother would, as you say, sell her own soul to fix her craving."

She might have gone further to explain, but suddenly a headache pressed in on her and she did not want to talk about her mother. "Please, Doctor Glenn," she said softly as she fussed about the bedclothes, "If you need to speak with Reverend Bristow, don't let me stop you."

Andrew watched her, seeing the signs of strain soften into lines of sorrow. This new piece of the puzzle surprised him. Why had he never known this?

Intuitively, he knew that she would have shared the story, but she had never trusted him. He could think of only one person to whom she would have confided and she was dead. Come to think of it, Lois had said very little about Avis' upbringing to him. To be fair, Lois might have tried to share the information, but he had been preoccupied.

"If you are done here, Robert, we can go to my office and talk," volunteered Andrew, hoping to ease her discomfort. He knew from his own experiences, that the doctor rarely minced words.

Andrew waited for the doctor, noticing that Avis bowed her head and rubbed her temples. The doctor stepped forward to embrace her in a fatherly fashion.

"I had no idea, my dear, and I am sorry for being so damned suspicious. Can you ever forgive me for thinking such unkind thoughts?" His voice sounded soothing as he held her tightly in his arms. "That's why you refused to return to North Carolina right after the baby was born?" He watched her nod and her shoulders slump. "And your mother, too, I suppose?"

The doctor hit close enough to the truth. Still, coming from a friend made it no less painful. She sniffed back the tears.

"Not surprising. The abuse is insidious and contagious Sadly, in the out-workings of life; one man's curse often taints another. You never did tell me if you forgive me, young lady." prompted the doctor gently, now better able to understand the young woman.

Impulsively, Avis threw her arms about the doctor's neck

to give him a peck on the cheek. "It's fine, Doctor. There is no way that you could have known. I just don't like to talk about it. I guess that I mostly try to forget, but sometimes I can't."

Andrew watched amazed, that she could she be sweet and forgiving to the doctor and shrewish with him. If he would have the same kinds of questions, she would have walked out. Suddenly disgusted at the way she fawned over the doctor, he turned away from them. "I'll be in the office if you want me, Robert," he called over his shoulder, certain the cozy twosome could get along just fine without him.

"I'll be there in a minute, Andrew, after I give Avis just a few more instructions," the doctor called after him.

Andrew tried to understand the peevishness toward his friend, or, for that matter, anyone else that she treated better than she treated him. He could have stood on his head for that woman and she would still treat him with contempt. Why, he asked himself, did he crave the familiarity and respect of a sporting woman?

To hear Bull tell it, she was chock full of tricks that he recounted to anyone who would listen. When he found himself in Bull's company, he made it a point to leave because the stories ate at his temper. Months passed before he finally figured out that Bull loved to corner him just to tell him the lascivious details. He was past caring.

Andrew turned the brass handle of the library door, comforted to know that things would be just as he left them. This was his haven and the place where he could escape to read, and meditate. Or, upon occasion, sleep undisturbed on the leather sofa.

Three walls were covered with six shelved rows of gold lettered leather bound volumes of books. Most of the books he had finished through the long quiet evening hours when there were no services or visitations to keep him busy.

The paneled room smelled musty, and he opened the patio

doors, releasing the protective netting over the gap to keep the bugs out. Folding his arms, he rested his head and shoulder against the doorjamb, as he peered out into the enclosed patio where fireflies beckoned. He parted the netting and strolled out onto the patio, seeking its coolness. Deliberately he ignored the open doorway to his bedroom and the subdued conversation within. Could he, he wondered, actually be jealous? Be jealous over a fallen woman? Not likely!

Hands shoved in his pockets, he strolled to a darkened corner to contemplate, again, the enormity of the universe. He stared into the unknowable expanse of eternity feeling insignificant in comparison. He decided, occasionally, a man needed to recognize his minute existence in the scheme of things to give a man perspective. Such a natural thing to do under the enormous expanse of star flung desert sky.

An insect landed in his hair and he tossed his head to dislodge the annoying critter. When it tangled itself deeper, he gave up, finally driving it away by feathering the strands away from it with his hand. He encountered his makeshift headband.

In one motion, he yanked it off, divesting himself of the ragged reminder of a miserable day. Holding it before his eyes, he laughed to think that this must have been what Amanda was staring at after all. She was unused to seeing her father garbed in any other way, but slicked down to a high gloss for services or always dressed presentable as a preacher should be.

Glancing down to where his shirt parted, he remembered too well the fiery line Delilah's finger had drawn as it trailed between his nipples to his belly. Hmm, and the feel of her knee pressed against his…

Pure lust shot through him. To dwell on such things was not good. He knew he should put the encounter with Delilah out of his mind and he would do just that.

Andrew closed his eyes, and lifted his face skyward. He inhaled the sweet fragrance of honeysuckle, wondering if Avis' touch could set him ablaze as easily.

"Andrew," came the voice, out of the darkness, shaking him from his reverie. "I am disappointed in you. I was hoping that you would have left that rag around your head. It makes you look rather the rogue, you know. Your devilish appearance did lend a slightly humorous lift to an otherwise unpleasant day." The Doctor laughed heartily, his booming voice causing the frogs to pause in their croaking.

"You reminded me of those wonderful pirates I used to read about and play as a child." The Doctor saw that his humor fell on deaf ears. Mildly disappointed, he cleared his throat. "Naturally, that was before I discovered the true nature of piracy, and how damned serious life is," he explained, miffed that his humor went unappreciated by the somber young preacher.

"Come, Andrew. It's been a long day, my feet are tired, and it's time for a sit," He clamped a brotherly arm about the shoulders of the younger man. "I know you are tired and probably hungry as well, but the quicker I get this said, the quicker I can get back to Em and you can get on with your business."

The doctor collapsed on the stone bench with a low groan. His head moved back and forth as he took in the big sparkling night sky. "I don't mind telling you that it has been a rough day, Preacher. When I was younger I thought that one day I would become so toughened that the tough days would not phase me."

He turned his head to focus on Andrew. "Did you know the Shipplett baby died today?" Surprised, Andrew shook his head. "I didn't think you had heard." He inhaled deeply of the fragrant night air. "Measles."

"No, I'm sorry. I did not know they had any sickness at all." Andrew realized how really tired he was. "I guess I'd better ride out there in the morning and see what I can do." Andrew paused, remembering the family. "If I recall correctly, they are part of Padre Juan's flock. Even so, I will offer help."

The offer, Andrew realized, was half-hearted and he felt suddenly ashamed for his lack of concern. The Lord knew he couldn't do it all, but he still felt guilty for not doing more. Andrew crossed his arms across his chest.

Robert recognized fatigue when he saw it. Andrew, with no helpmeet, was a man alone. The doctor tended to forget the preacher, wise beyond his years, was still a young man in his late twenties. Often, he had to send for Andrew in the wee hours of the morning because his patients needed spiritual help during their grief. The young minister had never once balked at the untimely request.

"Andrew, there is not a thing that you can do, but pray for the family. The baby passed on in my office and Padre has already seen to it that the poor mite was laid to rest properly. It was one of those times where the fever was out of control before they could get to me and all we could do was watch her slip away," explained the doctor, his voice distant and tinged with defeat.

"I was at the burying when Avis came to my office. Em had her wait for me." The doctor didn't need to keep score to know that in this wild country death won out more often than not. Robert Glenn took a deep breath enjoying the tangy scent of the rampant flowering vines and the solitude of the darkened corner of the patio.

"I am really sorry to have to burden you with the care that this girl is going to need if she is to survive. Until we get a hospital in this damned town, I feel that you are better equipped to see to the girl's needs than I can in my little clinic with Em near to birthing and measles on the loose."

He needed a nurse and thought of Avis and her fine nursing skills. "Especially, if you can get Avis to donate some of her time. Did you know her father was a physician, but wounded in the War?" He looked at the younger man to see, by the meager light, the blank look on his face. "Thought you might not know. The strain of healers must run true, for she is the best damned nurse I have ever had, trained or not."

Andrew grunted. He rested his elbow on his knee, and watched a horned lizard climb the patio wall. He grabbed a piece of honeysuckle and stripped it of its leaves. "Maybe you had better ask her to donate her time, Doc. I am not the most popular fellow with her right, now."

The doctor observed the sour expression on the younger man's face, and suspected his friend to be pouting. This particular glower always appeared with the subject of Avis Hollis.

"I don't know what happened between you two, but I think you should ask her to help out. If she says *no* to you then I'll ask. Maybe what you could do is sweeten the pot with a little green stuff. I mean that you can catch more flies with--" The doctor stopped seeing Andrew's lips twitching in a sort of tolerant, but bemused expression." Well, guess you have tried that."

Andrew knew that if money could lure Avis away from Bull she would never have left Amanda for that lecher. No, he knew what it was that sent her to the Bull. She was most specific about her needs the day she left and it wasn't money.

The murkiness that had clouded his brain after Lois' death and burying had to pass before he had figured out everything she had flung at him. She had challenged him to prove himself as a man and that chaffed at his manhood. For weeks he had been torn between proving himself to the woman and keeping himself worthy of the ministry.

"You think money would do it?" replied Andrew half-sarcastically trying to understand why his friend could not see that Bull's allure was not greed, but carnal. He knew well that lust could be a more powerful a reason than money. Long ago, he decided he would not play Avis' game. "Robert, I suspect she has more money than you and I together."

"Can't hurt anything to offer some stipends to her. Might even get her to change all together if we make the pot sweet enough. Seems to me, she'd do about anything for a buck." The doctor looked at Andrew surprised at his own words. "Didn't mean it that way, Preacher."

Andrew clenched his teeth, thinking that "buck" was not exactly the right word he would use to describe her price. Only how a man used his organ counted in her game.

"Bucks?" he sneered, wondering how wrong the doctor could be. She was as hot as a pistol, according to Bull, and couldn't get enough of any man. She needed a stable of studs to service her.

That she offered him Delilah this evening still rankled. Did she think he would be a failure if he wanted her?

He made too much of the incident in the hallway. Her low estimation of him was merely a blow to his pride. He had dwelt on it long enough. Vaguely he heard the doctor talking to him and forced his attention back to the conversation.

"But I just can't feature why anyone would do something so terrible to another human being as what was done to that girl. It's just more evidence that Darwin is wrong and man has truly hit a new low."

Andrew crossed his ankles and searched the expanse of heavens, this time he rewarded with a shooting star. "Doc, we have had this conversation before and I still maintain that Mr. Darwin would not have recanted before he died had he not sincerely believed himself to be wrong."

They fell silent, two friends listening to the gentle sounds of the evening. Little by little, their frayed nerves were soothed by the peaceful play of the fountain as it splashed from one level to the other.

Andrew studied the fountain. Funny, thought Andrew, how the natural routine of life had a reassuring effect that the world had not gone mad.

"The next two weeks will tell the tale for that girl." The doctor sat forward, palms turned under, grasping the edge of the marble bench. "If the shock doesn't kill her, I expect the infection will. It's pretty hard to find all those tiny grains of dirt. The only thing I'm certain of is that I couldn't get them all, but I tried. Kind of awesome to think that each grain multiplies the chances for infection many times over." He sighed deeply and rubbed his eyes.

"She is young, probably no more than sixteen or seventeen. A fool could see that she had not eaten right for a very long time, God help her."

The tall man stood and began pacing, one hand on his hip while stroking his forehead. "I can't help but wonder why she was beaten. What gives a man the right to flay a girl open as if she were a butchered steer, and then continue to beat her until she is a bloody pulpy lump, right on down to the bottom of her feet?" He stopped and looked at Andrew. "Tell me. I want to know what she could she have done so terrible in her short life that would make a man do such a monstrous thing to his daughter-I ask you?"

"Wife," corrected Andrew, cynically.

"Wife?" repeated the doctor, incredulously.

"I can see you're having a hard time swallowing that bit of information, but that is what I said...wife. I know it's hard to believe, but she's one of two wives."

Andrew watched the shocked disgust play on the doctor's face. "I can see by your shocked expression that you have not become hardened to the differences in people in this territory, either. It seems, according to her husband, that she is a witch and he was merely destroying the evil wife because she had put a curse on the good wife. The man's proof was in the birth of a deformed baby. That, my friend, is about all I know about our guest."

"My Lord, Andrew! I am sorry, but I hope and pray there is a special hell for people like him."

Andrew watched the angry doctor pace, his arms flung wide.

"It doesn't seem to be enough that wee ones die of measles, or that consumption claims fine wives and mothers such as your Lois, but now we have some medieval idea that a good scourging is some type of righteous act?" The Doctor pivoted and studied him for a moment. "You don't believe that bull wash do you?"

Daily, Andrew faced a new battle between good and evil, and tonight he sighed at the all the unanswerable questions in the universe. He flung his arms up. "Of course I don't believe such a thing as scourging purges the soul of sins, but Robert, this is a strange patch of country. I have met a few mighty odd folk since coming west, who do believe with all of their heart that such evil exists and the cure is to inflict pain on the mortal body."

The frustration evident in Andrew's voice, Robert patted him on the shoulder. "You did a good thing today, Andrew."

Light and even taps against the flagstone surface of the patio indicated that his black retriever, Bo, had come a calling. A cold nose nuzzled his palm, and Andrew obligingly scratched behind his silky ears. "I do regret forgetting about my daughter and her needs. It must seem to her that others have become more important to me than my own child."

He forestalled the doctors interruption with a raised hand saying, "I know it's true. I do have more outlying people now and have to ride longer distances to minister to them. I can't understand how other ministers do it without neglecting their families." Andrew slanted him a grin. "I suppose my predicament is one of those occupational hazards your Progressive Movement talks about?"

The doctor chuckled and jostled Andrew's shoulder.

"Listen to me, man! I'm a few years older and a bit more experienced in these life and death situations than you are. In fact, I dare say that I get called out more in the middle of the night than even you do. Today, had you delayed even so much as a few minutes coming to the aid of that girl, she would be gone from our help." The doctor grabbed a fresh cigar out of his pocket. He ran it between his lips, and bit the end off it, spitting the nub somewhere into the honeysuckle.

"I know, Robert, but where do my obligations stop? Where are my priorities: with my daughter or to my members? There is so much I want to do and I feel am but one person," he said, hitting his fist into his palm.

"I see. It is a matter of priorities," answered the doctor, studying the woebegone expression on Andrew's face. "Andrew, now that I think about it, I do believe I have diagnosed your ailment and know just the medicine you need!" he exclaimed, hiding his humor.

"Well, don't leave me hanging, Doc," he complained morosely feeling like the doctor's younger son. He watched Glenn take a match from his vest pocket, and pause before he struck it.

"Why, Preacher, I believe you an extreme case of *atrophia-absentia-a-wife-itis*," he announced with a flourish, punctuating his diagnosis with the rasp of the match and applying its flare to the Havana. "In laymen's terms that means, a wasting disease of the thinking parts due to inflammation of the plumbing parts."

Andrew watched the flare of the cigar noting that every time the doctor puffed, it flared brighter. "And just what brings you to that brilliant conclusion, Doctor?" he asked, irked that the doctor had suddenly become an authority on his personal business. Maybe he should join the traveling show for a quick turn as a sideshow freak. He could see it all now. *Ladies and Gentlemen, step right up and see the cherry nosed Protestant minister with the longest record for total abstinence ever held on the North American Continent!*

"Did you even hear me, Andrew?"

"What? Oh yes, Robert. I heard you. I believe you told me that I needed a wife and I asked you what made you believe this wife-itis was my particular disease."

"You are not paying attention, Preacher. I told you, before your mind slipped a gear, that you needed a wife because; you probably haven't had a woman since before Lois died. Your little girl, in case you haven't noticed, needs a mamma and we both know that as wonderful as Maria and Manuel are, nothing beats having your very own mother. Another important reason is that mother's make great child-keepers while we are out roaming the desert for the sake of the victims."

Why did Glenn think this should be news to him? "All right, Doctor Glenn, I'll play your game, but do you have any likely candidates for this honor?"

"Well, I don't rightly know of a wife, but there must be somebody. Hmm...how about Agnes Murphy? She's been playing the piano for you for four years now and been a widow almost as long. I think she has been sweet on you since the day after she planted Jake six feet under." Robert studied the tip of his cigar for a moment, snitched a look at Andrew, and went back to puffing on his cigar.

"I can see by the radiance of my fine cigar, that this suggestion does not make you at all joyful. Correct me if I am wrong, Bristow, but don't all preachers look for wives who can play the piano?"

Tired with the drift of the conversation and the almost overpowering fumes of tobacco smoke being pumped into his face as the doctor meddled with his personal life, he gave disgruntled snort and jumped to his feet. "Listen, Doctor Glenn, the only thing that the Widow Murphy is sweet on is being a preacher's wife and having a body to warm her bed. And no!

Most preachers do not look for piano playing wives, they just happen to play the piano. Sometimes they learn to play the piano later. There are--er--other considerations."

"Such as?" came the daunting rejoinder through the billowy haze of smoke.

Andrew shrugged and stepped away from the fumes. "Well, take it from me, Doc, the good Lord would have to throw a wife in my lap before I would ever marry again. Besides, the first time I married it was out of gratitude to Lois' father. I cared very much for her in spite of her illness, but I never had that attraction for her, like you obviously have for your Emily. Our married life was spent going from one physical problem to another." Andrew dropped into silence, reflecting on those few wrenching years that they shared. "I want what my father and mother had. Is that too much to ask?"

"Andrew," he cautioned, "don't go comparing, because you will never find the same thing. You need to make your own kind of ties that bind. And, like the cactus, with the proper care, most ties grow with time." Never one to waste a good cigar, the doctor stubbed his cigar on the bench and pocketed the remains. "Speaking of Emily, I need to head on home. She is too close to delivering to be gone long."

"I'll be praying for Emily, Robert, and if you need me, let me know, and I will be there," he assured the doctor as he opened the patio gate for him. The moment the doctor stepped through the door, he stopped and turned to Andrew.

"You know, Andrew," he began by shaking a finger in front of his nose. "I caution you not to believe all Bull's stories. Take my word for it that Bull is a sick old man, and he never liked women, anyway. Why Avis Hollis went with him, I am not sure, but a man could do a damned sight worse than to take Avis Hollis to wife."

Andrew tried to understand what Glenn had just said. "Of course, Trumbull likes women. What about all the stories?"

The doctor slanted a look at him. "Andrew, think for a minute. You know that not every man likes women." He put his hand up as if to ward off any more questions. "Let me speak. I'll not say anymore, but that Bull Trumbull is dying and he never liked women at all. To say anymore would be breaching my vows as a doctor, and those covenants do apply even to lowbred scum like Trumbull.

Stunned by the surety of his friend's words, Andrew watched him turn his back and step out into the night.

What was he trying to say: that Avis Hollis was not Bull's woman and that he should consider getting hitched to the town whore?

This was one of Robert's worst ideas. He appreciated the harlot's presence during some of his darkest hours, but Robert was a dreamer. Though she was a beautiful woman, he could never foresee any kind of relationship between himself and Bull's kept woman.

Maybe he languished for anything that was fashioned and plumbed like a female. The image of Agnes Murphy and her lantern jaw swam before his eyes. He shuddered at the thought of waking up next to her in the morning.

And what did Robert mean by those remarks about Bull? If anyone knew the town's secrets, it had to be the doctor who bailed everyone out. He should have stopped Robert and asked him to explain, but it was too late now.

Andrew raised his hand to stroke the coarse stubble of beard that had sprouted under the hot sun. His hands felt cool against his sunburned face and for the first time he was hungry.

He needed a bath, a shave, and food in his belly for straight thinking. Until then he flatly refused to think about anything more.

CHAPTER SIX

Curious, Andrew walked by his bedroom to discover if the sporting woman had stuck around. Except for the circle of light spilling from his doorway and the subdued voice crooning one of Stephen Foster's tunes, this part of the house lingered in quiet.

He realized, as he listened more closely that the melody was one of his favorites. He peeked into the room, to discover Avis rocking in the chair, her eyes closed, singing the melancholy words. He glanced at the bed to see that the Indian child slept.

Avis, he noticed, had turned the overhead light off, and set the two remaining kerosene lamps to low. The girl's wrists were tied to the posts to keep her from rolling from her stomach to her back. He hated tying anyone down, but there just wasn't any other way to keep her from hurting herself.

The girl's long dark hair, a filthy mass of tangles, was tied up in a ribbon away from the open wounds of her back. Remembering that sometimes Lois' hair could get impossibly tangled, he decided that he would ask Avis about cutting it to a more workable length.

Avis, he noticed, had taken her hair down, and tied it back with a ribbon. Andrew watched as the lamplight highlighted the fiery tendrils of hair to a coppery blush. The burnished curls trailed over her shoulder.

Turned away, she could not see him as he watched her. It was not every day that he had a beautiful woman in his bedroom, and grinned while he took the opportunity to look his fill.

He relaxed against the door, and folded his arms. At one time it had been Avis lying helpless in that bed while Lois, Robert, and himself stood the vigil.

He had been the one to spend the long hours nursing her. Lois had started failing with the birth of Amanda, before Avis arrived in their lives and could not endure the long hours.

He remembered how he had found her by the bloody flow that left the trail for him to follow. Moans, like a dying animal, had come from the crawlspace underneath the veranda, where she had hidden sometime early in the morning.

Later, after the doctor had arrived, Andrew had followed the trail back to the rear door of the cantina. He dropped the investigation there thinking that she would eventually explain who had torn her insides to the degree that she could never bear another child.

Instead, she refused to even discuss the attack and, not wanting to offend when she was at her weakest, he had not pursued for information. To this day the person who had done the brutalizing remained a mystery.

Andrew suspected the abuser to be her husband. He knew she had been wed and born a child to a man who had been killed in Texas a few months later.

He had always suspected that Lois knew more than she had allowed. But, even at the end of her life, she would only remind him that God looked on the heart, not appearances, and to have faith.

Andrew's eyes focused on Avis, who set a peaceful in the lulling sway of the maple rocker. But, he was remembering that naked and bloody victim he carried across his porch that morning. Having recognized her before as an uncommonly handsome woman in such a small community, he had known her to be fallen. Many times he had seen her entering and leaving the saloon.

Certainly she was one of the saloon hussies. Holding her,

broken and bleeding in his arms, he recalled the parable of the Good Samaritan and, laid her in the big bed.

Andrew shook off memories, reminding himself that the past was gone and only the present and future mattered. Could this occasion, he wondered, lead to a renewal of their friendship?

Should he care enough about her to take the opportunity to woo her off of Trumbull's table of delights? The disagreeable thought entered his mind, as it always did, that she might not want to leave. The doctor seemed to think the money kept her there. How did he know? He watched and waited, looking for an opportunity to really speak with her, but the moment she stopped rocking, he hesitated, unable to cross the threshold.

Avis stopped singing and slowed the rocker to a halt. She relaxed against the cushion puzzling over why she sat here, nursing the little Indian, when she should be out trying to find the information she needed to send Bull to jail.

She did not really begrudge the time, but a transport was coming up within the next few weeks. And she would not be present at the party to glean what information she could about the caravan into Mexico.

Yawning, she rested her cheek on her hand and savored the cool quiet of the evening. Through the netting over the doorway, she watched the flickers of light as the fireflies danced on the patio.

In the quiet, the familiarity of the room brought memories pressing upon her, but she kept them pushed away. Her stomach roiled, loudly complaining of its emptiness. She covered her mouth in a yawn. Her last thought before she fell asleep was that Andrew was a poor host for leaving her here and not bringing her something to eat.

Andrew watched the usually firm line of the jaw soften. The lines of bitterness around her eyes and mouth vanished into soft childlike ease that vanished when she was awake.

He recalled how, after she was beaten, the doctor had noticed that her breasts were hard and knotty from stored milk. He advised that Amanda be put to nurse to prevent milk fever.

This process had proven to be a blessing for both of them. Lois had no stamina to continue nursing the infant of three months, and Avis became more peaceful and even content when the babe was put to her breast.

In all that time, when he had been forced to do those intimate things for Avis, things that she could not do herself, he could swear that he had never once looked upon the woman with lust in his heart. Now, however, he found himself remembering her attributes in ways that he shouldn't. To prove it, now he remembered her breast for their rose-tipped beauty.

Why, he wondered, did the Good Lord not make ministers exempt from fleshly notions? He shook his head trying to rid himself of visions of times past that crouched in his memory, ready to tempt him.

His stomach rumbled painfully. He could not ignore his hunger. Avis, he thought, was likely as hungry as he was. If he didn't do anything else, he could see that she had dinner and maybe he could pay her for sacrificing her time to help him out.

Quickly he found Amanda, and Manuel in the kitchen with Maria and gave the three of them the evening's instructions. He hastened to the bathroom, knowing that he did not have much time before Manuel initiated step two of their little conspiracy.

Naturally, when he reached the bath, the water was cold, but perhaps that was a blessing to a man whose skin closely resembled a peeled tomato?

He stripped down to inspect his frame in the floor length mirror. He had a V-shaped sunburn, running down the center of his chest, small blisters dotted his face, and his nose did remind him of an overripe strawberry sitting in the middle of his face. But thank the Lord, he thought, as he touched the bridge experimentally; it did not appear to be broken, just swollen on the tip.

He promised himself that the next time he set foot on the veranda for any reason, he would wear a wide brimmed hat. But tonight, he looked as though he had gone a round with John L. Sullivan while roasting in an oven, and taken a punch between the eyes.

Looking as rough as he did, he would not blame Avis for running out the door at the mere suggestion of having dinner with him. But she would not being given a chance to escape. Democracy could just plain be inconvenient and this was one of them.

Andrew caught a pungent whiff of dinner cooking while he bathed and dressed. He figured Avis would have to be crazy to pass up one of Maria's dinners.

When he emerged, Amanda laid siege to his knees with hugs she transferred around his neck when he lifted her into his arms. He could always count on the sprightly Amanda for a rousing welcome. Her love for him was so sincere and honest there were times when he broke down and cried at what her mother was missing.

With a jiggle, he measured her weight. His *golden girl*, was as light as a fluff of cotton, but, thankfully, showed no signs of her mother's frailties. Golden blonde, her complexion turned the color of pecan shells by her daily frolic in the fountain. Her dainty looking bare feet were tough enough to walk unscathed through a bed of nails, he was sure.

"How are you doing, Toot?" asked her father, releasing her from the hug. He hunkered down on his knees to be eye to eye with the tot.

"Fine, Daddy, but I don't think you are doing so fine," she told him as she peered distractedly at his nose. "Why does your nose look like one of those red balls that grow on Maria's stickery plants?"

"Daddy had a little accident with a door, but see," he explained pointing at, but not touching the bridge of his nose. "It is not broken and will get better, but first it will look ugly for a few days."

Before he could stop her, Amanda Rebecca reached over, grabbed the bridge of his nose, and gave it a yank. Needles of pain barraged his face, shooting up behind his eyes, while he yelped and jumped to his feet grabbing his nose.

For safety's sake, he covered the bruised part with the palm of his hand. "Why did you do that, Amanda?" he asked, his question muffled by the protective hand.

Amanda's hands flew over her mouth. "Oh! I'm sorry, Daddy! It was an accident, but I just wanted to see if it really did hurt. I guess it does," explained his anxious daughter just before she plugged her thumb in her mouth.

Andrew stooped, ignoring the pulsing ache of blood rushing to his head. He tenderly bundled his daughter in his arms. Once at eye level, he gently pulled the plug of thumb from her mouth and prodded her head to his shoulder. "I know you didn't mean to hurt me, Toot, but you know that it will take a few days to get better and it will be sore to the touch, till then."

"Say," he said, as he set her firmly on her feet, "isn't that a new dress? I don't recall seeing one just that shade of blue before," he asked, hoping to divert her attentions from his aching nose. "Here, turn around for me, so that I can see how pretty you look."

Andrew exclaimed his approval while Amanda waltzed around the kitchen for him. Maria had given her the dress for her birthday and she had worn it at least six times since then, but he enjoyed watching her show off for him. Maria chuckled at the prissy antics, and he wondered if Maria had finished taking care of the arrangements for the next step of their little conspiracy.

At the end of the promenade, Andrew held out his arms to her and sat down at the end of the kitchen table with Amanda on his lap. "The girl in your bedroom is very sick, isn't she, Daddy?" When Andrew nodded, Amanda looked soberly at her father and replied, "I promise that I will pray for the lady, Daddy."

"Yes, Amanda, I believe that would be for the best. I want you to understand that if things are different here, for the next few weeks, it will be because it is so important to help her out in any way we can."

He looked at his daughter thoughtfully, "If it should be that I cannot be with you as much, remember that it is not because I want to be gone, but because there is only one of me to take care of you and others as well. You have Maria and Manuel, but some of the people I see have no one to help them." Amanda, her golden eyebrows drawn together, took all of this to heart. "You can be brave for a little while, can't you?"

"It's all right for a while, Daddy," she sighed, "but only if you still read me stories and rock me at night when I am afraid," she informed him, with a coy little pout, lowering her eyes and kicking her feet.

Andrew chuckled while tweaking a blond curl. "You silly child. You know you are never scared."

She giggled and shrugged. "I know, but that is because you always ask God to send His angels to watch over me." The child squirmed excitedly on his lap, "Daddy! I forgot to tell you that I saw an angel and he was as big as this house!" she informed her father, her arms stretched into a wide arc. "And he had gold bands around his dress."

"Did you really?" Astonished, Andrew gave her his full attention, listening carefully to every word the child said. When he was about the same size and age, he had seen a similar angel. He had also described the angel as being as "as big as a house."

"Come, *Meja*, help Maria with the food for your papa and the lady," instructed Maria, reaching for the child.

Obediently, Amanda hopped off her father's lap just as Avis

swept through the kitchen door, catching Andrew by surprise. Andrew jumped to his feet. "Hello, Miz Hollis," he greeted, aware that she must have been standing in the hall long enough for Maria to have noticed.

"Miz Hollis," he explained, clearing his throat, hoping his nervousness didn't show. "Maria thought you might be as hungry as I am, so she has arranged a late supper for us." Andrew hadn't realized he was lying until Maria was seized in a fit of coughing.

"Maria, are you all right?" he asked solicitously, knowing full well what was wrong. He could always hope that the housekeeper would take pity on him, this once, and not be his conscience."

"*Senor*! I am fine now, but how do you say... that something got stuck in my *claw* for but a moment." Her black eyes had him pinned as neatly as if he were a fly in her refried beans.

Andrew looked sternly at his housekeeper, hoping she had sense to play along. It wasn't like the fib was going to hurt anyone. "The word is not *claw*, Maria, but craw or throat. In your language *garganta*, he explained firmly, making it clear that he was not going to play her game.

"*Si, Senor*, but I prefer the word *claw*. It is, how do you say, easier to remember and sticks in my mind," she replied, determined to needle him, he was sure, until he repented of his sin.

Andrew's temper sparked, but he chose a tactical retreat over blatant conflict. "Very well, Maria. I will wait for a later time to discuss this with you, but for now, we will see to the dinner."

Avis, he saw, appeared puzzled by the strange conversation. "If you will allow me to escort you to the dining room, Ma'am?" he drawled, punctuating the invitation with a bow.

Avis stared at him. Wary of his courtly attitude she started to tell him to save the bull- but remembered that his daughter was present. Sometimes it was best just to play along. She certainly did not need to set a bad example for the child, by swearing.

"Sir, your chivalry is somewhat overwhelming' at the moment, but if you could direct me to the powder room I will promise to consider your fine offer."

She knew exactly where the bathroom was, but this was her way of telling him to back off. They stared at each other for a fraction of a second when energetic Amanda volunteered to show her the way.

"Why, how kind of you, Miss Bristow," acknowledged Avis. Avis stooped to become eye-level with the child. "Amanda is it?"

Andrew watched Amanda's curls jiggle as she shook her head agreeably. He thought the ruse that she was meeting Amanda for the first time-to be misleading, but noticed, annoyed, that Maria did not seem to have anything stuck in her *claw* over this fib. Maria, he discovered, had a double standard, and he hated double standards.

"Why, after I wash my hands, I'll bet you could show me to the dining room just as well as your father, and we won't even have to bother the poor man at all."

Amanda nodded, really liking this idea. The child took Avis by the hand and escorted her to the water closet making it very plain his services would not be needed. "Bet Avis thinks that I will go on and eat without her," he grumbled watching the females leave the room.

Andrew tried to sneak into the dining room. Maria stopped him by stepping in front of him and pointing a finger to the third button of his shirt. He might have been intimidated, but he winced, instead. "Maria, please. I am sore and tired."

"*Senor*! You lied. Don't you know the ninth law of God? Even I learned it in my catechism, and I will say it for you to remind you. 'Thou shall not bear false witness.' Have you lost what is important?"

Andrew watched her dark eyes flash while her finger drilled his chest like a woodpecker. Was he ashamed? Yes, but not to the point that it required repentance.

He rolled his eyes. "Maria, that woman does not like me and would not stay if she thought I had planned this out because I wanted to have dinner with her. Please, I am pleading for some understanding in this matter."

She studied him for a moment, and then launched into such a rapid spate of Spanish that he could not keep up. Finally, when she had finished and looked at him blankly, as if awaiting his reply he responded with, "Whatever you say, Maria." Again he aimed for the dining room.

"One moment, please, *Senor*. I am sorry I forget that you do not always understand the Spanish. What I said," she informed him calmly, "was that you are *loco*, if you think she does not care for you. It is impossible for most people not to have some regard for the person who saved their life, at least a little," she counseled measuring a small imaginary amount between her brown fingers. "Has it not occurred to you that perhaps the lady likes you too much to bring shame on you. Maybe it is that she is of another world and does not want you to be drawn into hers?"

Forced to listen, Andrew recognized the truth of Maria's words. Something resembling hope sprang to life inside him. Could she possibly be right? Could Avis be rebuffing him to protect him? Could the problem between them be her high regard for him?

Don't get too excited. She could be wrong.

Maria had provided fresh bait for his hook. Suddenly, he felt even more hopeful about the evening.

"Maria," he said as her words continued to bounce through his brain, "I love you," he added as he planted a resounding kiss on the smooth skin of her cheek. "But, Maria, am I forgiven my untruth?"

Her black eyes flashed and she pursed her lips. "Only if you tell her the truth, *Senor*," she replied with a bright smile as she patted his sunburned cheeks. "I think your nose looks more the red of a tomato to me than a cactus flower."

He cast an exasperated glance down at her and, once again, headed toward the dining room. Maria would not let him off so easily. "I will pray that God will lead you to tell her the truth tonight. You should explain that you wanted to have dinner with her," she called behind him.

His heart sank, because he knew that Maria was unbeatable when she took this tack into his conscience. "You win, Maria," he mumbled as he opened the door to the formal dining room. "Tonight, I will tell her it was my idea, but if she serves my *cabesa* to you on a platter, like John the Baptist, it may stick in your *claw*."

Maria's tittering giggle followed him into the dining room. Kneeling, Maria pulled a fresh blouse, skirt, and sandals from the cedar chest where she stored the clothes that she collected to give to the poor. They were lightly worn, but clean and she felt that *La Bonita* would enjoy fresh clothes after her bath. A true lady did not enjoy filth.

Avis could not help but giggle when she finally won her freedom from Amanda by closing the door. Amanda would not let her go until she had to assured her that she would be fine by herself and promised that she would call if she needed any help.

Amanda, she decided, resembled both Lois and Andrew. She had not really had occasion to talk with the child in nearly four years and found herself intrigued by the overly bright child and her direct way of thinking. Andrew, she thought, might have his work cut out for him.

She thought of her own daughter, feeling the keenness of loss at not being able to touch her or see her for the past two years. Tessa was growing up, just like little Amanda, and she was not there to experience all those wonderful stages. She could not even bear to think of how Tessa must feel abandoned by her mother. How much could a six-year old child understand about life? What did the good sisters tell her about her mother?

Gradually, she realized she was staring at herself in the mirror. Years of anger burst inside her and she found a damp cloth to throw at her image. The sodden thwack did not change her mood or situation, only left a damp smear across the glass. She shrugged off her ill humor, consoling herself that her situation with Bull would not last much longer.

She figured that, although Andrew owed her dinner, she would linger in here. Maybe he would be so hungry he would go ahead and eat without her.

Avis bent over the sink filled with water. There came a knock at the door and a little voice announced that Maria had sent something for her. She cracked the door to find Amanda with a stack of clothes almost as tall as the child. When she accepted the clothes, suspecting this might have been planned. "Miz Hollis, Maria also said to tell you that the tub has fresh warm water in it, if you would like to take a bath."

A bath? "Tell Maria that she is very wise and that I am very grateful for the bath and the clothes." She should have brushed aside the offered kindness, but the plain truth was that she hated being dirty.

Smiling brightly, Amanda departed and Avis closed the door. Going around the corner to the tub, she inspected the entire room to see if anything had changed through the years.

Everything remained in the same place. Apparently, Andrew had just bathed because the scent of bay rum lingered in the close air.

Damp towels hung, from a line strung in front of the high window set into the adobe. Her missing red silk hat, minus the feather, hung oddly in the midst of the array. Too bad that someone had quite ruined it by washing the silk and putting it on the line to dry. She would buy another in El Paso.

Avis gazed longingly at the fresh water in the filled tub. After ensuring that both doors were bolted, she shed the fancy clothes in record time. She placed the pistol in the folds of her dress, wrapped tightly in her stockings. After carefully folding them, she stacked them in a neat pile on the footstool.

Bending over, she dipped her elbow in the water. The temperature was perfect and the water scented with something flowery.

She stepped in, finding the big white enameled tub as deep and as wonderful as she remembered. Sighing with pleasure, she slipped beneath the water, melting into the tub's embrace.

Smiling, she wondered if Andrew knew that that his indoor privy was famous all over the Territory. Half the sporting women over at the saloon would marry him just to have use of the in-house outhouse.

There was another cake of soap waiting on the stool next to the tub. She picked it up and recognized it smelled faintly of bay rum. "Andrew," she whispered softly.

She liked the way he looked garbed in the loose, native fashion. He really looked handsome, relaxed, and not worried about someone else.

A smile flitted across her lips to remember how rakish he looked at the cantina, until she recalled Delilah's brazen display. That slattern deserved to have the spittoon dumped over her head for what she did. Messing around with a preacher like that! The woman had no respect for anything holy.

Avis could not understand why this little episode with Delilah irritated her, when just this afternoon she had encouraged the Bull to get Miss Silver Dollars for his fandango. Later, she had even offered to arrange a tryst for Andrew. How shameful of her! Why had she done such a wicked thing?

Before, when a man tickled Dee's fancy, Avis had been amused by the flirtatious antics. Like blind puppies, they fell all over each other to get her attention. Sure as shooting, all the men, to a man, had fallen for her brazen ways.

Tonight, there had been a difference. When she had seen Andrew's body respond to that slut's tricks, it wasn't funny at all. Was he, she wondered, just another man with the same failings? He had nearly fallen from his pedestal, but so far, he had passed the test.

What test? She had no claim on Andrew. She needed to understand her motives. She stopped scrubbing, pausing to watch the soap lather in the cloth.

Andrew she knew to be the rare kind of men who was truly good man. That his God had a prior claim on him, made her want to keep him from evil women.

For years she had refused to think about Andrew as a man at all. She had noticed the bulge in his breeches, and she was shocked to know that like any other man, he could be motivated by that thing in his pants.

He could deny it, but his body didn't lie. Doubtless, had she left them alone, he would have rushed the hussy upstairs to get his satisfaction? What then? Her illusion would be gone. She expected too much and refused to think anymore about the incident.

Reaching up, Avis grabbed a soiled towel to spread it wide, underneath the lip of the big tub. She stepped out, her mind buzzing, trying to sort out her muddled emotions.

She supposed she never really considered Andrew Bristow as human before, because he always seemed so perfect. Always doing the right thing and keeping his promises. If Andrew ever said he would do something he did it, and did it right.

The preacher was too hard up to see that that Dee was like the other women at the cantina and out for everything she could get from a man.

She knotted the leather tie of the sandal around her ankle, rechecked her appearance in the mirror, and remembered how proud Lois had been of her "water closet," as she called it.

She stopped, gazing in the mirror remembering when Andrew's frail young wife had led her about the big, square house. How she had pointed things out as though, giving her a grand tour.

Lois had stood in front of the bathroom, making a game out of it, asking her to guess what was inside, and then giving her hint after hint. When Lois had run out of clues, she opened the door with a queenly flourish. Avis had gasped when she saw the lavish facilities.

"My lands, now I believe in heaven," she had exclaimed making Lois giggle.

Lois, she sighed, feeling suddenly weepy. Avis gathered up her clothes recalling the truest lady she had ever known and the only best friend she had ever had

In all the time she spent in their home, living, eating, and suffering beside them, there had never been one reason for her to dislike either Lois or Andrew. Even now, Lois' death stung.

The trouble was, she decided, that the Reverend and his wife were perfect and she was not. "Who in the hell ever heard of a whore that was a lady anyway?" she muttered to herself opening the bathroom door. Her unworthiness before the memory of Lois' perfection bothered her as nothing else.

Before she knew what she was about, she turned around. Quickly, she hightailed it out the opposite connecting door into the hall that led to the front door. She would have made it too, if she hadn't run into Amanda, who grabbed onto her skirt.

"C'mon, Miz Hollis. I knew you would get lost," said Amanda, towing her back to the kitchen where Maria reached for her dirty clothes.

"I cannot do it today, but if you will return tomorrow, *La Bonita*, I will be glad to clean these beautiful things for you."

"*Gracias*, Maria, but they are stained with blood and I will take them home with me," she told her plainly, pulling the clothes back towards her.

Bewildered, Maria stepped back. "The preacher's clothes are stained and I have taken care of them. You may insist to take them home, but I am very good with those stains." She looked at Avis and smiled, her white teeth shining against her sun-darkened skin. "It is magic that my mother taught me, and I would like to do this thing for you for being so kind to the poor *chica*. And, also, for the other things you have done for my people."

Surprised, she drew back. Avis knew she was being charmed, but allowed the clothes to be taken from her arms, forgetting the derringer amongst the folds. She watched as they were carried away from her and stowed in the storeroom where Maria kept the family laundry. What, she wondered did Maria know that she had she done for her people? She dared not pursue the remark.

"You win this time, Maria. I will return tomorrow to check on the girl and pick up my things," she promised.

There came another pull on her skirt. Avis bent down to Amanda "I want to thank you very much for your help, Amanda," she told the child, "and now may I invite you to have dinner with your father and me?"

Amanda looked at Maria hopefully, but Maria's looked firm, her black eyes fixed upon the child. "You may show *Bonita* the dining room, *Meja*, but you know that we have already eaten and I need your help to prepare *galletas*."

Avis knew very well, that given a choice between making cookies and being the only child with two boring adults, Amanda would chose the cookies. "It's all right, Amanda. I would love to have some of the cookies that you make. Do you promise to save me some for after dinner?" she asked enthusiastically and watched relief flit across the child's face. What a burden it was to be an only child in a house full of adults.

"Oh, yes, Miz Hollis! I'll save you a whole passel of

cookies," she replied, her blue eyes round with excitement.

Avis stretched her hand out to Amanda's. "Are you ready to take me to the dining room so you may get on with cookie-making?" The child slipped her hand into Avis' palm, and Avis, recalling how very tiny those fingers had been when she left, gave them a gentle squeeze. She bit her lip, near tears to be holding them now, not really little any more, either.

When they reached the dining room door, she halted. "Wait! Just one minute please, Amanda."

Avis had to gather her courage to do this thing. Being alone with the preacher was hard, nearly unbearably so. She straightened her back, squared her shoulders, and raised her chin just a bit higher. She was after all, a wealthy businesswoman. She would survive.

When she marshaled her courage, she winked at Amanda. "On three, we go." Avis breathed deeply and fortified herself. "One, two, three. Let's go!" the counted together before they charged through the door to the dining room.

CHAPTER SEVEN

Andrew listened to the pendulum mark the time. Obviously, his houseguest wasn't exactly straining at the bit have a meal with him.

He opened the French doors onto the patio to wander about in the cool of the evening. This simple ritual allowed him quiet time to meditate or just let the pond scum settle.

Standing in the middle of the patio, he turned around, until he had surveyed every quarter of his home. He was proud of the big Spanish style hacienda that was built with mud into bricks baked by the desert sun. Had he not been called into the ministry, he likely would have aimed himself for a career in architecture or engineering.

The roomy house was squarely built, with both outer and inner verandas. An inner hall looped around the circle of spacious rooms. Rooms that opened onto the patio that set at the open center of the house.

Because of Lois' lung disease she had needed as much fresh air as possible and he arranged all rooms to have generously sized doors and windows. He had done all he could."

A familiar sorrow overtook him to remember his beautiful wife. Her hair had been the palest of blond and blue eyes that were not given to passion, but compassion. She had begun as angel and ended as a ghost.

He often thought she had battled consumption for so long by the time they had married that she seemed closer to heaven.

Lois had loved Amanda, but her affection for their child was of a different variety than other mother's had for their babes. Hers was a less possessive love, distant, as if she were near kin, and just visiting.

A few weeks after her passing, it occurred to him that she might have known she was not long for this earth. She had loved her family with open arms. Perhaps loving them distantly to avoid the pain of having to surrender them when the time came to leave.

Doubtless, giving birth to Amanda had shortened her time on earth. He had known the process would weaken her and had tried to dissuade her from having a baby, at all. She had stubbornly assured him that she would be well and had worn him down until he agreed.

The results of the pregnancy had been disastrous and Andrew had flatly refused to bed Lois after Amanda was born. She never regained her strength and everyday she wasted into a shadow of herself, too frail to be able to care for the robust infant.

However, Lois had left him with the greatest treasure of all. His precious Amanda had given meaning to his life in those dark and lonely hours. Lois had known that he would need the child after she was gone.

Even now he remembered to his shame, how he had, at first, resented the poor babe for no reason except the toll her birth had taken on Lois' health. In the end, he had been angry with Lois for abandoning him and, then, furious at Avis for doing the same.

Andrew lifted the netting and walked through the door into his bedroom to see if there had been any change in the girl's condition.

He looked at the girl as she lay peacefully on her stomach, her hands restrained by leather strips, cushioned by clothes wrapped around her wrists. "God help her," he murmured as he passed his hand over her forehead.

Manuel rocked patiently in the maple chair. "We need a miracle, *Senor*."

Andrew turned his head to look at him, sharing the uncertainty. "I agree. We do need a miracle, *Amigo*."

Manuel nodded and closed his eyes as Andrew softly prayed over the torn body of the sleeping girl. He spoke *the amen* and touched her brow one last time, hoping for a blessing.

"We have to have faith, and then only God knows, my friend." Andrew gave Manuel a sad but reassuring smile. "I think Father Juan will be here before long."

"Do not worry, *Senor*," he responded with a casual wave of his hand. "If Padre Juan is too long coming, I will simply get my knife and my wood to make a mess on my wife's floor."

Both men laughed, recalling how Maria heaped Spanish curses upon Manuel's head for dropping whittling shavings on the floors.

Andrew once asked his friend why he didn't pick up the curls, thereby avoiding those curses. He remembered the Spaniard's nonsensical reply vividly.

"*Senor*," he had answered after moments of thought and with a sly glint in his eyes, "I am the perfect husband. My wife is my heart. I do not chase other women or visit the cantina and its cats. I do not drink to go crazy. I am a most thoughtful lover, but I do not want my Maria to think that I am without fault, so I leave a little mess now and then. When she finds it, she will swear at me, and curses me, calling me the lowest and sloppiest sort of a pig. But soon, she is so sorry," he had said in his imitation of a high, simpering female voice. "There is nothing that she will not do for me and she is happy."

Andrew had thought Manuel's idea odd then, and the reasoning remained lost upon him. But, far be it from him to keep Manuel from making his wife happy.

Andrew gave his friend and employee a clap on the back before he walked through the patio doors. "Carve at your own peril, my friend, for I am powerless against Maria. One day, I fear that she will carve on you."

He ambled around the patio, breathing in the scents of the evening and exhaling the old frustrations of the day. Hands in pockets, he walked over to the fountain to contemplate the origin of the pure water high up in the snowmelt of the Sacramento Mountains where some adventurers told of seeing hidden tunnels that travel miles into the mountains.

The evening lengthened and still she had not appeared. His stomach lurched in anticipation. Anticipation of pleasure or pain he did not know which. Maybe it was just another reminder of imminent starvation in his gut that made him so jittery.

Often, he felt like an island; alone and cut off from anyone who understood where his life had been or cared where it was going. Why did he seek her out?

Maybe all he wanted from Avis was the friendship of another adult that had known Lois. Perhaps he had need of someone who had shared her life and death with him.

That could not be true, because Robert Glenn had seen the harrowing details most clearly. Andrew did not seek him out to rehash the painful past.

Could he be attracted to her mind? She possessed a clever mind to be sure, but one which seemed vengefully hostile on one hand, and impure on the other.

Maybe he just wanted the puzzle of Avis Hollis to be solved. Irritated with endlessly trying to reckon their relationship, he scowled, thinking that it certainly should not matter to him what a whore thought of a preacher.

He sat on the bench before the fountain, and propped his elbows on his knees. After rubbing his hands over his face, he shook his head to clear his mind of fuzzy thinking. Never before had his body been so at odds with his conviction of right and wrong.

He had better find himself a wife quickly. Perhaps a sweet-tempered seminary graduate that played the piano, taught church school, and fried chicken for Sunday.

The face of Agnes Murphy passed before his eyes. "Oh, Lord," he groaned, doing the impossible and making the word Lord into a three syllable plea, "anyone but her." The Almighty could not be so cruel and yet be a good God.

The identity of his prospective wife would have to be so obvious that he could not err in the direction of marriage. He stood, face upturned to the canopy of heavens. "All right, Lord, here is the deal," he declared to the twinkling audience. "Hand her to me or, if you have to, throw her in my lap, but make it so obvious that I'll have to take her to be happy."

He started to walk away, but stopped short, his eyes lifted imploringly to the sky. "That is, anyone except Agnes. Lord, I mean she is a fine pianist and a wonderful person I am sure, but some things are just too much to ask. You do understand, don't you?"

After scouring the heavens for some celestial indication that he had been heard, and with no great sign forthcoming, he shrugged his shoulders. He headed for the dining room, maximally lonely and minimally certain that by next summer, he would have his wife and a mother for Amanda.

CHAPTER EIGHT

Avis deflated quickly when, after screwing up her courage, she found the dining room empty. Alone, she walked to the French doors to see Andrew scowling at the fountain as if a giant demon had come to rest smack dab in the middle of his patio.

She turned away. Well, if the host was upset about her taking her time to get ready for dinner, then it was his own damn fault. He could have eaten without her. My goodness how she wished that he would have done just that. If he made one more self-righteous remark during the meal, she would light into him so fast he'd think his hindquarters were caught in a butter churn.

She gazed about her, marking the dining room for any changes. Everything looked perfect, too perfect, she thought, for the big room to be used much anymore. Lois had insisted that they dine around the formal dining table at least once a day.

The long glossy oak-slab table sat in the center of the big room. Around it were eight ladder backed, rawhide seated chairs, reflected the light of the lamp above. Her gaze traveled to the cabinet, which contained most of the earthly bequests by Lois to her daughter.

Avis pulled the brass ring on the door to the right. Lois had shown her that pressing a little lever on the inside would open the left door.

The cabinet held fine crockery, Dresden china, and a

variety of crystal and glass. Some pieces were delicate, while others not really pretty, but practical.

She removed the finely crafted cream pitcher. She held it in her palm and traced its gold etching with her finger, remembering how she had held it just so on the day Lois had acquainted her with the pieces.

Each piece, explained Lois, had its own story. No two pieces matched, being added to the collection by different women from each generation. Some pieces, such as the crystal decanter in the corner, had been in the family since long before her forebears left Ireland while others she began adding as a girl.

All the pieces Lois had earmarked as part of her legacy to her baby. Avis believed that Andrew should guard them to ensure that Amanda received every one of them.

Avis' personal favorite and the eldest of the collection, sat in back. The plain earthenware butter crock had been passed through Lois' Ulster Irish womenfolk since before Elizabeth was queen. She plucked the covered bowl from the back of the display, feeling the weight of the years in her hands.

More amazing to her was evidence of the continuing line of caring mothers and daughters that had added contributed to the collection through the centuries.

Though no two were alike, there existed beauty in the whole of the display. Breaking the chain of generations would nearly be a crime. If Avis did nothing else for Lois, she would see that Andrew made provision for Amanda to have her legacy in full: the history and heritage from a loving and gracious mother to her daughter.

The natural thing would be for Andrew to remarry one day. Likely, the small matter of heirlooms would not be an issue to a new husband. Experience had taught her that men usually did not consider such things as fine crystal or its history when spurred by a lingering arousal.

After the incident with Delilah, she was now convinced that Andrew would be no exception. She realized she had been unfairly expecting too much from him. A man, after all, could not be anything else, but...

Avis gave the crock a last appraisal and restored the cream pitcher to its special spot. Breathing deeply, she inhaled, for one last time the sweet fragrance of the aromatic dried flowers and herbs Lois had placed inside the china cabinet on that day.

She closed the door, gently, running her fingers over the seam where the doors met, lost in the recollection of that terrible time when Lois took to her bed. Avis sighed and closed her eyes. Time, supposed to heal all wounds, had done nothing to ease the pain and guilt as the memories returned.

Avis rested her forehead against the cabinet doors. Together, she and Andrew had endured the purgatory of waiting for the end and her doom. Only she knew Lois's death would signal her departure from his home.

She had refused to remember and survived by immersing herself in revenge. Tonight, her revenge nearly finished, she had dared to remember too much.

Avis straightened, sniffed, and wiped a tear from her cheek. She should leave. She turned to find the preacher watching her from the doorway.

He stared at her, his hazel-eyed gaze intense and speculating.

A rosy blush crept over her cheeks. Expecting to be rightfully rebuked for rifling the cabinet, she lowered her eyes. "Andrew, I wasn't stealing," she began, guilty to be found trespassing.

"Of course you weren't," he replied. He did not look away, but breathed in the beauty of her standing in the light of the lamp. Her stiff demeanor had changed with wearing a simple white blouse and turquoise skirt with her flaming hair pulled back into a black velvet bow.

His lips curved into a smile. She had called him Andrew. How amazing! He caught her red handed in the China closet and she called him by his first name. If he made her feel guilty enough, would she call him Andrew all the time, he wondered.

Moving to stand next to her, he smiled. "There is no need to explain, Miz Hollis. I don't think those doors have been opened since she closed them the day that you two cataloged the collection."

Her eyes slanted to him, but he was looking at the collection of glass behind closed doors. He looked not sad, but strong, as though he had made peace with the past.

"I understand that she went through all these items with you. I know that Lois explained every jot and tittle of detail. You didn't think I knew about that, did you?"

Avis shook her head. "No," she whispered.

"First, she told me that she bought extra insurance because you knew what was important and had more gumption than I did." His fingers lightly skimmed the smooth surface of the tabletop as he moved toward her. "She also left me a detailed list of the particulars in case you had not committed them to memory."

"I see," she said stepping back.

"Lois freely recounted most of what you discussed and the times you had together, but there were some things she never did tell me. You see, she believed in keeping confidences."

She inhaled the familiar scent of him. She noticed the pink tinge to his already tanned features and knew his nose must hurt terribly, for its end was cherry red. His hair lay slicked down, but she knew it had a mind of its own and would only stay that way for a little while. She would greatly enjoy disturbing the peace of those pasted down curls, but knew she could not be playful with this man. He was too good to mess with in any kind of funning way.

"But if you would like the piece as a keepsake, I am sure

that she would want you to have it. Take it," he offered, unknowingly illustrating her very thoughts of a few moments before.

Men! A thousand nasty words flooded her mind, but she bit them back. How, she wondered, could he be so damn careless with Amanda Rebecca's heritage?

He placed his finger in the ring to open the door. She placed her hand gently over his and took his hand in hers to keep him from making a mistake. His eyes followed their hands, folded together.

She shook her head. "Oh no, Andrew! You misunderstand what I was doing," she protested, avoiding his gaze. "These things all belong to Amanda. I was just remembering the details Lois told me that she wanted Amanda to know."

She tried to ignore the shock of the strong hand of the preacher beneath hers, but she had not realized that touching him could be greatly different from touching anyone else. His touch, warmer than when she had touched him on the veranda a few hours before, sent a little shock through her.

"I am sure," he mumbled his eyes focused on their hands.

She immediately released him, embarrassed to have grabbed without thinking. She looked down at the floor and clasped her hands together to keep them from trembling.

"I'm listening." Andrew turned, his attention focused upon her.

"If you must know, I was hoping that when you remarried, you would remember a mother's dying wish for her child and not allow some woman to do your daughter out of what is rightfully hers."

Her eyes grew moist and she refused to look at him for fear that he would see her weakness. "Family was so important to Lois…" She sniffed, feeling a fresh upwelling of sorrow for her friend who passed on before she could see her child blossom.

Andrew watched the beginnings of tears creep into her eyes. She looked away. Ill at ease, he suspected, because tears were strangers to the hardened woman she had become.

The last thing she wanted would be for him to see how much she had cared. "I'm sorry," she said, looking to the side while she wiped her cheek. "She was the only truly wonderful person I ever knew, and I still miss her."

Andrew had no idea that any feelings about Lois lingered, and he resisted the urge to take her in his arms and cry with her. He reminded himself that even a wild cat had a weak moment or two, but holding such a creature in an embrace did not seem like a good idea, unless one prepared himself to be mauled.

He sacrificed his clean handkerchief to her. She took it, lifting watery eyes to him and smiling shyly. For a moment he searched eyes of the deepest of blue, finding in them a haunting innocence. Even Trumbull's woman had her moments.

He knew better than to follow any momentary urge to be sympathetic. Perhaps it was the way her eyes too quickly shifted away from him. Maybe it was just a burst of good, common sensibility in his soul that persuaded him not to act on his impulse.

Andrew pulled the chair out for her. "Come, Miz Hollis," he said gruffly, unaccountably moved by the sentiment for his dead wife. "Let's eat before Maria looses her patience with us."

"Anything to keep the cook happy," replied Avis with a sniff and a watery smile as she seated herself on the offered chair. "Especially, a cook as good as Maria."

"If you will excuse me for a moment, I will tell Maria that we are ready."

Avis noticed that his place was set at the head of the table and she was seated to his left. He sat a little too close for her comfort, but at least he was not sitting across from her, making her self-conscious every time she took a bite.

When he returned, he picked up his eating utensils and moved them directly across from her. In one movement, he disposed of the distracting centerpiece by pushing it to the foot of the table.

"Why did you do that, Preacher?" she queried, unable to understand why he couldn't leave well enough alone. Maybe he read her mind? How horrifying it would be if he could read her mind.

He grinned broadly. "If you are asking me why I moved my things to this side of the table, as opposed to the end, then I can tell you that it is because I am always more comfortable sitting across from my friends than at their elbow." He settled the linen napkin on his lap. "It is not often that I have time to share a meal with my friends anymore, and I want to enjoy the meal when I do."

Andrew smiled innocently at her then sipped his drink. In truth, he wanted to move closer to discover if Maria's theory had any merit, and testing that theory required a strategy of closeness.

Above all, he would be patient and cordial with her. He would ignore any reactions from her that smacked of insult and consider any rude or offensive comment to be part of a well-constructed ruse to keep him away.

Her eyes would tell him what he wanted to know, even if her beautiful mouth said otherwise. He cleared his throat. "I prefer to be eye to eye with my friends."

"I see."

Essentially, his ploy was, to quote Shakespeare, *kill her with kindness*. Kindness required closeness, and an extra measure of perseverance to endure the barbs.

What, he wondered, would he do if she did care for him? She would still be a whore who had sold her favors to the highest bidder, and he would still be the Protestant minister who refused to forsake the ministry and his good reputation for the charms of an unrepentant harlot.

Avis lifted her head, focused not on her host, but on Maria and Amanda, who, ferried the various dishes from the kitchen to the dining room. Amanda paused just long enough to give her father a big hug before returning to the kitchen.

Suddenly they were alone. Two people sitting stiffly in an appallingly quiet room meant for intimacy.

Avis had no idea why, but when the child lavished the hug upon her father, she could barely stand to watch the affection that passed between them. Perhaps because she missed Tessa terribly? She ached for her own daughter, but until she settled the other matters Tessa remained safer far away.

Andrew smiled into the bemused expression in her eyes. She dropped her gaze to study the hands in her lap. Had Avis been embarrassed by Amanda's childish hug?

When she raised her head, to her credit, she smiled back at him. "She loves everybody and hugs everybody she loves."

"Yes, well, she is a lovely child." Avis sipped the cold drink. Chipped ice floated in the light brown lemony liquid. A drop of condensation rolled down the side of the glass and she caught it with her finger then touched the droplet to her tongue.

That simple gesture sent lust raging through Andrew's body. He nearly groaned out loud and tilted his head back for a moment to close his eyes and erase the image of the glistening droplet on her tongue. The woman, he decided, certainly knew how to seduce with the simplest of gestures!

Her gaze rarely met his and when she wasn't looking, he searched for changes the years had made. The lovely lady across from him made him ache for just one touch.

His eyes traced her form. Tonight, although she appeared disarmingly youthful with her hair held back in a simple ribbon, her natural curves were ample, and fully formed of a female in full bloom.

He sipped his drink, remembering the blue veined swollen

breasts he had seen that first night and how his famished baby girl had greedily claimed them. Looking away from her, he thought how strange that he remembered such things.

Amanda and Avis had certainly taken to each other. From that moment forward and until she left, Avis had Amanda near to her. His daughter grew healthy and brightened under Avis' lavish attentions.

Andrew purged such lurid thoughts from his mind. No woman should even be mentally ogled for nurturing a child.

He remembered catching them at play: Avis laying on her stomach on the floor, and Amanda crawling to her. When Amanda had advanced far enough, Avis scooped her up and rolled on her back to allow the babe to rest on her stomach.

"Amanda Rebecca," said Avis after kissing the baby's cheek and holding her above her head to look up at Amanda, "don't tell anyone else, but you, you round little baby, are beautiful and I love you." At that moment a long string of slobber dropped in Avis' eye and she bolted upright.

Plump cheeked and mostly bald, Amanda giggled while Avis wiped her eye. She stood the baby up in her lap. "You little stinker. I said I love you and what do you do? Slobber in my eye, but you will have to do something much worse than that to keep me from loving you."

Avis hugged the baby to her bosom. "I love my Tessa too, but I can't have her right now, so you will have to do. Is that okay?"

Not wanting her to know that he saw her crying, Andrew had retreated before she turned. That was the only time, he recalled, including the day Lois died, that he ever saw her weep.

A gentle breeze ruffled the curtains and cooled the dining room.

Andrew watched Avis eat, not in a dainty or mincing manner, but gracefully and with the enthusiasm of one who is hungry and enjoys food. Their hands collided as they both reached for tamale from the heaping platter sitting between them.

They smiled at each other and he politely withdrew. "You are, after all, the guest," he said, motioning for her to go ahead of him. He watched the long fingers with their tapered nails pluck a rolled morsel from the top of the pile.

Observing Avis had once been a favored pastime for him. His fascination had begun when she lay deathly pale and motionless, and he had hoped for any sign that she would fight for her life. Then, after she was well, there came riddles never satisfactorily answered. Over time the questions had not changed, only deepened.

Though the questions remained unanswered, in times past he had thought he knew her so very well that he could read her mind and even predict her next move. More fool he. He had never anticipated that she would desert them. Especially for the reasons she gave. He had been a fool and not known her at all or had he? Had she merely devised the scheme to keep them separated?

Now might be the right time to test Maria's theory. Besides, he thought ruefully, he might never get another chance to discover if he really did know what she was thinking.

Andrew cleared his throat. "Miz Hollis," he began, "you have really impressed Amanda and she asked me--actually whispered in my ear--if she might give you a hug before you leave tonight."

Avis paused, a fork full of enchilada suspended in the air, while she shot Andrew an irritated glance.

"I believe that she also wants you to sample her cookies as well, so you must not forget to do both," he continued, reminding her of what she had promised Amanda. The Avis Hollis he had known would never break her promise to a child.

Avis wiped her mouth with her napkin. There was

certainly no method by which Andrew could know her thoughts of a few moments ago, and if she made too much out of a childish hug then he might meddle in other sensitive places.

"That would be fine, Reverend Bristow," she told him, nodding her head as if it were the most natural thing in the world for a wicked woman, to be hugged by a child. "I'm impressed with Amanda. I think you have done wonderfully with your daughter, considering that she has had no mother. You do not object to Maria and Manuel calling her *daughter*?

Andrew opened his hands wide. "There are different kinds of love. Why should I object that the other two most important people in her life feel as though she is their daughter? No one fully owns his children. She is easy to love and she is, after all, God's gift to the world."

Avis realized she sounded peculiar: jealous, in fact. "But she has no real mother," she pointed out, thinking of her own daughter.

"But Miz Hollis," he countered, enthusiastically, "she has had three mothers and they all have left their mark." He lifted the bite to his mouth, but noticed the question in her eyes and then she evaded his gaze.

At last, he had caught her attention. His food could wait. He carefully replaced his fork on the plate, and rubbed his hands.

Placing his elbows on the table, he knit his hands together. "Let me explain," he volunteered, hastening on before she could choose not to hear the explanation. "As you know, Maria has been with us for almost four years now, and I find Amanda has adopted those practical and selfless ways that are the marks of Maria's sterling character. I am most blest to have such a good and caring woman as Maria to properly teach Amanda."

Avis stiffened, afraid of what might be coming. The last topic she wanted to discuss was long ago when hope lived within her.

He sipped his tea. "I am certain that she gets her beauty and intuition from my late wife, who always had a knack for disregarding appearances and knowing the true nature of a person."

He closed his eyes to reach far back in time to remember the woman he had married. "Lois had this inner voice, and always seemed to know a person's heart."

"Yes, I remember," agreed Avis, remembering the piercing pale eyes. "She never looked at the outside of anyone."

"I agree, but I only understood Lois after she had gone. I am sure that you would agree with me when I say that Lois had only one foot on the earth, because the other was in heaven. She could never really own anyone or anything, not even her daughter. I think she knew from the beginning that her days were numbered."

Avis stopped to gaze into the distance. She nodded her head. "Probably. I remember there was something otherworldly about her. She knew things before I told her."

Andrew paused. "Sometimes, toward the end of her life, I would hear her talking in the dark. When I would try to discover her companion, she would be radiant. The room would have a certain presence, but be empty. I have often thought, since then, that she communed with the angels even more than with us."

Avis shivered. She had never really considered heavenly beings real. Tonight was the first time she had heard this and to think she was living in the house, only a few rooms a way, and never knew.

"Amanda, I think is very like her. Sometimes she has an other worldliness about her, but she also has both feet rooted squarely on the ground."

Avis concentrated on eating. She resented the bonds he

tried to renew between them. Didn't he realize how difficult this conversation to be? Of course, he didn't. How could he know of her sacrifices? She shut her eyes, feeling the beginnings of another headache pressing in on her brain.

Andrew watched as she massaged her temples and he hesitated, wondering if he should continue on this tack. Everything within him told him to seize the moment. This time he would forge ahead and say the things that needed to be said between them.

He had languished for years, yearning to say the unspoken things to the one woman who had such a lasting effect on a man and his infant daughter. Whether she ever talked to him again was unimportant, for he would be satisfied with saying the words now.

"There was another young woman who nurtured Amanda for most of that first eighteen months of her life. I so appreciated her loving care for my child. She would rock her to sleep, sing lullabies and create a variety of pretty stories about errant stars or chivalrous frogs who turn into princes upon doing their good deed."

"Imagine that," she said stiffly. Why had she let him talk her into this? She didn't want to remember anything.

Andrew dared not look at her, but looked away and laughed softly. "I have a favorite story. I had thought Lois asleep and was sitting by her bed. The house was quiet. Amanda had awakened crying and this gracious young woman rocked her, speaking to her in a voice soothing to my daughter," he chuckled again, but occupied his hands by peeling fresh tamale, anxious for what he would see in her eyes. "The tale was about a little red dog with huge floppy ears. The dog would use the overlarge ears to fly about the country rescuing poor helpless rodents from carnivorous cats."

Andrew dared a glance at her, and saw that she had paused from eating. She was staring. Not angry, evidently surprised to know that someone had overheard the little tale she had spun to pass time with an infant too young to remember much but the soft timbre of the voice.

"My wife had been awake and listening. She told me to treat that young woman and our child as God's blessings to me. Now," he said, punctuating the air with a raised finger, "Lois, I finally understood to be right and that young woman probably influenced my Amanda above everyone else."

He sat forward, his elbows resting on the table. "Did you know, Miz Hollis, that though these things happened before her second birthday, Amanda still asks me about the singing lady and wonders if she was a singing angel." His eyes dropped to his plate and he busied himself with the tamale before it got cold and rubbery. "Isn't it interesting how much we remember as babies?"

The knot in her throat would not go away. For a moment, she thought she would cry, but she managed to raise her chin a little higher.

Avis wanted to surrender, to explain her actions, and share everything until he understood. She knew that, tonight, she had allowed herself too close. She longed to tell him how it almost killed her to walk out on the child and her father.

She betrayed her best friend. Lois had trusted, believing that she would be there for them when she was gone, but she couldn't have been."

Her consolation had been that she had saved their lives that day. He might never know what she had done and the pain of loss that plagued her for years, but she had done right by them.

"Yes, Reverend Bristow, it is amazing what fine imaginations small children have, and the story about the little dog was charming. Perhaps you should have said something, but it would have made no difference."

She knew she had hurt him again by not sharing the

memories with him. Avis watched his fine, symmetrical hands as they cut his food. He raised his soft eyes, filled with only tenderness and she wanted to cry or shout at God for the unfairness of the past. She tamped down her anger knowing that she should have never come. "But what do you tell her about the singing lady?"

Andrew stopped eating, and looked up at her, surprised. "I tell her the truth, of course," he answered lightly.

Avis' eyes narrowed. The last thing she needed right now was a complication. Though they both knew the truth, to agree that she was Amanda's singing angel would be too much of an attachment.

Andrew shrugged and grinned as if he knew a secret. "I tell her I knew of a lady who would watch over her when she was a wee babe, but I could not say that she sang, because I had never heard her myself."

Andrew took the pitcher from the edge of the table and refilled his half-empty glass of tea, then refilled hers "Tell me, Miz Hollis, do you sing?"

"Not one note," she responded blithely, her eyes fixed on her plate while telling him what they both knew to be a flagrant lie.

"Hmm. That could mean either that you don't sing at all, or sing many notes." He winked at her when she shot him an exasperated glare.

"Perhaps the problem is in your definition of a note," he suggested, a grin spreading across his face. "You see, a note is one of those dots you put on a paper and then decorate it look like it's a piggy coming through a barbed wire fence."

The vision of fat little notes, like chubby pigs with curly tails, stuck in a fence, caused her to laugh and sputter water from her nose. She clapped her hand over her mouth to stop the spewing fountain.

Andrew pulled back from the splash area too late, but

pleased that he had struck the humorous part of her that he thought had been swallowed up in her wicked ways, he ignored the spray of water. The delightful, giddy, and one hundred percent womanly sound of laughter had been missing from his home for too long.

"I want you to know that I make, Amanda leave the fountain on the patio when I bring her inside," he chided, blotting the liquid from his shirt. This brought on a fresh round of laughter that Andrew joyfully shared.

He quit laughing to enjoy her merriment. Taking a deep breath, he was vastly relieved that the tension had broken...at least for the moment.

"Very clever, Andrew," commented Avis, wiping the tears from her eyes with her napkin.

"Thank you, but I cannot take credit." He replied with a glint in his eye and a grin, grateful that he was back to being *Andrew*." That is a sassy little Amanda Rebecca special."

"Amazing! She is very clever, isn't she?" she said, thinking proudly of the child.

"Very clever and she would be the first to toot her own horn," he replied, enjoying her amusement.

Her eyes hid nothing, but were open with lashes dewy from tears. His gaze dropped to her lips to watch as she dabbed them with the napkin.

Idly, he wondered, how she would look sucking an orange? When, next he wondered how it would feel to be an orange being sucked by those lips, he bit his tongue at the fiery spurt that settled in his groin. "Yee-ow!" he barked.

"Andrew, are you alright?" she asked, anxiously, her eyes roving over him, looking for something wrong.

"Bit my tongue," he lisped, waiting for his tongue to recover from the insult...biting insult? He would have laughed, but it was just too painful.

Andrew lingered over his food, not wanting the evening to

end. It was good, he thought, to have a woman in the house again, even one of dubious repute.

"Do you think anyone was ever able to find the deputy this afternoon?" he asked, shifting his thoughts to something less likely to send him into the throws of carnality.

She set her glass aside, and pursed her lips. "I did, after it was all over."

Andrew frowned, perplexed because she had been with him just about the whole time since then.

"Do you remember when I asked you to wait for me? I went to Kate's rooms and there he was, naked and sprawled across her bed. She told me that he had run onto some money, and spent it all on liquor and playing around upstairs. She said he had been there since the night before, when one of the girls asked her to take care of him, because he was bad for her business."

Avis leaned across the table and pointed the fork at him to make her point. "Andrew, I am warning you that unless we do something about that lout now, somebody will suffer."

Andrew tried not to accuse, knowing that what she was saying was true, but not everyone walked on the wrong side of the law like she did. Herb was Bull's man and bad business. Andrew never intended to have a run in with him. "He is *your* mayor's man."

Avis ignored the pointed way he made Bull to be hers, as if she owned the snake. "Andrew, I could tell you terrible stories about the deputy that would take that curl right out of your hair."

Avis looked at the disgust in his eyes and she realized, then, she had ruined the evening by referring to her activities. Never mind that this was not the meaning she intended, but it was what Andrew thought about her that hurt. Why should she be surprised at the preacher when the whole damned world thought the same thing?

She folded her hands together in her lap and stared at her plate, knowing that even if those suspicions were not true, she had a job to do. She would have to let him think whatever he wanted until it was done.

"Thank you for the lovely dinner, I guess it's time for me to go," she informed him, feeling uncomfortable under his scrutiny and tired of the evening's illusion that things were good between them. She placed the rumpled napkin next to her plate.

"Nonsense," he replied good-naturedly. "Maria has a pot of excellent coffee for us, and don't forget about Amanda's cookies."

She watched dubiously as he spoke to her in calm and relaxed tones. Even his eyes, eyes that had, before, revealed his disgust and disapproval of her encouraged her to stay.

"Please sit down," he said softly, reaching for her hand. Amanda will be so disappointed if you don't stay. And so will I." He smiled at her. "Please stay." His eyes remained upon her. Eyes warm and inviting. "Besides, I miss having company over four years old."

Something good burst within her. Tired of being angry, she wanted to enjoy herself. True, it was nice to be able to visit with an old friend. No matter what she said or how she had acted in the past, he had saved her life and that made him the best sort of friend.

How could he believe the worst of her, yet still find her good company? Maybe he just needed a woman's company. Any woman might do. Good Heaven's! He might have invited Delilah to the same fine meal if she would have offered to help with the Indian girl.

Avis jumped when the door flew open and in bustled Maria with a steaming carafe of coffee and chocolate. The pungent and aromatic mocha brought her senses to attention. If she had two weaknesses it would be coffee and chocolate.

Only Andrew and Lois had known of her passion for chocolate and coffee. She had been served the combination only twice before and the last had been the evening before she left.

Avis watched, waiting as Maria poured the fragrant, bittersweet brew into Avis' demitasse cup and, then, into Andrew's. She leaned over and breathed deeply of the aroma.

"*Senor*," whispered Maria in his ear, as she poured the small cup brim full, "it is my duty to remind you of the ninth commandment, and that your time is running out to correct this sin.

Andrew nodded. She placed the silver vessel on the table, and he suspected Maria listened at the door. Thankfully, she did not wait for his reply, but retreated to the kitchen.

He sipped the rich drink, figuring how best to correct this sin. He needed to keep his vow to Maria without losing favor with Avis. He might as well come out with the truth.

Opening his mouth, he hesitated, becoming enthralled by Avis' tantalizing and perhaps unknowingly provocative enjoyment of the hot drink. The woman had a style of her own. She would sip the drink, but if there a drip clung to the side, she would capture it with her tongue.

Andrew stared, charmed by the sensual play of the pink tip catching the drop rolling from the golden rim of the cup. Before he could stop them, fanciful visions of a decidedly lustful nature snaked through his mind. Sweat beaded his forehead to imagine the wicked places on him she could touch with the tip of her tongue.

Andrew dropped his gaze and stroked his forehead. He was victimizing himself with vain imaginations, and could not look. He discretely changed position so that he turned slightly to the wall.

Andrew sipped the steamy brew from his cup. When he brought the cup up and looked over its rim, Avis was grinning at him.

"You fibbed. Maria did not plan this dinner, you are behind this evening." Her face tilted up and one burnished eyebrow arched, daring him to lie.

He set the cup down, chagrined to be caught in an untruth. He would have blushed, but he was not nearly as ashamed as he should be. "How did you know?"

"You are the only person in this town who knows how much I enjoy mocha. The only time I have ever had it was with you and Lois. The last time was the day Maria came to live here and the night before I left."

She sipped again from her cup, closing her eyes to savor the taste, and then suddenly opened them to stare at him. "What puzzles me, Andrew, is why you told me a bold faced lie and said the dinner was Maria's idea? You disappoint me. I never would have thought you capable of telling even a white lie."

He flushed and swallowed his drink. His nose itched and he rubbed, remembering to be gentle. "Honestly, Avis, things haven't been exactly agreeable with us for a while and I thought you would turn me down if you thought this was my idea."

"Really?" she said, leaning towards him. She propped her chin on her palm and fastened her gaze upon him. "Do tell."

She looked like she had years before with her hair down and tied back in a bow. The white peasant top dipped in the front displaying the warm, moist, fragrant line of cleavage between her breasts. Fragrant? How did he know if her cleavage to be fragrant? Andrew swallowed hard and looked above her head at the painting of the Organ Mountains hanging on the wall.

He shrugged, and looked at the fork in his hand. "I don't know, Avis. There were practical things to consider. I knew that you needed to eat just the same as I did." He couldn't believe that her first name kept popping out of his mouth, and she hadn't yelled at him once about the slip "I guess this is my way of saying *thank you*." He knew the other reasons were better left unsaid.

"Andrew." She called his name in a soft voice. He closed his eyes at the way the warm Southern tones of her voice poured over him.

"Andrew, look at me. Is that what was stuck in Maria's *claw*?"

Red rushed into his cheeks. He looked at her briefly then looked away. Andrew nodded. Feeling like a naughty boy, he looked up at her and the silliness of it all overtook them.

Their laughter blended and the years melted away. It was as if there had never been any anger or grief between them. They were still chuckling when Amanda burst through the door.

CHAPTER NINE

"Cookies!" announced Amanda triumphantly, bursting through the swinging door, followed by Maria.

Avis watched the child place the platter on the table and then climb on the chair next to her. Smiling, Avis leaned forward to smell the aroma of the warm cookies. "Hmmm. Did you make these cookies?" she asked, watching the anxious fidgeting.

Amanda nodded and leaned forward on her elbows, while her bottom squirmed against the back of the chair. "Yes, Ma'am."

Avis' arms snaked around the child, to pull the small body into her lap, hugging her until she squeaked. Next, she tickled Amanda until she begged for her to stop, and then hugged her again. Closing her eyes, she savored the warmth and genuine affection of a child.

The bond remained, as though the years had never come between them. Avis' throat constricted, and she feared she would cry. When she opened her eyes, she discovered Andrew smiling too sweetly at her. "Well," she said coolly, arching her eyebrow.

"Look! Your Daddy hasn't eaten his cookie yet," she whispered into the child's ear.

Andrew thoroughly enjoyed the tableau, observing that this was how he remembered her, affectionate, teasing and positively charming.

Her affection for Amanda was real and her enjoyment unfeigned. How wrong he had been to think that Avis would reject Amanda.

Now that he saw them together, heard his daughter's giggles, and the naturalness of their play, he concluded that the bond between the two had to be far stronger and more natural than he had supposed. With the bond between them so right why did Avis chose to give all this up for who knows what. He frowned, unable to understand.

"Daddy! Eat your cookie!" ordered his little magpie, her finger pointed at his nose. "Just like Miz Hollis is eating hers."

He watched his baby sprawl across Avis' lap. She picked up a warm cookie and handed it to Avis, leaving him to get his own.

"By all means, Daddy!" mimicked Avis. "Eat your cookie just like I do."

Andrew intercepted the wink from Avis, and watched her make the simple act of biting a cookie a long drawn out process, as she affected and exaggerated the mannerisms of crooking her pinky and waving the morsel around as if it were a bee buzzing through the air. Finally, and with a flourish worthy of a maestro, she placed the bite on the tip of her tongue and snaked it into her mouth.

Amanda watched entranced, her hands held up to her mouth, giggling at the silliness. Avis swallowed the sweet, and whispered into Amanda's ear. Amanda clapped her hands over her mouth in a childish fit of mirth. "Daddy, remember that you have to eat your cookie just like she did."

"But, Amanda," he whined, "I cannot remember all that. Maybe you have to help me."

Stretching his arms, he lifted her over the table and into his lap. Amanda helped by directing him through every movement. At last, when the sweet was swallowed, he pronounced it *deliciosa*, and proved it by eating at least a half dozen more in the space of a few minutes.

He suspected Amanda would soon be asleep. "I want Miss Hollis to hold me," she whined, rubbing her eyes with her fists. He passed her back, wondering how Avis would react to the tired child.

She looked down at Amanda, who lay cradled in her arms. "You make wonderful cookies, Amanda," she said softly, her mouth turned in a half-smile.

Amanda touched one of Avis' curls, then held it between her fingers, turning it over to study the curl in the light. "So bright. Pretty," whispered the child.

Andrew held his breath wondering if Amanda remembered the gesture she had made often as a baby.

"Please, Miss Avis, scratch my back. I am so sleepy."

He held his breath afraid to move for fear he would ruin the moment. He suspected that it would not take much to send the softness of this woman back into hiding.

He watched her hoist the child upon her shoulder. She held the child safely by one arm while scratching her back with the other hand.

"Miz Hollis," she said sleepily, "you smell so good. Like roses, I think." Amanda yawned. "And you scratch backs real good too, just like my mommy did," she added, before plugging her thumb into her mouth and drifting into sleep.

Avis jolted out of her ease, a bolt of understand had hit her. Even as she continued to soothe the child, she became aware of her folly. When she looked to Andrew for help, he was finishing a cookie and the last of his coffee, apparently unaware of Amanda's remark. He seemed more interested in the cookie than in her. He had set her up for this. "Andrew," she whispered.

He ignored her whisper. Andrew had heard, and saw the distressed look Avis sent his way. He had known that eventually Amanda would recognize the bond between them.

He could feel Avis staring at him. She willed him to deliver her from this predicament, but he was reluctant to have the evening end, lose the joy, and slide into loneliness again.

"Andrew," she said a little louder, "I do believe your daughter is asleep now, if you would like to put her in bed?"

He watched her draw lazy circles on Amanda's back, while her eyes begged him for relief.

He smiled at her, rose from his chair, and walked around the table to extract the clinging bundle her arms. Such a pity the night had to end, he thought. They had seemed so natural together, almost like a family. He could not remember when he had ever enjoyed an evening quite like this.

Avis rose to leave, and he stopped in the doorway with his slumbering burden. "Please, don't go yet. I have something I need to give you and then I will walk you home," he said, nearly in a whisper. He didn't wait for Avis to agree or disagree, but walked out, carrying his daughter to her bed.

Quickly, Avis flew out the dining room door and into the kitchen only to be stopped by Maria, who wanted her opinion of the cookies, the coffee, the tamales, and even, incredibly, her tortillas. Try as she might, she could not shake free of the woman and she liked her too much to hurt her feelings by walking away.

Too soon Andrew returned, stuffing something into the pocket of his white cotton pants. "Are you ready, Miz Hollis? O will see you home."

Escorting her home was a nice gesture, but it really wouldn't do for the preacher to be seen with her late at night. Especially to be heading in the direction of her house, but at the moment all she could do without making a scene, was to take his offered arm.

They checked on the Indian girl, who had stirred, but promptly fallen into a deep sleep when dosed with laudanum. Avis touched the cool forehead, reassured there was no fever. She bade goodnight to Manuel, who was concentrating on his whittling and making an awful mess on the floor.

As they walked out the front door, Andrew, again, offered his arm, but she declined. He stopped and pulled her arm to halt her charge ahead of him. "Miz Hollis, I would deem it a great honor if you would take my arm and allow me to escort you home," he told her formally, suspecting, that if Maria was right, and she cared about his reputation, she would refuse his offer and create a fight. He watched her wind up. When her face turned red, he knew didn't have long to wait.

"Cut it out, Reverend Bristow," she sneered, emphasizing his title. "I am quite able to make it home on my own, thank you, but I am not going home, because I have business to take care of at the saloon." Another lie, but Andrew didn't have to know that.

At this point, in the past, Andrew invariably became insulted and stomped off, but this time, he was determined to stay calm against the rebuff. He would be more insistent.

Avis Hollis had done exactly as he had predicted by turning him down and then offending him by the implications that she had something better to do than be with him. Tonight would be different and he was not about to lock horns with her.

Andrew firmly took her hand and tucked it under his arm, "Just tell me where to go, Miz Hollis, and I will accompany you," he responded pleasantly, determined to see the evening and his experiment through. "I refuse to allow you to leave my home unescorted."

She slipped her hand out from under his arm. "Reverend Bristow," she began, turning her gaze to meet his. "I want to explain to you that you, as a man of God, and I--"

He moved her hand back into the crook of his arm. "Miz Hollis, I agree and have noticed that you are not a man of God. Frankly, I had not thought of offering this escort service to Father Juan or any of the other brothers. I really doubt that I should, as they might think it a bit peculiar," he said comically.

She fidgeted by his side and he predicted that since she could not convince him with reason, she would counter with an assault.

"You dunderhead! Do you live in a dream world or something?" she exploded, jerking her arm away from him.

"Don't you know that there will be talk and that it is not good for you to be seen with Trumbull's whore? But if you are going to insist on throwing your reputation in the cesspit, then it is beyond me to stop you."

He winced that she referred to herself so unkindly. Fallen woman or soiled dove would have been sufficient. But, he thought wryly, that the Miz Hollis could rarely be compared to a dove.

He captured the waving arm and returned it to the shelter of his arm. "My goodness, Miz Hollis, your care for my reputation is commendable, but I had no idea that you were such a prude. Please, relax. Your nails bite" he told her, patting the hand.

"Tell me," he asked, in a subdued tone as he led her from the veranda, "are you really such a prude, or are you trying to impress me because you think I am a self-righteous prig?"

He heard her heave a sigh. When she relaxed, he drew her closer to his side, being mindful not to prompt her lethal elbows into action. The dim light of the street lamp did not provide enough light to see her, but his senses were alert to her nearness.

His senses quickened, his attraction to her undeniable, but there could never be anything between them because of how she had chosen to live. She did, however, stimulate his mind, and excite him like no other woman ever had.

Could Delilah fire his senses, *and* provoke him to thought? Could *any* woman do both, he wondered, or just this one. If only this woman, then had his boatload of hope sunk before he ever got it off the beach?

The unknowns of Avis' life bothered him. She had too many secrets. There was lots of loose talk about her. Of course, the wickedest talk came from Bull and his ungentlemanly boasting to anyone who would listen. Bull's skill with his member was at least as famous as Vittorio's gold. *With an unholy satyr for her lover, why would any woman need or want a short, dull preacher?*

He nearly stopped when he realized how good he felt. The *lady* by his side could not even be considered marrying material for him, but somehow, tonight, it felt good and natural to be walking beside her, taking in the coolness of the evening.

Fool that he was, even her stonewall silence contented him. It might be nice to have a little conversation dropped on him now and then, but for now, this was enough.

Too soon they neared the raucous saloon where the drunken merriment drifted down the street. The apron of light seeping out its windows and around the swinging doors served as a beacon to humans and insects alike.

He had lived in these kinds of places, it didn't please him one bit that Avis lived in this place. He bit his tongue knowing he had little he could say about her choices.

Just as they drew near the light, Avis pulled him backward into the shadows. "Wait here a minute please, Andrew, while I go get the lantern," she whispered. "I'll be right back."

She slipped inside the establishment, barely making the bat-wing doors flutter in her wake. Ill at ease, he stepped to the edge of the gallery, slipped his hands into his pockets, and peered into the heavens.

He asked himself: If God had thrown the stars in their fixed places in the same way that he had seen men shoot dice, was there a possibility that He was still throwing more stars around? His scientific mind liked the question, but, alas, all the stars kept their secrets and only winked at him.

Unexpectedly, one brilliant ball of white light followed by another, equally as luminous, arched across the heavens. The twin orbs turned fiery before colliding together. In a showy burst, they fragmented into a shower of thousands of tiny red hued droplets which passed from his sight to fall somewhere in the wide expanse of desert to the west.

His heart leaped to know that quite by chance, he had witnessed an unbelievably spectacular event. Immediately, he better understood the ancients and their fear of the natural forces.

Wishful thinking or not, fresh hope bubbled within him, for he felt as though he had been cosmically promised something. He was at a loss to know just what.

Close to him, he heard a timid voice call his name, and he peered down to his right side and saw Avis with a dimly burning lamp, staring into the sky. "What does it mean, Andrew?" she asked breathlessly, as she moved closer to him, her face pale in the lamplight.

Sensing fear, he threw a comforting arm around her and drew her into the protection of his side. He looked down and smiled into her blue eyes made bigger by fright. He looked up, waiting for another spectacle. "I don't really know, Avis, but whatever that meteor shower means, it must be good." Amused, he looked down at her.

"Will you explain to me how you know that?" she inquired, sounding like it was the end of the world.

Andrew gazed out into the western sky, and mulled the question. He looked for something more substantial than his feelings to give her.

"I don't know exactly, but I can tell you that my experience with fireworks is limited to Independence Day, which is a joyous celebration for our citizens. It would seem that if this meant anything at all that would have to be something happy, as well."

He studied her in the lamplight. He could see that even not buying all of it, did appear pacified for the moment. Again, he hugged her, intending to reassure, but she stiffened in his arms.

Abruptly, he released her and rubbed his brow in confusion. Perhaps the day would come when he could ask her why she avoided any closeness, even a sort of brotherly concern.

Avis snorted, disgusted. "If you are going to walk me home, Preacher, we'd best be about it. Most of those folks in the cantina aren't going to sleep over and we don't want them seeing us out here together, now do we?"

Andrew turned to her confused. "I thought you lived here," he said, his hand sweeping the facade of the saloon.

"Of course not, Preacher. The other girls live here. I make enough now," she declared, her voice ringing with pride "that I can afford my own place."

Andrew did not know whether to be happy or sad for her. What exactly did she do to be able to afford her own place? The unspoken words lodged in his throat and when he tried to clear it, the lump refused to leave. He couldn't get past the fact that she willingly gave herself to strangers. "That's wonderful," he croaked. "I had no idea that you had come so far."

"You hold the lamp, Bristow, and I'll lead the way," she said too brusquely.

Dutifully, after turning the lamp up, he allowed her to lead to the outskirts of town, where they turned east. They walked quietly together, nary a word or comment between them except for a direction or two.

They came to an abrupt end, facing small pale pink adobe surrounded by a grove of shade trees. Aloe, nettlesome cholla cactuses, and an ocotillo cactus framed the stoop.

Andrew had not known this place was here. He turned around guessing they were not far behind the Trumbull Lumber Company.

Now he understood how Avis came to have her own place. She, more than likely, owed it all to Trumbull. His offices were conveniently close. The thought of what passed here made him cringe inside.

He looked upon her home with a critical eye concluding that the one room house really was a lovely little bungalow, and supposed it even prettier in the daylight. Situated close to town, it was well hidden and that indicated, in his way of thinking, that it was a place of secrets. No one would ever guess there was a whorehouse here, one block from the mayor's office and two blocks from the mission.

Avis was proud of her home, and for some reason she wanted Andrew to approve of the symbol of her independence. She supposed the modest house was the one visible thing she could point to with a sense of accomplishment. Since it had been built, nary a man had trod across its threshold.

This isolated place, her home, made life bearable for her. She looked at Andrew, and saw that he silently studied her poor little house as though there were some mystery about it.

"So what do you think Preach?" she asked boldly, as she kept the threatening melancholy at bay, and told herself that it really didn't matter what he thought. "It might not be much compared to yours, but I do have running water inside and it's all mine."

Instead of replying, he passed the lamp slowly up one side of a pole that supported her stoop, disregarding her altogether. She watched him as he trailed his fingers along the pole in the wake of the lamplight, in the same way a blind person might feel his way in the dark. Just about the time he muttered "Eureka," she realized that he had been looking for a peg.

Was he planning on sticking around a few minutes? It had been a long time since she sat on a stoop and talked to a gentleman caller on such a nice evening. She bowed her head to hide the intense sense of pleasure that filled her at the thought of the simple gesture.

After hanging the lamp, he hunkered down in the circle of lamplight, on the top step of the porch. "Avis, I really think it's a lovely place and perfect for you," he told her sincerely, sensing that it was important to her that he should approve of her home. Carefully, he put aside, for the moment, any presumption about her homes origin or purpose.

"You really like it, Preacher?" she asked him again, sounding childishly insecure, as she seated herself beside him. She pulled her skirt over her knees with her arms embracing them.

"I sure do, Avis," he answered reassuringly, as he draped his arm over his knee. He turned his head to rest his gaze on the vision before him, made soft in the gentle glow of the lamp. "It's almost as lovely as you are." He watched her relax.

He imagined her at twelve or as an older adolescent; slightly wistful and dreamy eyed. Perhaps insecure about life, but hoping for the best. The sweet picture touched his heart. Even fallen women had dreams once upon a time, he supposed.

"Thank you, Andrew, I needed to hear that," she smiled at him.

"Avis, I want you to know that you did a remarkable thing for that young lady today," he said as he placed a warm hand on her shoulder. She didn't evade him as she usually did when he touched her, and she really listened to him for the first time in years. "The ordeal for you today could only be more difficult for you than it was for any of the rest of us, but I do want you to know that you did the right thing by helping that girl."

Andrew took a deep breath and continued to share with her his appreciation and admiration of her. The intensity of her gaze fell upon him, and he was keenly aware of the small nuances of her body. Even her breathing, while she listened to his words, drew him closer. "I thought you might be remembering Lois tonight, but you stuck it out, and I am proud of you for doing that," he finished, feeling that what he said had been inadequate.

Andrew heard her in drawn breath, and felt her withdraw from him. He should have never mentioned Lois' name. "Listen! What I mean to tell you is that you did a very unselfish thing, tonight," he explained, lamely trying to recapture the fast fading intimacy of the moment.

"Thank you for the lovely words and evening, Andrew," she responded coolly as she stood and turned to the front door. "I don't mean to be rude, but I am done in and I am sure you understand."

Andrew watched her as she turned away. He saw in the

lamplight the strain and weariness on her face. Finally, it dawned upon him that he was being dismissed and he had yet to give her the money. "Wait, Avis! Don't go in yet," he shouted. "I want to make a deal with you and give you this."

Avis waited. She watched, fascinated by the frantic way he dug around in his britches pocket. A smile quirked at the corner of her mouth to see the boyish tilt of the head, and the flying hands. Her brother John had dug around in his pockets just that way once, only to present her with a dead salamander that he thought a trophy.

Certainly, Andrew did not have a dead salamander tucked away. Her amusement faded at the sight of the paper money.

"Look Avis, I've got some money here and--"

"Reverend Bristow," she interrupted, spitting each word at him through clenched teeth. "I would not bed you here or anywhere else, for any amount of money." She turned her back on him and moved to the door in regal steps. "Leave, man of God!" she ordered turning around, and drawing out the words as if they were profane, "or I will sound an alarm on that bell over there that will raise unholy hell for you!"

Stunned and slow to react, he watched her walk through the door. There came a rattle and slam and he knew that she had thrown bolt on the door.

Andrew did not move until, much to his shame and humiliation, he understood what must have happened. A red flush crept up from his neck to the top of his head as he gained a better understanding of the hostile reaction.

Part of the misunderstanding was his fault for his poor planning. Knowing her distaste for him, and the way she'd eluded him for three years, should have prompted him to find a less shocking way to present her with money. He should have explained first.

The events of the day might have conspired to mislead her into thinking that he was desperate to offer money for her favors.

He in a sort of desperation, but not in the obsessive way that she thought. She would think that way because she lived off the obsessions of others.

Standing there, under the old cottonwood, it took only a few seconds to pick through his thoughts and conclude that what he wanted most from the woman was what he once had, but had been denied. More than anything, he wanted her friendship.

When she healed, and as they both cared for Lois and the baby, they worked together, then became friends. Often Lois herself threw them together, as she requested this or that from both of them. Often, Lois would simply want one to read to her, but require the presence of the other one, using her comfort as the excuse.

Together they had talked, planned, and cared for Amanda and Lois, but in the end they grieved separately because she walked out, leaving him flat. They should have grieved together. He buried his wife and lost his best friend in the same day.

But, here and now, for some reason, her friendship and respect was important to him and he refused to allow tonight's misunderstanding to further imperil their chance at friendship. It might take some real persistence on his part, but he would explain to her the differences between what she thought she heard and what he intended to say. No one could fault him for wanting to set the matter straight.

His attention was drawn to the humbled and rejected wad of greenbacks still at the tips of his fingers. The mute, remaining evidence of his futile gesture mocked him. The money seemed to burn in his fingers, and he felt now, more than ever, that it was important for her to have the money. If for nothing else than to make up for the money she would lose over the next few days. He riffled the bills and glanced over to the brass ship's bell, noting the rope that ran from the top loop of its freestanding carriage.

The cord extended from the bell and, in a loose fashion,

passed through the small hole in the lower corner of one of the shutters. If she had not pointed the bell out to Andrew, he never would have noticed her simple, but effective alarm hidden in the cluster of cactus.

As he debated exactly what should be his next course of action, a light flickered on in the house. *If you don't do something now, one-way or the other, you're going to grow roots a mite deeper than this cottonwood!*

Approaching it from the porch, where there was a break between the plants, the alarm could easily be disabled. He would untie the cord and retie it, temporarily, to its iron stanchion. He knew Avis would not be happy about it first, but maybe she needed to suffer a little for more than three years of unhappiness she had given him.

Inside the house, Avis waited until she calculated that he had left before she lit one of the kerosene lamps. She untied the full peasant skirt and let it fall about her feet. Absentmindedly, she pulled the string around the bodice of the light cotton blouse and lifted it over her head, pulling the tie out of her hair in the process.

Allowing the tresses to fan out about her waist, she scratched through her scalp, fluffing up her hair in the process. Iron springs creaked as she sat on the bed to unlace her sandals, releasing a breathy moan as weariness stole over her.

The day had been draining, and she could not muster enough energy to shed her chemise, complete her toilette, or turn down the lantern that she kept through the night. Everything could wait for tomorrow, she decided as she tucked her feet under the patchwork quilt folded at the foot of her bed.

Her eyes fell shut as she allowed her mind to wander into a peaceful place. For the first time since dawn, she began to relax.

She jolted awake at the violent rapping on her door. Surely, it could not be the Preacher. He would not be foolish enough to call her bluff and risk discovery by the good people of the community. It could only mean Bull had come or sent an emissary and that meant that she could not answer the door without protection. Thank heavens she had dropped the crossbar on the door to secure it.

Frantically, she grabbed the bell pull that was always tied to the bedpost, but there was only silence when she tugged. Again she tugged at the rope, but her heart stopped in fear when its loud knocker refused to peel.

Her gun! Too late, she remembered she had left the derringer at the Preacher's, stuck in the pocket of her dress. "Oh Lord!" she cried, feeling fear and panic overwhelm her. "What am I going to do without a pistol and with no way to get help?"

Afraid to answer the clamorous knocking, but afraid not to do something, she pushed her hair away from her face, and concentrated on curbing her panic. She recognized the voice pleading for entry, and immediately felt a surge of relief so great she had to grab hold to the headboard to keep from flinging the door open and welcoming the demented preacher in.

"Avis, it's Andrew," he called to her in that familiar baritone. "Avis, please, I want to speak with you." The thunderous hammering at her door belied his calm and cajoling tone. She listened, elbows propped on her knees and face cradled in her hands. The voice said, "If you are wondering why the bell doesn't work, it is because I fixed it so that it wouldn't. I'll fix it right back, I promise, if you will give me the time I need with you."

Avis stared unseeingly at the hardwood floor and mentally shook herself. Gradually, relief melted away, and fatigue fled until she was left with a burning fury directed at the hypocrite who was so determined to fornicate with her that he had dismantled her only available form of help.

Angry, and determined to get her revenge, she draped the quilted counterpane over her shoulders Indian fashion, and padded to the door. She stood for a few moments, listening to him pummel the door, begging her for time to explain.

"All right, Andrew," she called to him loudly. The infernal rapping ceased, and she raised the bar on the door. Finally, she gathered the quilt more closely about her and tugged on the rope pull that would open the door, her heart thumping crazily inside her.

Cautious, she waited while he stepped back. "Andrew," she said firmly, "since you will not give me my peace, I will give you what you want. Remember this, Preacher, that this thing is upon your soul, for it matters naught to me."

Avis allowed the colorful quilt to fall from her shoulders revealing her creamy white and lushly curvaceous body clothed only in a lacy undergarment. Three intricately woven roses covered the most interesting parts.

He gaped, confounded by such beauty. He could not think for the blood that thundered through his body. His head reeled, but a little voice kept telling him that his life, as well as hers, hung in the balance of this moment.

With more courage in the face of temptation than he thought he possessed , Andrew stepped forward. He plucked the quilt off the floor to gently draw it around her shoulders.

"Avis," he began, his voice husky with the desire, he hoped she did not detect. "You may be assured that I am not interested in your body. I wanted to pay you for your nursing services tonight because I know you that you send your money back east. Do you see?" he asked, holding the money before her.

Swathed in the blanket he held closed under her chin, she did not look at him, but nodded.

"I also wanted to ask you if you could or would be willing to help us nurse the girl over the next few weeks. Robert recommended you."

Andrew continued to hold the blanket snugly around her shoulders while he waited for her answer. His hands met together under her chin and he could feel the softness of her skin resting upon his fist. He wondered what she would do if he gave into his impulse and stroked the soft area of her neck with his thumbs. Better not. Her body, by lamplight, was an alabaster work of perfection, and he would not be able to stop.

While it wasn't precisely the truth that he wasn't interested in her body, it was the truth that he valued her friendship much more. He could be her friend by convincing her that her body was not a marketable commodity with him.

His eyes skimmed down, then up the long legs, finally settling on the bloom of her lips. Heat shot through out him kindling a slow burn in that often-ignored part of his anatomy.

Her breath, he noticed, came warm and chocolate sweet upon his face. He could barely see that little mark on her lower lip in the muted light, but knowing it was there was all that was needed for him to wonder for the hundredth time since this morning, how it would taste. A light smattering of freckles dotted the bridge of her nose and this was something that he had never noticed before. Even in the lamplight her somber, blue velvet eyes sparkled with tears.

This surprised him, for he had never before seen her shed so much as a tear through all her pain and suffering. Only that once with Amanda, but here she was, ready to cry because he wanted to give her money for honest work.

The silky texture of her skin teased the back of his hand as he held the blanket closer to her face, and felt the weight of the one enormous tear trickle down the side of her cheek to drop silently into his palm. He understood that she hurt inside. He might not know all the reasons why, but one thing he did know was that if the import of that tear could be measured then that - drop wrung from her soul, was weightier than the tallest mountain.

Avis could not understand why she was upset that he did not want her. She had always known that if the situation ever came around to this between them, he would turn her down. Her unreasonable reaction to the stab of rejection brought fresh misery.

She'd get even with him; maybe a little tussle in the dirt might help. "Please Andrew, let me go," she asked sweetly. She sensed his hesitation. Her rebellious heart pled with him to take her, but now when he could have her, he set her free. She walked to the edge of the stoop, keeping the blanket pulled tight around her shoulders.

Andrew followed her moves, relieved when she seemed to be content with taking the cool night air instead of heaping curses upon his head. "Come here and look at this, Andrew," he heard her say.

Once again, he shoved the money into his pocket and stepped beside her to see what she was talking about. Presently, she dropped the quilt, locked her arms about his neck and pulled his face to hers, finding his lips warm and sweet. She pressed herself against him, at last burying her fingers in the wealth of curly hair that had been tempting her all afternoon, finding him not only responsive, but detecting that manly hardness pressing into the juncture of her thighs.

She pressed her full weight against him causing him to lose his balance and plunge off the veranda, sending them both spilling over the edge and into the dirt. After he caught his breath, and the pain in his backside ebbed, he realized that Avis' bottom rested snugly in his lap.

Her body trembled, and for a moment he thought she was injured or in pain. He skimmed his fingers over her squirming body to make sure there was nothing broken. "Will you be still, woman!" he ordered sternly, "until I see if you are all in one piece." His hands gently drifted over her ribs, and climbed to the area between her breast and the hollow of her underarm when he heard her giggle.

Gradually he realized that her trembling had been nothing but restrained laughter. That he felt foolish shouldn't have surprised him. She seemed to have a gift for making him feel foolish.

When he jumped up and dumped her in the dirt, he was rewarded by her yelp, but she continued to laugh in fits and starts, much to his chagrin. He stood over her, glowering down at her, hands on hips watching her squirm and irritated that she had set him up to humiliate him. "Would you mind telling me what you were trying to prove, Miz Hollis?" he growled, not finding the situation funny at all.

After crossing his arms, he planted his feet wide apart, to study the wiggling woman. He could not see if she was hurt for her unbound hair had fallen forward to conceal her body.

She stopped laughing then, and, holding her hair back, looked up at him, his white trousers and shirt outlining his form in the darkness of the night. The meager light from the lamp set his face and hair in shadow, as he stood his ground, above her, his auburn hair appealingly tousled and boyish, ruffled in the evening breeze. The intense eyes, likely even now glared down at her.

Finally, she stood and faced him, hair tumbling about her shoulders and smudged from the scramble in the dirt. She planted a hand on each hip.

"Listen to me you good for nothin' do-gooder. You beat my door down, do who-knows-what to my only alarm, insult me and I'm supposed to be Miss Goody-goody. I'm a whore, Andrew, can't you get that through your thick head. To roll around with a whore in your lap is just like rolling around in that damned dirt under your feet!"

Andrew's fisted his hands at his sides, to keep from strangling her or making love to her. He really couldn't say which he wanted to do more and she tempted him beyond reason.

This female was driving him crazy. "I never did insult you, Avis, and you know it!" he yelled in her face, just as loudly as she yelled in his. "You're the one that goes on and on about *your calling*. You wear your chosen profession like the sheriff wears a badge." Andrew inhaled and frowned. "Infernal woman! You're the one who walked out that day for the likes of Trumbull."

She arched her eyebrow at him. "Why can't you just admit you need what any woman can give? Delilah or Jezebel or what ever name she goes by. They are all the same."

Andrew clamped his mouth shut, and crossed his arms implacably across his chest. "Because I can control myself, unlike some other people," he bit out. Never before could he remember being so angry with a woman. And she loved driving him insane.

She shook her finger before his nose. "That's another thing you heinous hypocrite. First you insult me by telling me you aren't interested in my body, then I proved you wrong, but you still haven't got the nerve to admit that you enjoyed a little petting."

Avis raised her chin defiantly, stood back, and crossed her arms under her breasts. Andrew looked away, lest he succumb to the temptation to touch.

Avis unfolded her arms and pointed below his belt. "I suppose that is one of those giant pickles in your pants that I see?"

Andrew groaned, and swept his hands over his face. He closed his eyes at the lunacy of the foolish conversation. She sounded almost jealous, but that was impossible. Gritting his teeth, he sent her a steely gaze.

"Listen to me. I did not come here to pay you to fornicate with me. I am not interested in using you for that purpose. I recall that you threw yourself at me."

His hand jerked forward, startling her, but all he did was shoo a mosquito away from the soft flesh of her upper arm. "Besides, "he said softly, his anger spent," what is a man supposed to do when a beautiful woman throws herself at him the way you threw yourself at me?"

Caught between determination to salvage some of her pride, and surprise that he thought her beautiful, words escaped her.

She flinched, surprised when he reached over and brushed a stray hair from her eyes. "Keep your hands off me," she growled retreating a step. He was just too damn good for her. In light of current events, maybe she was too good for him!

"All right, Andrew," she said smugly. She slowly walked circles around him, thinking. She raised her eyes to see him again. "I hate to disappoint you, but I think your flagstaff would wave for any female in the right situation. You know what they say, 'Put a gunny sack over her head and you'd never know the difference."

He thought about that oft quoted statement made usually by desperate men who wanted to keep their women in line. "No," he responded slowly, thinking how to answer. "I am not going to tell you that's not true sometimes, but I am going to remind you that you threw yourself at me." He watched her rounded bottom walk away from him and closed his eyes, groaning under his breath.

When he opened his eyes, he watched bend over and pick up the quilt off the porch. Merciful heavens! There were no roses on the rear end of the lacy thing. Blood surged to his loins as he watched her pretty bottom smile at him.

She straightened, and paused, with her back to him, standing in the lamplight. The cascade of hair blazed in the light, its brazen luster flaming next to the whiteness of her skin.

Just as she reached out for the door, she turned to face him and her hair turned into a burnished halo in the lamplight. "Yes Andrew, I admit that I did throw myself at you, but I want to remind you that I am a whore, and that is what we whores do best. You may comfort yourself with the thought that any hussy would have excited you. Just like Delilah did back at the cantina. I am sure that you are probably right, but just remember when you get next to whores, that we know all about you men. If you want to avoid temptation and a roll in the dirt with the dirt, then you need to avoid us." She turned her back on him.

"Avis!" he called, mildly gratified to see her halt in the doorway and wrap the quilt about her shoulders before she turned his direction. He stood in the shadows, where, at least, she wouldn't be able to see his rigid member. "Whenever you have need of it, Miz Hollis, I have two hundred dollars for you."

Andrew cleared his throat. "One more thing. Will I be able to count on your help with the girl or not?" Feeling as though he was standing on the edge of the world, he watched her step back a pace and close the door. With a final thud, the bar slammed into its brace, sealing her within and him without. *Really without.*

He waited a few moments and sighed when he realized how tired he was. Except, that is, for that part of his anatomy that had so recently sprung to life and did not seem to be fatigued at all.

She would be there in the morning. She had given her word and, once given, she had a habit of keeping it.

Turning to leave, it came to him that perhaps the evening had not been such a disaster after all. The most beautiful woman he knew had kissed him, and with not just any old kiss, but a kiss that fired his blood. He wondered if he had sampled the wine mark on her lip, and overlooked it. Another time, perhaps? Hmm. That was something to think about, even look forward too. Maybe things were better than he thought. One kiss usually deserved another.

It wasn't everyday a preacher got kissed by such a beautiful woman. He took three more strides and jumped to click his heels together. He landed feeling like the frog that became the prince.

CHAPTER TEN

With a rush and a rattle, the spate of water spilled from the hand pump into the tin pail that hung on its peg below the spout. Andrew cupped his hands and sloshed the soothing water over his face, directing most of the spray onto the new and sizeable lump on his brow. His formerly buoyant mood had vanished.

The pain when he accidentally brushed his nose with his fingers brought him close to shouting a long line of curses to the heavens. Instead, he grabbed the top of the pump with both hands and hung his head, waiting for the pain to diminish.

When the nettling stings blunted to a dull ache, he shook his head to clear the cobwebs.

He hadn't anticipated that it would be such a difficult thing to find his way home in the dark. "You'd think she'd have picked a better location for her establishment," he growled to himself, having observed that it wasn't exactly a well-worn path to her door. "Bull probably kept his end of the path worn smooth," he muttered, displeased for being bothered by what the town boss did with his ladylove.

Maybe he deserved the knot on his head for ignoring their differences. As much as he hated to admit it, they were worlds apart.

She had been right to remind him that she was a whore and he was a do-gooder. The only consolation; she was an unhappy whore and he was a happy do-gooder.

Was it possible, he asked himself, after all this time that

Bull's charms had become less than charming to her? Or could Robert be telling him the truth about Bull and he had only been fooled by loose talk?

Of course, directing his thoughts to her welfare would be easier if he weren't constantly aroused in her presence. Surely she understood that his was the purely natural physical response of a flesh-starved widower to having a woman--any woman--rub her body over him.

His body remembered too well just how Avis had done it too, judging by the sparks flying inside him.

He was just a man, after all. So why did she make him feel ashamed of himself? Perhaps she did know his reaction was natural and he was the one being foolish to deny the needs of his flesh.

He grabbed the towel from the nail and dried his face while contemplating his dilemma. If he were not a minister, he doubted he would have any of these feelings. He surely would be paying for her services right along with good old Trumbull.

Immediately mortified that he would stoop to having such unclean thoughts, he hastily repented hoping the Lord would understand.

Replacing the towel on the peg, he groaned at the combination of new aches and weariness of his body. He didn't have to worry about any loose embers of passion setting him off. The only enticing visions he had glimmering in his head were those of his fine eastern bed, until he recollected that it was occupied. Oh, well. He would just have to bed down in his office on his sofa.

He trudged to his office door, feeling much older than his twenty-seven years. He turned the handle and pushed. Finding it barred, Andrew, realizing what had happened, and hit the door with his clubbed fist in sheer frustration not even expecting anyone to hear for the deep thickness of wood.

Frustrated beyond belief, he stopped pounding, and bowed

his head as he pressed palms against the surface, equally as certain that the other three solid doors would be barred as well. He smirked, and shook his head sure that he had only to thank himself for the hard and fast rule that all the doors should be barred after midnight.

He had insisted upon the precaution, but surely they could have made tonight an exception. He kicked the door with his foot and jammed his big toe.

Catching the string of profanities before they escaped his mouth, he grabbed his foot. Shouting at both his pain and his discontent at the bleak prospect of spending a night in the hayloft, he danced a tight circle.

When his sanity returned, he concluded that everything was Avis' fault. He admonished himself that if the Lord was born in a stable then he could spend a night in one that was certainly cleaner and better equipped.

Before cracking the small door of the barn open, he checked the position of the stars and judged it a good while before dawn. He would have about five or six hours of sleep before he should be up. He slipped through the door of the tightly built barn, thankful to find the lamp and the matches in their proper places.

Carefully, he lit the lamp and hung it from a peg. Across a sawhorse hung the old horse blanket and he grabbed it up to use as a pad, careful to shake it out first.

There was a dependable livery down the street a few blocks and this allowed Andrew to use the barn as a combination storage area, and, frequently, as a haven for road weary travelers. The barn was even equipped with pots, pans, and a cook stove. An outhouse stood in the back of the barnyard, but there were no beds.

Andrew hauled the old horse blanket up to the loft. What, he wondered, really was her relationship with Trumbull now that he was sick? When he thought about their brazen affair, he fought the urge to break his vow to the Lord and take up dueling, again.

Extra linens were stored in the large wooden trunk that set flush against a wall of the loft. He opened the brass, pear-shaped lock. The pungent aroma of the herbal sachet that Maria placed in the bottom of the trunk to discourage the local varmints assailed his nostrils.

Knowing that some desert critters lived off those herbs, he shook out each sheet and blanket. He neatly placed the linens over the heavy horse blanket, preferring the faint odor of horse to itching through the night from irritating snippets of straw.

Dimly, he remembered Maria had mentioned that Artemis, their calico orange and black cat had her new kittens in the barn, but he was too tired to check on the whereabouts.

Andrew turned the lamp down to a soft glow and slipped out of his trousers, leaving them where they could be reached in a hurry. He needed to keep his long tailed and loose fitting shirt on over his newfangled knee length cotton under-drawers because it wouldn't do for the preacher to be found naked in case of an emergency.

He slipped his sandals off, tucked himself between the sweet smelling sheets with a sigh, making sure that there was nothing uncovered, and said a quick thank you that he had not heard or seen a rodent.

When he relaxed his body jumped once, startling him. Tired beyond belief, he surrendered to a dreamless slumber.

Always on the prowl, it wasn't long before Artemis discovered her old friend to be abiding in her territory. Thinking highly of her owner, she carried her five babies, one by one, and each by the neck, until she had her brood comfortable, purring and noisily nursing at Andrew's left ear.

Gradually, Andrew roused himself enough to recognize that what he thought to be rumble of a distant locomotive, were the purring sounds of a contented clan of felines. While his mind told him that he needed to move the brood elsewhere, his lethargic body refused to obey.

As he slept, Artemis became an elusive fantasy who wandered at will through his dreams. The deeper he slept, the more reality became entwined with his nighttime illusions. Throughout his sleep he struggled to catch the slippery phantasm of cat that couldn't stay in one place.

One part of his brain ordered him to wake up, while the other part pursued the calico through the desert, stalked her through a soggy jungle, and almost captured her in piney woods as she sniffed about the rotund trunk of a tree. But just as he reached the figment of a feline, the deep forest melted into the verdant fields of his childhood home in Virginia.

Andrew surveyed the familiar territory around him elated to be home. The irascible feline inspected the fortress he and his brother had built in their childhood.

Many years had crept by since he had been home, and he looked around him, excited to see the familiar things.

The burnished sugar maples wore their glorious fall colors, and the fishing pond of his childhood sparkled with the glittering facets of thousands of diamonds. Lost in the fulfillment of the fantasy, he absorbed his surroundings with a hunger created by the years of his self-imposed exile.

Andrew heard a subtle meow and turned to see the cat sitting on her haunches while the twin lamps of her eyes challenged him to follow. Although, already tired of the chase, he knew he would have no peace until he grabbed the pesky cat and put her far away from him.

Once more, he trailed after her. The feline only allowed him so close, then turned, waving her tail as though it were a guidon pennant, and walked through the door of his boyhood fort.

Had he not known its location, he might have missed the door because the vines and weeds had over grown the ancient log cabin so that only a small portion of the weather beaten door could be seen.

Andrew stood before the door. He touched the worn and weathered wood reverently, remembering how he and James had struggled together to build and hang a door that was heavier and taller than they were. In a flash, he understood that he need not open the door to see inside. This was a pleasant dream and he could walk through the door and not disturb the fragile wood or rotting leather hinges.

He took the imaginary step and, in that moment, was transported inside. The musty shack appeared exactly as he had remembered it on that last day. He touched the barrel table fondly and sat down on one of the four kegs that had served as chairs gathered round the table. Andrew rested his chin on his palm while he recalled the plots and campaigns that had been hatched around the table between the brothers and whatever cousin happened to be visiting. There had been lots of plans, lots of cousins and lots of fun.

Andrew surveyed the small space. The cane fishing poles hung on the walls. Beside them, hung the homemade bow and arrows, their colorful feathers sticking out from the sling.

His glance strayed to the cot that sat banked against the wall, and there, amidst the neatly folded woolen blankets watching him with a drowsy disinterest, crouched that infernal cat.

The cat turned her unblinking blue eyes to him once, and, then, turned away, closing her eyes as if tuckered from the chase she had led him.

Oh no you don't you obnoxious fur-ball. Andrew smiled his most gracious smile at her in hopes of winning her confidence. If he could get close enough to grab her and move her outside, he could lay down on that very cot and go to sleep.

He took it as a good sign when the closer he got, the louder she purred. Victory was but a grab away. He didn't know how cats thought, but she seemed not to mind when he sat down beside her and put his hands out to take her by the middle.

When he touched the cat, she changed texture and form. Startled to find his hands about the supple midriff of the bare bosomed Delilah, he could do nothing, but gape.

She faced away from him. He didn't need to see her face and instead of snatching his hands away, his fingers began to stroke the soft and supple flesh under her breasts.

He peered over her shoulder to fix his gaze on the breasts, whose out-sized nipples dared him to touch them. Oddly, even though his fingers itched, a certain reluctance stopped him.

This was a dream, for heaven sakes! And she was sweetly tempting. It took him a minute to understand that what he was being presented with was dessert when what he really wanted was a full meal.

Long, pale blond hair cascaded down her back. She tossed her head back and forth as she purred. He could feel the satiny hair on his cheek. She exposed her throat to his lips. Instead, he wove a hand through the silky strands at the back of her head and drew her forward, seeking her eyes.

Seeing they were closed, he placed light kisses on each lid, and then tasted her lips. She opened her eyes, and when he looked into hard, soulless violet eyes, desire dwindled. Even in his dream, this was not what he desired.

Disdaining the release the fantasy provided, he turned away from the vision, confused by his own actions. Surely the dream signified something, but he just wanted to sleep and not think.

But he wanted to continue the quest until he found that elusive something. Somehow he knew that until he found whatever it was he was seeking nothing else would suffice. Then he would have his peace.

Reminded by a lazy mewl coming from the cot next to

him, he turned his attention, once again, to the tricky cat. He grasped the furry, unusually complacent cat, and placed her in his lap. Gently petting her soft fur, he tried to bring some sense into this dreamy place of unreality where he found himself.

Artemis preened for him, arching her back and nuzzling his fingers when he scratched the sensitive area behind her ears. The cat, never leaving his lap, turned to peer intently at her master, her blue eyes watching him with a weariness that reminded him of Avis.

Next he found Avis sitting in his lap wearing that lacy see through thing. She watched him with eyes filled with sorrow and desire.

Surprised by the sudden transformation, he felt unreasonably happy that she had found him in his crazy dream. When she wordlessly turned in his lap, presented her back to him, and nimbly fitted herself onto his throbbing shaft, he moved to embrace her, craving this with the power of years of pent up desire.

Sleek and wet, she fit to him perfectly and in one urgent and uncontrollable surge the tension in his groin exploded causing him to find release in the same way he had found it as a randy boy.

Andrew's eyes popped open. He did not know whether to be ashamed or relieved, but shouted his surprise before he bolted out of bed. He flung the covers away from himself, causing the terrified felines to flee, pell-mell, out of his reach and into the safety of the shadows.

Groaning, he didn't know what to think about his returning to the fancies of his youth.

After rearranging himself, and his makeshift bed, he actually felt better. *Relieved*, he thought with a twist of a grin on his face.

He surveyed the area, and off in the shadows, here and there, he could see an occasional pair of luminous eyes observing him curiously. Maybe they would keep their distance now, he thought, happy to be delivered from being their early morning gathering place.

Settling down to a more restful sleep, he remembered thinking how odd it was that Avis had been in his lap twice this night. Once, she had her bottom fit snugly in his lap when they had fallen together in the dirt, and once in a dream.

CHAPTER ELEVEN

The dark hours of the morning passed dreadfully slow for Avis, as she laid first one way or another, endeavoring to find a more favorable position for her overtired body. She knew the real problem was not with her body, but the thoughts and recollections that tumbled randomly through her mind, refusing to give her rest. Fervently, she did hope that the preacher was having as much trouble sleeping as she was.

Clenching her teeth, she batted the down pillow in mock combat with the insipid preacher's head. So what if he got off a lucky shot when he helped the girl? A shot like that could happen to anyone--once. She gave the pillow another punch when she conceded it was a well thought out damned good shot.

He was not the weak-willed dolt that she had accused him of being three years ago. But her accusations had been insincere, devised as part of a ploy to make him miserable enough to let her go. It did bother her to think that Andrew might have had what it took to stand up to the Bull after all.

She could not have known that the day Lois was buried. Avis recalled the day of her last meeting with Andrew well, having relived it in her mind many times before. She sat up on her bed, hugging her pillow to her breasts, doomed, she knew, to reliving that terrible day one more time.

The day had been bitingly cold, when the bitter winter wind coursed through the canyons sending up a gritty spray of desert sand that pelted them, as they stood huddled around the gaping hole in the ground.

The mourners ventured into the bone chilling cold swathed in their heaviest winter gear to honor a lady whose graciousness had been an inspiration to the community. Most of the mourners were easterners who had migrated here when the railhead was established.

Avis could not remember a person present that day whose life had not felt a touch of heaven from the tips of fingers. That is, except for Bull Trumbull, who stood like Lucifer, bundled in a black traveling coat and black hat watching her, and waiting for her to fall from the haven of the Bristow home. She remembered thinking that he couldn't have her yet and she ignored him, focusing her attention of the fretful babe.

Avis recalled how she had hated the black bombazine gown she had worn under her dark cloak that day. She loathed black, avoided it because her mother, ever in mourning, had never quit wearing black. That day, the somber dress was a sacrifice to bid a proper farewell to her closest friend.

Amanda, too young to know better, had been grumpy. Squirming and whining under her cloak, she rooted at her bosom, not at all agreeable to being weaned.

The short service wore on and Amanda sent up a howl that defied everything she could do to make her happy.

Finally, in desperation, and because her breasts were still full, she stepped back, undid her gown and allowed the babe to suckle contentedly during her mother's funeral. Warm, protected, and hidden from the chill winds that swirled about them by the heavy serge cloak, Amanda did not make another complaint

Avis kept her eyes focused on Andrew, struggling to hear the pitiful words of comfort that he was striving both to believe proclaim and heed at the same time. The wind blustered, and whistled like a demon, determined to snatch his words away, while all the while, she was deceitfully and impatiently waiting for the ritual to end.

The deal could only be on Bull's terms, she reminded herself, again balking at the road ahead of her. Suddenly, the next moment, it was finished. She could feel Bull's eyes on her back. She did not look at him, but knew that, after that hour there would be no turning back-ever. All that remained for her was to bid farewell to the preacher.

The long and silent walk back had been a tiresome struggle for her. She handed Amanda over to the child's father, and remembered how he had carried Amanda in the folds of his great coat and the newly grown shock of golden curls that peaked out from under his chin.

A fresh burst of wind had blown the black bonnet from her head and plastered her skirts about her legs with such force that she had stumbled twice. Thankfully, each time she had stumbled, she had caught herself, knowing that Andrew could not very well carry Amanda and help her along, too.

She remembered thinking about what an appropriate day it was for the burying and the misery that was shortly to come. Life, she had decided when she had been forced to give Tessa up, was not fair at all, and now she was being forced, again, to sacrifice herself for the safety and welfare of someone else.

Andrew could never be any match for the demon. To defy Bull would have certainly brought death to those closest to her.

They trooped into the house. Andrew deposited the baby into Maria's waiting arms. Avis marched past them and went directly to the spacious room she shared with Amanda. Determinedly, she gathered her things, making sure to put Albert's death certificate into the worn carpetbag.

Pausing to survey the room one last time and determined to remember the most peaceful place she had ever lived, her eyes lit upon the maple rocker. Moving forward, she gave the empty chair a push, remembering that this was where she had spent so much of her love on a baby that could never replace her own, but loved as much as her own.

Things, important things, were ripping inside her. Tears of pain and desolation sprang to her eyes and she brushed them away with the back of her hand. She had to remind herself she was doing this for the babies, and everyone else. Even her mother, who was obsessed with dying, had to be protected.

If Bull Trumbull would murder his own nephew, there was no question that he would do worse to the others. Even knowing that she was doing the right thing, there was little solace for what was to come. Her heart contracted and she grabbed her stomach in a silent cry of agony. She had not even done the deed and she was breaking apart inside. When she could stand the pain no more, something inside her shrank into an immovable and steely kernel of resolve.

That, she thought, listening to the sounds of the night, was when she knew she could do it. She slipped down and turned over on her stomach, stretching her arms above her head, as she recalled her fateful meeting with Andrew.

Andrew's office door had been open, but he had not been inside. She ignored Amanda's crying for her and deposited the valise by the front door. Before she rapped on the bedroom door, she adopted the haughty role of the slatternly female that he abhorred. She had to be overwhelmingly repulsive to Andrew for him to let her leave. He understood her too well and he would see through a ruse, so she had to be good.

She rapped on the door, but not hearing a ready response, her determination ebbed. Her courage failed and she turned away, thinking that there had to be another way, but there wasn't, not here and not now.

Biting her lip, she had deliberately turned back to beat her fist against the solid panel of the door, demanding that he answer it. At last, she heard a faint shuffle and the door swung open to reveal Andrew, a pitiful stranger in the preacher's body.

The first thing she noticed was the contrast between the

somber, but collected preacher at the service, and the unkempt, discouraged and deeply unhappy man, who had taken his place in a few minutes time. For the first time, she noticed how the weeks before Lois died had taken a heavy toll on him. She had not noticed that he had lost weight or that dark circles ringed his eyes. There were hollows under his cheekbones, where before, the flesh had been tanned and firm.

Where was the stalwart man of God that force-fed his faith in his inscrutable and enigmatic Lord to her by the shovel full during her darkest hours? Apparently, devastated like all the rest of humanity during a crisis, she thought cynically, feeling nothing but pity for a preacher who couldn't practice what he preached like the physician who could not heal himself.

The black serge coat, vest, and tie were gone, flung across the bed in a haphazard fashion. All that remained of the dignified man of God were the woolen trousers and the suspenders over the linen nearly unbuttoned shirt. She could see the red top of his union suit from the opening in his shirt and the way he had carelessly cuffed the shirt above the red sleeves of the heavy underwear.

In the deep quiet, while she awaited that elusive thing called sleep, she recollected how her first impulse had been to embrace and comfort him. Instead, she kept her distance from his misery, knowing that she would inflict even more upon him.

His mournful eyes were puffy and swollen, while his auburn curls looked as though he kept them continually stirred by running his hands through them. The tip of his long straight nose was reddened as well. The long sleeves of his shirt and union shirt were rolled away from his cuffs, revealing tanned arms lightly sprinkled with dark hair. He stood at the door, slightly hunched over, with his hands thrust in his pockets.

Avis clearly recalled now, how he had not even been really aware of her presence, but peered through her as if he were not really looking at her at all.

"Sorry," he had said, opening the door wide for her as she stepped into the huge bedroom that had harbored such many sorrowful memories. Andrew pointed to one mauve colored horsehair armchair as he sat in the other. Many times they had done this when Lois was alive. But the bed between them was empty, her spirit having flown. And she was running out of time.

Before she could formulate her words, he spoke. "You know, Avis. I thought if I came in here, I could feel closer to her," he explained as he waved a hand about the room. Unable to sit still, he got up to pace. "But what I feel is nothing, but empty inside and wishing there were two things I had done differently."

He really looked at her, then and raised two fingers in the air. "Do you suppose that all my life I will regret not doing those two things?"

Avis held her tongue, patiently waiting for him to finish. For only these few moments, his need was greater than hers was. "Can you guess what those two things are, Avis?" he inquired, leaning toward her to watch her intently.

"No," she answered softly, not wanting or even able to second-guess the workings of his mind, after such a tragedy.

"Very well, I will tell you because, God knows that I need to tell somebody," he said, standing. He went to gaze out the French door, toward the fountain. He clasped his hands behind him, and he turned.

"The first regret is that I could never love her enough." Andrew turned away from her, his eyes watching the wind set the dead leaves on the patio to whirling and twirling. "I feel as though I cheated her of my love," he had told her as solemnly as if he had dispensed with Lois' life, himself.

This seemed a sort of dramatic foolishness to Avis, for she had never seen a man more faithful and devoted to his ailing wife than Andrew Bristow was to his. Why, the man had personally presided over Lois' medical care, and many times, he did so alone.

Even at the times of the flux, he would ban everyone else, from her room, and tenderly see to her needs. As Avis listened to his rambling, she suspected that he was a victim of a combination of his own personal grief and fatigue. The last few months had been harrowing. But she continued to listen, hoping that he would talk himself out and finally be able to rest. How foolish of her. Rest for what? So she could hurt him again.

"The second thing is that I never should have gotten her in a family way. I'm convinced that allowing her to birth the baby is what killed her." Andrew beat his fist on the back of the empty chair sending dust motes flying around him, and groaned.

He relaxed, slumping his shoulders and raised his head to look at her. He wiped the tears from his eyes with his hand. "I don't mean to say that I regret having Amanda, but my wife was progressing better than we expected. Stronger than she had ever been, until the strain of pregnancy wore her down."

Andrew took a breath and glanced at Avis. "You do understand what I am trying to say, don't you?" he inquired, his voice soft and questioning

Avis came to her feet. Her hands smoothed the pleats in her skirt in a feigned attempt to measure her words and not attack him for not practicing the sermon he just delivered not a half an hour before.

"Reverend Bristow," she began in a deceptively soft, almost flat voice, "You are a spineless, weak-willed fake, who prefers to wallow in his self-pity and decry your daughter's birth, simply because you are unable to allow your God to be God." She watched his face jerk back as though she had flattened her palm upon his face in one angry swipe.

Her anger pulsed not only for Lois, but Amanda, who had not one choice in her birth. Unlike Andrew, Lois had seen, in the infant, their hope for the future.

But Andrew was a man, and in his way of thinking the cause of his wife's death was not years of consumption, but the effect of bringing Amanda into the world on his wife's health.

Courage shot through her. He didn't know it, but he had morose guilt made her leaving a much simpler thing. Staring daggers at him, and notching her chin, she took a deep breath determined to pelt him with her words, in the same way that people were stoned to death: one by one, at first, then, building to a barrage.

She hated him for rejecting Amanda, and she hated herself for saying the things that could only hurt him. "I am insulted and offended for your wife and you daughter, sir," she informed him, drawing the sir out with a slur. "In all the months I have spent with your family, you have barely spent five minutes with Amanda at one sitting. I suggest Preacher that you take care of Lois' gift to you. She is the only part of your precious wife that rests above this earth, and I will not be here to do it for you."

Avis hurried to the door, but froze when she heard him cry out her name. The wrenching desperation in his voice had halted her so that she could not leave him. How, she had wondered, could one feel oneself wither like a rose in the desert wind? She stood quietly, unable to move at the pleading in his eyes.

"Why are you leaving Amanda and me, when we need you more now?" he had wanted to know, frantically trying to stop her. "I order you to answer me!" he roared, grabbing her shoulders to swing her around to face him.

It was then, when he pulled her into a desperate embrace, that she discovered that, although he had chided himself for his stature, he was stronger and much powerful than she could have imagined. He held her crushed to him, so that she felt his heart pumping wildly against her.

"I need you," he choked out, bringing tears to her eyes, but she could not afford to surrender.

The hands that had gripped her shoulders were hard and unyielding to the degree that later that afternoon she had found fingertip sized bruises pressed into the flesh of her shoulders. The dime-sized bruises were nothing, compared to the damage that had been done to her heart.

Courage and fresh determination welled within her and her weakening resolve forged itself into steel at the vision of fresh graves on that hillside. One weakness in her could prove fatal to them all.

Make him believe it, she prayed. "It's simple, Preach," she began with feigned lightness. "I am a hussy, Reverend Bristow, a whore, or a harlot if you prefer." She had lied to him then, knowing that he did not know any better...that her falsehood would soon become truth. He pulled back to look into her eyes, searching, trying to find the truth of her.

Avis stared down at him defiantly. "Just as you have chosen your profession, so I have chosen one as well." She watched for his reaction. He remained silent, not really listening to what she was saying. Maybe he had been trying to understand what was behind her words.

She watched his eyes tense in confusion at what she was telling him. "I don't understand. I thought you were happy here," he cried out, shoving her away from him. He stared at the floor, nodding his head back and forth in disbelief. His hands trembled as he forked his fingers through his hair.

Avis deliberately adopted a half-taunting posture she had seen the saloon girls do when confronted by an unwanted customer. She placed one foot in front of the other and her hand on the other hip. She pulled her head back, and raised her chin, to glare down at him, as though she were spoiling for a fight.

"Actually, Preach, here's the deal, " she explained, searching out anything painful to try to deal a death blow to their friendship, "you saved my life, and I have repaid you with a year of mine. Amanda needs weaning anyway, and Maria is well able to take care of her."

Again he reached for her and she shrugged away from him. "From now on, Preacher man," she informed him looking down upon him as though he were the lowest creature God ever created, "I belong to Bull Trumbull. He is able to give me everything I need. Do you hear, Preacher, everything! Including what you can't." She backed up, allowing her gaze to drop to his crotch.

Her only consolation had been that someday he would thank her for this. She would get over feeling dirtier than one of those bugs that lived in cow manure.

Those words, spoken so long ago, shamed her even now and she remembered too well. She buried her face in her pillow and wept.

Andrew pulled back, stunned, by the insinuation. He shook his head and cleared his throat. "And what exactly is it that Trumbull can give you that I can't?"

Avis recalled how she had flung her head back, and mustered up all the acting skills she possessed to glare down at his crotch in a most lurid manner. She licked her lips. "I'll give you three guesses."

The blatant perusal worked and Andrew fell back, to stare at her in a dazed fashion. "But I had not thought that--

Avis backed up and nearly yelled to stop him from saying anything he would regret on the day that his wife was buried. "Oh yeah. Be warned that Bull Trumbull doesn't share."

Avis found a hanky and rubbed the cloth over her face, wondering how Andrew could have believed any of what she had said that day. Though he might have saved her life, he really hadn't known her, at all.

"From now on I am Mrs. Hollis to you. If you so much as breathe my name, or try to see me, I will ruin your precious reputation and expose you as a cowardly yellow bellied muck worm."

Smiling ruefully into the darkness, she figured that he probably knew she had contrived the scene and that was why he was teasing her about it when she caught him on the veranda. "Hells-bells!" she said, flopping over on her stomach.

Had Andrew followed her out the door that day, she could not have left. They would have suffered together from Bull's wrath. But, then, as now, she wondered what kind of perversity caused her to break her own heart. She wept.

CHAPTER TWELVE

Pale shades of dawn were creeping through the cracks in the shutters by the time Avis decided that her best course of action was to forget the night before ever happened.

She had committed herself to doing her share of caring for the girl. If she ran into the preacher and he wanted to discuss their entanglement then she just might have to hurt his feelings again. Shameful though it was, she had become really good at hurting his feelings.

Mostly she would avoid him. Knowing Andrew, he probably all ready reminded himself that a whore and a preacher mixed about like oil and water, and would be avoiding her.

She smiled, thinking that the night before hadn't been a complete disaster. After more than three years of curiosity, she now knew the feel of his lips on hers, and the texture of those extraordinary curls under her fingertips. She also knew from the moments in his lap, that he wanted her, at least as much as he wanted Delilah...maybe even any other woman who might step off the train.

Closing her eyes, she again felt the sweet warmth of his lips and his hard length pressed against her. "My, oh--" she sighed, dismayed at the darts of excitement low in her belly.

"Men," she snorted, disgusted that he had the same reaction to that tramp Delilah that he had with her. Naturally, any nearly naked female would have done.

She opened her eyes, giggling to think it might be even

more interesting to see him today, and watch Mr. Perfect squirm a little. Alas, she was not vindictive about a man's normal inclinations, but she would never share affections.

Naturally, she would say nothing to anyone about what happened in those dark hours. The last thing she wanted to do was ruin the reputation of a righteous man.

She did not look forward to encountering Bull. He would be cranky and in a childish mood because she spoiled his machinations. Although he might be angry enough to want to hurt her, he would not lay a hand on her because she knew too much. He did not know anymore where the secrets were kept, and she knew most of them.

There was more to be learned, but she had discovered enough to board the next train to El Paso. The time had come to bring Bull down. The information needed to be retrieved from the hiding places and the letter picked up from Father Juan's friend in El Paso.

"Oh no!" she shouted, jumping out of bed. In all of the confusion of the day before, she had forgotten to check the post office for mail from her mother.

Usually, a simple thing, she stepped across the street from the saloon to the makeshift post office that had been parceled out of Dixon's General Store. She had not checked for the mail in two weeks.

She didn't mind missing her mother's letters, but she lived for the childish scrawl and gifts from Tessa. The little mementos faithfully enclosed within her mother's envelopes refreshed her, reminding her that soon they would be together.

Avis pumped clean water into the pottery bowl. Wetting a fresh cloth, she made a hasty bath, determined to arrive before most of the citizens made the streets busy.

Changing undergarments, she noticed a fresh scrape on her thigh. Maybe she got it when Andrew dumped her in the dirt.

She yawned, but the difference between day and night had blurred for her a long time ago. She could sleep later after she became good and tired enough to sleep through without the nightmares.

She snatched up the clothes and, after shaking them for any desert pests, slipped into them. The first stop would be the post office, then to the preacher's to see about the girl. She had not time for Bull.

Fitting her hands on her hips and staring into the freestanding mirror, she gazed into her reflection. "When do I ever have time for insanity?" she asked herself, knowing this would be inevitable. She would see him after siesta. But knowing Bull, he would find a way to meet with her first, if for nothing else than to threaten and berate her.

Quickly, she tied back her tangled mop of hair with a strip of turquoise ribbon. She grabbed her striped rebozo, throwing the woven shawl about her head and shoulders.

She stepped outside, where the morning air was redolent with the mingled scents of the nearby creosote bushes and purple sagebrush. She breathed deeply of the freshness; glad this began a new day.

The sun had not yet fully risen, and from the unusually sharp tang of ozone teasing her nose, she thought that they might be in for a cloudburst. Her eyes lit upon the bell and she frowned, thinking the reverend needed to keep his promise to fix it.

A fact of desert life learned quickly; if you had a business to run, you opened up in the early hours of the morning and late in the afternoon. In this town, Dixon' General Store was the earliest of all to swing wide their doors and her offices at Trumbull Lumber Company, the last. Every morning, except the Lord's Day, Judd Dixon would be out at daybreak sweeping the dirt from the front porch.

Avis wound her way through the streets and alleys of the

settlement, noticing how very little had changed in the *devil's thumbprint* of the Tularosa Basin."

She passed the offices of the Trumbull companies, and observed that Bull's shades remained drawn. She continued toward the post office, passing the place of yesterday's flogging marked by humming swarms of flies.

She hoped fervently that the frail thing could mend without the dreaded complications of infection and pneumonia. Eagerly, she waited to return the preacher's to get a report from somebody on the girl's condition. Maria would tell her.

Avis neared the store, and Judd Dixon, fresh in his spotless, merchant's apron, waged his morning offensive on the persistent dust that had collected overnight on his share of the wooden walk. "Hello, Miz Hollis," he greeted, as he continued pitting himself against ever present sands.

"Good morning to you, Mr. Dixon. Is your wife up and about as yet?" inquired Avis, knowing full well that Elsie Dixon was not the kind of woman to linger abed.

"Yep! " he replied not missing a stroke with the broom and keeping his eyes fixed on corralling the pernicious desert sands. "The Misses is up and I do believe she has mail for you. It's been awhile since you've been in, you know."

"Thank you for your concern, Mr. Dixon, but I was ill with the grippe for almost two weeks," she explained, walking by him, into the store.

Avis had always thought that Mr. Dixon would be embarrassed if she ever did stop to talk with him.

"We were expecting you yesterday." he called to her. "When we seen that you and the preacher was messing' with that poor little Injun', we figured you wouldn't make it in, so we set the mail aside for you."

"Thank you again, Mr. Dixon, for your thoughtfulness," she yelled to his back. If there was one thing she despised more than insufferable do-gooders, it was the narrow-minded do-nothings, such as the Dixon's, who had been able to lend Andrew a helping hand yesterday, but chose not to.

Keeping her feelings to herself, she walked to the rear of the store. She took note of the bolts of cloth, and pots and pans.

Instead of going to the long counter and the shelves of canned goods, she headed to the partitioned area, fronted by a barred cage, rather like a birdcage.

Avis was never sure whether it was a stroke of brilliance or lunacy, to appoint the town busybody's husband, the postmaster. Naturally, the postmaster appointed his wife as clerk.

No one worked as hard or as long of hours as the dedicated representative of the postal service Elsie Dixon did to keep everyone's business straight. She rang the bell in front of the cage.

Avis watched the top of her gray streaked, black pompadour bobbing up and down, lifting handfuls of mail from the canvas bag to the counter for sorting.

Avis had always gotten along with Elsie, but, looking at her now, Avis was reminded of a predatory bird plucking at a fresh carcass. She had the unsettling suspicion that Elsie and God were the only two all knowing beings in or out of this world.

"Why, howdy do, Miss Hollis. You're a mite early, ain't you?" Avis suspected that Elsie was suspicious of a known lady of the night out in the early morning hours.

Avis ignored her and smiled a greeting, instead. "Yes, Mrs. Dixon, I guess you could say that I am just anxious to catch up on my business."

"Yes, well…I see," she replied thoughtfully, as if that was a point to ponder.

Avis thought the postmistress must pucker her mouth a lot from the heavy lines creasing her lips.

"As it turns out, I do have a few pieces of mail for you."

Avis watched her hurry to one particular slatted cubbyhole where she extracted two letters. Foolishly, Avis wondered if her mail was slotted in a cubbyhole marked H for Hollis or H for Harlot.

"I believe I have a Sears book for you somewhere, as well. Maybe I can find it once I get this mail sorted through. That is, if you don't mind waiting."

Obviously, Elsie wasn't really concerned if she minded or not because she spared her not a glance to see otherwise.

"It has become so much more confusing, to get it all out. I mean, since the train comes three times a week now instead of two," she explained, nervously fluttering about her cage, picking through various stacks of papers and magazines. Avis expected this particular biddy either to squawk or produce an egg any second.

Frustrated by the delay, Avis poked her head around the corner. "Mrs. Dixon, the Sears book can wait. Don't worry about the catalogue. I know you will find it sooner or later. All I really need right now are my letters," she said, trying to soothe the agitated woman and coax her letters from her grasp before they were crumpled into deformed wads. "I can return for the catalogue later."

After enduring a few minutes more of the futile search, the deflated woman returned. Before she passed the missives to Avis, she sniffed the top one. "Your mother, I do believe."

Avis blinked, astounded at the observation. "How could you possibly know this letter is from my mother? Have you ever met my mother?"

"Let's see." Elsie tilted her head back and tapped her finger on her chin thoughtfully. "Wasn't it your mother who made the trip out here for your baby about five years ago. I seem to recall it was just after the railroad was finished?"

Avis paled and nodded woodenly. "Yes, it was," she answered, her covetous glance falling to the letter from her mother clutched in the Elsie's hands.

Mrs. Dixon pursed her seamed lips and thrust her beak-like nose in Avis' face. "Seems like just before the train was ready to leave, these two ladies came into the store with your baby and your mother bought a jar of Hessell's Lavender Bath Salts. Seems one of them couldn't find the salts between here and the Mississippi.

Elsie propped her elbow on the counter and cheek on the hand clutching the letters. "I guess, a few months later, when the letters started coming, it didn't take me long to figure out that it was your mother's letters that made all the rest of the bunch smell like lavender."

Elsie paused for a moment, glanced at Avis, and then threw her hand over her mouth. "I'm truly sorry, Miz Hollis. I forgot about your baby, and that terrible beating. Here is your letter. I never should have brought that up. Please accept my apology, won't you?" she asked, genuinely contrite, but none-the-less meddlesome.

Avis took a deep breath, accepted the letters, and shrugged as if the painful reminder meant nothing. "Certainly, I accept your apology, Mrs. Dixon, but we all do what we must to provide for the welfare of our children. I am sure that you, of all people, understand that."

Elsie Dixon's bespectacled eyes brightened with tears. Only recently had Elsie and Judd sent their deaf little Patricia back east to be taught at a new school for the deaf. Avis smiled understandingly at the woman's pained expression.

Too early for most everyone to be up and about, Avis parked herself on the bench in front of the saloon. Thankfully, the big inner doors of the slumbering cantina were closed at this hour.

She looked at the postmarks, and saw that one letter had been mailed almost three weeks before the other. The later letter looked to be addressed in a different hand than her mothers. Apparently, the first letter had gotten lost between North Carolina and New Mexico, which was not unusual. The postmark on the second letter, read only few days after the first.

Carefully, she peeled the end off the first envelope and blew into it to see if a surprise lurked in its folds. Sure enough, tucked inside the letter and folded in quarters, was a frilly handkerchief.

She spread the handkerchief across her knee and folded her arms, wondering about a child, sitting somewhere thousands of miles away from her, who loved her mother, enough to embroider her initials on the hanky. Tessa, she thought, with a smile, always managed to send little bits of herself in her gifts. She tucked the soft cloth safely between her breasts.

Avis unfolded the letter perusing her mother's standard list of grievances. Her new demand was for fifty dollars more a month to take care of Tessa's tuition. That might have sounded reasonable, but Avis had paid the year's tuition in advance.

Her mother must be farther gone than she had thought not to remember the arrangements that were put in writing for her before Tessa's nanny died.

Thoughtfully and carefully, she refolded the letter, afraid that her mother might have gone completely insane. Although her mother misused the money she faithfully sent every month, Avis usually gave in to the unhappy woman. She owed her at least some peace until he could be with her.

Could she be doing the wrong thing by giving in to her whims? She had no one to turn to for help. Morphine illness was not widespread enough to be understood.

She wished she had someone to check on her mother, but her brother, Johnny had gone to Oxford University, and she had not heard from him in years. Probably, still in England.

That left an easily intimidated maid and elderly

housekeeper who, along with the elderly cook and driver, would not withstand her mother's willful ways. At the very least, it would take Avis two more months in El Paso to tidy up loose ends, assuring that Bull would come to justice.

The address on the second letter was written by one of those typing machines. Avis' stomach flip-flopped at the feeling of dread and she dropped her hands in her lap.

Slowly, she worked open the letter, but it felt hot in her hands. Gathering her courage, she stopped to stare down the quiet street. Elsie Dixon darted across the street and Avis watched her, relieved that she had not come her direction.

What would she do, she asked herself, if something had happened to Tessa? Before the fear could overwhelm her, she unfolded the letter. Her eyes dropped to the signature on the second page. Seeing that it was from her Uncle Elwin, her grandfather's old friend, relieved her, but the letter was dated the twenty-second of July. Nearly an entire month had elapsed.

Avis read the letter over the first time. Stunned, she read them a second time, unwilling to believe the unmistakable words typed out so clearly.

The letter could not be a complete surprise. She had long feared that laudanum would eventually carry her tormented mother to her eternal rest. Now was she surprised that they were unable to locate John to settle out the estate. It was the last full paragraph that caused her to hold her breath. She read it again, to be sure and the meaning could not be mistaken.

Consequently, my dear I have arranged for your lovely daughter and myself to depart, by rail, three weeks hence. That is, Friday, 10 August, to arrive in Alamogordo on 17 August. I understand that schedules are not always reliable in that part of this country, but we shall hope and pray for the best. Tessa, while grieving for her grandmother, is overjoyed at the prospect of being reunited with her mother.

Avis dropped her hands, stunned, overwhelmed by the

circumstances set forth in the lengthy letter. Shocked and distressed, her wits scattered to every corner of her mind. She clutched the letter in one fist and the envelope in the other, raising them to her temples in a vain attempt to stop the panic.

Mercifully, after a point, she could not think. She slipped into mind numbing shock, sitting immobilized, while her mind wandered. The traffic on the street increased, but she ignored the passersby who cast furtive glances her way.

She did acknowledge any person; most of the good people plainly disdained any outright communication with her at all. The notable exception, the owner of the expensive elephant-hide boots that passed her once, only to double back and halt between the narrow margins of her vision.

"Ah, Miss Hollis," came the deceptively lazy and genteel drawl of Bull. "I was just thinking that we have some business to take up today." He waited for her to respond. "Avis," he hissed bending down to her ear, "You queered my deal last night. Don't think because you are sitting here in the middle of town that I will let you get away with it."

Bull, waited, fuming at her silence. Delilah had been good all right. An Eastern senator had fallen for an indecorous set of tits, and Bull had been not only obliged to watch the slobbering politician, but had to appear to enjoy the vulgar display, as well. The key would have been what happened to the senator and Delilah afterwards, but Avis had not been there to provide that information. His plans for blackmail had flown out the window, and, furious, he had abruptly ended the evening.

"Miss Hollis!" he bellowed, his voice ringing with self-importance. "I believe we have a few minutes of business to transact in my office."

When she continued to defy him, unfazed by his command, Bull reached down to take her arm. "Come on, Avis, it's time you came with me," he ordered, unaware of the puzzled crowd he had attracted.

A few of the folks had stopped to watch the mayor attempt to pull the unwilling harlot from the bench. Clearly, he was having a hard time because his whore was being excessively stubborn.

They grouped together to discuss among themselves the tug of war between Mayor Trumbull, and the rebellious nature of his sporting-woman. Bull overheard complaints regarding the indecency of the spectacle.

Gradually, Bull became more aware of the volley of conversation around him, and rightfully assumed he had acquired an audience. He saw the humiliating scene in the same way the onlookers viewed it and abruptly released Avis. He turned to the small audience, tipping his gray Stetson at them.

"Good morning, folks," he greeted in a parody of his normal salutation, figuring that he looked more undignified than ever. "Just trying to get the whore off the street. Seems she's over imbibed and has passed out."

He knew it was a stupid story, and he realized they didn't believe it for a jackrabbit minute. Probably didn't seem quite right either that the town mayor should be coaxing the unwilling harlot to go anywhere with him in broad daylight. Furthermore, how could she be passed out with eyes wide-awake?

"Come on, Eb," he called, spying one of his big strapping mill hands on the fringes of the crowd. "Help me get this floozy off the street, and away from these decent people."

The massive brute stepped forward and Avis jumped to her feet, backing herself out of Bull's reach.

"The only place you may go, Trumbull, is to hell!" she hissed, between gritted teeth. "The next time you treat me in such a high-handed fashion and insult me before the likes of anyone, I'll spread a true story so thick over this town that you will wish yourself in hell. Remember the boys in Juarez?" she taunted, in tones never rising above the level of a confidential whisper.

Her eyes flashed fire. He backed away. She smiled cunningly. "I thought you would recall that memorable occasion. I believe you called your play *the consummate experience,* but it wasn't really about consummation…at least not the normal kind?"

Bull recoiled, knowing that with a few cleverly placed words, his carefully constructed reputation would be in shambles. His life would be ruined.

Chin up, eyes narrowed, he glared down at her. "Very well." In a mock gesture of surrender, he tipped his fingers to his hat. The soft tone of his voice belied murderous intentions. "As you wish, Miss Hollis. I am sorry to have bothered you, but I will remind you that we have business to settle before this day ends."

The haughty way she turned to walk away from him infuriated him, but he kept silent. Bull replaced his hat, feeling the upward surge of anger. This was too much.

"Kill her," urged the voice in his head. Bull set his jaw.

"Just as I created you, Miss Hollis, so I can destroy you," he vowed under his breath, watching her figure disappear down the street. The game was over.

"Do you need me, boss," inquired the dullard.

When he looked around, he saw that all the gentry except Eb had proceeded about their business. Bull gripped Eb's shoulder. " I appreciate the help, but I do believe that the bad woman needs a lesson and you just might be the one to deliver it. She is an evil woman."

Eb gazed down at him, his pale blue eyes, wide and innocent. His mother had warned him about *evil women.* "Lesson? Sure thing, Mr. Bull, sir. Always glad to help you," replied the handsome youth, in his simple-minded way.

"Come on, Eb, walk with me, while we talk." The two men, one portly, obviously a man of wealth and power, and the other, born beautiful, but slow witted--a mooncalf--strode toward the mill, finding something in common.

Bull thought the partnership outstanding. Being a man who admired and lusted after handsome and brutish strength, he found a trainable disciple and a formidable champion in the powerful imbecile. The lonely idiot acquired a powerful friend and companion in him.

Avis traipsed the wide, hard packed streets of Alamogordo, oblivious to the constant traffic of heavily laden drays heading to and from the rail-yard. Twice, she would have been run down had it not been for the alert teamsters and their well-trained teams.

Vaguely she realized that her consuming preoccupation was becoming fatal. Having no desire to die meant that she could not afford to keep her thoughts imprisoned in a broken kaleidoscope of disjointed sights and sounds.

She found herself walking the deserted railroad tracks, seeing her only possibility of escape in the straight and parallel lines. Unfortunately, the tracks ran only north, past Tularosa, and south, to El Paso, almost one hundred miles away.

A short-line railroad climbed the Sacramento Mountains, but it only went so far as the timber country of the Apaches. Worse yet, Bull owned it all.

Bull had built the railhead from an oasis of fat cottonwood trees known to few, but the Apache and the Mexicans. The town had been named for the hospitable shade trees that thrived around the springs. The town grew, a narrow crescent of adobe buildings at the base of the towering Sacramento Mountains.

The basin's geographical peculiarity Avis often likened to living on the edge of the "devils thumbprint." To the west lay the wide and arid expanse of the Tularosa Basin. Craggy mountains ringed the basin in nearly every direction.

Towering gypsum dunes lay less than an hours ride away.

She recalled her amazement at the huge snow-white hills, and the fascination of their serpentine and undulating crests. In no way could she consider the basin, filled with hazards and desolate, as an escape route.

Legend held that the ghost of the great Indian marauder Vittorio jealously guarded his gold bars hidden away on Salinas Peak. Out here legends were founded in a bit of truth and had a way, if superstitiously heeded, of preserving one's life.

She turned her back on the desert and wandered towards the center of town. Still not knowing what to do, she bleakly acknowledged, that her haven of prosperity and security had, again, turned into a prison.

The sun had begun its climb into the sky, when she became aware that she had stopped her ramblings. She stared for some moments at the preacher's office door.

Tomorrow she would have to confront terrible falsehoods. She knew that Andrew would surely discover the horribly evil things she had been forced to do. After tomorrow, Tessa would no longer be respectable, but a whore's daughter and dear Uncle El would disclaim her as any offspring of her truly righteous grandfather.

The dry desert hair had parched her throat. Needing a drink of water, she aimed her feet for the only haven of cool and quiet that she knew on this end of town. She only needed a few minutes in a sheltered spot where she could sit in the quiet, drink of water and not attract attention.

Avis could hear Amanda's excited squeal emanating from the patio, but that was all she heard as she headed the south end of the house. She opened the gate, and stopped, fighting off a wave of weakness. Struggling with the sobs that threatened to explode, she forgot to close the gate behind her.

The pump-handle squeaked and groaned sending a gush of cool water into the tin cup that had been turned upside down on the top of the pump.

Carrying the cup with her, she dropped down on the long wooden bench that sat in the shade of the veranda. The air smelled sweetly of the fragrant vines that shrouded the walls of the big house. Here she could rest and think, sheltered from the rest of the world by the big house.

The water tasted sweet and refreshing, satisfying her thirst. Slowly, she let it trickle down her throat.

Setting the letters aside, she pulled the handkerchief from between her breasts and went to dip it into the bucket of water hanging below the pump spout. She swished it in the cool liquid, anticipating how refreshing the moistness would be on her neck. After wringing the excess water, she reseated herself.

She unfolded the handkerchief. With trembling fingers, she pressed her initials into view. Her eyes traced the lines of the lovingly embroidered letters that her daughter had taken such pains to stitch. Two years had elapsed since she had last seen Tessa, the child of her body and her heart. Closing her eyes, she imagined the auburn haired child bent over the hoop and sampler, innocently believing the best of her mother.

She gasped when a knot, hard and suffocating, grew in her chest. The next moment it shattered, sending her grief into the air like particles of desert sands blown in the wind. The first sob came in a violent tremor bursting the carefully erected stony place from her heart. In a few minutes, all her defenses and years of careful planning tumbled down around her.

"God, why are you so unfair to me?" she asked, pounding her fist on her knee. No divine word of explanation or accusation met her ears, only the familiar silence, hearing only the drip of water.

"I hate you, God!" she cried, clutching the keepsake to her breast. In the same way she was made to pay the price for her mother's failings, so her own daughter would pay the price for the sins of her mother.

Chapter Thirteen

Andrew awakened to the sensation of ten-grit sandpaper scaling upward on his neck. More obnoxious, the low hum of a motor in his right ear. He opened one eye to behold the brilliant, almond-shaped orbs of the overly affectionate cat.

"So you have forgiven me, huh, feline?" he teased, as she licked her whiskers, and then fixed him with a jaded stare. "I see you didn't bring your brood to visit this time."

He reached for her. "Foolish, Artemis," he teased with a gentle rebuff of his hand. He must have insulted her, for she blinked once, then looked away from him before tilting her coppery dot of a nose up in haughty disdain. Turning away from him, she swished her tail in his face, and skulked off to join her brood in the far corner of the loft.

"Faithless wench," he remarked with a laugh, watching her settle down to her kittens. "Sleep with 'em once, and off they go with their tail in the air."

The rising temperature in the airless barn made even the thin sheet draped from his chest to his toes become stifling. His nose twitched at a combination of the rank odor surrounding his body and the dry flyaway dust from the hay.

"Don't blame you for leaving, cat, I must be smelling worse than the chicken coop."

The bright light filtering through the cracks around the door told him that he had slept later than he had intended. Fortunately, he had no obligations for the day besides seeing to the needs of the Indian girl, and talking with Glenn about maneuvering Avis out of her cherished position on Bull's arm. In that, he was more determined than ever.

The prickle of straw poked the damp flesh under his shirt and he tried to swipe the nettles from his neck.

Hating the feel of the filthy, clinging, shirt, he stripped it off, to give it a good shake. Seeing how the minute pieces of straw still clinging to the damp material he concluded that he would be better off without the shirt. He stared down at his body, observing the grimy stripes where sweat had rolled streaks of dirt down his belly. No wonder the cat loved him. He probably tasted as savory as the salt lick down at the livery, and as aromatic as a three day-old catfish.

The pile of soiled linens presented a problem and he tried to figure a way to sneak the small heap into the wash under Maria's astute and intuitive eye. He did not recall sneaking around his intuitive mother being half as difficult as it was cagey Maria.

Many more occasions like this could reduce him to marrying Agnes Murphy and listening to her play the piano. He stopped to imagine himself shouting, "Play, woman!" every time he wanted to exercise his rights as a husband!

Nope! It would be better to make a trip back east. The time had come to mend fences with his family. He would introduce Amanda to her grandparents. Better that than to be saddled for the rest of his life with a woman he didn't love, whose face resembled a kerosene lantern.

He was sure his mother could find more than enough eligible women to keep him occupied for a few weeks, if not an eternity.

The Standish sisters loomed in his mind. Andrew chuckled to think of the aged, but adoring, "Belle" sisters who had shepherded him through school. The romantically inclined spinsters, DoraBelle and IsaBelle, would be more than happy to supply him with a few wifely candidates while they spoiled

Amanda.

He looked down where thorny bits of stubble sticking to the white trousers now turned powdery beige by his tussle in the dirt with Avis Hollis. Small spots of dried blood stained the leg: stains from his collision with an unseen wagon tongue in the lumberyard behind Avis' house.

Shucking the trousers, he shook the loose dust from his pants. After he slipped them on over his bare hips, he decided that a dunk in the stock tank might be the prudent thing to do with the whole lot. He could rinse himself, the clothes, and linens, then dump the wet stuff in the laundry on his way through the house with no one would be the wiser.

His problems solved and feeling more enthusiastic about the day, he tossed his shirt on top of the heap and thrust the crumpled drawers into his roomy left pant's pocket. The bulky wad of money that Avis had spurned was in the right pocket of his trousers. Since he was going to wear the pants and not the shirt into the tank, he transferred the hefty wad to the breast pocket of his shirt, and tucked the small heap of laundry under his left arm.

When he stepped into the area between the barn and the house, he the sobs of an unseen, but hysterical female greeted him. He stopped to figure the direction of the sobs. Listening closely, he thought they might be coming from behind the big, round water tank, under the shelter of the veranda.

Put off by the unexpected visitor, he tried to decide how best to handle the situation. Disappointed that he would not be able to take advantage of the tank after all, he also recognized that it was not proper to meet a woman nearly naked.

Visions of the injured Indian girl flashed through his mind. Thinking the worst, he decided he had better find out what was wrong, even if he wasn't presently suitably dressed for the occasion.

Highs walls and two solid gates protected the area

between the barn and the house from unwelcome visitors. A brief glance across the yard showed him that one of the two iron gates stood cracked open. Obviously someone had come through the gate this morning.

Regretting that he left his shoes in the barn, he angled off the brick walkway that led to the house, carefully picking his way around the chalky splotches of chicken droppings. He passed the creaking windmill that spat water into the tank.

Laundry still bundled under his arm, Andrew half-heartedly steered himself toward the pitiful wailing, amazed to discover the mystery woman to be hard boiled Miss Hollis. Immediately he knew something had to be terribly wrong.

The very woman who insisted that she enjoyed being a harlot, paid to give pleasure wept hysterically. What, he wondered, had so upset the woman who played the seductress nearly tempting him to sin? Probably old Bull found himself another heifer and the floozy wasn't happy about being discarded.

Immediately, his conscience shamed him for being both judge and jury. The best thing he could do was to repent of his own weakness, then, he could forgive her. He waited and the longer he stood before her half-dressed, the sillier he felt for supposing that she might need or want his help.

When she didn't notice his presence for what he presumed to be blinding hysteria, he shrugged and seated himself on the opposite end of the slatted bench.

His next challenge could be likened to deciding how to help a wounded porcupine. Naturally, the answer would be the same way one helped a wounded rattler...carefully. He stared, bemused to realize he would not help either a snake or a porcupine, but to aid a wounded human was his duty.

"Miz Hollis, is there something bothering you?" he inquired in his smoothest voice, immediately regretting his poor choice of words. He half-expected her eyes to fasten on him and word to berate him for asking her such a stupid question

"Miz Hollis," he repeated a little louder. With no response forthcoming, he sidled closer to her, set the linens in his lap, and carefully put his arm about the trembling shoulders to wait. Even fighting with her was better than this heartbreaking hysteria.

"Avis, is this about the Indian girl?" he wanted to know, getting as close to her as he dared. She did not answer his question. Nor did she spare him a glance, but continued grieving as though he were not present and not embracing her.

Andrew searched for reasons for her upset. He observed that she wore the same clothes she had been wearing the night before. Had she been hurt in some way when he fell into the dirt and she had fallen in his lap? His eyes raked her for any signs of bumps, bruises, or broken bones from their tumble on the hard ground, but he could find no discernable injury. She looked pink and healthy, if not splotchy from her crying condition.

He listened to her wail. The lady could not be considered a genteel sniveler. Avis had not attended the proper finishing schools, as had the Virginia belles of his youthful acquaintance, for if she had, she would know how to properly sniffle with a dab, now and then, at the corner of her eyes. In fact, the way she carried on made enough racket to awaken the hibernating denizens in the saloon across the way.

Short of slapping her, he didn't know how to ease her out of her misery. Instead, he pulled her closer to his chest, her flaming red hair spilling over his bare belly. Somewhere, in the back of his mind, it occurred to him that if anyone were to see them, their position would be considered scandalous. Thankfully, the high walls made that possibility remote.

Andrew expected her to fight him off, but, instead, she collapsed against him, draping her right arm over his stomach and laying her head against his chest. Her moist cheek pressed just under his right breast. He could imagine the layers of dirt and water making mud, and caking into some kind of cement between them: her cheek to his chest, bonded forever with a new kind of cement.

Andrew rested his head against the wall, forbearing the dampness of her tears. Stuck for the moment, he licked his cracked lips, regretting that he had not thought to get a drink of water before sitting down.

She snuffled. Her nose sounded stopped up so she could barely breathe, but he had no handkerchief to give her. All he had were the soiled underwear in his left pocket, and the dirty linens in his lap. About the best he could offer was an acceptable corner of his shirt. Extracting his shirt from the mess, he dumped the rest of the pile on the ground before his feet.

"Look, Avis, here, you may use my shirt to blow your nose." When she didn't respond, he adjusted his position to enable him to see her more clearly. He gently swabbed the flood of tears from her face. He cajoled her into blowing her nose in the same way he would his daughter.

Andrew continued to talk to her in low phrases. Occasionally, she would cry out as if some part of her were stricken in terrible pain, while at other times, she quietly listened to the soft words. But, for whatever the reason, the stubborn woman would not calm down long enough to explain her peculiar behavior.

Patiently, his arm around her, Andrew waited, growing thirstier and more uncomfortable. He considered the situation objectively. Perhaps he could retrieve the cup on the other side of her and get them both a drink.

"I'll bet you're as thirsty as I am, Miz Hollis. You are losing a lot of water with all these tears. I think maybe a couple of gallons at least. I do believe it's time for me to get some cold liquid in us. Do you think that you could hand me that cup on the other side of you?" he asked hopefully, trying to bring her around. When she ignored him and made no move to give the cup to him, he took it upon himself to reach around her and retrieve the cup.

When he turned to reach across Avis, he shot up, startled to hear an unfamiliar shriek behind him. Surprised, he shot straight up in his seat, momentarily covering Avis' body with his own.

He swung around to see Elsie Dixon swinging a book in her hand and huffily marching back through the gate. He winced when the gate banged shut behind her.

"Mrs. Dixon," he groaned, promptly realizing how compromising their positions must have looked to the woman.

He could imagine her shock to see her nearly naked preacher, bent over Avis in a suggestive manner. Amazingly, he had been more compromised than Avis. He wondered how hard it would be to get her to make an honest man of him to rectify the situation and rescue his reputation.

He nearly chuckled at the switch, but thought better of it, when reminded that there could be nothing funny about a fallen preacher, at all. He aimed to present a good example, not a stumbling block.

Holding the tin cup, his glance flickered to Avis who ranted and mumbled incoherent words. He didn't think she had even seen the gossipy Mrs. Dixon, at all.

Andrew shook the incident off, not having time to worry about the intrusion. Eventually he would have to make the situation clear to Mrs. Dixon and the others of his congregation, that he had been comforting her.

Andrew ignored the flock of hens on the prowl nearby and stepped from the veranda. The moment he intruded into the chicken's territory, his bare wiggling toes became fair game for their pointy little beaks. One full-breasted Rhode Island Red pecked at his big toe. He yelped, fighting the urge to wring the contentious biddy's neck.

"Confound it!" he yelled down at the clucking hens clustered around his bare feet. "I'm warning you, you dumb *cluckers*! You'd better leave me be, or I'm going to bring Maria's best skillet out here, and arrange for you to be Sunday dinner!" he shouted, hopping from one foot to the other.

Finally...desperately, he kicked the tormentors away, sending up a flurry of feathers amidst outraged squawking. Directly, laughter came from behind him.

Astonished, he swung about to see Avis laughing and crying at the same time. Hysteria and its conflicting emotions certainly brought strange happenstances.

He put his hand up. "Just a minute, Miz Hollis. My mouth is dry as cotton and I know yours must be, too. I'll get us water," he told her nudging a chicken out of the way, and racing to the pump, while hoping to hold her attention. "I'll be right there, so don't you move," he explained, uncertain when she would choose be contrary.

"I'll bet I looked pretty silly dancing my way around those chicken's," he prattled, as he pumped the cup full of cool water. "Maria tells me that if those critters don't lay, she comes out here and shows them the frying pan and it works every time. Didn't work for me. Guess they don't speak English. Maria talks to them in Spanish."

Andrew figured he had better drink his fill first. He didn't know when he would get another chance. He gulped the water while keeping his eyes focused on her. "Yes, sir! Sure is good water, and I'm getting you a cup right now!"

An eternity passed till he had cranked out enough water to fill the cup brim full, but when he presented her with the cup, her puffy eyes were closed, and her head rested against the wall. She took no notice of his offering.

He tried again to break through the stony silence. "Here's a cup of cold water, Miz Hollis. Do you think you might be able to take a few sips? It would do you good." When he saw her nod and heard the feeble whimper slip from her lips, something besides irritation, touched his heart. Poor woman probably got herself into a mess she couldn't escape.

He embraced her with one arm, and held the cup to her lips with the other, recalling the many times he had done just so, years before when she had to rely on him for her very life. The old feeling of protectiveness stirred him.

After she had taken a few sips, and rested her head against the wall, he returned for more water. He partially filled the metal bucket to bring it back, and set it between his legs.

He dipped the clean sleeve into the bucket and began stroking her face and neck, hoping the moist coolness would be calming to her. Thankfully wrung out, as he supposed she was, she did not fight the insistent caress of the cloth, but merely appeared numb to his ministrations.

His eyes followed the path of the cloth. Sitting with her head leaning against the wall, eyes closed and lips slightly parted, presented Andrew with an opportunity to sample her lips. Leaning forward, he stopped himself realizing that he would be taking unfair advantage of her.

Avis felt his breath on her face, but her eyelids pressed together, weighted like lead. She did not have to see Andrew to feel the damp of the cloth or recognize his caring touch. Long ago she knew his touch to be gentler and more comforting than Doctor Glenn's.

Frantically her mind searched for something good to come out of this catastrophe, but what? She had not been merciful to Andrew, how could not expect mercy from him.

Picking her own time for honesty had been taken out of her hands. The masquerade was over. No more she required to feed the preacher lies and taunt him with wicked and meaningless reproaches about his courage or his manhood.

There were those things she would never be able to tell him about Bull, but this was her opportunity to make a clean breast of all the other things that pertained to them. And then, she and Tessa would leave to start a new life somewhere else. That is, if Bull Trumbull didn't kill them first.

In that moment, she resigned herself to losing everything. Everything, that is, except revenge. With or without her presence, letters, safely hidden in El Paso, assured that the evil and perverse Bull Trumbull was bound to get his due.

Avis had no illusions that the preacher had any choice but to hate her after her confession. But Andrew Bristow was a man of truth, who only respected the truth. She could comfort herself that, before she left town, he would have that most rare of commodities that had been in such short supply around Bull's town.

Tomorrow she would board that train and leave town with Tessa. Leave before Bull would find a reason to take his anger out on Andrew and his family. First, though, the preacher needed to know as much of the truth as she could give him without risking his life. Bracing herself, she resolved to do the painful thing, but honorable thing.

The moment Andrew's hand reached to touch her face, Avis opened her eyes and grabbed his wrist, stopping him in mid-stroke. His eyes met hers, leaving the soggy shirtsleeve dangling between them.

She couldn't stop the shudder that wracked her shoulders, but she fixed him with her gaze. The tenderness in his eyes replaced by a questioning gaze more akin to confusion. "Andrew, we have got to talk now." She released his wrist. He dropped the shirt in his lap.

"Very well," he replied, annoyed that when he wanted to talk, she foiled him, but now that she wanted to talk, it was another thing all together.

He dropped the material onto the pile at his feet and

moved away from her. "Fine," he muttered, wary of anything this Pandora might have to say to him. "We shall talk, Miz Hollis, but after a night in that oven called a barn, I am not exactly properly attired for counseling." He shifted to stretch his cramped legs before him.

What an ungrateful female she was, not even giving him a thank you, but staring at him with that *it's now or never* expression. "Surely this conversation can wait until I've had a chance to get decent."

Avis rubbed her forehead, tired beyond belief. "All you have to do is listen," she sighed, worn out from lack of sleep and the years of lies. She turned slightly to face him, and watched the strength of his shoulders as he crossed his arms over his chest in the masculine attitude of impatience.

Avis noticed he had acquired a farmer's tan: hands, and forearms darker brown. The firm, muscled flesh of his upper arms and chest were lighter, more bronzed.

Tawny bits of straw festooned his thick, dark auburn hair. Dirty patches showed around his radish-red nose and a fresh goose egg sprouted on his brow. She almost smiled, thinking he looked more like a battered cowboy than a pious preacher.

"I understand your discomfort, Preacher, but what I have to tell you is a damn sight more important than proprieties. If it's your state of undress that concerns you, I've seen men in less than you are presently wearing, but--" she said, her head turned away, and her hand thrown up before his eyes to stop anything he might say. "I promise I won't stare or, better yet, here," she said as she slipped the shawl from her shoulders and offered it to him. "Here, Andrew, if it makes you feel more decent, you may use my *rebozo*."

Andrew looked away, wondering why the thought of her encounters with naked men should seem like a personal offense. In his youth, he would have taken it as a dare and stripped down to his altogether, but now he tugged at a corner of the linen wrap and playfully fingered the coarse material.

"Really, Miz Hollis, I much prefer floral to stripes. However, if you do not care for the sight of my naked, but manly chest, and if it would make you more comfortable, then I will gladly wear your wrap."

He glanced down at the almost hairless flesh of his chest and arched an eyebrow at the dirty streaks. Andrew clucked his tongue. "I'll admit that you have probably seen hairier, more manly chests than mine, but rarely one as dirty. I mean, if it is stripes you want, won't these dirty ripples down my belly do?"

She watched amazed when Andrew made the muscles in his belly roll. "Hmm! And there is the added advantage of having my sweaty fragrance wafting about us."

Avis glanced sideways at him and huffed, irritated by his feeble attempt at comedy when she did not feel the slightest bit humorous. "Can't you be serious? Your chest is perfectly fine and I've smelled worse. Although I admit that I can't remember when," she snapped. Too late she saw him grin. "Oh, hell! That's not what I mean, and you know it, Preacher."

He grinned, his teeth even and white, in that cocky way all men have when catching a female with her foot in her mouth. "My heart is rent," he told her, feigning sorrow by laying his hand over the spot where his wounded heart resided. "First you say you admire my chest, then you tell me that you don't, and then you swear at me. Truly, I am heartbroken, Miz Hollis. I had never before realized you were such a fickle female."

She yanked the wrap away, irritated. "Will you hush? Why can't you be your usual solemn self?" she said, clenching her fists. "Can't you see that this is no time for jokes, Preacher!" she nearly shouted grabbing her head in pain at the pounding behind her eyes. Her eyes felt gritty as though they had been through a sandstorm. "I'm too hot and too tired to fool around."

A long, loose curl drooped before her eyes. Before her

fingers moved to tuck the lazy strand behind her ear, Andrew's finger's reached the stubborn lock to gently place it behind her ear.

"Better?" he asked, smiling. "Just trying to help."

Her fingers rubbed her temples. "I'm sorry, Andrew. I don't mean to yell." Her shoulders sagged, and she bent forward.

"You are welcome, Miz Hollis. Now, you may have your say, so that I may get on with the day."

Avis fortified herself with a deep breath, but the words refused to come. Frustrated, she looked up at Andrew as if he could help. "I don't--"

"Wait!" Andrew raised a hand to stop her. "Sorry, but don't start until I am comfortable."

Sitting down, he balled the shirt into a sort of pillow and stretched his body out in a reclining position. Again, he folded his arms across his chest. "I am ready. You may get on with it," he told her with a wave of his hand. "Don't mind me, I listen better with my eyes closed."

Frustrated, Avis might have yelled at him again if it would have done anything except worsen her headache. "Confound it!" she sighed, burying her face in her hands, then throwing her head back. "Why can't you pay attention?" She began to count to ten.

He opened one eye; aware she sought to provoke him. Somehow it was easier for him to deal with her bouts of temper than the few episodes of tears he had witnessed. "Are you counting for my benefit?"

She arched her eyebrow at him. "You are taking this too lightly, Andrew."

"You have five minutes, and if this story isn't good," he growled, keeping his eyes shut, "I'm jumping into that tank over yonder."

CHAPTER FOURTEEN

He opened one eye to see her throw her hands up in the air, then, drop them in her lap. "Damn!"

"Having a problem, Miz Hollis? Is your vocabulary limited to one curse word?" he commented dryly, looking away from her. "That must be the third occasion, at least, in the past five minutes that you have uttered that particular profanity."

Exasperated, Avis slapped her palms on her thighs and glared at him. "No, my vocabulary is just fine. I guess my problem is that now that I have your attention, I don't know where to start."

He shrugged, recalling recent events. "Normally, the beginning would be a good place to start, but perhaps the end would be a more appropriate place?"

"Why do you say the end?" she asked.

"Simple...because, whatever has gotten you all worked up, must have happened after I left you early this morning. However, I must warn you, that I would find it dubious that our little squabble produced this kind of upset from you. And--" He turned his head to deliver a long, nearly lecherous appraisal with his eyes, "you don't seem the least bit banged up or bruised, or worse for the tussle. Slightly mussed, perhaps, but dented and banged up, no." Andrew winked at her. "Unless, of course, you're broken-hearted because I rejected your advances" he jested, a half smiling.

"How could you bring that up? You have no idea," she groaned, fresh tears leaking from her eyes. She opened her mouth to tell him what she thought, but decided better when his humor turned into a warning glare. "Tell me, Preach, don't you get tired of always being perfect?"

Andrew closed his eyes and resumed his relaxed position. "Only when I am perfectly wrong. Now get on with it. The stock tank over there, beckons, and if you swear at me, again, I may have to wash your mouth out with that cake of lye soap over there under the pump-spout."

She retrieved the fallen handkerchief and letters, reminded that this was not the time to argue. "Very well!" She would have plunged in, but the words stuck in her throat like hard candy gone down the wrong way. Gathering courage, she faced straight ahead and refused to look at him. "I received two letters this morning, one from my mother, demanding more money, but the other was from a close friend of my grandfather's telling me that mother had died and he was bringing Tessa to me."

Much about her family remained a mystery, but now, with the death of her mother, all hope of having peace between the two women had fled. Andrew sat forward, opened his eyes, and turned his gaze to where she sat nervously stroking her forehead.

Her fingers toyed with the wealth of hair, loosely tied back with an Indian turquoise bow barely visible for the tangle of curls. Andrew had long ago observed she had the kind of hair that, wildly thick, screwed into wispy curls around her face. The feathery bits never staying tamed for very long, rather much like their wayward owner

While he watched, the usually proud shoulders sagged and her eyes squeezed tight. Thinking she was going to cry again, he reached out to her, turning her to face him, ready to give her the much-needed shoulder to cry on. After all, a pastor should give consolation and consolation was one of his better talents. "I see. I understand now. I am sorry about your mother. Please accept my condolences. Is there--"

She pulled away from him and placed her hand over his mouth. She scowled at him. "Will you ever hush?"

Surprised, he released her like he would a wild cat. He watched her blue eyes turn icy. She put a hand to his chest and pushed him till he moved further away from her.

"Save your pity until I tell you the rest. I am running out of time." Avis fell silent. He waited, watching her chew on the sides of her cheeks to keep from crying.

Stung, Andrew leaned forward and ran his hand through his hair. Maybe she would like it better if he pushed her around a little and told her she had gotten what she deserved. Immediately guilt poked him. That was not his way. He relaxed and folded his arms. "Maybe there's time to--"

"There's no time for anything. Tomorrow, my grandfather's best friend is bringing Tessa to Alamogordo. He's bringing my daughter on the El Paso coach to be with her mother; the low bred harlot." Avis hid her face in her hands and shuddered.

She dropped her hands to clasp and unclasp them nervously in her lap. "Can you believe it? My uncle thinks he is doing the right thing by bringing her to me," she explained bitterly, sobbing into the handkerchief.

"A-a-a-," she stammered, blinking back the tears. "I will not cry!" she vowed, her hand fisted above her head. She dropped her head back, and clamped her eyes shut. "I'm stuck in this hell-hole and now Tessa will know her mother is a whore."

Andrew winced at the cruelty of the words that flew from her lips nearly in shrieks. He watched icy Avis Hollis again melt into a teary puddle.

The moment Andrew's arms reached out in comfort, she slumped back into the wracking sobs. "I am so sorry," she cried, turning her face to hide in his shoulder. Andrew could only imagine how the fear for her daughter must tear at her.

Inevitably, the price of sin always became too dear. He held her tightly, with his chin propped on top of her head while she cried in his arms.

A problem solver by nature, his mind worked to understand the situation and find a solution. To be known as a whore's daughter was calamitous. Although he never understood why she had given up so much, he would help her for a child should never have to pay for the sins of the parent.

"Avis, listen to me. I promise we will find some way through this thing." He hoped he sounded convincing. The whole town knew Avis Hollis to be Bull's woman, and keeping the secret from her daughter would be nigh too impossible.

Humiliated by the pity in his voice, she sat up, and opened her mouth. She wanted to tell him the rest, but every time she tried to form the letters with her lips, a sob would carry them away. "Oh, Andrew, that's not the worst...I lied." she croaked out.

Although he had many questions, he maintained his silence. He felt around for his shirt, pulling it into his lap. He found the sleeve and dipped it into the water. More coolness on her face might help calm her. He would like for her to be able to carry on a decent conversation.

Angry, Avis grabbed the shirt and flung it to the ground. The forgotten greenbacks fluttered like leaves like leaves from his pocket, falling unnoticed about her feet. "Andrew quit placating me! Dammit! I'm trying to tell you I have done the horrible thing of telling my family that you and I are married and Tessa thinks she is your daughter. All you can do is think about my runny nose and coddle me like a teeny baby."

She hiccupped once and stared, stricken by the words. She clapped her hand over her mouth.

Andrew gaped at her and drew away from her. "I don't believe it," he replied shaking his head.

"Look, I--" she began, holding her hands in a plea for understanding. Fresh tears pooled in her eyes. "I didn't mean for it to come out like that, but you were being so nice...too nice.

Seeing he wasn't accepting her words, she studied her hands clasped calmly in her lap. "I just can't stand it when I'm so mean and you're so nice. Seems like the meaner I get, the nicer you get. You know what I mean?"

They both heard the childish chattering at the same time, looking first at each other and then up in time to see Maria and Amanda round the corner. "Daddy!" called Amanda galloping into his arms.

"Daddy, I was worried about you," she said, throwing her arms about his neck. "Did you sleep over last night with Daddy?" she asked Avis. Her father set her down on the ground.

"No, she did not!" he answered quickly, leaving no room for speculation.

"Daddy had to sleep in the barn because all the doors of the house were locked," he explained, glaring at the housekeeper.

Maria crossed her arms under her bosom. "Not all of them, *Senor*. Did you not check the kitchen door?"

Feeling like a simpleton, Andrew shook his head. "No, I admit I didn't. I assumed you followed my instructions and bolted all of the outside doors." Andrew's eyes narrowed. "You mean the kitchen door was open all night?"

They fell into silence as Maria and Andrew battled for victory. Avis looked from one to the other as Amanda sat at Avis' feet, and played with the money.

"Daddy! Looky! Lots of money," she sang out, gleefully throwing greenbacks up in the air.

Maria stared at the money floating about like confetti from and *piñata*, and the argument ended. Maria said nothing, but that disturbed Andrew. The disapproval that passed over her face moments before she reached her hand down to reclaim Amanda said it all. She extracted the money from Amanda's fists and towed the protesting child away from the damning evidence strewn around Avis' feet.

While the story about locked doors was certainly true, it sounded silly. Especially, when presented with greenbacks lying around like salad makings. Not even faithful Maria could believe he had spent the night alone in the barn.

He moaned and ran his hands over his eyes. Avis bent down, frantically gathering the loose currency. "Don't," he said softly.

"Maria!" she called, running after her with the bills clutched in her hand. "It's not the way it looks," she shouted, her voice trailing off when Maria disappeared around the corner. Shaking her head, she made to follow, but a firm hand on her shoulder held her back.

"You might as well save your breath, Miz Hollis. You and I both know Maria will believe what she wants to believe and no amount of talking is going to change her mind until she's ready to listen." He stood close enough behind her that she could feel his breath ruffle the hairs on the back of her neck.

Avis closed her eyes. Dispirited, her hands fell to her sides. "I'm so sorry," she whispered, turning to him, her eyes filled with pain, "but I really can explain. The last thing I wanted was to sully your name." Before she could think, she turned into in his shoulder.

"Now, now, Miz Hollis there is no reason to cry. It is only a reputation, after all." Andrew patted her back, distracted by his thoughts of Elsie Dixon and Maria.

Maria sometimes knew him better than he knew himself and asked too many questions. Elsie Dixon, on the other hand, loved tasty gossip. How diabolical to be framed between the two women!

"I'm sure you can explain and so can I...later, but in the meantime, we have got a few things to settle between us, haven't we?" he asked pointedly, steering her toward the bench and urging her to be seated. Andrew smiled at her hoping to reassure her that things were not as bad as she might think.

Defeated and too tired to argue, she resumed her seat, pushing the money back at him. Andrew collected the money and folded the bills neatly, returning them to the shirt pocket. This time, he remembered to button the flap.

She tilted her head back to stare at the eaves of the veranda. "I knew that one day I would besmirch your reputation. I just knew it." Avis turned her head away from him, to wipe the tears from her cheeks.

He folded the shirt and tucked it neatly under the bench. "Yes, well...You have done a lot more to me these past years than ruin my reputation in this one day."

He leaned forward, resting his elbows on his thighs. "How about the time you returned the birthday gift? The times you refused to walk on the same side of the street and jumped to the other side when you saw me coming? Or the occasions we met at the store and you walked right out the door, leaving your purchases sitting on the counter?" The rancorous words, once uttered, sounded harsh even to his ears and provoked a new round of crying.

"I am so sorry for all those things, but you don't understand."

He studied her, where she sat, sort of shriveled and childish, blowing her nose. "Really, you will pardon my incredulity. When you are done crying, I am waiting to hear what I assume, to be the interesting tale of how I acquired another daughter, and wife when you couldn't stand to be on the same street with me."

Andrew's mouth set in a hard line and his eyes, did not look at her, but focused on the shimmering water rippling in the tank. "I can explain all that, if you will let me?" She rubbed her nose, hating that it was stuffed.

He looked at her, his eyelids half lowered. "Why don't you try being honest, for a change?"

Avis pulled herself from her piteous huddle. Anything he wanted to dish out, she deserved. Honesty was hard, she knew, the best she could hope for was that he would do the courtesy of hearing her out. Hadn't she known what to expect from the beginning?

"I am waiting for the truth," he said sternly, his voice sounding harsh and uncompromising. "I think, for once, I deserve the truth and all of it. You have drawn me into a mess and I want to know why and how you have done this thing?"

Avis leaned towards him, her eyes smarting with dried tears. "I will tell you, I promise, but please, I beg of you to listen and don't be angry with me until after I leave," she said, her eyes imploring while gently touching his forearm with her fingers.

Andrew focused on the arc of nails lightly resting upon his arm. Heat simmered under each pad of her fingers. He focused on the contrast of her pale skin against his sun-darkened flesh, and then pulled his arm away.

"I'm not promising anything, Miz Hollis, but to listen. I hate dishonesty," he informed her coldly, disgusted with years of half-truths and dissembling." To be honest, I doubt that you are even capable of telling the truth."

She crumpled her hand into a fist and put it to her mouth to stop her lips from trembling, then, her face flushed, she pulled it away. She faced him, her eyes shooting sparks. "It's not like I planned for it to happen, you know!"

"If you didn't plan this, then point the culprit out to me?" he shouted in return. Surprised at his outburst and the way she retreated from him, he turned away from her. "You still haven't clarified what happened, have you?" he reminded as calmly as he could. "I'm willing to listen, if you will quit beating around the bush."

"Very well." Avis shifted in her seat, and sat up straighter. "I guess I should really begin with Albert Hollis, my late husband."

Andrew crossed his ankle on his knee and angrily slapped at an ant that had blundered up his leg. Avis jumped at the noise. "Whatever makes you happy," he grumbled, his gaze lingering on the tank of cool water, thinking what a fool he was to be sitting here listening to a woman who could not tell the truth if her life depended upon it.

He closed his eyes. "Please God," he prayed silently, "this once just let this woman tell me the whole truth."

CHAPTER FIFTEEN

When Avis promised to tell him everything, she meant exactly that. She bubbled out with her story like a cherry phosphate that had been shook too long.

He listened patiently as she recounted the tragedies of her childhood beginning with the sad tale of her father, Jeremiah Ashton.

Her eldest brother died at six years old, when he accidentally poisoned himself with the painkilling drug her father had taken.

Andrew listened quietly, observing deep sorrow. Avis Hollis, he decided, could only be a woman of strength to have survived such an intolerable life. "I can see why you are upset. So sad...too sad," commented Andrew slapping at a biting fly. The next moment, there was another sting on the back of his neck. "Hold up a minute, Miz Hollis, I'm drawing flies. You will just have to talk with me while I scrub."

Not waiting for her to answer, Andrew grabbed the soap from the tray under the pump handle, and mounted the steps to the tank. He glanced back to see that Avis deflated like a popped balloon. "I promised I would listen, but if you want to talk to me, you will have to sit by the tank. Andrew paused on the top step, and pointed. "Look, there is a nice shady spot over there with a chair right in the middle of it. Or--" he suggested with a waggle of his brows, "you can come with me and wash my back? Wives do those things, you know."

He meant to be funny, but he could tell by the dead-eyed

stare as she marched toward him, that he had deceived himself. He flopped, stomach first, into the water, sending spray shooting in all directions. *Take that.* Hearing the anticipated feminine shriek pleased him.

Avis was not prepared for the wave of cold water that hit her. Her body stiffened when the flood splashed against her. "Andrew!" she screamed at the shock. "Why can't you be serious?"

He could hear her even under the water. Andrew ignored her and took pleasure in the feel of the cold water on his heated skin. "I *am* serious," he replied, after coming up for air, and turning to face her.

He dashed the water out of his eyes, and forked his hair back amazed at the job the water had done on her blouse.

He stared at plump breasts, revealed in their glory, by the wet, clinging blouse. He gaped at the pebbled nipples beaming at him. Fresh heat of the carnal kind, poured through him.

"Marry her," a voice said from behind him. Andrew turned around to find the source, but saw no one behind him or anywhere else.

After wading to the side of the pool, he propped his elbow on the edge of the tank. Refusing to take another look at the magnificent breasts, he focused on the floating bug he was splashing out of the water. "Ah, I am really sorry about splashing you."

She glanced down to see herself exposed from the waist up. "Hmm, I'll just bet you are," she replied angrily, covering her embarrassment by turning her back to retrieve the shawl. She swung its long length over her shoulders and sat on the stool beside the pool.

"Marry her," came the voice, again. Once again Andrew turned around, but found no one.

"Huh?" he said, totally mystified.

"I didn't say anything," she said, focused on rearranging

the rebozo to cover the important parts.

Curls bobbing in his face, Andrew put his fingers in his ears to clean them out, tilting his head one side and then the other until the water trickled out. "Pardon me, I thought you were talking to me."

Avis sent him an exasperated look, and stuck her nose in the air. "I was, but you're not listening."

"Sorry, I will come closer." He sloshed around the shallow tank to stand next to where she sat. "Go ahead. I had to get away from the flies."

Avis looked at where he perched. Her brows lined in consternation. She pointed a finger at him. "What I am telling you is very serious."

"Yes, I know it is," he agreed earnestly. "And I am sorry. I am sure you had a good reason to tell such an outstanding lie?"

"I had to tell my mother something for my daughter's sake. You could not possibly understand what was happening. How could I possibly tell my mother that Albert had threatened to kill Tessa if I didn't get rid of her?"

Andrew stared. "You think he meant to kill his child?"

Avis looked at Andrew soberly, her eyes open and intensely blue. "I have no doubt, but that Albert meant every word. He was a wicked man, who held nothing sacred, except his uncle."

"Uncle? Does he live in this part of New Mexico?"

"Sure does. His name is Bull Trumbull."

"I see," he replied thoughtfully, unable to keep the astonishment from his face. "Where is your husband now?"

"Dead," she replied tersely with a careless shrug of her shoulders. "He got in the way and Bull had him killed."

"I see. Bull Trumbull had blood kin killed. Are you sure he is dead?"

"I have the death certificate. Bull had Albert killed because talk had started about how he had beaten me." Avis stood, sweeping the rebozo around her shoulders. "At least that is what he told me when he gave me the ultimatum."

"Well, well. That is pretty amazing, all right. Bull Trumbull got rid of one of his own."

Avis stood, her hands clasped in front of her, watching the puffy clouds in the morning sky. "Not really. Albert had only followed Bull's orders to fix me so that I could not bear more children." She turned to him, a sad smile on her lips. "Bull killed Albert because Bull Trumbull wanted me and for no other reason."

She stood in the sunshine, back straight, head up and hair radiant in the morning's brilliance. He listened while she related the facts coolly, as if the attack on her had been a petty nuisance.

"Knowing that he had done that to you, how could you have gone with Bull in the first place?" he asked incredulous. "How could you have stayed with Bull Trumbull all this time?"

"At first it was hard, but I had my reasons." Avis tilted her head.

This was incomprehensible! What kind of woman was she? He moved forward.

"Woman! What reason could be good enough to stay with such a person and be his kept woman even after you knew that he almost killed you?"

Avis trailed her hand in the water, as she slowly walked around the tub. "Murder," she said softly, watching the water trickle between her fingers. "Amanda, yours, Tessa's, anyone close to me. He promised to make me pay. He knew Lois was dying and gave me only one hour after she was gone to come to him. I even threatened to kill myself and he vowed he would come after you anyway."

"Murder? Amanda's and mine?" he repeated in stunned surprise. The spark of anger kindled a flame inside him. "I'll kill him," he said quietly moving forward to get out of the tank.

"The man deserves to die. I'll kill him right now." Andrew waded to the steps, but stopped to find Avis standing at the top, blocking his way.

"No you won't."

"Move," he ordered, stepping upon the first step.

"No. Not until you hear it all."

"I don't need to hear anymore to know that the man is a menace. What else do I need to hear, but that he threatened my family?"

"Bull is sick. Dying, probably with one of those awful diseases." she replied, dropping her shawl and then her shoes beside the tank. Gathering her skirts around her legs, she sat on the top step to dangle her feet in the water. "Mind?"

Andrew backed down a step. "So what if he is sick? Coyotes get rabies and we kill them. Why keep me from plugging him between the eyes?" he asked, his jaw clenched. Was she protecting him? His eyes narrowed in speculation.

"Because the matter is in the hands of important people and if you kill him, they will never get the rest of the men who come in on the train and disappear for days. Important men who wear the ring."

"Ring? What are you telling me, Avis?"

Avis gathered the long skirts in her lap and leaned forward, meeting Andrew's gaze. "What I am saying is that it took four years to set the trap that will snare Bull Trumbull and his brothers that wear the ring with the Minotaur. They are evil, Andrew. They steal lives and if you kill Bull, they will scatter, only to come together again, somewhere else. I beg of you not to do anything. Wait until the trap is sprung."

His eyes searched her face, noting the expressive brow, and the straight nose. Beyond that, he recognized the honesty in her eyes. "Four years?"

She nodded, and smiled at him. "From the very hour I left here, I have lived for nothing else, but to see him locked up, and regaining my freedom."

That didn't change the stories he had heard...four years worth of stories. "How could you be intimate with a man you intend to betray?

The smile left Avis' face and she pulled back. "You are so innocent to believe everything you hear. I would have done anything! Do you hear me, anything, to gain my revenge and my freedom? If entertaining his intimacies had been part of the price, then so be it, but the stories were talk.

Avis stood looking down upon him. Andrew, a good man to be sure, had feet of clay. A naïve man, he could not see beyond the lies to the truth.

"Bull is not interested in women at all. I was his ruse. A way for him to look as normal as he could." Avis tossed her head then rested her chin on her hand. "But Bull was right about you. He said you would believe anything about me and you did. Didn't you?" She shot him a scornful smile.

"I wondered how you could have allowed me to mother your daughter and nurse your wife. How could you have provided me a place in your home and with your family, yet willingly believe a lie?" She pulled back from him, her gaze frosty. "That does not say much for you does it?"

Rendered speechless, she threw her shoulders back and stare down at him. He didn't know whether to feel relieved or ashamed, but he could see by the stubborn set of her body, that he would not be given the time or chance to do anything.

"I guess that is all." Her arm came up to push the hair from her brow. "I am tired and I have packing to do. I must go."

Avis turned. A vice-like hand grabbed at her ankle and she fell backwards into the water.

She came up sputtering, her skirt billowing around her. The blouse sagged with water and she held it over her hand with one hand. "This is not funny, Andrew," she said, spewing water and pushing her sodden hair out of her face with the free hand.

Andrew dodged the shapely legs bared by the skirts floating on the water. Also, he refused to even chance a glance alabaster mounds exposed by the drooping blouse. He looked above her head, instead. "This was not meant to be funny. Since you have had your chance to speak, fairness dictates that I shall have mine."

"What could you possibly have to say to me, Andrew? I don't need apologies or your permission to leave." Dismayed, Avis watched her skirt float about her, knowing it was useless to try to tamp it down. "I don't even know why I came here in the first place." Avis reached for the handrail leading to the bottom step. "I do to remember. I came for a drink of water. I have had enough water for one day.

Andrew shot ahead of her and blocked the steps with his body. "Oh, no you don't, Miz Hollis. Not until I have my say."

Mrs. Dixon has seen you. Maria has seen you, and you wanted your choice of wife to be obvious. Now ask her to marry you and don't release her until she agrees.

The voice came to him clearly, but this time he did not need to search out its source. He knew the voice came from inside him. He looked at Avis, really seeing her for the first time in years. "Don't go, until I explain," he said, clearing his throat.

Avis shrugged, and raised her hand. "So, have your say, Andrew. I haven't got all day."

For a moment, he could not speak. His eyes roved her face, seeing the sadness and confusion in her eyes. "Please wait," he whispered, reaching out, he took one of her hands in his and studied the long, tapering fingers. His gaze moved to her face. Curly strands of hair were plastered to her cheeks. Gently, with his palms, he pressed the hair from her face. He cupped her face between his hands so that he could look deeply into her eyes.

"Marry me, Avis and put an end to this," he asked softly, barely above a whisper. She turned away from him, but for a moment he glimpsed the bitter sweetness of her soul in bottomless blue eyes.

Avis stepped back slowly, shaking her head, and eyes wide with shock. "Preacher, you are mad, like the Indians say, *tonto*." She moved around him to reach for the rail. Wrapping her hands around the rail, she pulled herself half out of the pool.

Andrew grasped her by the waist and pulled her back into the pool. "I am not finished speaking my piece. I will have you know that I am not crazy, but I am practical. Amanda needs a mother and your daughter needs a father."

Leveling a hostile glare at him, she moved closer, shaking her finger in his face. "Shame on you. What would people like Elsie Dixon think? You could never hold your head up to those people." She escaped the force of his gaze by looking up to the eave of the barn where a finch had built a mud nest.

Andrew saw Maria and Amanda emerge from the side door of the house carrying food scraps. Desperate to win her, he pulled her into a crushing embrace. "Avis, if you want me to write poetry to the blue of your eyes or sing songs to your beauty, I am not so gifted. But, if you need a shoulder to cry on, a friend to lean on in times of trouble or a father for your daughter then marry me and put an end to this."

At first shocked, she stiffened in his arms, but yielded with pure sweetness when his lips claimed hers. Pure pleasure seized him when her arms wound around his neck and she kissed him fully in return.

She couldn't think. His lips tasted of fire and honey at once. And when he held her like this, his strength enveloped her. She sighed when his kiss deepened bringing forgotten simmer of desire low, inside her.

NORA FLETCHER

"Maria! Looky at Daddy kissing the lady!"

From a distance, Andrew heard a shocked gasp. "*Senor* Andrew, have you no shame? Two women from the church have been here asking what happened to their preacher and why he was with *La Bonita*. Do you not know the Ten Commandments?"

Andrew tried hard to think of a commandment against kissing, but he could not recall one in the heat of the moment. Maria, he thought, was stretching the point. He pulled her closer and she pulled back.

Horrified to be caught by Maria and Amanda, Avis pulled away, only to be held in place by his unyielding arms. "Let me go," she hissed into his ear while pulling against him.

"No," he answered firmly, grinning that cocksure grin of a man who is on the verge of getting exactly what he wants. He leaned down to whisper in her ear after nipping at a pearly earlobe. "Avis, do you hear? Elsie Dixon was here earlier and the people in the church already know. They are coming to my house to find out if the rumors are true."

"How could Elsie be here?" she wanted to know, not believing him. Hadn't she been here as well? "I didn't' see anyone, but Maria and Amanda.

He nuzzled her throat. She shivered in his arms. "Stop. Please stop, Andrew," she insisted, going limp against him.

"*Senor* Andrew, I am shocked," said Maria, sounding not shocked at all. "There is only one answer for this and that you know very well."

"Yes, Maria," he replied dutifully, not looking at Maria, but trying to see beyond Avis' glare. "I understand, Maria, but your *Pretty Lady* is being most stubborn."

"Stop it, Andrew!" she shouted, bringing her arms up to shake free. "Why do you lie? Elsie wasn't here."

Andrew gave her an innocent look. "Why can you not believe that Elsie Dixon was here carrying some kind of book

238

and marched right back out through the gate you left open? Everybody in this whole town knows by now, except you, I am sure."

"Come Amanda, let us feed the chickens," Maria said pulling Amanda down from where she was perched watching her father.

His breath was warm in her ear and Avis shivered. "Save me. Marry me!"

She closed her eyes and shook her head. "I can't, Andrew. What would they think?"

"That I am a hero who has saved the beautiful, but brazen dove from falling any farther. People love those kinds of heroes," he assured her, moving to sample her lips. He touched her nose with his and stared into her eyes. "Please marry me and save my reputation."

"Stop it!" She pushed his face away and looked away. "I can't think when you kiss me."

Imagine that! She can't think when I kiss her! Andrew grinned, but did not release her. His hazel eyes held hers. "Pay attention to what I say, Avis. To hell with Bull and his gang! If you do not marry me today, I will find Bull, kill him and then shout his wickedness to the town?"

Avis gasped, seeing years of work and the sacrifices come to naught. "How could you jeopardize the work? Don't you understand that this is more than just you or me or our children? Until they are gone, no one is safe, or don't you care?"

Andrew looked at her thoughtfully before backing away. He folded his arms across his chest and watched her try to pull herself together. He observed the way her breasts plumped when she moved and swallowed his desire to touch. To taste and bury his face in… He shook his head to clear the tempting thoughts from it. "How could I not care when my reputation is at stake?" he countered, snapping his eyes away, only to look back.

"This is blackmail, and I understand about blackmail," she replied, following Andrew's eyes to see the shocking amount of breast she displayed. Quickly her fingers worked to knot the blouse tighter.

Ashamed, Andrew looked away. "You are certainly right about that."

"Bull won't like it. He will probably try his best to kill you and your family." She stepped up, intending to leave.

His eyes hardened and he held her back. "Bull belongs in hell. You said yourself that he is sick. If you think I cannot protect my own, then you underestimate me."

"No," she said, shaking her head. "What if Albert--"

Andrew jerked her from the step, his grip around her arms making her squirm. He relaxed his hold. "Look at me!" He held both her arms and she stopped fidgeting to stare up at him. "You said it yourself. It has been four years, and you have not seen, nor have you heard from him. You have the proof of his death in your possession. You cannot do any more than that. We, that is you and I together, must get beyond this."

Avis dropped her eyes to stare at his throat. She could not say the words he wanted to hear. Marriage, for her, meant humiliation, and pain. If she married him, her one chance at freedom would be gone.

Did Andrew deserve to be one more victim? Hadn't he proved that he could defend himself and others? She swallowed hard, and, unaccountably, her head began to nod, slowly.

Andrew's heart bounded with jubilation to watch the rich red crown at the top of her head. Was she nodding? He swallowed back the shout of victory that lodged in is throat. "Avis, look at me." When she raised her face to his, he could see the sparkle of tears shimmering in her eyes. "Is it *yes*?

Avis could not speak, but the thin line of her lower lip surrendered into tremble. "What ever you say, Preacher. It is you reputation." She tried to smile, but found herself crying instead.

Everything within him wanted to scoop her into his arms and shout the victory. Instead, only his heart beat with excitement as she cried against his shoulder.

CHAPTER SIXTEEN

He paced, anxiously waiting for her to return the pink house with suitable clothes for the wedding. Finally, he heard the knocker at the door and moved purposely to the carved, oaken door.

Andrew held his breath as he threw the door open to find her standing, both hands gripped around the leather handles of the bag. He nearly sighed with pleasure, eternally grateful that she had chosen not to humiliate him once more, he grinned, welcoming her back to his home. Reaching down, he relieved her of the carpetbag, and carried it back to Amanda's room, as she followed behind.

"How is the girl?" she asked, as they made their way through the corridor passing the sickroom.

"I checked on her after you left. She's a real fighter that one is. Robert is going to change the bandages after the ceremony, and we will know more then." Andrew dropped the bag at the foot of Amanda's double bed and turned to Avis.

They stood facing each other, the air between them thick with tension. Avis opened her mouth, wanting to warn him about marrying her. Instead, she turned to hang the gown in the wardrobe.

She turned; he watched her, arms folded, shoulder resting against the door, staring at her. Surprised by the intensity of his gaze, she turned away to check the hem of her dress for loose strings.

"I'm glad you came back. Any regrets?" he asked, probing

for that thing she had been about to say.

Avis bowed her head, intent on the skirt. "I am the wrong person to ask. If I had any regrets, they would not matter one jot." She stepped closer to him, but carefully stayed outside of his reach, having learned her lesson from their dip in the pool.

He moved closer. "Why is that?" he inquired, nervously drumming his fingers on the nearest bedpost.

She shrugged. "Everything is happening too quickly. Blackmail does not leave any room for misgivings, does it? Tell me, your disgrace by design or chance? I am not sure I have ever heard of a man requesting to have his reputation saved before."

His eyes lit with a certain impish glint. He moved closer and she stepped back. "What do you think?"

"I think you had better get out of here so I can get dressed, otherwise I will not be able to keep to the groom's schedule of events." She stepped to the standing mirror and piled her hair upon her head. Looking first to the right and then to the left, she settled in the middle allowing her hair to fall passed her shoulders. "I believe I have less than an hour to perform miracles with my hair." She wasn't trying to be vain, just hoping he would quit looking at her in that sappy way and leave.

Andrew stepped forward, and held the rich weight of the tangled mass in his palms. He looked in the mirror at their reflections and grinned.

"You know your hair really is like fire…especially in the light of day. Wear it down for me, please." Andrew placed his hands on his shoulders and kissed the top of her head. "But you know better.

Avis turned to look at him wearing the first real smile of the day. "Why Andrew, thank you! I never knew you admired my hair. But I'll never make it on time, if you don't leave me be."

Avis noticed that while Andrew had already shaved and changed into fresh white trousers and pale blue shirt, he hadn't yet slicked his hair down. "I promise I will not wear my hair up, if you will not slick yours down. I have always admired your curls."

He pointed his finger at her and grinned. "Ha! It's a deal! But I had no idea you admired my locks," he mimicked in a falsetto voice, checking the poof at its sides with playful, female mannerisms.

She giggled at the silly way he minced around the room. She pointed her finger at him and then at the door. "Before they put the dress on you, you best leave. Out I say!"

He halted and moved closer to her. "Oh, yes," he began and then cleared his throat. He pulled her hands to his chest and held them fingers entwined, over his heart. "I almost forgot." He hadn't really. He did want to forget saying the words all together, but decided he must make his feelings absolutely clear to relieve the pressure on her. "If you would feel better about delaying consummating our marriage until you know me better or get used to me or--"

He couldn't his embarrassment! His tongue refused to say the words! After going over his considerate little speech, his mind suddenly blanked to see her focused upon him and hanging on every word. Shadows diminished the brightness of her blue eyes.

He released her hands. "All I am trying to say is that I am willing to wait until we are both comfortable with each other to know each other in the--ah--Biblical sense." Quickly, he gulped a hasty breath. "Now I'll get out of here, so you can get dressed," he said, hightailing it out the door faster than she could muster a reply.

What the hell is that suppose to mean, Bristow! "Just the sweet-nothings a woman wants to hear on her wedding day," she growled yanking off her clothes, donning her wrapper, and heading for the tub.

For the next hour, busy with her toilette, she had no time to ponder the implications or inferences of his pessimistic counsel.

Two rooms away, Andrew paced back and forth in his office. But he only paced after having tried vainly to read the same usually calming passage from his Bible no less than twelve times. Thankfully, Amanda, meanwhile, had fallen asleep in the living room with her favorite doll and thumb in her mouth.

After what seemed like an eternity, Andrew heard the grandfather clock chime the half-hour and began dressing. A knock at the door. He opened the door relieved to see Manuel.

"*Senor*, the patio is arranged. I have come to help my friend."

"Good! I think I have got it all under control, Manuel," he answered calmly. "My nerves are as steady as those mountains out this back door, and I'm doing fine."

The tall Spaniard entered the room to lean against the dresser as he studied his friend. "Are you sure you don't need my help, Preacher?" he inquired skeptically, after he had given the harried groom a hasty perusal.

"Certainly, I'm sure. After all, this is the second time around for me," he reminded Manuel, as he tried to make the proper knot on his tie. "I mean that it's not as though I don't know what I am doing."

Manuel clasped his hands before the slight pooch of his belly. "I happened to notice you are wearing two different boots." His right finger pointed at the left foot as his left finger pointed to the right. "I think you have one of your work boots and one of your dress boots on each foot. This difference in boots is an Anglo ritual of the *Norte Americanos*?"

Andrew looked down at his feet and back up at the *omniscient* Spaniard. His fingers fumbled for the last time and he slumped. His steady nerves had fled and he wasn't fooling anybody.

"I guess it's pretty obvious, isn't it?" Andrew collapsed on the sofa and rubbed his face in his hands. "I don't even think she really likes me, Manuel. We're marrying because we need parents for our girls. I have to be *loco* to do such a thing?" He buried his face in his hands then jumped up to pace a few more feet. "I really am crazy, that's what I am."

"Here, *Senor*, allow me to help you with you boots." After some investigation, they found the correct match to the dress boot. The next step; Manuel reworked the tie, to save Andrew further frustration of being too fumble-fingered to knot it properly. All the while Andrew voiced his frustrations and insecurities on his stoic friend.

Manuel silently endured the anxious ramblings of a man who cared more for a woman than he was willing to admit. He thought the *Senor* lovesick, but graciously said nothing.

Andrew, having run through his doubts, remained silent. Manuel stood back and folded his arms across his chest. "If I understand you correctly, you believe *La Bonita* is marrying you, not because she cares for you, but because of this bad situation with *the lizard*?"

Andrew nodded. "That is essentially correct, but sounds a little too simple when you put it that way." Andrew brushed the pestiferous curls from his forehead. "That and I used some blackmail, but not a whole lot."

"It is interesting what you think, but I believe, you are incorrect." Abruptly, Manuel stopped and snapped his fingers. "The ring. Where is the ring?"

"Ring? Ring! On no! I don't have a ring," bellowed Andrew, frantically ransacking his desk for something resembling a wedding ring.

"Thunderation, Manuel! How could I forget such a thing?" Andrew gave a hard yank to a drawer. It flew out of its slot, spilling odds and ends of things over the floor, sprinkles with taps and clatters. Not taking the time to reassemble the things in the drawer, he dropped to his knees to sort through the disorganized mess until he found two rings. "Here are some rings, but I can't very well give her Lois' ring. What am I going to do?"

"Did Lois give you a ring?"

"Yes, why?" he asked plucking both rings from the mess on the floor.

"Give her yours. It is a plain gold band and she will not know from where it came. Tell her it was your father's and he handed the ring down to you. This one will do until you can get one that fits her better."

"Well, that's not far from the truth, because it was my father-in-law's band and he handed it down to Lois." Andrew pocketed the circlet before stepping outside the door to clip a white rose bud from the potted rosebush. He stared at the bush, distressed to see most of the blossoms gone.

Where there had been a profusion of the white, fragrant blossoms, now remained only a few buds. Never mind, he couldn't worry about the rape of the poor bush right now. He tromped back into the room.

"Manuel, I just realized that you never finished telling me why you feel that my fears are not justified," he said, rosebud in hand, closing the door behind him.

Manuel gave a subtle shrug. "I could give you many reasons, *Amigo*, because I have given this much thought, but the best one is the most obvious one." Manuel accepted the boutonniere that Andrew handed him and set it neatly in the buttonhole, anchoring it with a pin.

"For years she has gone out of her way to avoid you and Amanda for your protection. Her life has been miserable, but not once has she come to you. She is a woman of means, who is independent. The sensible direction for her to take would be to board the train tomorrow with her family and never look back." Manuel stepped back. "*Bueno*! No, the easier road for her would be to board the train. The harder road would be to stay and fight this evil."

The clock struck three times, and they looked at each other. The preacher checked his French cuffs, tugged at the lapels of his suit coat, then squared his shoulders, as if going into battle. "Ready," he announced nodding to Manuel, who watched, amused to see such nervousness. Andrew patted his chest with both hands and breathed deeply. "Courage, Bristow!"

Manuel grinned and rumbled with laughter. "Why do I suddenly think of poor beguiled *Don Quixote* when I watch you?"

Andrew drew back, nearly insulted. "If I am *Don Quixote*, then who are you?" Andrew headed for the door. "Come, *Sancho Panza*, let us do the deed and rescue fair *Dulcinae*." Andrew halted in the doorway, took another breath, and hastened to meet Padre Juan in front of the fountain. Manuel's disconcerting chuckle echoed after him.

A quick perusal showed him that nearly everyone, including Emily Glenn, had arrived. Everyone, that is, except the bride.

Maria and Manuel provided for the seating to be in the shade of the veranda. Excellent idea, considering it could be a long wait in the sun for the woman to make her appearance. She might just leave him at the altar.

He looked around for Robert, thinking he should have been sitting with Emily. When he didn't see him, he turned to Manuel. "Did Robert have an emergency?"

Manuel shrugged his shoulders. "I do not know, but surely, he would not have allowed *Senora* to come in her condition, by herself."

For the first time, Andrew observed that Manuel dressed

in the traditional Spanish garb, with the wide, silver-laced sombrero and the fitted pants with pleated cuffs. Manuel looked romantically dashing and grand, he thought sourly, when compared to his plain self in a drab Sunday suit.

He spotted Maria fanning herself dressed in red silk with a black lace mantilla. She sat in the shade by Emily. He could not locate Amanda. Amanda would have to be with Avis or Maria would not let her out of sight.

Usually collars didn't bother him, but Manuel must have pulled his tie too tight for he could not swallow easily. He ran his finger around his collar, pulled, then reached for the kerchief he kept in his pocket only to find he had neglected to stuff one in his pocket. Sweat poured from his brow and he regretted forgetting such an important thing as a handkerchief.

Manuel's hand jostled his elbow and he glanced down to see a white square of cloth resting in Manuel's fingers. Grateful, he gave Manuel a weak smile.

Father Juan, not at all upset by the wait, smiled in his best beatific fashion as if to reassure the groom that all progressed nicely.

Inanely, Andrew thought it a real blessing that the friars shaved tonsure was covered by the disk shaped hat. He could still hear the barkeep complaining about his baking baldness and Avis' lack of punctuality from their sojourn in the sun the day before. Had it only been yesterday when all that happened? Impossible for it seemed as though years had elapsed.

Time continued to drag for him. The moment he decided that his bride had deserted him for good, the patio doors from Amanda's room swung open.

What a surprise to see Amanda step through the door, golden ringlets tied with a big pink bow, and dressed in a white frock made of some kind of material poked through with little holes. Her fingers wrapped around the handle as she clutched the full basket of honeysuckle blossoms and white rose petals.

Andrew thought she was supposed to be the flower girl strewing the petals before the bride, but, instead, grinned at him in a conspiratorial way that melted his heart. Certainly, he had never seen her look so fetching and happy, nor had he ever seen a poorer flower girl for she had not sown one petal on the bridal path.

Next came Avis, her left arm tucked into the crook of Doctor Glenn's right arm. He *would* be the one to give the bride away. How stupid of him not to have guessed. Somebody, thankfully, seemed to think of all the details he had missed.

Finally, his gaze fell upon Avis, her hair down, curls pulled back with a black velvet ribbon. The light green gown had tiny flecks of blue that brought out the fire in her curls. In her hands she held a bouquet made up of red and white blossoms, tied with a green ribbon.

Ah ha! The mystery of the vanished blossoms was solved. Lois and Avis had planted roses in separate pots that day so many years before, the white rose bush being for Lois and red for Avis. Andrew stood amazed and wondered if she, too, remembered.

Andrew waited till the doctor had deposited her next to him that he dared meet her eyes. She smiled at him, her eyes alight with mischief of some sort. "Sorry, we were late," she whispered, "but Amanda didn't want to walk out here in front of everyone. I promised her a prize."

Andrew squeezed the trembling hand that was now tucked into his arm, and nodded agreeably to her. His own nervousness faded as the priest began the solemn and sacred ceremony.

Not motivated by flames of passion, this marriage would be different. This would be the binding of two good friends united in a common cause, not the wayward whim of two love-struck young people who did not understand that everything worthwhile required an investment.

Avis studied her groom to see if he had any lack of resolve, but he listened calmly. He repeated the words loudly and firmly, pushing threatening insecurities farther away.

Although she knew lingering doubts, she felt more confident because he took his commitments very seriously. He would stand his ground to assure that his vows were carried out. That is, until the marriage lost it's interest to him.

She reminded herself that they were two partners in a business deal. She was not contracting to this man for a lifetime, only until they were safe and able to give her up.

Avis listened carefully to the words. When she turned to him, gazing into kind eyes the color of warm tea, he took her left hand in his, and it trembled. The ring, too big, floated on her finger, but she would fasten it on a chain to wear around her neck.

Her eyes were drawn to his rich thick curls. The sun gave them a luster that reminded her of the warm, but subdued coals of a banked fire. He was handsome, she decided. Not the tall, roguish looks of Manuel, but the attractiveness of a strong, broad shouldered, slim hipped, well-put together man, unshakably secure in himself.

From somewhere she heard a voice say that the time had come to kiss the bride. She had forgotten this part. She hated the thought that he was forced to kiss her in front of the others, even if it was a customary part of the service.

Andrew must have sensed her timidity. His eyes searched hers before taking both of her hands into his. His hands covered her cool ones.

She smiled at him, but her eyes were veiled and she hesitated. His new wife obviously did not want to be kissed. Andrew kissed her brow, in a sort of blessing and then, to satisfy the onlookers, dropped an off center kiss on her lips to seal the marriage.

Andrew opened his eyes to find her face turned pink and a

surprised, but with a hint of curiosity in her eyes. This time around, he remembered to taste that little mark at the corner of her lip where he had aimed, and he winked at her, thinking himself to be quite clever.

Avis allowed him to turn her about to face their friends as the priest proclaimed them married. Her mind fumbled to discover exactly what was so different about that kiss from the ones other men had given her. Once more, he pulled her close to his side, the squeeze reminding her that they were in this together. He whispered an apology in her ear for upsetting her, before releasing her to talk with Emily Glenn. He hoisted Amanda into his arms.

"Are we married yet, Daddy?" chirped the child from her perch.

"Yes, we surely are, Toot. I am proud of you and I have never seen you look so pretty. Is that a new dress?" he asked, watching the excitement in her eyes.

"Yep, it sure is. Did you like the way I carried the flowers, Daddy?" Andrew responded by nodding his head. "Did you notice that I didn't throw the flowers down like they wanted me to?"

He tilted his head back to better watch her face. "I was wondering about that. Is that what you were supposed to do?"

"Yes sir, but I didn't, did I?"

"Now that is a mystery. Isn't it?" Andrew nearly bit his cheeks to keep from laughing. "Just why didn't you?"

"I didn't want them to get stepped on. If I dropped them on the ground I wouldn't have any left, and they would all be stepped on and get dirty. Besides, you know how Maria acts when Manuel gets his pieces of wood on the floor."

Andrew burst into laughter, thinking about how funny it was that Amanda should notice such things. "Yes, Amanda. I do know how upset Maria gets about that. By the way, Missy, who gave you the new pretty dress?"

"Isn't it pretty, Daddy? " she said, her eyes sparkling and brimming over with enthusiasm. "Miss Hollis brought it to me. She said she had been saving it for Christmas, but that I had grown so tall she thought we could be married in it." Amanda leaned her head on her father's shoulder. "Daddy, I'm sorry we were late. It was my fault because I got scared."

"That's fine, Amanda. It's kind of scary being in front of people for me, too," he explained enjoying the blessed warmth of her.

Sister Agatha, ran out of the bedroom, panicked, and fluttered around Father Juan. "Padre! Padre!"

All eyes turned to fasten on the flustered nun.

"Padre, come quick, she is fighting and will hurt herself! Come we must do something, quickly."

Andrew handed Amanda to Maria. The priest, Manuel, and Avis lifted the net and entered the room.

Emily remained on the patio with Maria and Amanda, aiming to soak her swollen feet in the cool water of the fountain. Soon Maria had taken Amanda's clothes off her, and the child played in the fountain, careful to mind her swollen feet.

"Maria, what do you think about the preacher and Avis making a marriage?"

"What do you think about it, *Senora*?"

"No fair, Maria. I asked you first," she told her, laughing at her friend's evasiveness, as she dabbled her feet in the soothing water.

"He has loved her a long time, but he has yet to find that out. I am so relieved and happy for them. It is a good day. A very good day." A sudden splash from Amanda alerted Maria to move her bench a few paces back.

"That child is part duck, you know." Emily laughed, thinking about the hasty marriage. "I'll bet Avis has loved Andrew for a long time, as well. I wonder which one will realize it first," she mused. "I remember when Lois was ill, there was not an extra thought that one of them had except for the other's comfort. I remember how all their time and efforts were taken up caring for Amanda and her mother. I wonder when this feeling between them first happened?"

Emily glanced at Maria and realized she needed to change before Amanda ruined her red silk gown with water stains. "Listen, Maria, I'm going to be here awhile, and I will be glad to watch Amanda while you change into something cooler. You look so lovely in that gown I hate to see it ruined with water spots."

Maria glanced over her shoulder at the bedroom, to see that the group remained clustered around the bed.

"Don't worry about them, Maria. They'll be in there awhile. I know Robert had planned to give her a pretty good look over, and that takes time," Emily explained, as she paddled her feet.

"*Gracias*, I will hurry," she called. Emily thought it sad Maria and Manuel had never had children. Maria had told her long ago that after nine years of marriage, she had given up, preferring to care for other children, than be frustrated by her barren womb.

Manuel had been stricken with the mumps when he was a youth. It was a terrible and painful condition for the mumps to go down on a young man. After the swelling left, the disease usually left him unable to sire a child. Emily thought this sad for Maria and Manuel would make wonderful parents.

Emily watched Amanda attempt to catch the overflow as it spilled over the edge of the topmost basin to fall into the lower basin. She envied the child's compact size and boundless energy. Robert was right; she thought as she tried vainly to see her feet, carrying this baby was different than the way she carried the other six. But she was also forty- two years old.

There came a gentle jab at her belly, just above her navel.

She spread the cloth of her cotton skirt tight across the place of the bounce, and watched the material flutter, smiling at the energetic evidence of the life within her. "Don't you ever get tired? You keep me awake at night and insist I remain awake during the day. Tell me, Junior, when do you ever sleep?"

Who are you talking to, Mrs. Glenn?" inquired Amanda, thinking it odd that she looked at no one, but down at her very fat belly, and spoke to it as though it was a person.

Startled, Emily's gaze went to the golden haired, nut brown nymphet and laughed, wishing that she had been given time before this hasty ceremony, to round up her brood to give Amanda a little company. "Why, Amanda, I was talking to my baby. There, did you see the baby make the skin of my stomach move from the inside out? You didn't? Watch closely and in a few seconds my stomach will move again."

The child stood on tiptoes to look at her belly. "There, I saw it!" she exclaimed, bouncing up and down, and splashing water all over them and the pavement."

"Here. Let me have your hand." Gently, Emily took the child's hand and placed it over the hard mound of her stomach. The baby, unusually agreeable, kicked at Amanda's hand.

"Oh! I felt it," she exclaimed as she jumped up and down, clapping her hands gleefully.

"So did I, Amanda." Emily enjoyed the child's delight.

"I'm getting a sister," announced Amanda.

"You are? You must be excited." Emily shook her head, amazed, momentarily forgetting about Avis' older daughter. How, she wondered, there could have been any carrying on between the two, because Avis had sidestepped the preacher like the plague for years, refusing even to mention his name.

"When are you getting your sister?" she asked the child, as Amanda kept her hand over the spot, anticipating another movement from the babe within.

"She is coming on the train, tomorrow," quipped Amanda

unable to understand why that was so funny to Mrs. Glenn. "Shh," she said, Mrs. Glenn she would keep still and quit laughing so she could feel the baby.

"Child, are you bothering *Senora* Glenn?"

Amanda, staring at the roundness, put her finger to her lips. "Shh, Maria! I am waiting for the baby."

"You don't mind, *Senora*?" asked Maria, sitting down beside Emily and Amanda.

"Of course not," she replied. "My children do it all the time. I forget Amanda has not had any brothers or sister to see for herself."

"I do so! Did you forget, Mrs. Glenn, I told you my sister was coming tomorrow on the train." Amanda stared at them bewildered by their laughter.

"There is much difference between coming from a train, and coming out of your mother's belly.

"I think he went to sleep, Amanda," explained Emily after a few moments. Amanda waited a few moments then scampered away.

"Maria!" called Amanda, from the other side of the fountain, her fingers pointing to the corner of the house. "There is water coming from under the gate, again."

Maria sighed, before mumbling something in Spanish and walked to the gate. Turning about, Maria hurried from inspecting the gate, to the bedroom. Not wanting to upset everyone, summoned her husband quietly. When he stepped out, she drew him to the side. "Manuel, the stock tank is overflowing once again. Can you see about it, please?"

"Has the child been playing dolls in it, again?" he asked, hands on his hips. He remembered the time Amanda left doll clothes in the tank that plugged up the drain that permitted the excess water to be channeled off to the garden, and the house.

"No, I don't think so, but who knows with that active child. Will you go and see about it, please?" she asked, thinking her husband truly handsome, dressed in his finery and looking strong and tall.

Manuel looked down at his little woman, grabbed her hand, and pulled her into a corner. "There is such romance in the air today it sets me on fire for you. I will do as you ask only if you give me a kiss now, and promise me more later," he told her, nibbling her ear, and giving the lobe a teasing bite.

Never let it be said his wife was easily led. Her black eyes flashed with temper, and she stamped her foot. "I shouldn't. You made another mess on the floor last night with your little pieces of wood."

"Have I told you how beautiful you are and how pleased I was to see you in the gown you wore when you became my lover. Did you know that you have only become more beautiful with the years," he told her smoothly. "I have been thinking, little wife, that we should get the padre and repeat those love words that we vowed fifteen years ago."

Maria, all ire gone, leaned into him. "I thought you didn't notice me at all," she told him, standing on tiptoe and planting a light kiss upon his mouth.

"Forget you, woman? I will show you that I have not forgotten anything. Have you forgotten the time I first kissed you in the confessional? I even remember how your braids were entwined with pretty ribbons. No, *Senora*! Not one thing, have I forgotten!" he proudly declared.

Maria's eyes widened when he pulled her toward him, pinning her against him in his embrace, and capturing her mouth with such a manly, ferocious kiss, waves of desire to surge through her. "Now, I will check the foolish tub, but I promise you there is more that I have to share with you later, and I expect for you to do some remembering as well, eh?"

Flustered, Maria watched him stride gracefully away from her and ease himself out the gate, hardly making a sound. When they were children, she called him *El Gato*, for he could walk as soundlessly as though on cat's paws.

Her cheeks warmed to recall his words and the memories of their times together. Her man was true to his word, and if he promised her *later*, he meant exactly that.

Even now, after long years together, her body prepared for him. But though their love grew more splendid, it remained that she was unable to give him the child of his heart. God knew best, she told herself, and God knew the years of running from the law were behind them. But if He chose not to bless them, who was she to question the reasons of God?

Maria glanced into the room, and saw the little group remained huddled about the girl. She returned to sit beside the fountain. This time she allowed her feet to soak in the sun-warmed water. She had prepared a feast, but until they were finished with the girl, she would allow herself a moment or two of rest.

"I wonder why the two of them decided to be in such a hurry about getting married?" Emily mulled aloud, handing Amanda her hanky to dampen it for her. She had gotten too big to be able to bend over and do the simplest of things.

Maria did not know how to answer, equally puzzled by the sudden turn of events. "I agree, this is most strange, but after so many years of angry silence between them, only God can say."

They heard Manuel approach, bearing something wet, dripping a trail across the patio. "Ladies, pardon me, but do either of you know who matches this garment?"

As Manuel held the sodden cotton under-drawers before them, the two women looked at each other and burst into giggles. "Maria, I believe we have before us the answer to that puzzle."

Amanda's head bobbed up when she heard the merriment. "Looky Maria! Aren't those Daddy's new drawers?" The child's eyes skimmed the three adults, and noticed even Manuel laughed now. She sloshed over to them, spraying the surrounding patio with sparkling droplets, and put her hands on her hips in outrage. "Maria, you have never laughed at my daddy's panties before!"

"I am sorry, truly I am, *Chica*, but you see, we are relieved it was not your doll clothes that were found in the tank this time," explained Maria, soothing the chick's ruffled feathers. "If you will give them to me, husband, I will see they are put in the laundry."

Manuel grinned at his wife, but instead of handing them to her, he twisted the water out of them. Half-embarrassed for his friend, gave his wife a wink. "I will see to it that the *ropa* are put in the proper place. It is understandable our *amigo* was not thinking clearly today?" The women watched him swagger toward the area of the storage room that was set aside for the dirty laundry, and laughed together.

"It is now understandable why our *amigo* got married today?" commented Emily mimicking Manuel's softly accented baritone, prompting Maria to new levels of hilarity. "*Machismo*, that is what it is. They really do stick together, don't they, Maria?"

Maria's dark eyes glinted with humor, the knowing look passed between them. "*Si*, but, in my language *machismo* not only means man, but he-mule. You decide which."

Amanda watched the two women giggle, thinking they must be pretty tired and need a nap to get so silly over her daddy's panties.

CHAPTER SEVENTEEN

Scissors in hand, Avis listened for a change in the girl's breathing, as she sheared the dark mass of dirty and tangled hair. The heavy ebony hair had probably been beautiful once. Maybe the girl would wake up and hate her for this, but for now, they all agreed, it the most sensible and healthiest thing to do in her behalf. Perhaps someday the girl would forgive her.

The sun dipped lower in the sky, and she supposed it would be suppertime soon. She needed to return to the house to pick up a few things. She needed the heavy gold chain for the ring, as well as the copy of Amanda's dress she had commissioned her dressmaker in El Paso to make for Tessa.

Never had she thought that one day, Tessa and Amanda would be sisters. She smiled, anticipating what a convenient and excellent welcoming gift the matching dress would be for Tessa, tomorrow.

Tomorrow, she thought. Good Lord! Here she was, anxious about tomorrow when the topsy-turvy changes of today had yet to be mastered. To think, this morning she had been a fallen woman, with no thought of marriage, and by this afternoon, she had become a married woman with a readymade family.

She had been with her groom for all of about five minutes before Sheriff Bookhout showed up at the door. Andrew had been closeted with him for the past two hours, discussing yesterday's events... she assumed. Hopefully, Andrew got a few good licks at the sheriff about Herb, but she knew it was hopeless. Bull gave Herb orders and insisted on keeping the sot around. Worse, she only had contacts in El Paso.

The connection between Bull and Herb had been a puzzle. She never could figure what Bull got out of one lousy deputy in a town that already jumped to his command. Knowing Bull, however, he had to be getting something.

Avis stopped snipping when she heard the even breathing change. The girl moved, agitated, but quieted when Avis' gently stroked her forehead and spoke to her in a low voice.

She could see the girl's pretty face had been left untouched by the whip. It broke her heart to think of the girl being young and made to live with such an animal, but well she knew that life wasn't fair at all.

Soon the girl was asleep again, and Avis finished cutting her hair. She surveyed her handiwork, and although she had clipped the hair short and pixie-like, it rather suited the girl's slim face and fine features. She smiled to think she might have set a new mode for the Territory.

Her wrists remained tied to the bedposts to keep her from flipping to her back. Avis thought she must be very uncomfortable, but sleeping on her stomach was the only way that would allow the wounds to air and heal naturally.

Maria entered the room. Avis had wet a cloth and put it to the girl's lips. They watched her respond to the moisture by attempting to suck the liquid from the cloth. The girl wasn't asleep after all, thought Avis, marveling at her endurance.

"This is the first time she has done that, *Senora*," Maria told her coming to her side. "I believe Manuel is right, and she will not give up, for she is a fighter."

Quickly and efficiently they changed the pads beneath her.

"*Gracias*, Maria," she said, when they were done. "It is also a good sign that she is able to wet, don't you think?"

"*Si, Senora*. A very good sign and she is eating, as well. It is not much, but yet she sucks the broth from the tube. If you would like to rest, I will see to the girl. There is plenty of food left over from the feast, and you will find it in the kitchen on the table."

"Are Andrew and Sheriff Bookhout finished?" inquired Avis. Andrew must be hungry since it was their wedding meal had been cut short by the unexpected arrival of the lawman.

"No," she replied, shaking her head and rolling her black eyes. I cannot believe the sheriff came today of all days, to inquire about that *beast*." Avis watched Maria's brown, nimble fingers straighten things around the room. Now would be a good time to walk to the cottage and pick up those few things.

"Will you be able to stay with the *chica* for a few minutes, Maria?"

Avis stood at the window that faced the alley and yawned remembering that she had never had a chance to sleep. She thought it funny that she had been awake over twenty four-hours, until now, without realizing it.

This made her more determined to get her chores at the little house done, because once her head hit the pillow there would be no waking her.

"*Si, Si... Nina* is asleep in the little bed in my room, and she is so tired from her big day, I am sure she will not awake till the morning. Manuel is with Padre distributing victuals to the poor, and the padre has already said that he will return at dark to care for the pitiful one through the night, to give us rest. He is such a blessing, that one."

"Maria, there are a few things I have forgotten at the little house. I will only be gone an hour, perhaps, but I need to get them before tomorrow. Will you tell Senor where I have gone, please?"

"But, the preacher is now your husband and don't you think you should inform him yourself before you go?" From the way Maria studied her, she could see the housekeeper thought it funny when she unthinkingly referred to her husband as *the preacher*.

Avis laughed at herself. "I guess I forgot I was married today and then, to boot, forgot I married the preacher. I still haven't figured out how it all happened, but I am sure I don't feel any differently than before the ceremony."

Maria laughed as she touched the patient's brow with compress. "It is understandable, for it has been a most peculiar day. But I think you will feel differently in the morning, *no*?"

"Yes. No! Oh, Maria, I don't know," she replied, allowing her frustration to show.

Avis truly did not know what to think after that odd declaration from Andrew before the ceremony, but, then, she had always thought that bedding a whore would be repugnant to him. Maybe he thought his speech would keep her from being disappointed. "But I do need to get over there and get back before it gets too dark. Maybe I should tell Andrew on my way out the door."

"*Si!*" That is the best way." Immediately, Maria had her hands full with the girl who had begun groaning loudly. Avis started to stay and help, but Maria stopped her saying," Go on, *Senora*. The child is fine with me, and it will help her to have her medicine."

"You win, Maria. I will go now that I can see you can handle her. *Gracias*," she said, turning to Andrew's office. Instead of knocking on the door, she listened for a moment and overheard the two men loudly discussing the deputy. It was not a good time to interrupt.

Knowing she would be quick, she snatched her *rebozo* from the big bed in Amanda's room. Not stopping, she headed out the door, thinking if he knew where she was going, he would feel obligated to accompany her. Right now he had more important things to do than escort his wife on a short walk.

Tinkling sounds of piano mixed with the raucous noises of partying cowboys. Drifters drifted down the empty street. Avis had intended to bypass the cantina, but the instant she stepped past the swinging doors, she remembered she had left the silk fan her grandfather had brought from China up in her suite. It took only a few seconds for her to pass, unnoticed, through the cantina, up the stairs, and return with fan in hand.

She walked out, overwhelmed by the sense of freedom bursting in her soul. The other things, the fancy clothes, and undergarments she would leave for Kate and the girls to parcel out, but no one else would ever have her fan.

Avis reached the small house and let herself in. She would miss her little hideaway, she thought, placing the fan on the dresser, but Andrew had promised she could keep the pink bungalow. Moving her belongings a little at a time, made more sense.

In the meantime, the girls would enjoy playing under the big cottonwoods while she packed. That would leave Andrew free to do as needed for his people. The last thing she wanted to do would be to interfere with parish business.

She found the extra carpetbag shoved under the bed. Two years worth of dust had collected on it, and it made loud *whamps* as she beat it against the bedpost, sneezing at the puffs of dust that billowed from the heavy weave of the fabric. When that was done, she opened it and checked inside for any desert critters that might have taken up residence in such a perfect spot. Finding none she opened, it on her bed.

She didn't feel the thud on the back of her head, or the impact of her fall for the darkness.

Eb watched her wilt like a dying flower, and pocketed the borrowed pistol at the back of his waistband. *Bull will really be proud of me for this.*

He tossed the whore over his shoulder like a gunnysack. Bull had told him to take her to the mill office, not far, and ordered him to make sure nobody saw him take her there.

He heard then glimpsed, in the twilight, a body running through the trees towards him with a gun in his hand. "Shee-it, Bull! That man will kill me, and I ain't getting killed, even for you," he complained, dropping her with a thud onto the porch. Hightailing into the copse of trees, he lost himself in the dark.

Andrew arrived to see his wife lying still as death, and to catch only a glimpse of a blue shirt as the culprit fled away from him and through the trees. Andrew started to give chase, but thought better when he realized he could not leave her.

He placed the pistol on the ground as he knelt down by Avis to check to see if she were alive. Mercifully, she was breathing and her pulse was strong. He put his hand behind her head feeling the wet, sticky blood and his insides turned to jelly.

"Avis! Please, God," he begged, noticing the ominous swelling below her crown.

"Avis, can you hear me?" he repeated, frantic to bring her around.

In the back of his mind, he recalled someone telling him, that if it swelled on the outside it was a much better sign, than for it not to swell at all. The sense of it: swelling on the inside of the brain would be more dangerous. Small comfort, for no one had ever told him how to tell if it swelled both ways.

He looked around, reminded by the uselessly mute bell that he had not fixed it as he had promised. "Oh, God!" he prayed, resting on one knee and looking down at her."

The drying blood became tacky between her hair and the porch. He paused, afraid to move her, but he knew he had to get her off the dirty stoop.

Racing through the front door, he threw a carpetbag off of the bed and pulled the covers down. Returning to the porch, he pulled her into his arms, and carried her across the threshold, placing her on the snowy linen sheets.

Gradually, he unbuttoned what, he thought sadly, had

been her wedding dress, now stained with blood. He slipped it off her shoulders then peeled the dress the rest of the way down her body, pulling it off at her feet. Not bothering to look for a place to put it, he flung the dress over the foot rail.

In a few minutes he had pumped water into a mixing bowl and set about cleansing the dried blood from the back of her head. His eyes scanned her body, noticing that everything else about her appeared to be normal, but she remained dead to the world.

Andrew got up and lit a lamp, feeling foolish when he recalled he had left his gun out on the porch. He stepped outside concerned that might be gone and stared, bemusedly, to find the weapon just as he left it.

Immediately, upon reentering the house, he threw the bar across the door, placed the weapon on the nightstand, and checked again on his wife. He drew back disappointed she hadn't awakened.

Although the bump had grown to a sizeable goose egg, the bleeding had stopped, and he rinsed out a clean cloth and swabbed her face with the cool water, hoping to rouse her. If he didn't know better he would think that she only slept.

This time he grinned when she rewarded him with a distinct expression of displeasure. Hope burgeoned and he tried again.

"God bless you, Avis. Now, Sweetheart, if you will give me another dirty look, I gladly let you sleep as long as you want." He held the sodden rag over her head and watched her bland expression change into an irritated frown as the droplets fell randomly across her face.

"Avis listen, you have a nasty bump on the head," he explained, not really knowing if she could hear. "I'll understand if you don't want to open your eyes, but here is my hand and squeeze it if you understand what I am saying." He held his breath when she gently squeezed his fingertips.

"Good for you! I'm going to turn the lamp down and let you sleep, but I will be here if you need me," he assured her unable to remove his hand from her grasp.

My head, she wanted to say, but could not form the words. Avis' head pounded, hammered with one of those big sledgehammers men used to lay track. Her ears rang, and the one time she tried to open her eyes, she saw four of Andrew, his back to her, walking out the door.

Sleep provided the only way she could avoid the clamoring ache inside her head. Andrew would make everything fine. She continued to clutch his hand fearing he would leave her, and walk out the door for good. "Andrew." She formed his name in her mind, but they would not come.

He waited, not knowing why she held his fingers, but he would like to think she wanted to touch him. He waited but a few minutes more. When her grip went slack, he extricated his fingers.

Before he left her side, he smoothed the hair away from her face. He took a long look at his lately avowed wife-for better or for worse. The wine stain on her lower lip beckoned, and he planted a kiss on it, feeling rather like the frog prince come to wake up the fair maiden.

But, his kiss availed not for she did not waken. Mildly disappointed, he reminded himself that this was no maiden. Worldly women did not waken to chaste kisses from frog-princes, anyway.

Reluctantly, he stood, turned the overhanging lamp down, and looked for something to fill his belly. He lit the kerosene lamp that hung from the peg above the sink and began foraging for food.

Avis kept a stocked pantry and because he had barely eaten all day, he helped himself. He made a meal out of long slices of yellow cheese from a wheel, soda crackers he found in a tin, and a half of pecan pie.

"Great way to spend your wedding night, Bristow," he grumbled stacking the food on a blue willow plate. The night probably wouldn't have been much different anyway, after that self-sacrificing speech he made before the ceremony. The more he thought about it, the more the words stunk like fresh horse manure.

Andrew looked to see if she had stirred. He nibbled his food, mesmerized by the rise and fall of his wife's breasts as she slept on the bed across the room.

Andrew stopped eating and slapped his forehead in disgust. *You bastard, how can you be thinking of your lusts at a time like this?* He quit eating, his appetite gone, to comprehend how close he came to losing his wife.

Who, he wondered was the man he saw run into the trees... an old lover perhaps? Had she come here to meet him? Many questions plagued him and no one but the slumbering princess could answer them.

He put the food aside and rested his head on his hand, tracking the rise and fall of the shapely breasts barely hidden by the scooped out neck of that skimpy thing women wore under their clothes. Fiddling with a cracker, he wondered how long would elapse be before he could touch them.

"Now is not the time for this, Andrew," he admonished himself as he picked up his pie and navigated around the one room house, focusing on the gallery of childish artwork pinned to the walls. He bit into the pie, enjoying its sweetness.

Strange decorations for a woman who's business it was to please men. In all his experience he had never met a harlot with their child's artworks on the walls above their bed.

One whimsical watercolor he especially liked, that of a little girl--he could tell by the long hair and the dress--painting the sky blue.

A fancy silk fan lay on her dressing table. The blades looked to be ivory and the crimson silk webbing was trimmed in black lace. The Oriental fan, an expensive gift, likely came from Trumbull.

Just the thought of the things she must have done for Bull to obtain the fragile frivolity made his stomach revolt. He lost his taste for the pie and set it on the table, thinking he might finish it later.

Maria had been as disturbed that Avis had left without telling him, as he had at finding her gone from the girl's room. Their first thought had been for the danger lurking in the dark streets and allies, but Andrew reminded the housekeeper that Avis always carried her little pistol.

"But, *Senor*, I have the gun. She forgot it in her skirt."

Knowing that, Andrew figured that one encounter with a disgruntled lover could spell disaster.

Somehow he had known that she needed him. The vision of the disabled bell had flashed before his mind, and he had been stricken with guilt when he recalled he had failed to keep his promise to restore it before he left. Determined to meet her at the house and fix the bell, he borrowed one of Manuel's pistols. A few more minutes and he would have been too late.

Andrew paced the room trying to put his feelings aside and think coolly. His head reeled with questions that tumbled through his brain. The attacker could have been a jealous lover; he supposed for surely, there could be no other reason someone would want to hurt her. Was there something else he didn't know? Had Bull been that anxious to be rid of her?

Was it Trumbull? How much of a hold did Bull still have on her life, and what did she know about him? His gut told him there had to be something more, while his mind counseled patience. Patience, he thought irritability was getting scarce as hen's teeth.

Andrew went to the bed to consider the woman who, so recently, had become his wife. What he did not know about her overwhelmed him. Truthfully, the history he did not want to hear, but were extremely important. Perhaps, even a matter of life and death.

Avis turned away from him, rolling onto her side. She appeared to be out of danger. Maybe he could use the time to nose around and see if he could learn anything that might lead to the identity of her attacker.

The bell! Before he did anything else, he needed to get that bell put back together. Before he stepped out the door and onto the porch, he shoved the Colt in his waistband and grabbed a lantern.

After finding the loose end to the bell, he began reattaching the pull cord to the loop at the top ring. The task took only a few minutes.

He walked around the outside of the house a few times, checking the dark corners and taking care of his needs. Back home, a patch of woods this size would hardly be worth considering, but the dense brush would hide a few men and their horses.

Satisfied they were alone, he reentered the adobe and threw the bar across the door, sealing them in for the night. Within two days, he promised himself that he would have a lock on the outside of the door, and a real bolt on the inside. If she wanted to keep this place, he would make it safe for her.

Andrew surveyed the neat structure. Compared to this hovel, his home, and now hers, was huge. This place, however meant something important to her, and he would do everything in his power to keep his promise to her and keep the bungalow safe and in good repair.

He dropped into a chair to consider the problem. When it occurred to him that it would be a long while before Avis trusted him enough to come forth with any secrets about her dealings with the Bull, he arose to nose around the room for clues.

A few people had come right out and confided to him that

Bull Trumbull, nasty as a mountain badger, was a man killer. Thankfully, he had never had to deal with the man, but if there were dangerous secrets lurking between Avis and Bull, and, if she were a threat to him, she could well be dead before he fully recognized the danger.

Andrew glanced at the bed, and admired the lush bottom temptingly displayed before him. He pulled the sheet over her and kissed her forehead, not surprised she didn't move. The longer she slept, the longer he had to search out her secrets.

The small house had only a few places where she would keep documents, papers, or anything of importance. A woven basket full of mail from back east set on top her dresser. The vanity held her passbook and a few legal papers right along with her cosmetics.

Andrew, in a bold but ungentlemanly move, opened her passbook to find a much healthier balance in her savings than he would have thought. Avis, a wealthy woman in her own right made the last deposit of five hundred dollars to the Lone Star Savings Bank in El Paso, on Friday, two weeks before. He put his finger in the crease of the ledger and wondered if it bothered him that his wife, a woman of independent means, did not have to rely on him for everything?

He shook his head and folded the book up. No. Hadn't his mother and her mother been women of wealth? But, he wondered, how she had come by her money.

Next came the documents, one being the written proof of Albert's demise and the other being a will made in her name. A quick perusal showed that she had left her fortune to Tessa, and named her brother, John, as executor. A small key with no identifying tag winked at the bottom of her drawer…a safety deposits box.

The wardrobe contained little else but prim walking clothes and not even one hurdy-gurdy outfit. His search continued until he discovered the photographic portraits in the bottom drawer of the dresser.

Dismissing any remaining feelings of guilt, he snatched them up, and placed the set on the table where he could examine them at length. The four pictures would be of some importance in understanding his bride.

He lifted the lamp from over the sink and set it on the table for a closer look at the black and white images.

The first was a family portrait that bore the signature of Matthew Brady. He well remembered the fame of the photographer who chronicled the Civil War, and points west. His name had become so well known that any picture by the man was now considered a keepsake.

This picture seemed to confirm the very things Avis had spoken of this morning. Her dark haired, frail looking father stood behind a settee upon which sat the members of his family. Andrew noticed right away that her father smiled, despite the afflicted expression in his eyes.

That Avis' mother had been beautiful did not surprise him. Her face was heart-shaped, and sausage curls trailed down her back. In her arms, she held a dark haired infant of less than a year. She laughed openly into the camera, obviously tickled.

To her left stood an older boy with springy fair hair and light eyes. He too laughed, but with the kind of impish glint in his eyes that was trademark for adventurers and makers of mischief. The boy could have been Puck in Midsummer's Nights Dream, and it was a heavy thing to think his joy died with him likely short time after this picture.

Occupying the other end of the seat was a grizzled old man with mutton chop whiskers who held a fair-haired, curly topped tot in his lap. Though he smiled toward the camera, his eyes were slanted toward the tot who seemed fascinated with his beard. Her round face turned in profile from the camera while her pudgy hand reached to grab a handful of whiskers.

This, he realized, would be Avis at about three. He

chuckled to himself at the thought that her desire to tempt fate had changed little from the tot to the adult.

The second of the sequence was counterpoint to the first. The old man was there, made wizened by the white hair and beard. The eyes looked doleful. Hunkered next to him, and looking as if she wanted to disappear in his pocket, sat Avis. Older, her face had lost its cherubic quality and her smile had vanished. No impish twinkle lurked in her eyes and the child clung to her grandfather.

Avis' mother did not look at the camera, but just below it. She smiled, but the eyes were sunken, flat, and expressionless. The shadow of a beautiful woman, if her eyes were the windows to her soul, the candle of life had been extinguished.

The boy, John, appeared to be the least affected, having a sincere grin and enthusiasm in his expression. His eyes lacked the impishness of the elder brother's, and tended to study the photographer, but an amiable smile lit his face. Andrew paused, thinking law had been a wise choice for him.

He concluded the photographs affirmed what Avis had told him earlier in the day. The close bond between with grandfather readily apparent while the unknown character of his new brother-in-law was less discernable. The intervening few years had not been kind: her mother had changed profoundly, even aging beyond her years.

A Kodak of a child was next. She had dark, nearly straight hair, big serious light colored eyes, and except for a slightly fuller lower lip, her features were a miniature replication of Avis'. This must be Tessa, he thought, with some satisfaction. It will be interesting to see how Amanda and Tessa fare together as sisters, their shape and coloring so different.

He contemplated the image of the dark haired child wistfully wondering if a child of their union would be as lovely. That could never be, but if a miracle happened, would the child have flame red and eyes the color of the desert sky at twilight, or brown hair and eyes the green and brown of summer grasses. Would their child even resemble Amanda?

The speculation was futile for they would never have any children of their own. Lois and Andrew had been the first to know, but Doctor Glenn had long ago told them after he had stitched her up that he had done as best as he could, but she would ever conceive again.

Andrew recalled that Lois had wisely chosen a time when he would be gone to tell Avis she could have no other children. When he returned, she related to him, that after a few tears, Avis told Lois that it was just as well anyway.

Andrew got up and paced around the room, thinking how this marriage had spelled doom to his desire for a large brood. He consoled himself with the knowledge that the disappointment he felt at this minute, could be nothing compared to what Avis must have felt on that day.

He said a quiet thank you to the Lord for being even handed and seeing that there were two girls-one his and the other hers. He settled back in his chair thinking that adoption might something worth considering. Once he had even considered opening an orphanage.

Avis and a dower faced man with frosty eyes and fair hair stared back at him from the last picture. The young man, his very light hair parted in the middle, was slicked back and looked severe.

This must be Albert, he thought, surprised at the contrast between his fair, almost too white complexion and his daughter's darkness. Then he recalled, according to the first picture, that Avis' father was dark, bearing the wide mouth and broad cheekbones that bespoke an Indian heritage.

Andrew studied Avis' expression. Her eyes were somber, her mobile mouth, pressed into a straight line. The possessive grasp of his hand on her shoulder must have caused some pain.

Albert's emotionless eyes stared to the left of the camera.

Their paleness reminded him of the thin light of winter reflected through icicles. Most telling was the cruel tension of the hand pressing into Avis' shoulder. Pressed until the fingertips disappeared and the knuckles too apparent.

He could discern little resemblance between Trumbull and his nephew, except for the eyes. However, there was no reason to disbelieve Avis' story, and from what he had seen so far, every reason to accept it as the truth.

Andrew flipped the frame over on its front to see if there was a date on the back and sliced the corner of his finger open on a loose tack. All of the tacks around the picture had been loosened, and replaced, but not securely. He grabbed a tea towel from the shelf and wrapped it about his finger as he secured the tacks.

By the time he had fixed the frame, his finger had stopped bleeding. He rinsed the soiled towel with a combination of spit and cold water, counting himself fortunate he had not bled all over the pasteboard backing of the picture. Bloodstains would certainly set Avis wondering.

Thoughtfully, Andrew replaced the pictures in the drawer in the same order he found them. She had told him the truth, but he also believed she withheld some of the truth. His hopes were gone that he would stumble across the rest of the information this night.

The past days had been long and eventful him, he reflected, finishing his pie. He looked at the open timber beams of the ceiling and the earthen walls of the adobe, wishing he could open the shutters for fresh air. Safety, not comfort had to be his primary concern.

The solitary bed occupied, this gave him a choice of using the floor, the chairs, or daring to crawl in beside his bride. There appeared to be room on the other side of the bed.

Sleeping on the floor was out because of the crawling desert critters that lurked in every home. The chairs were too uncomfortable and that left the narrow strip of bed. He yawned, certain she would understand. He was, after all, her husband.

Andrew took a final drink of water, and turned down both lamps for the night. It didn't seem likely Avis would waken. If he needed brighter light, he would take care of that by placing the lamp and matches on the nightstand by the bed. The gun rested next to the lamp, within reach and loaded.

Gently, Andrew checked the swollen knot on her head and listened for any hitch in her breathing. He didn't want to check anything else more closely, anticipating sleeping next to her difficult enough. He sure didn't want to dwell on things that could not be.

In a few seconds he had removed his shirt, and shucked his trousers, leaving his cotton drawers on as some kind of chastity belt, he supposed. He tried to slip under the cool sheet as discretely as he could, but the steel coiled springs groaned and creaked loudly every time he moved.

He settled on his side, facing away from Avis and to the wall. He sighed with pleasure at the luxury of stretching his body on a real bed.

The minutes clicked by as the chirrup of the cicadas, which neither slumbered nor slept, and the bullfrogs from the nearby springs teamed into such a chorus, his body refused to relax. His thoughts turned again to the woman next to him, and the ripe pale breasts, which promised to be more than a handful. His groin throbbed with wanting, but he immediately doused the heat reminding his better sense of her feeble condition.

Andrew grumbled to himself. Tonight he would concentrate on the tangle of laws in the Old Testament, the ten tribes, and the books of the Bible. If he failed, he would have to try sleeping in the chairs.

He did sleep, but not by force of his stalwart will. Sleep claimed him at the book of Lamentations, but the result of two days worth of accumulated fatigue.

Long after the good citizens of Alamogordo had doused their lights, and the frolic at the cantina began to wane in the early hours of the morning, two men with the Circle T brand on their horses rode out of town into the inky blackness of the moonless night.

One person, keeping watch in front of the lumber mill, saw them leave. Sly as a fox, Herb made it his business to know more than he ever said about Bull.

"Hot damn!" he swore, spitting a wad of tobacco into the sand. "It's about damn time I got me some more bucks."

Herb headed back to the saloon. He passed through the swinging doors aiming to find himself a good whore.

Thanks to Bull's nasty ways, he'd spend his last gold piece for that *Frenchy* that Bull liked to use when he couldn't get none of his purty boys.

Bull talked a hell of a lot about the Frenchy and he said that her mouth had the power to sump pump the Rio Grande. Bull lied a lot, and this was something Herb had to find out for himself.

Eb was hungry. His stomach growled, but they kept riding. He told the boss, but Mister Trumbull said nothing.

They had ridden straight up the mountain, using an old logging trail, and then angled off to follow a winding ledge a few hundred feet. At last, they dismounted, and led the horses the last few feet to the place the trail led into the narrow mouth of a cave.

"Now I am telling you boy, you'll see more gold here than anywhere else in the world. If you do what I tell you, part of it is yours. Remember what I said," he told him, throwing his arm around him and leading him into the cave.

When they had entered through the mouth of the cave,

Bull lit one lamp, and then four more spotted around the huge chamber. The brilliant sight that met Eb's eyes made him gasp. He stepped forward, wondering that so much gold could be in one place.

The gold was not only in bars, and chests, but there stood a gilded throne at the end of a path of gold bars. Everywhere he looked either gold or red velvet shown brilliant against the dark walls of the cavern.

"Come with me, you adorable boy," urged Bull, taking the giant by the arm, he led him into a second chamber. The centerpiece of the room a massive canopy bed dressed in elaborated hangings of gold and red velvet. "Splendid isn't it, Eb?"

Eb tried to take in all the bright and shiny things. "It surely is Bull. I ain't never seen the like." Many of the things he saw on the walls and in fancy golden jars were strange, too. Some of them looked like golden whips, but the golden loops and chains dangling from the ceiling and walls were peculiar.

He had never seen golden chains before, and stared in wonderment at the way they shimmered in the lamplight. His gaze stopped everywhere he found something new. "Pretty hanging things, Bull," he murmured, entranced by the glittering spectacle.

Bull followed Eb's gaze, enjoying his consternation over the toys. "These trifles are some of the playthings I acquired from my trips abroad. You do like them, don't you?"

When the wide-eyed, but handsome simpleton nodded, Bull smiled. "Good, for you! I trust you to rule over my little empire, when I cannot be here. This is the safest place for you, until we have thought of a plan for the whore and her husband. You shall be my Minotaur and all this is your Labyrinth," he declared flinging a whip around as if it were a sorcerer's wand.

"My food?" whined the anxious oaf, unable to see any provisions within either chamber.

Bull smirked, thinking that Eb had just sold his soul for a mess of porridge. "Right this way, you big, strong bull," he directed, exchanging the cat-o-nine tails for one of the smaller whips. "I am sure you will be more than satisfied with all the pleasure you will find here, my boy." He led him to the storage area and opened trunks full of rations. "And here are things you may use to open the cans."

Had Eb been able to read, Bull realized he would have recognized them as foodstuffs issued by the army. Food, to him, was better than any gold.

Starving, Eb lunged for a can. Bull flicked his hand playfully with the whip before he could grab the can or the opener.

"First comes my pleasure and then you may eat for your pleasure," he instructed, leading him back to the bedchamber and the gold manacles on the wall. "You'll find I am an easy man to please, my strong Minotaur."

CHAPTER EIGHTEEN

Avis gradually became aware her headache had gone. Except for a curious and tender swelling on her head, she felt refreshed for the first time in days.

She opened her eyes to the blackness of the night and focused on the thin white cord of the bell tied to the bed. She breathed deeply, relieved that the double vision had gone.

Avis breathed in the scent of bay rum and remembered that Andrew rested beside her. She smiled to recall the furtive way Andrew had tried to sneak into her bed.

She had not bought the metal springs because they were quiet, but because they were more comfortable than the crude bed frames made locally. But they were noisy enough to wake the dead. Had she known she would have company in her bed, she would have been more particular about the kind of iron springs she bought.

He faced away from her, but she could hear his rhythmic breathing above the combined din of the night creatures. The measured way he breathed meant that he was asleep and it was safe for her to use the chamber pot.

Gingerly, she sat up on the side of the bed allowing the dizziness to pass. She tried to recall what she had been doing to get the lump on the back of her head.

The last thing she could clearly recall was beating the dust out of the carpetbag. Had she passed out and fallen on her head, or unknowingly bumped her head on the bed rail? None of these possibilities seemed very likely to her.

Andrew must have come at precisely the right moment. She remembered the comfort of his voice reaching to her through the intense headache.

She thought about Andrew lying next to her. For the first time in a very long time, a gentle peace resided within her at the long forgotten comfort of not being alone.

Rolling to her side, she cuddled up to his bare back, throwing an arm around his waist. She turned her ear to listen and be soothed by the steady beat of his heart.

Her fingertips lightly stroked the firm rangy muscles of his shoulders and traced the hard rigid surface of collarbone, thinking how deceptively solid he was.

Recalling the speech he made to her before they said their vows, she realized he had spoken about building trust in each other before sealing their marriage by consummating the vows. That only mattered to noble Andrew because she knew that nothing lasted forever.

They both knew she already trusted him therefore he could only be talking about being able to trust her. Though understandable, it did not seem very desirable.

His body, she knew, needed release. This sharp wanting had to put a great deal of strain on a man who could not admit to being blatantly randy.

Even if they were not in love with each other, they were friends. Certainly as both friend and wife, she could fulfill her marital obligations to him. After all, the act was mechanical; a simple thing to perform for a man she liked, instead of one she despised.

The more she gave her fingers expression over his warm flesh, the more intrigued she became with variations in the feel of different parts of his body.

This blissful thing called "mating," she had come to understand," had less to do with emotions and more to do with petting the right areas.

This separation of the two ideas of mating and love in her mind enabled her to skillfully calculate a man's need, yet, allowed her the distance from them as persons. But could she keep that protective distance with this man, she wondered?

He saved her from a terrible fate and did she not owe him this at least? Though she dared not trust him forever, she could relax for with him for a while: until it was finished between them.

Kate's girls always liked to say that a man could get it off in a knothole, if he could find one without splinters. "Would Andrew be any different?" she asked herself, as her fingers began to work slowly downward, now, having a definite goal in mind.

Her fingers deftly tracked the line of coarse, springy hair from his chest to where it swirled around his navel. They lingered there, fondling and gently caressing the solid flesh of his abdomen, as she listened, alert for some sign of wakefulness.

She pulled the string holding Andrews drawers in place. It was when she slipped her hand in the soft warm area below where the waistband had been, that he sprang to life. She felt him draw in a breath as if to speak.

"Shush! Not one word," she cautioned, continuing to massage his groin, "or you'll spoil it."

Happily surprised, he certainly had not wanted to spoil anything, but instead sought to participate. He attempted to roll over to face her, but she held him in place, with the pressure of her body next to his.

"No, you can't roll over yet," she whispered, drawing her hands back to cup his muscular buttocks, and knead the solid and compact flesh.

"Let me do this for you," she whispered seductively, "Don't think about me or you, just think about the feel of my hands on your body," she whispered, working her thumbs around the creases of his bottom.

Her hands moved to travel down the outside of his right leg all the way to his foot, where she began to massage it in the same manner, paying particular attention to the ball of his foot and his toes. "You may lay on your back now," she urged, her voice low and throaty.

Uncomplaining, he did as she instructed, savoring the excitement of her hands on his neglected senses. His body tingled and even if he had wanted to stop her, he would not have had the power to deprive himself of the knowing hands that made him throb in anticipation of her next touch.

She was between his legs now, stroking her fingers downward. Her fingertips climbed upward slightly higher with each movement. Her thumbs rubbed circles into the bunched muscles of his calves with sharp, almost, painful pressure. Then, she stroked the area with subtle caresses made more sensual by the heightened sensitivity of his flesh.

The random brush of her hair against the soft skin of his inner thighs brought fresh surges to his mounting passion. He ached to take her, but feared she would stop and there would be no relief for the hungry throbbing in his groin. "Too long," he moaned.

When her probing fingers began to touch and manipulate the innermost areas of his thighs, his body quaked with the need.

His lusty organ, hot and hard, strained for release. He feared that any moment he would shame himself.

It was when he thought he could stand no more, that her finger drew a line from beneath his glands to the tip of his rod. If she did that one more time, he knew there would be no stopping his release.

When he grabbed for her hand to stay the fiery touch, she evaded his grasp. In one move, she mounted him and moved to sit astride him. She did not fully sheath him, but teased him by keeping him poised at the entrance to her moist warmth. He groaned, begging for the finish.

Avis could feel the tension build in Andrew's body. She knew she enticed him to distraction by not allowing him fully to enter, but she wanted to prolong it for him. When his hips pulled back to surge into her, she would parry, lifting herself away from him.

Hands came around her waist and she knew that he reached for her to hold her down upon him. Taking his hands firmly, she moved them above his head.

"No, this is on me." Her lace covered nipples teased at his chin as she pinned his hands above his head. He pulled forward, wanting to taste them with his tongue.

She straightened her back to fit herself smoothly around his length. He groaned his surprise. "Come with me!" he urged feeling the tight warmth of her enclose him.

Pausing for a minute, she anticipated that cool, sober-sides Andrew, the man who always approached each crisis with such calm was about to loose control. Stroking his face and passing her fingers across his lips in the dark, she eased herself up slowly. She sighed at the length and breadth of him, before settling back upon his manhood.

Again, he groaned, grabbing her hips to stay her. "Wait. Come with me. Together," he urged.

The next moment, she, again, raised herself above him. Coming down, she heard him shout as she met his thrust upward on her downward stroke.

Avis could not see him for the dark, but she felt him spend himself within her. She rode him, amazed that the quiet and dignified man she knew was not at all that way when he released his seed.

Andrew loudly bucked and writhed beneath her, pushing into her with all of his might. He touched the top of her, and she knew that he had touched her womb.

As his passion ebbed, she bent over and planted a light kiss upon his damp forehead.

She nearly groaned aloud at the pain behind her eyes. Bending over had been a mistake. The headache returned sending sword points behind her eyes.

Avis pulled her leg back across his body. "Sorry I can't linger." she apologized, immediately feeling weak and nearly nauseous. She rolled to the far side of the bed hugged the pillow and curled into a ball.

Andrew, sated, exhausted, but confounded, stared into the darkness above him, marveling at what just happened, but something was missing. She had not called or spoken his name once and the terrible thought that she might have thought he was someone else lurked in the back of his mind.

Avis, unconcerned with anything but the piercing ache in her head and the disagreeable urge to upchuck, impolitely fell asleep.

This is foolish, he thought, unmoving and staring at nothing. I have just enjoyed the experience of my dreams, and now I am worried my wife does not know who I am.

The longer he thought about it, the sillier it sounded, and the less it mattered. Still, it rankled his pride he had not pleased her, but shot himself off like some stick of dynamite with a short fuse. She deserved better.

After he had cleaned himself up the best he could, he turned toward Avis and hugged her womanly body close, feeling the fine smoothness of her bottom against his thighs. He also felt the weave of the lacy thing she was wearing against his chest only then realizing she had worn it throughout their lovemaking.

Lovemaking? Did he consider that lovemaking or something else? He rather thought it was the something else. They should at least have called their names.

Why am I disappointed, and why must everything have a

deeper meaning?

Frustrated with the direction of his thoughts on his tired mind, he determined to put his vain imaginations away. Knowing she slumbered, he lightly ran his fingers over the velvety underside of her forearm. The feathery touch did not even produce a stir.

His fingers trailed over her shoulders. Soft, so very soft and years had gone since he had the luxury of touching such a fine feeling bit of womanly flesh. But he had not pleased her and in this, he remained unsatisfied.

Andrew closed his eyes, savoring the nearness of her, while his anxious pride wanted this woman to come alive for him. He yearned for her to desire him with the same intensity he had wanted her just a few minutes before.

Was it possible for him to touch that distant and aloof part of her? His thumb tried the sensitive flesh beneath her breasts.

Realizing where he was leading with the ever more daring strokes of his thumb, he withdrew and contented himself with holding her close.

It wasn't long before she stirred in his arms and turned to face him, prompting him to lift his chin. She buried her face into the hollow of his neck. Her breath warmed the sentient flesh of his throat, while his mind focused on the hot friction of her firm breasts pressed against his chest.

He had been only casually contemplating thoughts of arousal. But, now fully erect, he calculated when and how best to seduce the seductress.

He did not know how long he held her this way, his arms wrapped around her and snug into the curve of his body. Half-listening to the early morning chatter of birds, he debated whether to let her rest, or dare to put his stamp upon he. Seduce her in the same calculated way she had branded him by driving him to the brink.

Such an inconsiderate thing it would be for him to take

advantage of her while she had that lump on her head. But it certainly hadn't stopped her from taking unasked for liberties with him, had it? Should he be any more concerned for her than she was toward herself? The next moment she stirred, shifting out of his arms and onto her back.

Outlined in the morning light, he reached for her, nearly touching her lips with his finger. The possibility she might turn away from him stilled his fingers and he moved his hands to rest under his cheek.

Finally, when his fruitless musings were exhausted, he fell into a light doze, mentally registering every move she made upon the cranky bed.

Near dawn, she again rolled to face him. Feeling her breath on his face, he opened his eyes to find himself staring at lush, ripe lips slightly open. He moaned, again rock hard with need.

This time he did not hesitate, but lowered his lips to her breast and, with blood singing and thrumming through his veins in anticipation, he took a lace cloaked nipple into his mouth, suckling hungrily, while manipulating the other nipple between his thumb and finger.

As he laved her breast, she gave a soft, promising sigh and felt her arch her body against him. He pressed his ache against her thigh in effort to assuage the fresh surge of desire that darted through his body.

Sweat popped out on his upper lip and forehead as he continued to tease at the buds through the barrier of the delicate material. Unexpectedly, she drew away from him, slipped a strap off one shoulder, and pushed the garment down to bare the fully for him.

He held his breath as her fingers wound through his hair. Again, he gently pressed his mouth to the nipple, while encouraging the other hand to continue the stimulating friction of the lacy cloth against the other.

Avis arched toward him, thrusting the sensitive nub further into his mouth. Long ago she had denied herself the exquisite thrill of having a man do the things Andrew was doing so well. Nor had she welcomed the hungering ache it produced between her legs.

Down came the other strap from her shoulder. His rigid member strained against her thigh. In a moment, she offered the other globe to him, and moaned in delight when he took the sensitive nipple between his teeth, gently nipping it before laving the swollen nub.

Suddenly, Andrew pressed her to her back, and gathering both breasts to his lips, suckled both at once. The insistent hardness begging for entrance between her legs sent shimmering sparks of tension through her body. At once, Avis raised her hips and locked her legs about his back. She wanted him insider her, where she could feel again, every part of him. "Please," she begged straining toward him.

He did not fully enter her, keeping the stiff head of his erection at the threshold of her center. The barest feel of him, enticing her, seducing her, and bringing her to an unexpected but heady climax.

At the moment the pleasurable spasms began to pulse through her body, that he moved higher within her, increasing her pleasure so that she screamed her ecstasy. Then, when he embedded himself inside her to the hilt, and paused for a few moments, she feared she would die for the exquisitely lingering contractions.

Andrew heard her cry of surrender and smiled in the night at the small victory he had wrung from her. She bore down to meet him. He grit his teeth, working to maintain control as he perceived the rhythmic clenching and unclenching of her swollen sheath around his shaft.

When she lay spent beneath him, he eased himself slowly in and out of her. He closed his eyes to remember the wanton vision she had been when caught away by passion.

"So beautiful," he whispered aloud, to realize the consuming fire she had drawn from him a few minutes before.

He closed his eyes, maintaining the steady stroke. He sometimes whispered to her bits of a poem, while at other times, he confirmed to her the many ways in which he admired her and desired her. He continued until he felt the damp of fresh arousal.

If he could bring her around twice, he reasoned, then he could possibly have done something no other man had done for her. Being different from the others had suddenly become very important to him.

Andrew watched, beguiled by the myriad of expressions as they flitted across her face. Her eyes were closed totally absorbed by the sensations he produced in her body.

When she began to move with him, he lifted her legs over his shoulders, and pounded into her. At last, she came again, drawing her bottom tight around him, as she frantically grabbed at his arms.

"Andrew!" she called to him, straining to push herself against him. His heart leaped to hear his name, knowing now that she did know who she had been with this night and morning.

He threw his head back and closed his eyes. Good! Immediately, he came, breaking forth with a roar of triumph. "Avis," he cried, shouting her name to the heavens.

CHAPTER NINETEEN

Her intuition told her he was watching her, staring at her with sappy adoration and gratitude in those soft, puppy dog eyes.

Andrew probably wondered if she thought he was as good as he thought himself to be. She smiled to remember the feel of him surrounding her: the velvet in steel inside of her.

Such unexpected passion lurked inside him! But she would never tell him of his masculine beauty or how he had pleased her. She didn't want him making too much out of what she considered legal fornication. Nor did she want him gloating that he had pleased a woman he considered jaded.

"Listen, Preacher," she began gruffly, keeping her eyes shut. "Don't go getting worked up over what happened between us. As far as I am concerned we both had an itch that needed scratching, and that's that. We only did what comes naturally."

When he didn't immediately respond, she rolled over and opened her eyes, disappointed to find his back to her. Avis nearly giggled at her conceit.

Truth to tell, she might even be a trifle piqued he appeared to be unfazed about the *event*. This meant the end of a long dry spell for him, and she had thought he would be bursting with compliments and gratitude for what she had done for him. Indeed! He snored.

He'd be puffier than a two-day-old corpse if she told him how really wonderful he was. She did not wonder even for a moment where he had learned those skills, but doubted he refined those sensual touches in a seminary, or even the hayloft.

Though she might be curious about his *higher education*, she would never ask. The past had little bearing on the here and now. In fact, she'd just as soon let her past die. She owed him the same opportunity.

She turned to face his back, unabashedly scrutinizing what the darkness had hidden from her. Her eyes wandered over the man from the breadth of his shoulders, down the smooth, but muscular back to his firmly rounded hips.

Her fingers itched to touch him, again. She pressed weight of her breasts against the brawn of his back. Moist rivulets of perspiration ran between them. She wrinkled her nose at the unmistakable stink of unwashed bodies, in the shuttered stuffiness of the room.

Turning around, she sat on the edge of the bed, planning the morning. She would open the rear windows to allow fresh air inside and prepare for herself at least half a tub of water. She ran a dubious glance over the naked body beside her and decided Andrew could sleep. The longer he stayed out of her hair, the better.

The train would be here in the mid-afternoon. That gave her only about four hours to gather her things here and make preparations for Tessa and Uncle Elwin's arrival at the big house. Tessa! She pressed her heart with her fist to slow the burst of anxious thumping.

Avis pulled her hair into a pile on the top of her head then yelped when the hairpin rudely reminded her of the knobby bulge on her head. The source of the tender spot continued to puzzle her as she pumped six pails full of water and dumped them in the huge copper-lined tub hidden behind the Chinese screen.

Facing away from the bed, she peeled the sweaty, damp, and clingy chemise down her waist. She wriggled the chemise over the curve of her hips and, then, bent at the waist to slide the garment down her thighs. She stepped out of the lacey black puddle unaware of her rapt audience on the bed.

Andrew remained still as stone having nearly spoiled the show by groaning at the sight of her winsome rump staring him in the face. Merely watching the pale behind and shapely legs made his member run up like the Stars and Stripes at San Juan Hill.

When his new wife stepped behind the screen and into the tub, Andrew shook his head and rolled to his back. He pillowed his head on his arms to consider her words. She had called what was between them an itch. Maybe *itch* explained that brand of lust best, but the term was shallow, not adequate.

To expect love would be asking too much, but he would settle for anything above friendship. Even Adam had needed a friend. Perhaps friendship and the carnal attraction would be the place where they could start to build their marriage. Scratching their respective *itches* could be the best way of avoiding forbidden subjects, and, yet, still build closeness between them.

The fresh evidence of a burgeoning *itch* had developed the moment he saw her wiggle out of her clothes. Would his bride be as accepting of him in the daylight, he wondered? She'd probably be more accepting if he didn't smell rank. Perhaps a bath would be in order?

Soon humming and splashing came from behind the screen precisely drawn with Chinese women walking over arched bridges. He rose from the bed and padded to the tub. Slipping behind the screen, he halted, startled by the mirror image of her, seated in the tub with the washcloth over her face and him standing behind her. The reflection showed the only part of his body hidden from view to be the arrogantly waving staff. He grinned to realize that the puffy mound of hair on her head concealed the unusually notable of his manhood.

Maybe he could jump to the side, stand spread eagle and yell surprise!

Andrew chuckled at the image in his mind. Avis brushed the damp cloth from her face. She straightened, to meet his gaze reflected in the cheval mirror.

"Excuse me, madam, but I seem to have developed an *itch*," he informed her, grinning. He stepped to the side exposing his *pride* to her, "and I was wondering if you might take pity on me and scratch it?"

Her eyes narrowed at his grin. "You were listening!" she hissed.

Andrew winked at her. "Naturally, and I heard every word. But I have developed this new *itch*, would you be a good wife and help me?"

Astonished at his boldness, Avis laughed into their reflection, her eyes glinting up at him. "I tell you what, husband. You get into the tub with me and I will be glad to take care of your itch. Firs, though, you have to promise to wash my back for me," she answered sweetly, while her eyes danced.

Grinning arrogantly, Andrew dropped into the tub, forgetting how cold the water from the pump could be. He gasped as the shock of the cold water puckered and shriveled him to nothing. He stared at himself in mute surprise.

Avis giggled and pointed her finger at him. "I told you I would take care of your itch, didn't I?" she teased, between fits of laughter. "Now you have to wash my back, please." She handed him the soap and cloth. She scooted around to present him with her back.

"You aren't angry at me for tricking you, are you?" she inquired innocently, craning her neck to see him.

Andrew cocked an eyebrow at her thinking she sounded a little too meek. "No," he answered, spreading the rosy smelling soap over her back into frothy lather, "just a mite surprised, I guess."

Avis burst into a fresh bout of mirth. "I suppose so. *Mite* is right word for it. Only, I think you should have better stated that your *might* was a victim of surprise. You do understand how amusing words can be?"

She squirmed when he snaked his soapy hands around her to lather the already puckered nipples. "Just remember, Wife," he informed her, lowering his lips to her ear. She shivered when his tongue explored the shell of her ear. "You have a comeuppance awaiting."

She would have laughed at the humor, but instead she closed her eyes to savor the touch of his hands on her breasts. When he released her, carefully washing away all that remained of the lather from her body; she simmered with unexpected passion. "When do I get my comeuppance?" she whispered scooting her bottom against his groin.

Andrew heard the quick surrender in her voice, before he felt the warmth of her bottom hard against him. "When do you want it?" he asked first admiring the graceful tilt of her head with his eyes, then, nibbling at her neck.

"Do you suppose I could have it now?" she answered thinking it silly to be so nervous about asking for something he seemed more than willing to give. "Quick. Before the needs of the day make me forget, how wonderful it is to feel good."

"Mm, you smell good," he replied, his warm breath in her ear. He turned her around to face him. His arms closed about her, while his mouth sampled the curve of her neck.

"Let me please you, Andrew," she offered, kissing him, while enclosing the evidence if his need in the warmth of her hand.

"Let's please each other," he countered, feeling each stroke of her hand herald the fiery return of his arousal.

"We don't have much time," she said, between kisses.

"This won't take much time," he said, as he pulled her up from the water.

"You promise?"

They stood eye to eye, the distended tips of her nipples brushing against his chest. He glanced down at them, then at his , and grinned impudently at her.

"I would say, my dear, that would depend upon you," he informed her taking the bud into his mouth while his hand explored the springy red curls at the juncture of her thighs.

She gasped when he slipped his finger inside of her, at he moment she plunged her hips to meet the heel of his hand. "You are most beautiful right now, Avis, he murmured, watching her move into the throes of ecstasy.

His wife was a sight to behold as she melted before him. He watched her, head thrown back and eyes pinned shut. Deep in concentration she moved with him, pressing against his hand as he stroked the liquid warmth. He watched the emotions flit across her face, becoming even more aroused by her evident passion.

"Ladies first, Sweetheart." His voice became husky with his own barely controlled passion. Presently, the sheath around his fingers tightened.

"Suck," she begged, urging his head to her breast. Immediately, he latched onto the erect nipple. "Andrew!" she moaned, adding fresh kindling to own desire. She sagged against him, and he waited before he gently extracted his fingers from the musky dampness.

"What about you?" she asked, weak as a kitten.

Andrew held her in his embrace, standing ankle deep in cold water. "Turn around and grab the sides of the tub with your hands," he whispered, gruffly. Avis' head shot up, nearly clipping him in the chin.

"No!" she shrieked, nearly falling as she scrambled out of the tub. "Not that way."

Avis," he said, gently pulling her back into the tub. "Do you think I would hurt you?" When she didn't answer or even turn about to face him, he turned her about, tracing the worry lines on her forehead with his thumbs. "Listen, Mrs. Bristow. You're forever mine now and I would sooner hurt myself than I would hurt you. Can you understand that I don't hurt those I care about?" Head bowed she didn't answer, but stared at her feet, all passion drained from him.

Avis turned away. "I am sorry, Andrew, but I have to be able to see you."

Avis didn't want to speak of *forever*...people change. When Andrew talked like they would be married forever she wanted to run from him. How naïve he was to think that humans kept their vows and never changed.

"My goodness. Well," he said, sucking in a deep breath. "I think we better get a move on, or your daughter will be here before we get out of this big bucket."

He kept his tone light hoping to distract her from a subject he really didn't relish thinking about, even on his better days. They both had pasts, but irrationally, he found he resented hers.

"What about you?" she asked, her blue eyes filled with apprehension. Could she be afraid because she felt obligated to please him?

Andrew could understand how she could be concerned for him not getting his release, but she appeared to be genuinely fearful about it. He pushed the hair back from her face and kissed her lips. "You worry too much. Seems like I remember that it wasn't so special for you the first time around last night. Am I right, or were you quieter than you were later?"

"No, I didn't, the first time." she replied, lowering her eyes. "But I wasn't expecting to please myself, either."

"Then you may consider us even."

"Oh, but my job was different."

"Job? How so?" he inquired as he reached over to grab a towel from the short stack kept on a shelf above the tub. "Turn around and I will towel your back," he offered, hoping to distract her.

"Thanks for the offer, but I have been standing here so long, the only thing that is still wet is my feet," she told him, as she snatched the towel from his hands. She held the wadded towel pressed to her bosom. "Now will you let me explain?"

"Only if you will dry off my back," he replied turning around to face the mirror.

Avis pursed her lips. She crossed her arms across her chest making her breasts bounce upward in what Andrew thought resembled fresh baked dinner rolls. He licked his lips and closed his eyes.

"Your back isn't wet, either," she said speaking over his shoulder, to his reflection.

"Yes, but I like attention." He cocked his head over his shoulder and grinned. His bride was a woman, he decided, who had learned all the wrong things about married love. Foremost among them would be fear.

Andrew turned about and slipped the towel from her hands, throwing it over the side of the tub to spread its length onto the floor. He cupped her face gently in his hands. "Touch me, Avis, anywhere."

Andrew took her warm hand, and kissed her palm before moving it down to cover his flaccid organ.

Her eyes registered surprise as they darted to the shriveled organ now fully enveloped in the palm of her hand. "I still don't understand if you are telling me if you want it or not," she told him. "Either you want it or you don't. What is so damn complicated?"

"I see we are back to swear words again," he rubbed his eyes and put his hands on his hips. He tilted his head to look at her. "The human body is a marvel, but I'm telling you neither thing. What I am telling you are the facts of life. We cannot allow our lives to be ruled by the tyrannical and fickle whims of my organ. It is insatiable at times, while at other times, impossible to arouse." He paused and looked away from her, thinking how to make himself clearer. "I guess what I am trying to say is, simply, that it is fine for you to say *no*. Andrew crossed his arms. "Coming together can only be right for both of us and only mutual choice."

He could see the wheels turning in her mind as she considered his words. "I notice that your breasts are very sensitive, is that correct?"

"Yes," she told him, amazed to feel him stir in her hand.

"Do you think about your breasts all of the time?" he inquired glancing at the exquisite, rose tipped pair, and finding himself more than excited by the fetching display.

"No! Of course not," she answered hotly, not understanding what he was trying to tell her about her breasts.

"When you nursed the babies, did you think about your breasts all of the time?"

"What are you saying Andrew?" she asked, drawing her hand away from him horrified at what he implied. "Are you suggesting that I--"

"Hold on." Andrew cut her off before she could finish working up to a good mad. "If you don't think about your breasts all of the time, what in the world makes you think I think about my organ all of the time?"

Avis recoiled. "Are you telling me I insulted you just now?"

"Wouldn't you be insulted if I thought that all you thought about were your nipples? Aren't you much more than the total of those little nubs?"

"Little nubs, is it?" Avis picked up the wet washcloth and threw it in his face. "They are little only when compared to Delilah's deformities, you--you *bellicose ba...ooby*." That was not exactly what she was going to say, but that was the only "B" word she could muster clean enough for Andrew's ears. "I understand your attraction to her but why do you have to make everything spiritual? Sex is a fact of life and I can understand your attraction to her..."

"Come here, " he urged calmly, standing with his arms outstretched.

Avis reached for the partial bucket of cold water and dumped the remaining water over his head. "Ugh!" he growled, trying to recover.

"But you married me!" Before he could stop her, Avis jumped out of the tub with the empty bucket, and worked the pump handle at the sink overtime. When Andrew took the bucket away from her, dumping the water down the sink, she began to slowly back away from him.

Andrew stalked her around the room. "*Bellicose booby*, am I? For your information the word bellicose means warlike and I have not said one unkind or rotten thing to you all morning." He wagged his finger at her as if she were a child. "In fact, I have been very patiently trying to explain to you that what is important between us is not what is swinging between my legs, or hidden between yours, but in our relationship."

She backed into a table and he nearly laughed out loud when the corner stuck in her hip and she yelped. "For the life of me, I can not even remember one time I even remotely thought or brought the name Delilah into the conversation. I am struggling to understand why you bring her into our conversations."

Avis watched him fling his hand up in frustration but had backed up to the bed and could go no further unless she went over the bed. "I am warning you, Preach! If you lay one finger on me, you will be sorry," she shrieked putting her hand up to ward him off.

He allowed her the safety of the few feet between them. Andrew shot her an arrogant smile, thinking how he liked it when her hair was sort of wild, and the way her eyes sparked angry fire. Her body dared him by her defiance, to take her: to master her, once and for all with force, but, he would wait. In time she would come to him because she wanted to belong to only him.

Right now, the animal attraction drew them together, but in time… He turned his head slightly. What a pair they were; he thought nearly smiling as he studied her, while she glared at him with that haughty, rebellious look. Andrew crossed his arms across his chest, lecherously watching her breasts heave, entranced by their beauty. He smiled.

Avis watched him swell before her eyes. She looked down to see that her own nipples betrayed her by popping to attention. Confused, she looked back at his organ and, then at her nipples, again. A nervous giggle rose in her throat, but biting her cheeks, she looked at Andrew to see his reaction. "Well?"

"Ah ha!" snorted Andrew, wanting more to give his bride freedom, than to win--for now.

Andrew brought his arms up. "You see what I mean? Clearly, they know what they want, and they will drive us crazy if we let them. But you are not here to service my whims. I give this choice to you. What do you want?" he told her, keeping her out of his reach. Noble sentiments aside, he flat out didn't trust himself within firing distance.

Avis considered his words. She wanted the wonderful feeling again and craved to escape into mindless pleasure. But, to have a man care enough to put his immediate desires aside to please her? She wanted too much and knew that she could not have them both.

She dropped her eyes, ashamed to be undecided as to where she wanted respect or sex. "I want to get dressed, and prepare for my daughter's arrival."

The words rush out of her mouth. She averted her eyes, fearing he would see too much. When she finally did meet his gaze, she saw he understood.

He gave a curt nod of his head. "My sentiments exactly. Let's finish dressing and I'll help you however I can." Andrew headed back for the tub to finish his scrub while Avis donned a fresh skirt and blouse.

He sang in the bath. She smiled to herself to think that God might have shortchanged this otherwise perfect man with a five-note range in two registers.

"Avis, do you know who it was who hit you on the head?" he called from the bathtub. She did not answer him. He waited, hearing the sharp intake of breath, and the squeak of the bedsprings. He thought she had known.

"Did someone hit me in the head? Is that what happened to me, Andrew?" she asked, limping to him with a lone sandal in her hand and the other on her foot.

"You didn't know? Of course you didn't know." He should have been less obtuse, he thought disgusted with himself for getting caught in unimportant things. He should be finding out who wanted his wife badly enough to cosh her over the head and make off with her. He stared, especially disturbed when she tried to hide the fear he saw in her eyes.

"Maybe he wanted money," she said, but in her bones she knew Bull was behind it. Mechanically, she slipped the sandal on and, then, frantically started pulling things from her wardrobe, and drawers, anxious to be away from this place.

Andrew stepped out of the water and finished dressing. They had fallen into silence, each thinking their separate thoughts, and wondering how to start sharing with each other.

Andrew tried again to get the important information from her. Judging from the frantic way she pulled things from the closet, and tossed them into piles, there was something very wrong far beyond what he knew.

Andrew moved closer, so that he spoke over her shoulder. "He was a big man, Avis. When I came upon him, he was carrying you off the porch and you were already knocked out."

She froze, and folded her arms in front of her, rubbing her forearms. "I'm thirsty," she said, her voice weak.

He turned to the sink and pumped two glasses of water. He offered her one. "Drink this," he said, hoping to calm her.

She accepted the glass with trembling hands, sipping the water slowly. "Do you know of a man, at least a foot taller than I am and about two hundred fifty pounds?" Andrew thought a minute as he drank down the cool liquid and placed the used tumbler on the edge of the sink. "Light haired and wearing a heavy work shirt. Like one of the workers at the yard might wear."

Trying to appear calm, Avis singled out a short pile of clothes and pointed to them. What was she going to tell him, she wondered fighting through a fresh wave of panic?

"If you want to help, you may fold these and put them in the bag over there."

His back to Avis, Andrew did as he she instructed, first placing the Colt in the bottom of the bag, then carefully folding the undergarments and putting them in the bag.

Avis kept her hands busy while she mused over the short list of candidates. The only person she could think of who might fit that description was Eb, and he worked for Bull.

She had thought him sick and too ill to complete any evil against her. Everything, she realized, from here on, would lead back to Bull Trumbull. Apparently, Bull was not far enough gone that he didn't still want his revenge and now that he had made his move. His man had failed, but Bull would never let her out of their deal alive. Maybe she needed to hurry up with the plans, but how?

Would he kill her? Never had she seen Bull kill anyone himself or even heard a whisper that he did his own work, but she knew he had often paid others to do the deed.

Now she had to worry about Andrew, and the children, as well. Maybe she could talk Andrew in to moving back east.

After all, Virginia and North Carolina shared borders and maybe he could preach back there in some remote section of the mountains. Could Bull find them even in the heart of the Smoky Mountains?

"Avis, did you hear me?" asked Andrew curtly, dropping the bag on the bed beside her. "I asked you, does the guy in the blue shirt sound like anyone you know?"

Andrew watched Avis bustle about in a flurry of activity, pulling things out of drawers. He watched her place the fancy fan in the top of the bag.

She stopped to face him, pressing the fingers of one hand on the top of the bag. "Can't think of anyone off hand, but if I do I'll let you know."

He knew she was lying. Avis had never been good at telling a lie. "Andrew, if you will carry the bag, I will carry the dresses. The other things can wait until later."

Everything about the brusque way she went about things displayed her upset. That is, everything except hearing it from her mouth. They were about to walk out the door when Avis halted.

"Oops! Almost forgot. Hold these," she exclaimed shoving the mound of dresses into his free arm.

While his head peaked over the accumulated gewgaws and fripperies he watched her turn back and pull the pictures out of the drawer, save one, that she perused for a moment, flipping it from front to back and she returned to its nest under the linens. She carefully stacked the pictures in the bag. It was not hard for him to guess which one she had declined to bring with her, but he would check on it later. If she was going to withhold information he had better do what he could by sneaking around, to save her life.

"I promise I will have a lock on that door by tomorrow, Avis, and see, I fixed the bell for you last night."

Andrew walked over to the bell. Arms over burdened,

pointed to where he had retied it, but instead of thanking him, she went down the steps calling over her shoulder, "Fat lot of good it did me last night. Let's get going, Preach!"

Andrew grimaced. One of these days he was going to have a talk with her about calling him Preach. It didn't bother him when others called him Preach or Rev, but somehow, when Avis said it, the subtle mockery behind the word left a bad taste in his mouth.

Also, he would have to talk with her about lying, but first he wanted to think on the problem. His gut told him all her secrets had to do with Bull Trumbull. He ignored his vow and the admonishments from scripture about killing, deciding that he would be saving the world from evil.

She walked too far ahead of him and it made him nervous. The Colt was buried in the bottom of her carpetbag and if he had to get to it quickly, he couldn't.

"Avis!" he called, catching up with her. "Do you think we could slow down a pace? I mean, I look kind of silly carrying these frilly things following you around, while you stalk off ahead of me. Besides, you're my wife now, and I would like for people to see us together."

Avis stopped, and turned to glare at him as if he had gone daft. At that moment the Morgan family marched between them.

Deacon Morgan eyed the bouquet of floosyfied dresses overflowing Andrew's arms and shot the preacher a sympathetic glance. "Morning, Reverend Bristow." He turned to Avis, courteously tipping his hat to her. "And congratulations to you, Mrs. Bristow, on your nuptials."

"Congratulations on your wedding,' Mrs. Bristow," said Mrs. Morgan smiling at the preacher.

"Come along, children," she called to the six little Morgans who trailed between them.

Andrew watched, amused when he saw the last Morgan,

Nathaniel by name, lisp his congratulations to his new wife. He watched Avis smile down at the boy's charming, but toothless grin up at her.

"What did I tell you, Avis Bristow? I am now the town hero," he crowed, flourishing and waving his arms, dresses and all, around in the air. "Didn't I tell you that they love reformed sinners?"

Avis joined in the laughter and relieved him of the dresses. She took his free arm and they properly acknowledged all of the congratulations from those they met on their way to the big house.

Even Elsie Dixon came out to greet them with the *Sears Catalogue* in her hands, and an "I told you so" look in her eyes. "Aren't you two the sly ones? I tell you, Preacher, I wouldn't have believed it if I hadn't of seen you two lovebirds with my very own eyes. But why the rush?" Before the newlyweds had time to formulate an answer, she added, "You ain't got a surprise on the way, do you Miz Avis?"

Andrew watched the gossipy harpy sidle up to his wife. The woman caught up in her prattle remained oblivious to the warning signals he saw popping out all over her face as she restrained her temper.

Avis felt either a rosy blush or livid fury creep up her neck and suffuse her face at the insinuation that she might be expecting. Before she let her temper run away from her, Andrew slipped the catalog from Mrs. Dixon's hand and replied, "Why Mrs. Dixon how did you ever guess?"

When he saw Elsie's smug inspection of Avis' figure, it made him angry, but he maintained his cool cordiality. "We sure are! We've got a new arrival coming."

Elsie grabbed Andrew's arm, her face tilted up at him, watching him avidly. "When, Reverend Bristow? I promise I won't tell a living soul."

He leaned close to the biddy, as if to share a secret.

"Today, Mrs. Dixon, she's coming by train." When he saw the confusion, he explained, "Avis' daughter Tessa is arriving on the El Paso coach today."

"Well, Lordee! Isn't that wonderful for both of you," she replied, clapping her hands once then folding her hands in front of her. "If there is anything we can do for you, don't hesitate to let me know. Come to think of it, a new batch of notions and baubles arrived today."

They breathed a mutual sigh of relief when she moved away from them, but held their breath when she stopped, abruptly to return. "I just wanted to apologize about the *wish book*, but my boys made off with it."

"That's fine, isn't it, Sweetheart?" Andrew smiled bemused by the meddlesome female.

"Oh fine, dear," she replied, cloying sweet while wanting to give the woman hell.

Elsie's face brightened. "I am so glad all is forgiven. Now, if I can just figure out how to keep the boys from takin' the wish books to the privy," she mumbled, returning into the store.

Andrew and Avis looked at the catalog tucked under Andrew's arm then at each other. He snatched Avis into the nearest ally where they both laughed uproariously at the woman's outrageous behavior.

Andrew held the catalog before her. "Do you really want hang on to this book, Avis? If you don't, I have the same issue at home," he informed her, between fits of hilarity.

"Hell no! Not now, and surely not from that snooty woman who doesn't know why her sons have it." She hadn't realized she had sworn again, until he shot her a stern look, which only brought on more giggles. Before she knew what happened, he had dropped the book and the bag to pull her into pressing his lips to hers, until they opened to his seeking tongue. Then, he released her, dazed and befuddled. He stole her breath and her hand came out to balance herself against the building." What was that for?"

Her blue eyes looked at him curiously. "I was expressing my gratitude to you for giving me the inspiration for the midweek sermon." Andrew moved to retrieve the bag from the dirt, beating the fresh dust out of the carpet with his hand. He left the book in the alley by the store for the boys to find. "I haven't preached on the ill effects of a vulgar mouth in a long time." Before she could give him another illustration for his sermon, he had marched down the walk, heading home.

"Wait, Andrew!" she called to him as she hurried to catch up, while tamping the dresses down and out of her face. "You wouldn't humiliate me like that would you, Andrew?"

He heard the accusing tone in her voice, and felt the beginnings of guilt, that he quickly squelched. He stopped to face her upturned face. "I cannot understand why an intelligent, and well-educated woman such as yourself, continually passes herself off as a bawd with the education of a gutter snipe. Words are very important, especially as they outwardly indicate intelligence. You know once can get away with saying about anything if one knows the right words?"

He ignored her bid to say something and traveled on. When they reached the verandah, she stopped and threw the dresses down on the bench located by the door. "How could you think of embarrassing and humiliating me like that," she yelled accusingly, pacing back and forth before him.

"The same way you embarrass and humiliate yourself, that's how." Andrew opened the door for her, and waited for her to walk through, but she remained stubbornly rooted to her spot. "Come on, woman! Let's get out of this heat."

She folded her arms, tilted her head and stomped her foot. "Andrew Bristow, I never once told you I would attend your silly little services have I?"

Andrew continued to hold the door open for her. "No, I

guess not," he replied. "I am sorry, my mistake. I thought we were a family now."

Avis swooped to scoop the dresses into her arms without comment. When she walked passed Andrew and swept through the door, she had a message for him. "Andrew, I have but one thing to say to you before we get on with this day."

She smiled at him, and he answered her smile with a grin his own. "I bid you fornicate with thyself," she told him sweetly, not missing a step as she walked away from him, regally and with her head held high. When she reached the end of the entryway, she turned to face him. "Was that little bit of prose done in King James English refined enough for your tastes? I realize that God only speaks in King James English and--"

Andrew stopped to gaze back at her, amazed. The laughter erupted from him so that he leaned against the wall to keep his balance. "I predict, Avis Hollis Bristow, that you will never give me one dull moment."

"Humph," she snorted, moving by him in the narrow hallway. At the door of Amanda's room, she paused. "You may bet your both your sweet right and left buttocks on that, Preacher man."

She dropped the dresses on the bed, and listened. The fresh round of laughter caused her lips to curve upward. He had the most wonderful laugh--just completely him.

CHAPTER TWENTY

Andrew at first, astonished, became too tickled at her indecent comment to censure his laughter. "What am I going to do with you, Wife? Come..." He grabbed her from Amanda's room and pulling her past the sick room, to pull her into his office, shaking his head.

"Please, have a sit." Deciding to be agreeable, she sat down in the armchair. Andrew tucked the bag into an available corner. "Let's get this straightened out, before we get busy with other things."

Andrew, instead of sitting in a chair, sat on the corner of his walnut desk, swinging one leg as he folded his arms across his chest. A quick glance at his wife told him she her mood might have lightened, but there lurked a tinge of annoyance in eyes.

"I owe you an apology," he began sheepishly, as he tried to make peace between them without loosing ground. "I mislead you. I don't have a service tonight. We decided not to have one, and I want you to know I would never want to humiliate or embarrass you in any of my sermons."

Andrew took a deep breath and studied her for some kind of softening toward him. "It would have probably been better if we had discussed a few things before the ceremony, but my mind wasn't thinking quite straight," admitted Andrew running his hand nervously through his hair.

Avis thought she might not have been thinking quite straight either, but not because she was thinking below the belt.

"Anyway, having said all that, I would like to ask you and the girls to attend the services, but if you choose not, then I will see to it that Amanda continues to come with me. And Tessa as well, if you so choose."

"I thought the issue was my language, Preach, not whether I take in your services or not." Avis' fingers fiddled nervously with the crocheted antimacassar on the arm of the chair. "Oh, very well! I might as well tell you, Andrew. I believe in God, but I am what you would call a Deist. I have never been able to see that God has concerned Himself in my life. To the contrary, I can see many times in my life when I asked for Him to change things and He didn't."

Andrew heard the unmistakable brittleness of longstanding bitterness in her voice. "I apologize for not being able to believe as you do. I know it complicates things for you."

"Avis," he replied gently, "I only asked for you to attend the service, not swallow everything whole. Not one person believes exactly like another one does about anything in or out of this world." She glanced at him suspiciously while he continued to assure her that it was not his job to change her mind, either. "You have the freedom to believe as you want, but I have always thought my job was to present or explain various precepts pertaining to salvation to those who want to hear."

He saw a movement on the patio and went to the window in time to see Amanda wade into the fountain. "Now, about your language."

"The only reason you want me to clean up my language is to keep people from thinking badly of you," she replied, convinced his reputation mattered.

"Wrong," he replied tersely.

Why, then should it matter what I say?" Avis moved to the window, to stand beside him, and watch Amanda play. Would she ever get used to thinking of Amanda as belonging to her, she wondered.

Because, I don't want people thinking badly of you, that's why." His gaze locked with eyes as bright and unforgiving as the desert sky. "And often times people form opinions of us from what we say. I do want you to have good standing with them. But for your sake, certainly not for mine."

"Have you forgotten it was barely twenty-four hours ago I was a paid harlot sold to the highest bidder? Doesn't that matter to you at all?" She turned away from him and walked to the back of the desk, staring unseeingly at the leather bound volumes of books.

"I suppose you did what you felt you had to do in order to survive," he told her softly. He turned to her and put his hands on her shoulders, rubbing his cheek against her hair. "What is in the past is gone and cannot be changed. I want us to start fresh."

Avis stared at his face, seeing nothing but tenderness in his eyes. She shrugged her shoulders. "I can't change what I was, and I am merely being honest with myself and everyone else when I say that."

"That's true. We cannot change what we were, but only what we are, and if I had any doubt that you would return to that life, I would not have married you for any reason. No matter what."

"How do you know I won't, Preacher?" she taunted hearing the doubt creep into her voice. Maybe he would expect too much of her and make too many demands? Worse, Bull could blackmail her into returning by threatening the family. The obstacles too huge even to consider making their relationship permanent.

Andrew gave a snort. "It's easy. I know you would not willingly return to that life because you are a bigger prude than I am. Even more prudish than Elsie Dixon, I'll bet," he joked, leaning down to give her nose a tap with his finger.

Avis resisted the urge to reciprocate by biting his finger. She folded her arms. "I am not a prude!" she retorted, unable to understand why she should be so upset that he thought her a prude. To be a whore and a prude are contradictory.

"You are, too. You are not a whore anymore, but my wife," he maintained calmly.

"I am not!" she insisted, her voice rising with her temper. "I mean, I know that I am your wife. There can be no such thing as a *prudish* whore and you know it, Preach. They are understandably exclusive."

"That may be the trend of thinking, Avis, but if you are not a certifiable prig then why did you not want me to walk you home the other night."

She gave a small shrug and pulled up the shoulder of her blouse that had ridden down, exposing bare skin. "To save your reputation, of course!"

"To save my reputation from whom?"

"The townspeople, of course." The man could not be totally ignorant of his reputation, but he was being too damned stubborn for his own good. "There are certain times and places whores and preachers should not be seen together. Everybody knows that, you dumb a--" she was going to call him a dumb ass, but thought better of it, "posterior of a moronic mule. I don't think I was being prudish to remind you of that fact of life."

He could not believe that she just called him a dumb ass without one using profanity. "Ah ha!" he exclaimed, raising his finger in the air. "That is exactly my point. You thought the townsfolk would feel that way because that is exactly what you would think if you saw a preacher and a soiled dove together, isn't it?"

Avis thought a minute and then, shook her head reluctantly admitting he was right. How mind boggling for her, to say the least, to accept the idea that a whore could be a prude.

"And you felt that way for better than three years, which is why you would give me the cold shoulder and ignore me, right?"

"That and to keep you all from getting hurt by Bull," she answered, her eyes looking beyond him. He mind latched onto what Bull could still do, if he had a mind to do it.

"What are you telling me?" inquired Andrew, grabbing her by the shoulders, picking up on the slip of the tongue. "Avis, you need to tell me everything!"

She could feel the anger mounting within him. "I want to you remind you, that if you know something you need to tell me because we are not just speaking about you or even me, but our family. If there is a threat looming, I need to know about it."

Avis clamped her mouth shut at a loss as to how to answer him. There were some things she had to keep to herself, and she couldn't have him running over to kill Bull. She looked at her husband and smiled, taking her hand and running it across the stubble on his cheek. "You need a shave, you know."

He saw, and then felt her index finger rest softly on the tip of his nose. She was changing subjects again.

"Your nose is still a bit red, but getting better, I think. How did you hurt your nose anyway? You never did tell me, you know," she told him, hoping to put him off.

Andrew pressed the narrow ridge of her shoulders, feeling the crinkle of cloth underneath his fingers. He looked into her eyes, and saw shutters close over them. "Stop evading the issue! If there is something I need to know, you have got to tell me, Woman. Don't you understand that?"

His face lined with urgency, she felt the pressure of his fingers at each joint of her shoulders. She heard him reasoning with her, and realized he might be right.

Once she began to reveal the sordid story, she feared her mind would run away with her and then she would tell him too much. Andrew could not kill Bull and not expect to ruin his reputation and his career. No, the authorities would have to take care of Trumbull.

"I really don't know anything right now, but I promise Andrew, when I know more myself I will share it with you. There too many things I don't know for a certainty."

Avis opened the patio door, and deserted him. As he watched, she joined Amanda's play in the fountain by slipping off her sandals, hiking up her skirt to wade in the shallow water.

The woman dismissed him again, and it stung that she did not trust him. Andrew heard giggling from the patio and Amanda and Avis boisterously targeted each other with splashes. He walked to the door, trying to enjoy the sight, but his insides were in an upheaval, more convinced there was something terribly wrong.

Andrew made up his mind to get himself a set of pistols like Manuel's. In the meantime, he would borrow one of Manuel's guns. The worst thing he could be was unarmed and undefended.

Grasping the suitcase by the handle, he set it on his desk, and opened it. The portraits lay on top. He carefully removed them, and then extracted the Colt from its nest. He examined the oval, wood-framed pictures, checking the backs to see if they had been tampered with and saw that they had, their tacks not fixed securely. What, he wondered, was beneath them? Expecting her to return, he didn't have time to check.

Just as he had anticipated, the only one missing from the collection was the one of Avis and the man he assumed to be Hollis. There was something strange about that picture and if he had not been so tired and distracted he would have taken the already loosened back off to check when he had the chance.

When he fixed the lock on the door at the little house, he would have another look at the frame, this time from the back to the front.

CHAPTER TWENTY-ONE

Andrew anxiously prepared for the weekly arrival of the southbound coach for El Paso. Unlike the northbound coach, (which was same train, turned around), was always an occasion of community interest. Even if the inconsiderate two o'clock arrival time did interfere with the sanctity of *siesta* there was always a group to view the coming.

The reason for this preference was the likelihood of back east news and wares being brought in from the north, rather than making that long trek over the unreasonably wide, desolate expanse of the staked plains and deserted spaces of Texas. The local gentry often remarked that "nothing good could ever came out of El Paso and Juarez, except for the victuals, and even then, you had to be careful.

Because the train, like a Baptist revival, notorious for running late, occasionally early, was never on time, the three members of the Andrew made sure the Bristow family arrived early, prepared to stay late. Andrew jiggled the pocketful of change he had brought to keep Amanda occupied with trips to the little depot store for penny candy.

Occasionally, he glanced, frustrated, at the only public timepiece in town. The ornate clock, conveniently located under the gabled eave above the front door of the cherry red brick depot never kept time. A nasty thunderbolt had hit it one day about four years before, and the curly cued hands always read twelve nineteen in big, black Roman numerals. No one was really interested in fixing the expensive clock because the train never ran on time and that was the only thing you really might need a clock for around these parts.

But, whenever Andrew was down at this end of town he always checked it to see if it was keeping time. He found it irritating that it remained stuck. Not because there was no other reliable way to tell the exact time of day in the town, but because it was a broken piece of machinery that needed fixing. Andrew truly appreciated well-running machinery.

He looked down at the on his pant's leg. "Daddy, I'm thirsty, can I have some money to go get some sarsaparilla, please?" Andrew looked down at the cherubic face, fringed by golden curls peeking out from beneath her pink bonnet, and over at Avis, who squirmed more nervous than the bait in a bear baiting contest. He reached into the pocket of his denim trousers and pulled out fifty cents.

"Bring back eight sticks of peppermint candy with you," he instructed, watching her go to the store in the depot. Avis and the newcomers might appreciate a taste of sweets, as well. The chances of him being able to talk his wife into taking one step away from the station to buy her a drink were dismal.

It must be nearing arrival time, observed Andrew. The portly stationmaster, Amos Dunbar, and his helpers emerged from the station rolling the loading carts to the edge of the platform. The helpers left while the stationmaster checked his pocket watch.

The crowd grew and milled about, but Andrew's eyes were focused on his jittery wife, who jumped from spot to spot as though she had ants in her pants. She stepped a few feet beyond him, paced back and forth, occasionally stopping to peer down the tracks.

He looked to see Amanda speaking with Martha Arnold, the lady behind the candy counter. Andrew relaxed, having concluded long ago, that you didn't see the train before you heard it. The smoke belching monsters did not quietly creep up to the station, but heralded their impending arrival by rumbling and thundering from great distances.

He would have told Avis that pacing was useless, but decided, as anxious as she was, it would be better for him to let well enough alone.

Andrew watched her with pleasure. Avis, he thought, looked quite the docile wife, dressed in a simple cotton dress. She wore a bonnet with tiny pink and green flowers to match the glossy green ribbons tied under her chin. The distinctive curls were hidden under the crown of the hat.

Though he preferred her hair down and flowing, intuition told him that the covering of her hair was more her concession to affect the look of respectability than an attempt to avoid the effects of the sunshine on her face.

The third time he saw her standing in the middle of the tracks, and staring up line, he stepped forward to pull her back. She looked at him, bewildered. "You are not going to make that train get here any faster, and you might trip."

"Andrew," she fretted, burying her head against his shoulder. "I am so afraid something will go wrong! What if she doesn't like me?" she wailed into his shoulder, the sound of her voice muffled by his shirt.

Daddy," interrupted the child, "I got the peppermint sticks like you asked me to." Andrew looked down to see Amanda proudly holding the required number pieces of candy, and smiled reassuringly to his daughter.

"Thank you, dear," he replied patting Avis on the back.

"What's wrong with her?" asked Amanda worriedly.

Avis pulled away from Andrew's shoulder, and gave Amanda a tremulous smile. "Nothing really, darling, see?" she answered, kneeling before the child. "Oh look, Andrew! Peppermint sticks. Is one of those for me?" When the child nodded enthusiastically, Avis slipped one from the child's grasp. "What a treat, Amanda. How did you know that I love peppermint?"

"It was Daddy," she responded proudly, looking up at her father. "He told me to bring eight sticks back after I got my root beer. See I can count to ten because I have ten fingers and eight is before ten, so I knew how many. Daddy says that I am pretty smart for being four"

"Well, as usual, your father is right." Avis laughed and untwisted the paper from around the stick. "I must thank your daddy for his thoughtfulness." She straightened "Thank you, Andrew," she said softly, feeling humbled and filled with gratitude to him, "for everything." She leaned forward and pressed a kiss on his cheek.

He noticed that the glow in her eyes bespoke things that could not be described in words. "My pleasure, ladies. Now, if you will follow me, I have a demonstration for you." Andrew held out a hand for each of his girls, but Amanda was the only one to accept.

"What if we miss the train?" asked Avis, worrying her lip, and wringing her handkerchief.

"We are only moving a few feet into the shade. Do you seriously think I would take you away from all this excitement? I am aiming to get us into the shade, because these rails are hotter than a firecracker, and I can't show you what I want you to see."

"Very well," she sighed, impatiently taking his arm. "Don't you think it must be past two, yet? I mean, doesn't it seem like the train is late?"

"You weren't really expecting the train to be on time, were you?" he chided as they strolled into the shade. "Now then, if you ladies will watch closely, I will show you a better, more scientific method of predicting when the train is about to arrive than trying to see around that bend, out yonder."

Avis and Amanda watched silently while Andrew stooped down beside the track and put his hands on the polished steel of the nearer of the two rails. A crowd formed around him, curious to see what the preacher was up to. The chattering stopped. All remained quiet and expectant for a few minutes, as Andrew continued to concentrate on the track.

"Come here, Avis. Put your hand on the rail. Tell me if you feel anything." They knelt, with their heads together, his larger hand closed over hers as they waited for the track to pulse beneath her hand.

Not to be left out, Amanda hopped down and knelt at the rail, in imitation of the adults. "I don't feel anything," she piped causing the bystanders to smile.

Avis looked to Andrew, who shook his head. "No. Sorry, but I don't feel a thing."

"I don't either for now, but we will wait a few more minutes and then try it again." The disinterested crowd drifted away leaving them clustered by the tracks.

Mayor Trumbull strode across the dusty street, his boots crunching the pebbly surface. He expected the new roll top desk he had ordered through the catalog to be on this train. The fine crafted piece needed to get the eight blocks to his office in worthy shape.

When he walked into the depot office to see Amos Dunbar, he thought he spied Avis Hollis through the wide expanse of observation windows. He was not used to seeing her with a collar up to her chin or a prim bonnet on top of her head.

She had the preacher's pretty little girl by her side and was talking with the preacher. Maybe Eb was right and she did marry the preacher.

He watched when they stepped out to feel the rails. Bull smiled to himself, remembering the old Indian trick, deciding it might be interesting to spy on them awhile. They were such a wholesome looking little group.

He watched the beautiful, blond Bristow child, thinking of

her value. She would fetch a good price in certain markets.

Heedless of being observed, the trio sucked on peppermints and tested the rails periodically. Avis remained nervous, but thankfully distracted from multiplying knots in her stomach by a combination of Amanda's blithe chatter and Andrew's talent for making a game out of anxiety and boredom discovered that time past a little swifter.

Cleverly, he had them imagining a trip to Virginia, reciting what they would take with them and the sights they would see along the way. Andrew provoked Amanda's chatter and encouraged by Avis' willingness to enter the spirit of the game.

Taking the family home soon to meet his family was something he intended, and the way Avis jumped onto the idea with such enthusiasm gave him something to plan for the future. After Christmas, perhaps, when things settled down to a dull hum they would make the long trek back to Virginia. He watched Avis, certain that his mother would like her.

After a few more minutes elapsed they stepped to the track to feel the rails vibrating. "There she is, Avis!" He met her wide-eyed surprise with a reassuring smile.

"I feel it! I feel the train, Daddy. My sister is coming!" squealed Amanda as she jumped up and down in a joyful abandonment of propriety. People chuckled and continued to chatter in small clusters.

Assured end of their vigil was near they stepped back onto the platform. They waited, straining their ears to hear the hoot and rumble of the engine as it pulled its varied entourage of cars and equipment along the tracks.

"Do I look all right, Andrew? Do you think she will know me?" Avis pressed her hand to her heart, feeling it race and fearing it would stop altogether.

Andrew pursed his lips considering. He grinned as she

fidgeted before him. You look beautiful, except for one thing."

"What is it? Oh! Andrew," she yelped, "I haven't got time to run back home and change now. You should have told me sooner," she whispered through clenched teeth as the roar of the approaching train became louder and more deafening.

Wasn't it just like a man to wait? Soon the train would be coming around the bend, and Andrew waited until now to tell her there was something wrong. Exasperated, she started to swear at him, but thought better of it when she remembered Amanda listened to every word.

"Look at me, woman!" he ordered, nearly screaming in her ear to make her hear. When Avis turned to face him, he untied the green bow under her chin and pulled the bonnet away from her hair. Then, just as the engine cleared the bend, he pulled the pins from her tresses, allowing the brazen mass of hair to fall free.

At that moment he dropped a kiss on her astonished lips. "That's better. Now your daughter will know her mamma." He tied the bonnet to her wrist as the sooty, smoke-belching dragon snaked its way into the station.

Bull watched the affectionate exchange between the two. "How charming. So the simpleton preacher did marry the whore," he murmured, stepping onto the platform.

He'd see the desk got to his office and, then he would write that letter, but first he'd do a little needling. A little testing of the waters, to see how much the preacher knew or even cared about his wife. If that failed he would focus on the child.

Avis waited, almost not daring to breathe as the engine bypassed them and drew the passenger cars in front of the sooty plank platform. There were only three Pullman cars for them to watch, and few passengers ever got off at the stop on the edge of no man's land.

The porter set four pieces of luggage on the platform, and then offered his hand up to take the hand of an unseen passenger. Avis held her breath as a blond haired young woman, emerged and to be greeted by an older couple she did not recognize. Must be from out of town, she thought, her eyes moving to the second car.

A garishly attired man with a handlebar moustache stepped onto the platform with a suitcase and a larger square display case. Only a drummer would dress in such a brash manner, she decided, as she focused upon the last car.

"Looky! There is a girl," cried Amanda pointing at a child, of similar age, just stepping down from the first Pullman.

Avis' gaze swung back, following the Amanda's point and saw the girl, surveying the crowd and looking confused. For a moment fear and desire warred, pulling her in different directions. She wanted to run to her daughter, but what if Tessa pushed her away?

Her child, with alabaster complexion and long, thick dark hair, looked lovely as a fairy princess. More beautiful than even Avis had imagined, she held her breath.

Everything around Avis fell away as she stared at the child clad in blue gingham, who had produced a lace edged handkerchief from her cuff to delicately dab at her face. Standing behind Avis, Andrew put his mouth to her ear. "If you don't step over there and rescue your daughter from her discomfort, I am going to carry you over there, do you understand?"

Avis shot him an angry glare, but took one step forward and then another, until she stood at the front of the milling crowd. As Andrew had anticipated, when Tessa caught sight of the red hair, she identified her mother and ran into her arms. Avis knelt to catch her.

Tears stung his eyes at the lovely scene. The child was a beauty all right. He glanced down at his own blond daughter and thanked God for the twin blessings of having two beautiful daughters. Andrew reached down to loft Amanda into his arms for a better view, when he heard her ask, "Who is that man, Daddy?"

As soon as he lifted her up into his arms, he looked up in time to see Avis throw her arms about a tall, dark stranger. Andrew clenched his jaw. This couldn't be the Uncle Elwin. Avis had very specifically explained, was an old man.

"Who is the pretty man who is swinging her around like that?"

"Men aren't pretty, Child. They are called handsome." Andrew watched jealously as the long legged gentleman swung Avis in a circle that revealed her bloomers to all the interested bystanders, before putting her down.

"I don't know the man, but I do think we should make it our business to find out," he remarked jealously provoked by the liberties this stranger took with his wife.

Avis reached up and cupped the stranger's face in her hands, sliding her hand along his jaw, admiringly. To Andrew's possessive gaze, she appeared to be petting him…touching him intimately in the same way she had caressed him a few hours before.

Carrying Amanda, he marched closer to the three of them. Andrew wondered derisively how long it would take for her to finish fawning over the new gentlemen in her life. At last, Andrew stood behind her and cleared his throat. Avis turned to him, and said something lost in the piercing burp of the train whistle.

Amanda eyes fastened on her new sister and she insisted on being put down. Amanda promptly extracted a peppermint stick from her frock and handed it to Tessa, while Tessa, unmindful of the adults, grabbed it, frantically untwisting the paper. The next moment she plugged the sticky sweet into her mouth.

At that moment the train wailed again and the tall stranger led them away, and in the process picked up the two bags he had dropped at his feet. Andrew kicked himself for being so eaten up with jealousy that he had not thought about moving everyone away from the noisy area around the engine, and helping with the bags.

"Why, if it isn't Mrs. Hollis." Andrew watched Avis stiffen at the sound of Bull's voice. She whipped around to face the mayor.

"Mayor Trumbull, you have not heard the news, but I am Mrs. Bristow now," she informed him putting her arm through the crook of Andrew's. "And this is my husband, Reverend Bristow."

Andrew knew very well that the mayor knew who he was, but Trumbull did not recognize him, but offered his hand to the stranger. How strange for Bull Trumbull had known him since he moved to this town four years before. Maybe Avis was telling the truth.

"So glad to meet you, but are you related to our minister, Mr. Bristow?" he inquired, sounding too cordial.

"Well, I guess I am related to Reverend Bristow, but my name is not Bristow, but Ashton. I believe the good reverend may not know it yet, but he is my brother-in-law."

Andrew caught the humorous twinkle in the stranger's blue eyes. Relief filtered through him to realize that this must be John. He might have recognized him from his boyhood picture, except for the moustache. Well… he might have if he hadn't been uselessly preoccupied with his own jealousy.

"Ah! I see," declared Bull, eyeing the stranger speculatively. He admired a man of quality. "You are an Ashton then and related to the lady?"

John nodded, wondering why he thought the man odd. Perhaps because the eyes leered at him in a suggestive way he had rarely encountered apart from certain places in Europe.

Bull turned his attention to the girls. "And who might these lovely misses be?"

Andrew watched the girl's eyes round in fear. They backed away, frightened by the intimidating manner in which he insinuated his beaked nose face so closely to their faces.

Bull extended his finger to tickle Amanda under her chin. The child hunched her shoulders and drew back. Avis looked to her husband who turned livid. Using both hands, he pulled Amanda back and entirely away from Bull.

She had never seen Andrew really angry before. Avis nearly panicked to see Andrew visibly angry. There could be no telling what Bull would do to Andrew if he lost his temper and made a scene in public.

Andrew inserted himself between Bull and Amanda. "These are *our* daughters," declared Andrew, as he drew both girls away. "Come with me girls. I am sorry, Mayor, but we really must be going now." The girls followed Andrew.

Bull stepped into their path. "Perhaps your lovely daughters would care to stop by my office sometime for candy from the jar I keep on my desk. We could even make ice cream, if they preferred. Occasionally, I enjoy a bit of ice cream in the afternoons, but find myself disappointed that I have no one to share it with. I don't like to waste ice cream by throwing it out. I would like to get to know my--"

"No!" Horrified that he would reveal his relationship to Tessa, Andrew cut him off, pulling Tessa back. "Absolutely not!" shouted Andrew, above the din of the train.

The smile on Bull's thick lips, belied by the evil intent in his eyes, John watched drool slip out the side of Trumbull's mouth. Given the wild-eyed way the eyes wandered, he guessed the man might be insane. Syphilis? John moved forward.

Tessa and Amanda joined hands where they stood sandwiched between Andrew and John.

Andrew studied Bull with loathing. "That is a very kind offer, but we have an ice cream maker of our own, Mister Mayor. We do not encourage our girls to eat with strangers no matter who or how important they are in the community."

Shocked at the intentional insult, Avis looked around to see other citizens watching them. She glanced first to Bull, to see his face redden, then at Andrew.

Seeing this new protective part of her husband and brother, she remained silent. When she looked into Andrew's eyes they had gone as brittle and brown as desert scrub brush. The fine muscles around his eyes were tensed, while the appealing softness of his mouth had changed into an unyielding stern line.

Avis had not thought Andrew could be capable of such a defense. At that moment she had to wonder what he knew or suspected. Maybe she had underestimated him again.

Would Bull, she wondered, understand that had Andrew delivered a warning to him. She shivered to see Bull's black eyes narrow into frog-like slits. Having seen that look before, she knew he had not only understood the threat, but also taken up the gauntlet.

Haven spoken his piece, Andrew stood ready, but determined to ignore the hatred in the man's eyes. "I do believe Mayor Trumbull, that we understand each other very well, don't we?" Andrew asked pointedly, pushing Bull even further.

Bull nodded once. The blinds descended over his eyes as he calculated that the sissified wimp apparently knew something he shouldn't. He figured right when he figured that the bitch couldn't keep her mouth shut.

"Of course, you are so right to protect your sweet little daughters, Pastor," he conceded. "This is such a perilous time and the Territory is such a dangerous place to live. It would be a grievous thing if anything happened to these lovely children, like what has happened to the others. Why, I recall the time, a few years ago, when a little boy just about the age of your little one, wandered out in the desert never to be seen again."

Bull looked around him and clenched his teeth together when he saw there were witnesses to the little scene. He smiled as he replaced the hat on his head and bid each a good day, vowing that he'd get the preacher, eventually. Maybe have a little fun with that handsome brother up at the Labyrinth. In the meantime, he had a letter to write and some plans to make.

Andrew kept silent as Trumbull retreated. He had nothing more to say, because now it was clear that lines were drawn. He was certain that the well being of his family had been threatened, and resolved to protect them at all costs. He surveyed the protective stance of his newfound brother in law and wondered if he had been gifted with an ally.

The Bristow's watched as Bull angrily strode through the door. He mounted a wagon, posted in front of the depot, shouting instructions to the two men who were hunkered around a large desk in the rear of the wagon.

All followed Andrew's lead, waiting silently for the buckboard to pull away. When he had gone, Avis' mystified brother broke the silence.

"What the hell was that all about?" John's blue eyes traveled from his sister to his brother-in -law for some explanation.

"Daddy, that man just said a bad word," complained Amanda, horrified.

"Shush, Amanda! I'm sure he didn't mean to. Finish your candy." Andrew looked around for a quiet spot, but the stuffy depot was no place for this discussion and the girls did not need to be listening. "John, I will explain it to you later, but first, unless these two cases are the only baggage you have, we need to arrange for some kind of transport with Mr. Dunbar."

"We should have two trunks on that train." replied John, sheepishly hanging his head. "But, I suppose I should apologize to everyone, especially Miss Amanda for my language. I forget."

Amanda's face brightened, but she pursed her lips primly. "My daddy says we shouldn't talk that way anywhere." John's face reddened, at a loss to know what to reply to the tactless child.

Avis smiled, but Andrew frowned, not really seeing any humor. "Amanda," he said sternly, "that will be enough."

"But Daddy, you said--"

Andrew shook his head. "No, you are a child. He is an adult. We will discuss this later when it is just you and I. Right now we have a whole bunch of other things to do, right?"

"Yes, Daddy," she replied with a windy sigh.

Avis and John exchanged conspiratorial glances, while Andrew went to make arrangements with the stationmaster. Avis sidled up to John, and hugged him. "I guess you haven't had much of a welcome, have you little brother?"

Amanda, overhearing the exchange looked at him curiously. "You mean, Miz Avis, this man is your little brother?" Amanda and Tessa looked at each other and giggled as they stroked the peppermint sticks with their tongues.

"What's so funny about that?" questioned Avis, as brother and sister peered down at the girls. "By the way, where are your manners, Miss Bristow, you have not offered my baby brother even one piece of candy?"

At the mention of her really tall baby brother, both children laughed merrily at the idea of the tall man with the dark, fat moustache ever being a baby. Amanda reached into the pocket of her frock and fished around, finally producing the last peppermint stick. "I'm sorry, I forgot a--what is his name again?" she whispered to Tessa.

"Uncle John," whispered Tessa, in return.

"Is he my Uncle John, too?" she wanted to know, holding the candy towards him with her head turned toward Tessa.

"He's awfully tall and pretty. Not my uncle," she decided, shaking her head.

The two girls comically debated John's attachment to the family, while John leaned forward and snatched the candy out of the child's already sticky palm. "Hmmm. I love peppermint. Remember how you used to feed me these when I was a baby, Sis? I don't' remember ever having a stomach ache either."

Avis' face lit up, and she chuckled poking a finger in his ribs. "I remember how baby Johnny turned the sticky sweet into a paint brush over Mamma's freshly waxed floor."

"You mean that he really is your little brother, Miz Avis?" asked Amanda, pointing her hand with the candy the length of his tall frame.

"He sure is, Sugar!" she retorted, pride shining in her eyes. "But you know it's almost not as nice to point as it is to cuss." Avis watched Amanda snatch her hand away and shared a smile with Andrew.

"Sorry," said Amanda, hiding the offending hand behind her back. "It's just that he is twice as big as you and Daddy."

Tessa pulled the candy from her mouth and studied her new sister. "Isn't my mamma, your mamma, Amanda?"

"Yep! She sure is," agreed Amanda, nodding her head enthusiastically. "We all got married."

"Then why don't you call her Mamma, like I do?"

Avis held her breath while Amanda's eyes got big. She turned to Tessa, and fisted her hands on her hips. "She wasn't my mamma till yesterday when we all had a wedding, and I got to be flower girl."

Avis did not have to look at John to feel his questioning eyes upon her. Perspiration beaded on her nose and neck and she dabbed at the beads with the handkerchief she pulled from her sleeve.

"I don't understand, Sis," she heard her brother say. "I thought you and--"

"Johnny please," she began, taking a deep breath. "The story would take some time and it will have to wait," she replied, smiling weakly at him. "I forgot to ask about Uncle El. Is he ill? Is that why he sent you?" She should have asked about him sooner, but now provided a handy distraction away from John's questions about her.

"Not unless you consider arthritis an illness. Sis, the old man is seventy-six and was not looking forward to making this trip at all. He was only doing it for you and Tessa and overjoyed when I came along."

Avis wanted to ask him if he had made it home in time to see their mother before she died. "Johnny," she said softly, touching his arm lightly, her eyes moist with unshed tears for her mother. "Did you get to see--"

John shook his head, sadly. "I know what you are going to ask. I was too late. She died the day I got off the ship in New York Harbor. But aren't you the least bit glad to see your baby brother, you old married lady?" he added, spreading his arms wide and razzing her.

John watched his sister's face brighten. It didn't take too many brains to see that something was going on here. He had no alternative but to be patient to hear the whole story. After all, he had been gone for more than five years.

"Why, John Ashton! What kind of a fool question is that? You cannot know how I have missed you," she told him tearfully, outraged to think he might think she wasn't glad to see him. If it weren't for the other things, she'd be walking on air.

She looked away, her attention falling on her husband who spoke animatedly with Amos Dunbar. "He sure is taking a long time, isn't he? You don't suppose he's having some kind of problem, do you?"

"Blast! I forgot. Uncle El sent you a surprise." Avis watched, perplexed as John rushed into the depot and wedged himself between Andrew and Mr. Dunbar. Together, they went to one of the loosely slatted box-like cattle cars, set up a ramp, opened the door, and disappeared inside. They emerged leading three horses, a sorrel and chestnut mares, and a Morgan gelding.

Avis listened to the girls exclaim over the pretty horses. The men transferred the reins of the gentle, but spirited horses to the helper's hands. The men led them away from the train and toward the street.

The train belched and the gelding fought his handler by pulling backwards, nearly pulling free.

To Avis' surprise, Andrew rescued the handler cowering before the frightened horse. Reins firmly in hand, he expertly strove with the nervous horse until he gentled.

It was also Andrew who led the gelding into the street. Grabbing a hunk of mane and the reins in one hand, he swung onto the horse's back, and then worked the excess energy off the energetic horse by running him in the empty street.

The girls ran ahead of Avis to the front of the depot, and stood in the shade. Together, they ogled Andrew as he expertly put the horse through his paces a safe distance away.

Avis put her hand to her forehead to shade her eyes from the harsh glare of the sun. She found herself pleasantly awed by the spectacle, as well. She had never seen Andrew in anything but a buckboard, and stared, amazed to find Andrew an expert horseman. Quite dashing, in fact.

In a few minutes he returned, cooling the horse down by walking the horse, using the pressure of his knees more than the reins. He drew up to the hitching post, away from the other horses and threw one boot-clad leg over the withers to dismount, noticing for the first time he had acquired an admiring audience.

He smiled jauntily at the mesmerized females before sliding down to the ground. Turning, he tied the reins around the well-worn rail. "He was stall soured, I think. Seems to handle very well. Good lines," he commented coming to stand near Avis, and admire the well-appointed horse from a distance. "Why would your uncle send such a fine horse out here, I wonder?"

"Why *did* Uncle El send the horses to us?" asked Avis, her eyes squinting in the bright sun to watch her brother mount the Morgan, while the young helpers walked the mares.

She glanced over to see the poor girls sitting like two wilted lilies on the stoop of the depot. Avis' eyes sought out Andrew's and she whispered, "I think we have some tired girls."

Andrew surveyed the droopy, bedraggled children. "John! What do you think about letting the girls ride a mare home? We can lead them. The Morgan needs to be back, though."

"Fine with me." John dismounted. The girl's energy miraculously revived at the prospect of riding a horse for the first time.

The buckboard, with two wooden trunks jostling in the back, rounded the corner. The creaky wagon halted in front of them.

"You want us to carry these trunks on over to the house, Preach?" called Amos Dunbar from the buckboard, his lower lip puffed with chaw. "I'll be glad to take your young'uns in the back, if you've a mind. They must be plum tuckered from waitin'."

Andrew looked from Amos to the kids. "No, Daddy!" objected Amanda, "we want to ride the horses don't we, Tessa?" All eyes turned to the dark haired child expectantly.

"Yes, Father," she replied formally, eyes demure and downcast. "I believe I want to ride the horse with Mandy."

Andrew shrugged, throwing up his hands. "So be it. The young ladies have spoken, Amos, and declined your generous offer in favor of a horse." Everyone chuckled, knowing the predictability of children. "But you may cart the trunks over to the house for us."

Amos spat into the dirt. "That is the first time in my life I ever lost out to a horse. Say, why don't you tell that tenderfoot to throw them bags laying' over there in the wagon and then you won't be worrying yourselves with them."

In three strides John had the bags in his hands and in five he had them placed in the bed of the buckboard. "Thank you Mr. Dunbar, but maybe the lady would like to ride?"

Amos eyed the stranger. He looked at the whore and spat pithy juice into the dusty earth. "Cain't do that, son. The company don't allow for growed women to be hauled around in its wagons."

Before John could point out the inequity of the policy, Amos prodded the mules and moved the wagon down the road.

Avis and Andrew exchanged glances, knowing that Amos' wife would not take kindly to him riding with a *sporting* woman. "I think we need to be honest with your brother, Avis. It looks like he's going to find out one way or the other," he commented in a low voice, while John walked toward them shaking his head in confusion.

"John, you never did tell me why Uncle El sent the horses," she asked as she handed the horses reins to him.

"Uncle said that he did you a disservice by allowing Mother to sell your horse off that time. The Morgan and the mares are to make up for it. John dropped his voice appropriately, in a dramatic imitation of the politician. "The west is a better place for good horseflesh than the south has been since the *Yankees* moved in. You take these out to the Territory, son, and your sister will find something to do with them, I'm sure. And her tell that fickle female to write!"

Avis and Andrew laughed at the way John modulated his voice into that of a thunder voiced orator. "You know the war will never be over for him," he said, speculating if the war would ever be over for the south in general. "The fighting might be over, but the war remains to be won. I can't help but think that something will happen to even the score."

They put the girls together on the sorrel's back. John fixed the bridle; informing them her name was Firefly. The three adults each had a set of leather reins in their hand as they traversed the quiet street, leading the horses. Andrew stayed to the outside and to the rear with the Morgan.

Avis led Firefly with the children happily clinging to each other and clutching the coppery horses mane for dear life.

Andrew smiled as he listened, watching after the children. It seems he not only had acquired a wife and two daughters, but three horses and a brother-in-law, as well. The Apache would even approve of the generosity in the deal.

When the caravan arrived in front of the cantina, Sal came out to greet them. "Congratulations on your nuptials, Preach," he called as Andrew came even with him.

"Thanks, Sal," he replied, nodding his head to him. Andrew held his breath, thinking that Sal might spill the beans about Avis before he had a chance to prepare John.

His gaze flickered ahead to Avis, who, from the back, seemed to be in conversation with John. When Sal opened his mouth, again, Andrew cut him off by waving an arm and putting his finger to his lips.

Sal stopped chewing when he saw the preacher's signal and did a little ruminating. It was pretty darn clear the Preach didn't want him to say nothin' more. That was fine with him, cause he knew Preach had his reasons.

He heard the scrape of the windows above him. "Oh no," he groaned. He ran out into the street and looked up at the open window.

Delilah's voice floated into the street. "Hey girls! Do you see what I see?"

"You floozies better get your windows shut now!" Sal

shouted up at them. "You know how Miss Kate feels about lettin' the hot air into your rooms in the afternoons."

Out of the corner of his eye, he could see Preach and his family had about made it out of shooting range now. "You best get your ass back in that room afore you wake Miss Kate, Delilah. You know what Kate is like when she gets woke from her *siesta*."

The window had not closed, but he heard only silence as the Preach and his little family rounded the corner-out of ear and eyeshot.

"Hey, Sal! Seein' as how I saved this for a special occasion and I don't want to waste it, I guess I'll spend it on you," called Dee, dumping the contents of her washbasin out the window and onto his head.

Sal yelped at the shock of the cold water as it bombarded his pate. "Thanks gal," he hollered back up at the smirking female. "I always did think Hollis was worth two of the rest of you and now I know it's true. You best be gettin' your ass inside, cause I aim to wake up Miss Kate right now!"

Sal snickered when he heard the window slam shut. Boy them gals hated to have their pay docked, and that is just about what Kate would do to one of her gals for causing a brawl in the street.

The barkeep didn't rightly know why he felt like he needed to protect Hollis, but maybe he was just repaying her for protecting him when he needed it way back when. It didn't take a real mind to see she wasn't born bitchy. If anyone deserved a chance at happiness, it was the woman who was going to put things right.

Sal climbed the rough plank wooden stairs to Kate's apartments. Kate owed Hollis a bunch and he'd have himself a little conference with Kate about some of the women. He would put a stop to things before they got started. Them hens were purely jealous of Hollis.

When he reached the landing he looked down the gallery. Delilah's door cracked open. He raised his hand and knocked on Kate's door. "Come in," beckoned Kate.

Before entering, Sal looked at Delilah's door. He hit it with a brown stream of spit, before it slammed shut. Sal smiled, knowing that sure as hell, that Jezzy was gonna be the first to get it.

CHAPTER TWENTY-TWO

The fiery rod sizzled as it seared its path through flesh, burning away pockets of infection. Avis turned her head, averted her eyes, and tried to think of anything but the sweet stench of the smoke.

Avis clamped down, as the girl screamed and bowed herself off the bed. Twisting and jerking she fought against the thin padded leather straps restraining her limbs.

Avis could not know if the wretched girl understood that they were inflicting this pain for her good. She knew this medicinal searing represented the girl's best chance to escape putrefaction and the killing fever that came with it. The reasoning sounded terribly flawed in the face of the sheer agony and the nauseating smoke.

God help her, but she hoped the poor girl's recovery would justify all her suffering. However, as Doctor Glenn would say, *only time would tell*.

"It's finished. The hell's over," declared the doctor grimly, cooling the rod in a bucket of water before returning it to Manuel.

The two women, who had been bent over the girl, gently released her. Mercifully, the girl must have lost consciousness, for she did not respond at all to the final application of the purifying heat.

"I hated to do that," commiserated the caring physician, his face pinched. "Her life depends upon the cleanliness of the wound. I'm afraid, that some cures are more painful than the

337

disease."

Satisfied that he had not left any infected areas untouched, the doctor turned around to the vanity to wash in the speckled, enamel basin. The sleeves of his white shirt were hiked up passed his elbows as he soaped, working the yellow bar till his hands and arms were covered with pale yellow lather. After rinsing and capturing a snowy towel from the small pile beside the bowl, he surveyed his handiwork while drying his hands.

"If you ladies would have asked me yesterday whether or not I thought she might make it, I'd have not been optimistic. Today, I think she's got a chance. The question is going to be infection." Long fingers choked the towel in one hand while he counted the fingers on his other. "Let's see. This is the third day?"

The doctor peered over his spectacles at the women. "Yep. Now, mind you, I am not predicting she will pull out of this. I am only telling you she has a fighting chance, and that chance depends on whether we got all the deep infection."

The doctor dropped the soiled towel in the galvanized bucket and began rolling down his sleeves. Buttoning his cuff, he turned to Avis.

"Sugar, you might tell Andrew to get on with that mountain moving praying he does. This child is going to need all of our prayers because in a few days, we are going to begin weaning her off her pain medicine. Giving her opium sickness would even be worse."

The doctor stepped back to the inert form and gently brushed the dull black bangs from her face. He surveyed the fine features of the girl, noticing in particular the thin, straight line of her nose and the absence of raw cheekbones. "She's a pretty thing...probably a breed. It's a real blessing for her that the lash did not catch her face."

Avis, excessively nauseated from the smell, needed to escape the room before she lost her supper on the floor. "Yes sir," she muttered, pushing a loose strand of red hair out of her eyes. Hands trembling, she picked up the enamel basin, intending to escape the stuffy room to dump the water in the bushes.

Robert Glenn noticed the pallor of the new Mrs. Bristow and put a restraining hand on her arm. "Please accept my apologies. I guess I pulled you away from your reunion with your daughter to do this, but the poor thing was quite a handful." He took the basin and escorted her into the free air of the patio.

"Come with me. I can hardly stand the stink myself and this room is filled with it. He stopped abruptly, pitched the water into the honeysuckle, then handed her back the basin. "Let me speak to Maria first."

Obediently, Avis waited, staring vacantly through the netting. Her arms embraced the bowl, but her mind was preoccupied with the room down the hall, where Andrew and John had been cloistered. Her husband and her brother had been talking for hours and she knew the engrossing topic could only be her scandalous self.

She had been a coward to be so relieved when it had fallen to Andrew to disabuse John of the notions of his sister's virtue. Now, she regretted leaving the task to her new husband.

Maybe she should just march into the room and make a clean breast of everything the right away. One trip to the saloon and John would discover that his sister was not the lily-white daughter of the south he supposed.

"Did you hear me?" queried a male voice at her side. She looked to see the doctor studying her face. "You're tired," he observed. "I reckon you haven't had much sleep in the past few days?"

Avis smiled, and dropped her eyes. "No, Doctor. Maybe I am a little tired, but just more concerned about the girl."

She hated telling another untruth. After all that had gone

on, she did not dare share her unhappy thoughts with another soul.

"Let's step outside and we'll talk about the next few days. I've been looking for a chance to get you alone. I have a proposition for you," he said, lifting the net for her to pass.

When he saw her astonishment and the way she balked, his laughter rumbled. "I assure you my proposition is quite honorable, Mrs. Bristow. But I do admit to being guilty of using a bad choice of words."

Avis giggled, relieved. "It *was* only the words. Considering I know your wife and her temper, I would not have thought otherwise," she countered primly, over-stepping the threshold. Hastily, she walked across the patio, her blue cotton skirt swishing around her ankles.

They walked to the far end of the garden. She turned around to find the doctor had picked the nearest shady bench on which to sit and had a cigar forked between his fingers.

She set the empty bowl on the edge of the fountain. In the struggle with the girl, her hair had come undone and the lopsided tangle was becoming a nuisance. Twisting the long hair, she tried to poke the red mass back into place.

"I'm surprised Em hasn't taken those foul smelling old things away from you yet," she chided, wrinkling her nose. "Sometimes, Doc, I wonder just how she can stand you and those awful things at the same time." She sat down beside him, stretching her legs out, and leaned back to catch a deep breath of the perfumed air before the cigar spoiled her breathing space.

"If it's any consolation, I don't know why she puts up with me either, but I surely am glad she does." He struck the match on the flagstone pavement, and put it to the stub of his cigar.

Avis twitched her nose at the pungent stink of the sulfur, and prepared for the vaporous odor of the cigar. "Did you ever think, Doc, that the reason you're going bald is because of those vile cigars?"

Irritated, he shunted his eyes down at her. A cloud of fumes swirled about his head. He stuck the cigar between his teeth and snorted.

She lofted a haughty eyebrow at him, her eyes sparkling. "See," she said, pointing to the fertile crop of dark hair on his forearms, "I expect you've got more hair on your arms than on that sparsely vegetated dome you call a head."

He chuckled at the foolishness. "Can't say as I ever made that connection, Sugar, but now that you've brought it up, I'll give it some cogitation." He proudly blew a wispy smoke ring.

"Maybe my hair is disappearing, but these stogies, sure as shooting, haven't stopped me from making babies." He chose that moment to run his hand over the wispy thatch of hair on the top of his head to see if he had lost any more. "Haven't lost anymore lately," he laughed. "If I'm losing my hair, it's over dealing with the likes of you, and my children."

Avis covered her mouth and yawned. "Doctor Glenn, if you don't get on with your proposition, I'm going to desert you and go take a nap with my girls."

"Your girls, Avis? You claim them hellions?" he teased, looking down at her, his eyes narrowed.

"My girls, Doc," she answered proudly. The next moment she wondered bleakly how long it would be before fate tore them away from her. Oh Lord, but she had never been so afraid to be happy. Her chin tilted at a stubborn angle. "Have you got something against me laying claim to them?"

"Nope. Just checking," he declared, with the soggy end of the cigar locked between his teeth, and one eye closed.

"Avis, let's get to it. I guess you could say that I'm a desperate man. Now, Sugar, before I tell you what I need from you, I want you to remember all the times you got me involved in your shenanigans. Like the time Minnie got in a family way and used a crochet hook, or the time Kate was slicing bread and shaved the end of her finger off. Or the time Dicey got--"

Avis remembered each incident vividly, and knew that at least one of his patients had quit this world before he could be paid. "Hold on there, Doctor," she responded, raising her hand in protest. "You don't have to list them for me. I know you worked on them all, and I also know that I owe you."

"That's what I like about you, Avis. You aren't some cracker who runs around with feminine fickleness. You are an educated woman with a heart of gold."

Avis gaped at him, frankly amazed to find that the town doctor held her in such high regard. Swiftly she chided herself for being taken with the doctor's words. How many times, she wondered had she been called the whore with a heart of gold, when they usually called the *norther*?

"Not to mention, a boldness that keeps you from running at the first hint of a fight. I admire those qualities. I need your help," he continued with a sigh. "You've seen Emily. When you saw my darling, did you notice anything different about her?"

"Only that she is big with child."

"That's what I mean. She's only five months gone," he clarified, his forehead furrowed into a frown. "She has never been this big so early on. Her feet are swollen, sometimes twice their normal size. Not good signs at all. But, my Emily is full of Yankee stubborn and I can't get her out of my office long enough to rest."

He took a long, thoughtful drag on the cigar. "The woman should be taking care of herself, not others, but she refuses by telling me I don't have anyone else to assist me." The doctor shifted on the bench. "Even our children are able to take care of each other if they have to, but that woman is as stubborn as Balaam's ass, and I'm afraid I am going to lose her."

Avis marveled at the difference between the doctor and the other men in town. One of the first lessons a fallen woman learns is that no woman ever understands her man, but here sat a man who had nothing, but love and concern for a wife. They were positively strange in their devotion to each other.

"I don't know Balaam's ass from Adam's, but if you want me to help her, I will." She watched, bewildered by the laughter. "I'll have you know I was being serious. Why are you laughing at me?" The doctor shook his head as though he didn't believe her. She supposed she'd spoken something ignorant, again. "I don't see what's so darn funny," she snapped.

"Avis, when I said *Balaam's ass* I was referring to a donkey, not part of someone's anatomy. It's in the Bible."

She folded her arms and looked away. "Humph. Well, I guess by now you know that I'm not exactly up on the Bible."

"Entirely understandable, my dear, considering your recent profession."

Irritated, she sat straighter and pulled her skirts tighter around her legs. "What the hell has my past got to do with a mule's hinder parts?"

He shook his finger in front of her nose. "Don't get huffy with me. In case you have forgotten, I'm your friend and your past has absolutely nothing to do with my offer."

Glad to hear it," she grumbled.

"The way I need for you to help is to work in the office with me in the mornings when I see my patients, and be able to assist sometimes in surgery."

"You're joking. Surgery?"

"No I'm not joking," he replied, before taking a puff on his cigar. "I already explained the situation to Maria and she has volunteered her time for three mornings a week. That leaves two mornings for you as well as one afternoon for surgery. That is, if you are agreeable to the plan."

"Why now?" she asked cautiously.

"I figured now that your circumstances have changed, you might be more available."

"My circumstances?" she repeated. Only her newfound

respectability changed, as her circumstances worsened. On the other hand, here was the chance to do something with her life. He provided a way to gain an education for her notion of a place where injured families could come and be helped.

She would not do it if she would be robbing her family of precious time. Just now might not be a good time to commit. "If Maria is helping out three days a week, I assume I would have Tuesdays and Thursdays?"

"Tuesdays and Thursdays," he confirmed with a nod. "Good guess, but does that mean, that you agree?"

The doctor was right; she did owe him a great deal, including her own life. More than that, she would enjoy learning the healing arts.

One day, when she had her home for orphans and fettered women, the nursing experience she could gain now would be valuable. She met his gaze, her voice firm in her commitment. "That means that I will help you, Doctor Glenn, if it doesn't interfere with my family."

Robert Glenn reached around Avis to give her a hug. "I promise, Mrs. Bristow, not to interfere with your family."

"Mrs. Bristow?" She paused thinking how amazing it was to be Mrs. Bristow, even for a short time. Her heart nearly burst to realize that she had a family. When the time came, could she leave? She refused to think about the future. She sighed and shook her head to clear it of the dark shadows.

The doctor stood. He breathed deeply of the fresh air, puffing his barrel chest, while he put his hands to the small of his back, and rubbed. It had been a long day, but a good one. "You think you could start tomorrow?" he asked, turning slightly to glance over his shoulder at her.

He saw her nod and wondered, by the glazed expression in her eyes, if she wasn't about to fall asleep. "Good. Emergencies, by nature, are unfortunately unpredictable." He felt a pang of guilt seeing how tired she was and thinking he should let her find some rest for her obviously weary head.

Sitting, in the cool shadows of the patio made her lethargic. Avis watched, mesmerized by the faint drone of a bee browsing through the honeysuckle. Her shoulders and her eyes half-closed.

"Oh! Yes, well!" continued the doctor. "I almost let it slip my mind. Since tomorrow is Thursday, and it will be your first day to work, I think we should give you a thorough examination. I got to thinking and I haven't really given you an examination since you recovered from the ordeal four years ago. Have you any objections?"

Her eyelids fell shut. "No, not really. Probably would be a good thing," she replied, her voice fading. She leaned her head against the cottonwood tree, allowing her eyes to rest.

"Also, if you have no objections, would you provide me with the names of every man you have been intimate with in the past year and a half?" Avis' eyes popped open, startled by the tactless request. "If I knew who you're a...gentlemen friends were, it would help a great deal. I'm the only doctor and if one of them has fallen ill to a disease, I would probably know.

Fully awake, she bolted upright. She bit her lip; not humiliated, but knowing the knowledge was dangerous to the doctor. "I--"

"I can see you're concerned, but I promise it would be in the strictest confidence," he assured her.

The faces darted through her mind. What he was saying was correct and only commonsense, but how could she explain? "I know what you are saying is right, Doctor, but you don't know what you're asking. That information is not for anyone to know, but myself," she informed him curtly.

She sprang to her feet, pulling at a runner of Trumpet plant. She tucked the bright orange blossom behind her ear.

"Stop avoiding me!" he ordered, grabbing her by the

shoulders and making her face him. She dropped her eyes. "Hear me out, Avis. I know Bull's not been using you himself, because he's only interested in what a man can give him. But his perversion is not commonly known here."

Her shoulder's relaxed and the doctor watched surprise light her blue eyes. "I didn't know anyone knew. How did you know?" she whispered, knowing that Bull would share his most closely guarded secret with the upstanding doctor.

Doctor Glenn snorted, clearly disgusted at the remembrance of the occasion. "Let's just say he got caught and I was the only one around to help him out of it. Sometimes, I think we'd all have been better off if I had let him rot." The doctor chuckled. "You forget, I am the only doctor around."

Her brain reeled at the notion that all this time someone else knew that the repulsive perverted toad had never touched her. Gad! But he has taken his filth to new heights. "When, exactly, did this incident occur?"

"I can't give you the exact date, but I can tell you it was about the time you sent Tessa back east. Maybe a week or so before you were beaten." sighed the doctor dropping his bulk on the bench.

Avis picked a flower tearing the petals to strip it down to the furry nub. So he had been the only one to know.

"You weren't a child very long were you, Sugar?"

Struck by his words, she slanted her eyes to him. "Did you know Bull was my husband's uncle?"

The doctor shook his head and Avis thought about how much to tell him. "Did you know it was Albert who tore my insides out that time I almost died?" Avis discarded the useless remains of the posy by flinging the scalped nub into the thickly carpeted border of the patio.

Surprised by the shocking information, the doctor straightened and fixed his eyes upon her. "No, Avis, I'm sorry I didn't, but I always wondered who could have done such an awful thing?"

"Bull spent a great deal of time in his sister's home when Albert was a child. It seems Bull believed in getting his victims while they were young and Albert became his willing, if not ardent disciple. In case you didn't know, Bull prefers them younger than most of the men who come around."

The doctor's gut clinched at the obscenity of a man who seduced boys. Anger, white and hot, jolted through him. "This is incredible. Boys, you say?" When Avis nodded, he knew that that the only thing that would stop Trumbull and break his hold on the town was a bullet. "Did Hollis, per chance, have any medical training?"

Avis paced in front of him. Her eyes downcast, she focused on each step. "No, I don't see how he could, because I married him just out of the academy. I learned that Bull very nearly completed medical school in France, and then, for some reason up and quit."

Avis raised her eyes and saw understanding crossed the doctor's face. "I suppose it has occurred to you that Bull might have had something to do with your beating?"

Avis dropped onto the bench. She grabbed the edge of the bench, her knuckles white as her fingers pressed in a death grip. "I'm positive Bull had something to do with what happened to me."

"He did ruin you for childbearing. Let me ask you this, Avis. If you suspected Bull was somehow involved with what Hollis did to you, why, then, did you go to work for him? After all, Andrew had a ready made place for you in his home and he would have protected you."

Avis smiled sadly at her friend. She squared her shoulders and notched her chin. "You're wrong. No one could protect me from Bull. Not then and I fear, not now. We married for the sake of Tessa and the effects of my reputation upon her. All for nothing now." She brushed a fly away from her face.

"I don't understand? Surely, your circumstances are better? I can affirm that Bull is sick and not long for this world."

Avis held her hand up to stop him. "I have put those I care about in harm's way. But," she sighed convinced that eventually she would have to give the devil his due. "The deed has been done and there is no way, at the moment, to correct the grievous wrong I may have done them all. You see, even if I left, he would send messengers to kill those I care about."

Bowing her head to hide her tears, she brushed them away with her fingers. "I was a few weeks from giving the final information to General Brokaw, when everything collapsed around me. All because of the girl…"

Bitterly, Avis realized it was just like God to let her toil for three years, four months and thirteen days. Years of sacrifice and then ruin it in one fell swoop.

"I guess you could say my house of cards took a tumble," she said. "But the foundation I've set remains, with or without me because I've arranged to pass the information on in case something should happen to me. My worst nightmare has been for him to attack me through the people I care about, and I now know he has not given up."

The doctor's head jerked back. "Pardon my surprise, Gal, but let me see if I understand you right. You think that Trumbull might try to get at you through the children?

The burden seemed too heavy for her to bear alone, and weary beyond belief, she rested her head against his broad shoulder. "He threatened before, and exactly as I told you. Except for the details, that's about it. I should have left on that train, yesterday," she whispered.

"And Andrew has no idea of any of this, does he?"

"Some, but not all. I am afraid to tell him everything. He has sworn to kill Bull and that would be wicked."

Robert jumped to his feet. "My Lord, woman! Don't you

understand what kind of danger you're in? That bugger is not going to give you up. The sicker he gets, the more suspicious he becomes."

Not waiting for an answer, his thoughts rushed forward, irritated at himself that being aware of Bull's persuasion, he had not guessed at Avis' sham long before now. "Why in heaven's name, have you kept it secret for so long? What in hell are you--

Avis didn't like this any better than he did, but repenting again of her hasty actions wouldn't do a damn bit of good. Right now she was worn out trying to think of something that would do some good, and damned angry that it had taken a bump on the head for her to see that Bull was not about to release her alive from their deal.

"If you will remember, Andrew was not involved until yesterday. If I had been in my right mind, I sure as the world wouldn't have married him." Her voice came strident and harsh. She reached for him, begging him to understand. Could he not see that she had been backed into a corner? "It's bad enough that the preacher married a whore."

"Don't you realize how people have misjudged you through the years or doesn't it matter to you what other people think of you?" He glanced from the fingers gripping his forearm to the sincerest blue eyes he had ever seen.

"I know, but listen, Doctor. I have asked myself those questions many times, and I certainly know what people think of me. In the beginning I used to lay awake worrying about it. Then, I figured out that someday all those other people who looked down their noses at me, would thank me for what I was going to do for them."

The doctor rolled his eyes and grunted. "If you survive. Avis, human nature isn't like that, you know. They will only remember the bad things."

He reached to pluck another cigar from his pocket, and

she, in turn, plucked it from his fingers. "Oh no! You're not going to smoke one of those smelly things." She deposited the stub in her apron, and then, brushed the residue from her hands. "But, now let me ask you a question. Did you know Bull would kill to keep his secrets hidden?"

From the blank look on the doctor's face, she could see that he was stumped and had not one clue that Bull would kill to keep his secret. "How am I supposed to know something like that? I'm a doctor, not a sheriff. I only know about healing and cigars," he growled at the irksome woman. Frustrated by his unmet need for a smoke, he frantically patted his pockets hoping that he had brought two cigars instead of the usual extra one. "I don't suppose you'd give my cigar back?"

She merely smirked at him and continued her story. "I know you're not a sheriff, the same way Andrew is not a sheriff, but both you and Andrew see to the needs of the people on earth and the hereafter."

She looked up at the gruff, but gentle bear of a man. "Do you now understand why I can't tell Andrew? He's a babe in the woods compared to Bull."

"You think Bull will try to remove you and will hurt Andrew in the process?"

Her heart thumped and a shiver of dread crept up her spine. "I'm afraid Bull tried to get me last night. I have a bump on my head to prove it."

The doctor stood reaching to feel the knot, and then dropped his hand on his thigh. "Very well, Mrs. Bristow, but perhaps you need to share this confidence and should tell me what has Bull been up to that he would kill for?" He watched Avis' eyes and saw the shutters close before her gaze evaded him and rested on the fountain.

"Why do you need to know?"

"So that when they find your corpse out in one of those canyons, I may at least be able to explain it to your family when we bury your remains."

She turned her head to face him. "It would do you a disservice, Doc, if I told you, but I will tell you this much. I have made full reports to my contacts--"

"Lovers?" he interrupted.

Avis rolled her eyes and shrugged. She learned long ago that her reputation was beyond salvaging. She brushed it off. "Think what you like. As I said, up to now I have made full written reports to my contacts. But the last report I won't be able to hand over unless I have some help. Two more months and we will get him red-handed. He won't be able to talk or buy his way out of it."

"Red handed at what?" He stared at this woman he had thought he had known so well and he discovered he really didn't know her at all.

"I can't tell you," she answered. "It could mean your life."

When the stubborn woman refused to reveal all the details to him, he pulled himself straight and thought he should demand the full story. But reasoning won out when he realized that she had been doing exceptionally well by herself for a very long time. "I suppose you want me to help you?"

"Only if you want to," she told him meekly, as if the nasty business were a petty game to be played out until the winner prevailed. "But if I have to tell you all the details, I would rather do the deed without your help. You see, Doctor," she said, her eyes wide and pleading. "I care about you too much to tell you what you want to know."

"Well." The doctor stared, his lips pursed in bemusement. "I suppose, if you had to make a list of your lovers, you wouldn't have any names to put on it either, would you?"

Avis recalled the discrete southern ladies of her upbringing who would never kiss and tell. "The ladies of the South say, "kiss and tell, repent in hell." Her eyelashes lowered demurely.

The doctor grinned and chucked her under her chin, playfully. "I'll just bet you miss them magnolia trees, 'bout as much as I'm missing my see-gar."

"Why no, honey. Those fragrant white blossoms make me sneeze."

"You don't say! A fair southern belle, who is allergic to magnolia? Impossible!" Robert Glenn teased her, deciding not to press for more, preferring to believe she was telling him the truth. "But you must promise me that you will let Andrew in on your secret at the soonest moment."

"I promise, Doc, that I will tell Andrew at the soonest possible moment. I know it's hard for you to watch and not to do anything, but please remember our lives are in your hands," she whispered to him.

"Well, I am going home to my peaceful abode. I might even give each of my children a special hug before I have myself a long smoke." He stepped, once, in the direction of the big bedroom to retrieve his coat, but stopped short, returning to stand in front of her. "I still think you are doing you and your husband a grave wrong by not telling him about the goings on. I order you to tell Andrew at once, young lady."

Avis drew herself up to stand before the doctor. "You see, I have to consider what Bull would do to me if he were to discover I had been playing him false. Also, there is the matter of the evidence I have collected."

Avis stared into the sunset as if trying to see into the future, trying to ignore the cold hand that clutched her heart. She wanted to be free. "Someone needs to be around to raise the children, Doctor, and if I am not here for them, who will do it?"

She looked off toward the office where she could barely discern the two heads in conference. "I'm in too deep. Now it has become either Trumbull or me." With a shrug of her shoulders, Avis gave the doctor a weak smile. "And, I thank the

Lord every day of my life that Albert is dead, for if Bull is from hell, Albert was his demon and a true devil to be sure."

She paused and took a deep breath. "You reminded me that I had been ruined for further childbearing. You have acted as though the unspeakable deed left me cursed, and maybe it was a curse in the beginning, but the way I see it, my barrenness has been a mixed blessing. That deed has been the force that has held my resolve when I was alone, and set me free from future encumbrances." Avis walked to the fountain and gazed at her reflection in the water.

"For better than four years I have tried to understand why Albert Hollis ruined me that night," she explained, turning to the doctor, her voice low and with determination forged through pain and bitterness. "I thank God, if He exists, that I have a piece of paper from Raton verifying Albert's death, but I swear to you if he weren't already dead, Doc, I would kill him myself and I would start with the bastard's balls."

The doctor winced at the hate that drove her for revenge. "I insist that you tell Andrew, Madam, or I will."

Feeling woozy from fatigue, she put her hand to her forehead to stop the spinning. "You best go, Doctor Glenn, it'll be pitch black soon, and your Emily needs you." She turned her back on him, feeling weariness sap the remainder of her strength.

"There is something you need to know," he told her placing his hand on her shoulder. "I will keep your confidence as long as you tell him. However if I see things aren't going right and your lives are threatened, or out of control, that will be the end of our agreement."

"I understand," she said meekly. "Give me a week, and thank you." Avis stood on tiptoe and kissed his cheek. "If it gets out of control, it will be because I am no longer around. If that happens I will have not one thing to say about it."

The doctor reached into her apron pocket and extracted his

cigar. He put between his lips, holding it between his teeth. He heard her husky laugh as he walked away. "'Night, Mrs. Bristow, I'm going home to a woman who loves and appreciates me, with or without my smelly cigars."

In less than five of his long legged and loping strides, he was through the netting and giving his patient a parting examination. He headed out the front door, not bothering to let Andrew know he was leaving.

He felt a bit ashamed when he realized he hadn't really gotten but one good look at Tessa, the baby girl he had delivered nearly six years ago. From what he had seen, she looked to be a lovely thing, with long dark hair and intelligent eyes, if not a bit on the shy side.

When he passed the saloon, he heard the usual doings. He glanced in the window and saw Trumbull in conversation with Herb. They were standing in the far corner of the hall. An unlikely pair if he ever saw one. Something was going on, and feared that the new Misses Bristow was smack dab in the middle of it.

Avis, he decided, needed all the help he could give. He just wished he had a twin.

CHAPTER TWENTY-THREE

Dusk descended into twilight as Avis strolled around the patio, sampling the sweet mix of the aromatic flowers growing over the patio walls The floral scents were keener in the evening as they mingled with the freshness of the evening air.

She tried to decide whether she should help Andrew explain things to John. Every time she looked in the direction of the lamp-lit office, and saw two heads in conversation, she lost heart.

Occasionally, John's voice, loud and demanding, would carry over the chorus of crickets and frogs. His agitated rumblings reminded her their fragile peace. Those times, when she heard his outraged bellow, her heart dropped in fear and shame.

She moaned aloud, the ache of her past haunting her with the ferocity of a howling banshee at an Irishman's wake. She wanted to still the accusing voice, and pressed her fingers to her temples to exorcise the harpy, but to no avail. She was tired, perhaps too tired to make any sense at all.

Looking up, she spied the whimsical fireflies swarming around the fountain. She smiled at the sparkling flickers dancing in the fragrant air.

Avis remembered when her older brother had trapped one in a jar for her to see. She could not have imagined that a brilliant firefly was really an ugly little bug with stripes. The familiar sadness stole through her to realize the fondly remembered occasion had occurred only a few days before he died.

Her daring brother most certainly would have been an explorer, had he lived. Her gaze fell to the room where Andrew and John remained cloistered. What a peculiar thing to mourn for the brother, lost to her, while avoiding the one sitting a few feet away.

She brushed her curls from her forehead. "Right now the only thing I need is rest," she declared, stretching her arms and yawning. "Let them figure it out for themselves," she grumbled, tripping over the upended corner of the flagstone.

Maria emerged from the kitchen, engaged in the nightly ritual of lighting a few of the lanterns. She stopped when she saw Avis approaching.

"*Senora*," she called to her as she came to the light above the fountain. "The girls are asleep. The men have much to say. Would it not be a good time for a *siesta*?"

Avis rolled her eyes toward Maria and smiled. "How I wish, Maria. Did they ask for me?" Relieved when Maria shook her head, she aimed for the bedroom. "You're right. I think I should rest. Perhaps the weight of the world will feel lighter after I have a little rest?" Avis hugged Maria, thankful for her friendship. "Don't wait dinner for me," she told her.

She experienced an unfamiliar thrill of pleasure when she entered the girl's room and found them both asleep. So much had happened in such a short time, she still had difficulty thinking of these two angels as her daughters.

Tessa lay curled on her side, chin resting on her hand. Little pink toes peeked out from her white nightgown. Avis wondered how many times Maria had to lather Tessa's hair before the soot and grime washed out of its dark thickness.

She marveled at the deep auburn of Tessa's hair, until she remembered her half Cherokee father had hair the color of polished cherry wood.

The deep auburn hair made a fine display as it lay on the

snowy pillow. The porcelain complexion had been her own mother's gift to the child, she supposed.

Thankfully, she saw nothing of Albert in Tessa. But any resemblance would not matter, for Tessa, she determined long ago, would be her own person.

Tears of gratitude welled in her eyes. Gratitude for whatever power arranged this restoration of her daughter to her.

She swiped at the salty tears that trickled down her cheeks as she continued to absorb the sweet vision before her. *Imagine, both children in one place at one time, and both, mine.*

Amanda lay curled away from Tessa her thumb plugged into the corner of her mouth. If Tessa, with the long dark hair and pale complexion, was the snow queen, then Amanda was a golden pixie: all sunshine and rainbows. Never did Amanda have a thought that didn't escape her mouth and her laughter was abundant.

Though thinking about her girls lifted her sinking spirits, the sweet memories were not enough to stave off the overwhelming weariness.

She could probably move a child in either direction, but between her two angels was a space made just for her. Forgetting she had a husband and a brother, she slipped off her sandals and shrugged off her dress, leaving it in a heap on the floor. Carefully, she crawled between them, tucking only her feet under the folded quilt at the end of the bed.

She bestowed a kiss on each of their cool, cherubic cheeks and extracted Amanda's thumb from her mouth without waking the child. Another tear crept down her cheek, to realize that for the first time in years she knew happiness.

She thought of Lois, who had given her so much and wasn't here to enjoy them.

"Drat!" grumbled Andrew, spreading the horse blanket on the hay. "I hate sleeping in barns!" he informed the feline family.

Crouched in a half-circle, they were more interested in watching the flutter of the linens he was spreading than listening to his bluster.

He had gained new roommates. He could hear the two horses placidly munching on the oats Manuel hastily bought from the feed store. The Morgan was stabled in the roomy paddock at the *smiths*.

It wasn't bad enough that he had spent the better part of the evening shuttered with John, answering every probing question imaginable from every angle his brother-in-law, the taciturn lawyer, could devise. The worst came when he had found that his bride had thoughtlessly, and inconsiderately, bedded down with his daughters instead of her husband.

Finding her contentedly sleeping between his two daughters was the last straw. Straw? Did he say straw? He put his hands on his hips, gazing at the mounds of yellow straw, hating the stuff.

If he had possessed one overriding desire, one goal he was aiming to achieve for this day, it would have been to have his way with his bride, again.

Angrily, he shucked his trousers and cast them to the side, thinking how far the day had fallen from his expectations. He watched amused when the kittens scurried to safety.

Andrew lay on his back, staring at the rafters in the dim lamplight. Maybe if his emotions were a little less involved, he could see the day had ended better than he would have expected.

But, considering the potentially unhappy state of Avis' affairs and the disagreeable news John had to accept about the one and only living member of his immediate family, the conversation had ended in a grueling form of torture. John asked endless questions for which Andrew had no answers.

John cross-examined him until he had become convinced that Andrew had very few answers. If his experience with the man was any indication of him as a barrister, John had chosen the perfect profession for himself.

At first, John had not believed him, determined to hear the

story from his sister's lips. But in the end, after Andrew had explained the story, John had become more understanding and even sympathetic to his sister's plight. There would, he was sure, be a future confrontation between brother and sister, but it would be tempered with mercy and understanding.

Andrew rubbed his nose to relieve the itching brought on by the hay, reminded of the prior insult to his nose. Artemis settled on top of his chest, her slanted eyes staring into his accusingly until he began to pet her behind the ears. The cat purred, closing her eyes, and slipped into some kind of blissful trance.

"Lucky you," he grumbled.

What had Avis had told him yesterday morning in the tank? Was it something about Albert coming from a family of twisted men? He shook his head to clear his tired mind, realizing he was too tired to think clearly, at all.

"Boy howdy! I must have really made an impression on her last night for her to choose to sleep with the girls tonight," he grumbled, placing the cat away from him. "Find another bed, feline."

He smiled to remember the cozy scene of the three sleeping beauties he had found after the long day. Avis had been laying in the middle, on her right side with her knees drawn up and her arm thrown over Amanda in a protective fashion.

The children had looked prim in their cotton nightdresses, but Avis had not bothered to do anything but strip down to her bloomers and that white gauzy under thing on top. Tessa had her thin arm thrown over her mother's waist in a slumberous hug. There hadn't been room for him.

Hope stirred. Suddenly proud to be the only man in their lives, he said a quiet, but sincere thank you to Providence.

Tomorrow, he vowed that he would put a lock on the door at the bungalow, measure the windows and order glass. He and Avis would at least have that little house to themselves at night for their honeymoon. While he was at it, he would give that picture-frame a browse and see what was underneath the backing.

CHAPTER TWENTY-FOUR

Andrew awoke early, remembering his vows of the night before. Fetching the buckboard, he gathered his tools, stopped by the general store, and made his way to the small house, determined to make it safe. He did not bother to awaken his family who remained asleep. This should be quick and he would only be a few hours.

Tonight, he intended to have his wife to himself. Maybe he was being selfish, but he had grown tired of fighting for her attention. How, he wondered, could the honeymoon be over when it hadn't even begun? They needed time together to sort things out.

He measured the windows for glass and netting, then replaced the ragged leather hinges on a shutter. Next he installed the lock on the outside of the door, to prevent any surprises lurking inside. Working on the lock, he glanced to the clock, seeing it a few minutes before eight. His family, he expected, would just now be waking up. He smiled, anticipating Avis' surprise at the improvements.

Perspiration made his job more difficult. Looking through the top drawer of her dresser, he found a rag to wrap around his forehead. When he opened the folded cloth, something fell on the floor. He stooped to pick the oval disk up and held it between his fingers. He flipped it over to see that it was the miniature of baby Amanda and himself that he had made for Lois when the artist had come to town.

Andrew mentally thumbed back in his mind to see if he had

ever missed the small picture painted on porcelain. Why had she kept the picture if she had not cared about them all these years? Clearly she had, and he grinned as hope sang through his veins. He wondered whether to confront her now or another time. "Later," he said softly, knowing that for now, this was enough.

Quickly, he replaced the portrait, tucking it back into the folds of the cloth. Going to the kitchen drawer, he pulled out a rag and tied it around his head. Filling a glass with water, he set it on the porch to sip on it while he worked. The next time he looked up, he was amazed to discover that an hour had flown by.

After mounting the lock, he moved up to the inside of the door to mount the hasp. He hammered the nail into the soft pine door, only to hear a crack and watch the wood split. With one hand, he pulled the rag of his head, and glared at the wood in frustration. He thought about walking away from the project, but knew he had to finish what he started.

After another trip to the store for more wood and hardware, he began to shore up the weak places on the door. By the time he finished, the wind up clock declared it to be noon.

He gathered up his tools and piled them into the wooden tray he used for a toolbox. He picked up the handles to the tray and walked through the door to meet Manuel coming down the trail.

"Manuel?"

"*Senor*, one moment please. We have received a sad telegraph message from your friends in Texas. You have to go to Amarillo. *Senor* Malcolm has fallen from a horse and is not expected to live. His wife and family need you."

"Oh Lord help," he groaned, looking up to the heavens. He squeezed his eyes shut, remembering his fellow minister, the pregnant wife, and the children that lived on the plains of Texas.

"How can I go? I can't leave my family now."

Manuel shrugged. "How can you not? It is a promise you made long ago when you agreed to come west together, *no*?"

Andrew did not answer, but set his jaw. He ran to the buckboard and Manuel hastened to catch up with him. "I have two *amigos* who will help me watch over *La Bonita* and the family. They will never be unguarded."

Angry, Andrew pitched the tools into the wagon, uncaring if they scattered or not. He grabbed the side of the wagon and rested his forehead on his hands as he weighed his options: a man pulled in two directions.

Avis returned from the doctors to find the house in a flurry of activity. She found Andrew packing his bags in the girl's room and her heart sank. She waited a few moments, trying to understand what her eyes were telling her. "Why are you are leaving me?" she asked, her voice sounding small and uncertain to her ears.

"Where have you been," he growled, piling his clothes into his bag. It is nearly one and you have been gone for four hours, Maria said.

"I had to see Doctor Glenn. I promised him I would come in and get a look over. He wants me to help in the office. I went to the barn to tell you, but you had gone."

Andrew raised his head to stare at her. She stepped back to see the angry look on his face. "Why didn't you tell anyone you were leaving? Did you think we wouldn't be worried?"

She could feel the color leech out of her face. Tear came to her eyes. "I am sorry. I thought you would be glad that the doctor told me my health is excellent." She bit her lip, refusing to cry.

His shoulders slumped and he dropped the remaining clothes into the bag. He pulled her to him, wrapped her in his embrace, and rested his chin on her head while she cried. "I am sorry. I was worried, that's all."

"I didn't mean to make you leave." She sniffed, wiping her eyes with the *rebozo* dangling from her hands.

"You, for once, don't have anything to do with it. Manuel brought me bad news. My best friend has had a riding accident and his wife has asked me to come to Amarillo. The information is in a note I left for you. I gave it to Maria."

Avis drew back, seeing the regret on his face. She shook her head. "No, it can't be. Not now. I have so much to tell you."

He released her, and sealed up the bag. He moved to the door, turning the key in the lock. "I guess it will have to wait. My train arrives in forty-five minutes."

"What about Bull?"

"Manuel has arrangements made. At no time will you be alone or undefended. When you leave, someone will be with you and remain with you." He set the bag on the floor and dropped onto the bed. "Come here. We need to talk about a few things before I leave."

Avis set on the bed next to him, all the terrible possibilities for conversation turning her thoughts bleak. "I--"

"Shush, not now," he said, kissing her. "Before I leave, I want you beneath me." His fingers began unbuttoning her dress. "Now."

Avis' mind tumbled with things that should be said. "But there are a lot of things that I need to say."

He pressed her back on the bed and slipped the dress over her shoulders. "Later, when I return there will be plenty of time to talk. Now I want to remember you like this."

Andrew seduced her first by stealing her determination, then her whisking her thoughts from her. When they lay spent, he did not immediately move from her, but raised his head up to look at her. "Will you be here for me when I return?" He caught a curl in his fingers, and rubbed the silkiness between them.

"Yes," she replied, tears shimmering in her eyes.

His mouth crooked in a wistful smile and with the pad of his thumb, captured a tear. "Does this mean that you care for me, at least a little?"

She nodded. "A little."

"You promise to be here, then."

Instead of being annoyed, Avis smiled brightly. "If you promise to bring me a surprise."

"Mercenary woman! You will be the death of me yet," he groaned, rolling over on his back. Dampness rose to his eyes that he erased with his fingers. He had to be strong.

He heard a wail from the other side of the bed. What he meant in jest had brought hysterical sobbing. He turned his head to see that she had turned away from him. "Avis, what's wrong?" he asked, rolling over on his side to lean over her. "I was only teasing."

"That is nothing to tease about! Just go and leave me alone," she choked out.

"I can't until you quit crying."

Avis pulled up to sit on the edge of the bed. She stood, holding her hair back as she recaptured her clothes.

"I have about ten minutes before I have to leave. Sit down. I want to tell you something." She held her clothes up to her chest, giving him a sharp, skeptical look. She picked up her robe from the footboard.

"I promise that I will not touch you again, but I do have something that I want to say."

"Promise?" He nodded, no humor in his eyes. Avis knotted the robe, and sat down on the bed.

Andrew did not look at her, but fixed his gaze upon the cross on the wall. He cleared his throat and glanced at her once to see if she was listening. Nervous about what he was about to say, he looked at the floor. "I just wanted you to know that I think I am in love with you and have been for a long time. The knowledge came to me today while I fixed up the little house. I am tired of secrets and I thought you should know."

Gathering his courage he looked at her to see astonishment first on her face, before she dissolved into loud sobs while beating the bed with her fists.

Angry, and humiliated he rose from the bed. "Well, I can see that you are really pleased about this. I have to go." He grabbed the handles of his suitcase and unlocked the door.

"Andrew!" she shouted, running to him. He dropped his bag to catch her. "Thank you," she said, hugging him around the waist. She raised her face and he kissed her again, this time with promise. Her kiss tasted salty.

"Be here," he ordered sternly, fighting his own tears.

"I will," she promised, looking up into his face.

He tapped her on the nose and grinned. I will only be gone a few days at the most. I promise to bring you a surprise." Andrew placed his hand on the doorknob.

"Wait, I will go to the station with you!"

"Absolutely not. Remember what happened at the station the last time. With any luck, I will be gone a while before he finds out."

Avis held tighter. She wanted to say the words, but she could not. "Andrew, I--" She refused to let him go before she told him.

He looked down at where her head rested on his shoulder. "Hush…later. Have faith." The next moment, she released him and he walked through the door into little two girls, one begging for kisses while the other hung back.

Andrew stooped to administer a resounding hiss on Tessa's cheek. "Take care of your mom, and when I get back I will have surprises for all three of my girls."

Avis cried a little more at his thoughtfulness toward her daughter. She trailed after him, through the ritual goodbyes to Maria and Manuel, and to the front door. She wanted to tell him, really she did. He opened the door and stepped out on the porch.

"Andrew, please. Wait." He halted, turning around to look at her. "I want you to know--" she began, but she stumbled over the thorny words.

His face softened as though he understood. The approaching train whistled, and he looked in that direction. He turned to her, frustrated. "Wouldn't you know the train would pick today to be on time?"

Avis squeezed her eyes shut trying to say the words caught in her throat. "I want you to know--"

He dropped the bag, but the train whistled again. "I know," he replied stepping closer to give her a last kiss. "Things really are better now that you know. I have no more secrets" He grabbed his bag and began running. He turned, running backwards shouted, "Promise me that you will be here, Avis."

She held the robe closed about her. "I promise," she shouted in return.

Avis watched him disappear. The third rain whistle blew, echoing the loneliness in her soul. He had time to make it.

"Promises," she repeated miserably, letting herself back into the house. She might have failed to keep her promise to Dr. Glenn to tell Andrew everything, but she would keep her promises to Andrew and be here when he returned. He deserved that much.

ABOUT THE AUTHOR

Nora Fletcher is a very strong woman with the determination to do whatever she puts her mind to. With the desire to write comes a plethora of ideas that are destined to be monumentous works of fiction.

Nora lives in Northeast Texas with her husband. With three grown children and two grandchildren she strives to maintain a healthy outlook, a firm family hold, and a brilliant writing style.

You can visit her online at: http://www.NoraFletcher.com

You can email her at: norafletcher@echelonpress.com

You can write to her at: Nora Fletcher
c/o Echelon Press
PO Box 1084
Crowley, TX 76036

Leslie Burbank
To Tame a
VIKING

"Charming...a true excursion into a fantasy world, a delightful read."
--Heather Graham, author of *Knight Triumphant*

Lord Steele meets his match when he takes Viking warrior Queen, Silke, prisoner. Promised to one another in a pact for truce, the couple face off in a battle of desires that will have them risking everything they believe in--and then their hearts.

Lady Thunder will do whatever necessary to save her people from the Viking berserkers ravaging her lands. When her salvation shows himself, she finds her destiny in the eyes of Aragon, the wolf. Not even the elements can save her heart.

ISBN 1-59080-101-9

To order, visit our web catalog at
http://www.echelonpress.com/catalog/

Or ask your local bookseller!

Dana Elian

Music of my Heart

"A keeper!" --The Word on Romance
"Four stars!" --ScribesWorld

Adrianna Whitaker has a lot of thinking to do. Staying behind at the hotel while the rest of the band and crew flies home for Thanksgiving sounds like a great idea. Luke Preston needs a break after five months on the road, and a week of uninterrupted peace and quiet is just too good to pass up. So much for solitude.

Without the band and crew around for distraction, Luke and Adrianna find that mutual admiration and respect is only the tip of the iceberg. A wonderful sonata of passion and compassion sizzles just below the surface. Soon the unexpected symphony has Adrianna wishing for things that can never be, and Luke entertaining thoughts of fatherhood.

With the help of one very sassy angel, perhaps these old friends will finally see what's been right in front of them for years.

ISBN 1-59080-035-4

To order, visit our web catalog at
http://www.echelonpress.com/catalog/

Or ask your local bookseller!

SECOND CHANCE at FOREVER

NATALIE J. DAMSCHRODER

"Highly recommended." --WordWeaving

Having just moved to a new city, Angie Detmer is determined to get on with her life. After being left widowed and penniless by her cheating husband, she has nothing but the unborn child she carries and a scant few possessions she has managed to save. She will never again be owned by a man, and that includes the sexy superintendent for her new apartment.

Michael Ripley can't seem to get on with his life. Left to his own grief by the death of his wife and their unborn baby, he's bent on working himself through his debts and his despair. In order to do that, he holds down four jobs, the most lucrative as a male dancer. Even still, he feels compelled to take care of his new tenant, whether she want him to or not.

Neither expects the gentle bond that grows between them as Michael fights against his growing attraction to Angie and as Angie fights to maintain her independence.

ISBN 1-59080-005-2

To order, visit our web catalog at
http://www.echelonpress.com/catalog/

Or ask your local bookseller!

Pamela Johnson
Unfinished Dreams

"A delightful story, full of charm and warmth!"
--Holly Jacobs, author of *I Waxed My Legs For This?*

Gabe Russell is a product of the land, where respect for the earth and family are one in the same. But life takes both from him, leaving only shattered dreams and a deathbed promise in its wake. Now the promise to his father is all he has, but even that is as tenuous as his hold on the house he calls home.

With her spirit nearly broken by an abusive ex-husband, Tess Graham is given another chance--a chance to reclaim her life and find happiness. But in doing so, she risks stealing the dreams of the one man she finds herself drawn to. How can she make things right without losing her own dreams in the process?

Unable to ignore the passion between them, Gabe and Tess seek the comfort of one another in a quest for fulfillment of the ultimate dream...Love

ISBN 1-59080-045-1

To order, visit our web catalog at
http://www.echelonpress.com/catalog/

Or ask your local bookseller!

Secrets of the Sea

Leslie Burbank

Lord Nerus

When an assignment leads Theodora "Red" Redmon, a skeptical reporter to Scotland, her main goal is to debunk a myth. But then she finds herself in a place that time forgot and attracted to Lord Nerus, a legend destined to steal her heart. Can this merman prove that love is real, no matter what?

Lady Syren

Seeking a prize more valuable than anything, Lady Syren makes a bargain with a notorious pirate. How bad could marriage to Keirnan "The Black" Macleod be, he is after all human, and that is what she wants more than anything. Will the treasure of love make a woman of this mermaid?

ISBN 1-59080-193-8

PAMELA JOHNSON

White Eagle's Lady

"Sure to leave a sigh on your heart."
--Lora Kenton, author of *Sinfully Delicious*

Embarking on a journey to meet her father, Sarah Reynolds heads into the untamed lands of Georgia. She sets out, eager to take her new position as teacher for the white settlers who, according to her father, are living peacefully with the Cherokees on their land.

Rescued from certain death by a bold Cherokee warrior, Sarah is thrust into the turmoil of the forced emigration of his people. Injured in the attack, White Eagle fights to survive while Sarah learns the hard facts of life.

Thrown together by circumstances beyond their control, White Eagle and Sarah overcome betrayal and tragedy to find a love strong enough to bring nations together.

ISBN 159080-114-8

To order, visit our web catalog at
http://www.echelonpress.com/catalog/

Or ask your local bookseller!

Alexis Hart, Pamela Johnson, Blair Wing

"A magically woven tale!"
--Kathleen de la Lama, author of *The Fool's Journey*

It began in 1799 with the love of Ian MacLachlan and Elizabeth Sinclair. Two lovers whom fate cast into a curse that would test their love through time.

The Sinclairs and the MacLachlans will see their clans joined in peace on Christmas Day, but when Elizabeth bursts into her intended's chambers, she is shocked to find him in the arms of another. In a moment of blinding jealousy, her doubt sets the star-crossed lovers on a journey through time with a mission. They must correct the errors of fate by bringing three lost couples back together. Only when the quest is completed can Ian and Elizabeth be together again.

Join Ian MacLachlan and Elizabeth Sinclair as, through the centuries, they help Lucinda and Flynn, Maggie and Ryan, Chandra and Duncan, find the love they lost and thus right the wrongs of the past.

ISBN 1-59080-025-7

CRUMBS IN THE KEYBOARD

Stories From Courageous Women Who Juggle Life & Writing

"This is wonderful!"
--Fern Michaels, New York Times best selling author

Eighty authors come together with words of wisdom, encouragement, humor, and true-life stories of what it is like to juggle the demands of a career and maintaining relationships with those around them. Each author is donating 100% of her royalties from the sale of Crumbs to The Center for Women and Families in Louisville, Kentucky. Echelon Press is matching those monies dollar for dollar. By purchasing Crumbs, you will help in the fight against domestic violence.

ISBN 1-59080-096-6

To order, visit our web catalog at
http://www.echelonpress.com/catalog/

Or ask your local bookseller!

Printed in the United States
6630